THE DROWNING MAN

THE DROWNING MAN

MARGARET COEL

THORNDIKE PRESS

An imprint of Thomson Gale, a part of The Thomson Corporation

THOMSON

GALE

Detroit • New York • San Francisco • New Haven, Conn. • Waterville, Maine • London

Fic
Coel
[Large Type]
[Mystery]

i1499065?

THOMSON

✶   ™

GALE

Gale 2/07 $31.95

LIBRARY OF CONGRESS CATALOGING-IN-PUBLICATION DATA

Coel, Margaret, 1937–
    The drowning man / by Margaret Coel.
      p. cm. — (Thorndike Press large print core)
    ISBN-13: 978-0-7862-9321-6 (lg. print : alk. paper)
    ISBN-10: 0-7862-9321-7 (lg. print : alk. paper)
    1. O'Malley, John (Fictitious character) — Fiction. 2. Holden, Vicky (Fictitious character) — Fiction. 3. Wind River Indian Reservation (Wyo.) — Fiction. 4. Arapaho Indians — Fiction. 5. Petroglyphs — Fiction. 6. Large type books. 7. Wyoming — Fiction. I. Title.
PS3553.O347D76 2007
813'.54—dc22   2006033325

Published in 2007 by arrangement with The Berkley Publishing Group,
a division of Penguin Group (USA) Inc.

Printed in the United States of America on permanent paper
10 9 8 7 6 5 4 3 2 1

For Jane Love and the late
Dave Love,
who first introduced me
to Wyoming's petroglyphs.

ACKNOWLEDGMENTS

Many people helped to guide me through this story. I thank them all.

In Fremont County, Wyoming: Merle Haas, director, Sky People Higher Education, Northern Arapaho Tribe; Julie Edwards, county librarian; Ed McAuslan, coroner, and his wife, Roni McAuslan; Edward L. Newell II, county and prosecuting attorney; Capt. David Good, sheriff's department; Todd Dawson, special agent, FBI.

In Rawlins: Linda Bryson, corrections officer, Wyoming Department of Corrections.

And for the always gracious hospitality of St. Stephens Mission on the Wind River Reservation, I want to thank Ron and Laura Mamot; Sister Monica Suhayda, CSJ; Rev. Ronald Seminara, S.J.; Rev. Robert Hilbert, S.J.; and Rev. Dan Gannon, S.J.

And thank you to my good friends, many of whom read and reread the manuscript and offered many excellent suggestions that helped shape the story: Karen Gilleland, Beverly Carrigan, Sheila Carrigan, Anne Stockham, Virginia and Jim Sutter, members of the Arapaho tribe, and Rev. Anthony Short, S.J.

Ho'hou'!

The rock, the rock,
I am standing upon it,
I am standing upon it.
By its means I saw our father.

My children, my children,
I take pity on those who have been
taught,
Because they push on hard.
They push on hard.
Says the father.
                    — ARAPAHO SONGS

PROLOGUE

Now something wasn't right.

Brian Little Wolf squinted past the pock-marked windshield at the mountain rising over the road and tried to put his finger on what was different. Something out of kilter, he could feel it in his gut. Red Cliff Canyon looked the same — the road snaking ahead around a hump of mountain, the sun beating down through a sky as blue and clear as glass. He adjusted his spine against the hard seat of the pickup and squinted into the sun that glistened in the streams of runoff tracing the road. He had the odd sense that he'd never driven up this road before, never been in *this* canyon.

Well, that was ridiculous. True, Red Cliff Canyon was a sacred place, which always filled him with awe, as if, in the midst of the vast isolation and silence, he was not alone. Spirits dwelled in the canyon, and that was a fact. They had carved their own images on the boulders that jutted out of the mountain as proof of their presence, so the people would know they were always with them. They had watched over the canyon, the elders said, from the beginning of time when the Creator made the Arapahos — before He made the other human beings. Every time Brian Little Wolf drove through the canyon, he looked for the images, comforted by the flash of light-colored figures carved into the rocks. He'd always felt safe in the canyon, comforted. Not like today, when he felt bereft, alone in a strange and lonely place.

He'd been driving through Red Cliff Canyon since the summer he was thirteen years old, hired on as a junior wrangler up at the Hidden Lake Dude Ranch where the road narrowed into two tracks that loped into the Shoshone National Forest. The foreman had tossed him the keys and said, "Kid, go down to the Taylor Ranch and get a couple extra bales of hay for the horses," and he'd said, "Yessir," and jumped into the old black pickup, this very pickup he was driving now, half sitting and half standing, hauling himself upright over the steering wheel so that he could see the road. He'd turned the key in the ignition and stomped on the gas pedal, the way he'd seen the

12

cowboys do, and bumped across the field, hoping he'd make it to the road before the foreman realized he'd never driven before and called him back. He'd driven down the canyon, picked up the hay, and headed back to the dude ranch, fighting the steering wheel all the way to keep from plunging down the mountain into the creek.

That was ten years ago, and ever since, he'd been in Red Cliff Canyon so many times that he could find his way blindfolded. In the summers, as soon as the tourists arrived, he stayed up at the dude ranch, looked after the horses, took the guests out on trail rides. Sometimes a whole week went by before he drove down the canyon. But during the winter, he'd drive up to the ranch two or three times to knock the snow off the roofs so they wouldn't collapse and fix the fences around the corral. A thousand tasks, just to keep the place from being swallowed in the Wyoming blizzards.

He knew this canyon, he told himself. He'd seen it in all kinds of weather, from a hundred different vantage points. Why did he feel as if he were seeing it for the first time?

He pulled himself over the steering wheel and scanned the boulder-strewn slope. Ah, there was a petroglyph, and another right beside it. And up ahead, as the road started to curve, yes, there it was, the long wall of carved pictures that looked like humans with squared heads and rounded eyes and short, sticklike legs, and arms and fingers like twigs floating in the water.

Water. That was it!

He hadn't seen the image of the Drowning Man. It was always the first petroglyph that came into view, looming over the road not more than thirty feet up the slope. The guardian of the canyon, welcoming visitors into the sacred place of the spirits. The image gave permission to proceed, and one shouldn't proceed without permission. Yet somehow he'd driven right past. He hadn't paid the proper respect. That explained why he felt so uneasy.

He pressed hard on the accelerator. The tires skidded in the dirt as he drove around the curve, keeping his eyes glued on the road for the turnout ahead. He had to go back and pay his respects, ask the spirit to grant him a safe passage through the canyon.

He pulled into the turnout, an apron of land that jutted over the steep drop-off into the creek below. Moving the gear — reverse, forward — he carved out a half turn until he was back onto the road heading downhill.

Calmness began to settle over him. The other spirits had shown themselves — that was true, wasn't it? He hadn't just imagined them, or seen the figures that his eyes had seen so many times he'd assumed his eyes were seeing them again. Yet he had failed to see the Drowning Man.

He came around another curve near the mouth of the canyon, crossed the lane, and bumped to a stop. This was the place. The pickup tilted sideways toward the barrow ditch. He got out and started up the slope. No sign of the image.

He bent forward and kept going. There was a steep pitch to the slope, and he had to dig the heels of his boots into the soft earth, still moist from the snow that had covered the ground all winter. He could see the road unwinding below. The petroglyph had to be here somewhere. He kept climbing, struggling to fight off the panic that grabbed at him, like the branches plucking at his arms and pant legs. Why would the spirit refuse to show its image?

It was then that he saw the rock where the image should have been. His breath knotted in his throat. The face was a raw wound with pink and white stripes running like blood and water through the stone. The edges were jagged, broken by the deep thrusts of some kind of weapon. Beyond the rock was nothing but piles of other rocks wedged among the scraggly brush and pines. There was a hollow sound in the breeze sweeping through the canyon.

The Drowning Man was gone.

1

He wasn't sure how long the gray sedan had been behind him. Somewhere along Seventeen-Mile Road, Father John Aloysius O'Malley had glanced in the rearview mirror and seen the vehicle hugging his bumper. He'd turned right onto Blue Sky Highway, the sedan following, then pressed down on the accelerator and lurched ahead. The sedan had dropped back before sprinting for his bumper again. The noise of tires humming against asphalt drifted past Father John's half-opened windows. He caught a glimpse of the driver in the mirror: dark eyes that flashed in a square, brown face and black hair cut long, tangled around the collar of a reddish shirt.

Father John held the old red Toyota pickup steady at about forty miles an hour and kept driving north. *Turandot* blared from the tape player on the seat beside him, mingling with the rush of wind through the cab. He'd just visited Hiram Whitebird, who had gotten out of the hospital yesterday. And he'd promised Mickey and Irene Wolf he'd stop by to see their new son this afternoon. He glanced at his watch: almost five o'clock. He didn't have time for the gray sedan.

They were the only vehicles on the road. Outside his window was a stretch of scrub brush that bumped into the barren foothills of the Wind River Range, and on the other side nothing but the flat, open plains of the Wind River Reservation melting into the blue sky. It was the third Monday in May, the Moon When the Ponies Shed Their Shaggy Hair, in the way that the Arapahos kept track of the passing time, and the wild grass that checkered the plains looked green against the brown earth. Houses were scattered about, set back from the road with rounded white propane tanks, pickups and old cars dropped onto the bare dirt. An assortment of clothes and towels flapped on lines strung between poles.

The roofs of Ethete flashed ahead, and Father John started to ease up on the brake pedal. The sedan stayed with him, the driver staring into the specks of sun that danced on his windshield. He was Indian, Father John was sure, but no one he recognized.

No one from the reservation. He considered pulling over to let the pickup shoot ahead, then thought better of it. There was a chance the vehicle might put him in the ditch. He could almost feel the resolve and — that was it — the anger in the man's stare.

Anything could have triggered the anger. Father John had been the pastor of St. Francis Mission on the reservation now for almost nine years. Nine years of counseling parishioners, listening to a hundred different problems — the alcoholism and abuse, the breakups and divorces, the lost jobs and rebellious teenagers, the lingering despair. And he, a white man, trying to talk Arapahos through to the other side where there was hope. But there was always the risk that when someone found the way to go forward, someone else was left behind, someone who blamed the pastor and decided to look for revenge.

He followed the road through the outskirts of Ethete, mountain peaks floating into the sky on the west. The sedan was still on his tail. Ford, with an out-of-state license plate. A couple of houses passed outside his window, kids playing in the yards. A truck was stopped at the light swinging over the intersection ahead.

Father John made a sharp left turn across the highway and into the parking lot of the gas station and convenience store on the corner, the sedan right behind. He skidded to a stop at the curb that ran alongside the sidewalk in front of the store, got out, and walked around to the car drawing into the next slot. The license plate was from Colorado.

"What do you want?" he said as the Indian lifted himself out of the front seat. There was a defiance about the man in the way he thrust his shoulders forward, tilted his head back, and stared straight at him — the cockiness of a bully, Father John decided, sizing up his opponent. The leathery look of the Indian's face, the weathered hands and tobacco-yellow nails might have put him at about fifty, but something about him — an uncertainty just below the surface — made Father John think that he was younger. No more than forty, a good eight or nine years younger than Father John, and close to the same height — six feet, three and a half inches — with rounded, muscular shoulders and brown, powerful-looking arms.

"Thought you was never gonna stop," the Indian said. The hard stare dissolved into a grin that seemed to affect only the lower half of his face. "I seen your red pickup back on Seventeen-Mile Road. Saved me drivin' over to the mission."

"Do I know you?"

The Indian jutted out his chin and let out a guffaw. "Me and the mission priest friends? I don't think so."

"How did you know what I drive?" Father John knew the answer even before he'd asked the question. Whoever the Indian was, he'd been watching the mission.

The man shrugged.

"What's this all about?"

The Indian let his black eyes roam across the parking lot: people banging in and out of the front door of the convenience store, two pickups parked at the pumps, blue sedan sliding next to a vacant pump. A car door slammed shut, and there was the muffled sound of a dog barking in one of the vehicles. Out on the highway, a line of pickups waited for the traffic light to change.

"Man I know," the Indian said finally, "has a message for the Arapahos and Shoshones here."

"You need to talk to them." Father John jerked his head toward the Indians moving about the parking lot and coming out of the store. "The Arapaho tribal offices are down the road," he said. "Shoshone offices are over at Fort Washakie. Take your pick."

"Well, I got to thinkin' about it, and you know what I come up with?" The Indian was grinning again. "Soon's this here Indian walks into one of them tribal offices and delivers the message, they're gonna call the cops and slap me in their jail. I betcha they got one, right? And I don't much like the idea of goin' to jail, so I called up the man I know and said, 'You gotta deliver your own friggin' message 'cause they're gonna throw me in jail.' Well, he starts shoutin' why the hell'd he send a dumb Indian like me on this job, and if I didn't deliver the message, he was gonna take the pay he give me outta my hide, and I was gonna wish I was in jail, and a lotta shit like that. So I says, 'Hey, take it easy; take it easy. I'm gonna deliver the friggin' message.' "

The Indian hesitated, as if he'd gone further than he'd intended and wasn't sure whether to go on. His gaze ran around the parking lot again. After a moment, he shrugged and brought his eyes back to Father John. "So I got an idea. All I gotta do is tell somebody else and let him tell the tribal mucky-mucks. Who better than the mission priest? So I checked out the mission yesterday, seen you comin' out of church with all them people around, seen that beat-up red pickup in front of the house, and I put two and two together. I was on my way over to the mission when I seen you comin' the other way, so I turned around."

"Find another messenger." Father John started back toward the driver's side of the Toyota, taking in the Indian's license plate as he went, fixing the numbers in his mind.

"I think you're the messenger." The Indian's boots scraped the pavement behind him. "I think," he said, "that you, bein' the mission priest, are gonna wanna help these Indians get back what rightfully belongs to 'em. Get my drift?"

Father John turned back and faced him. "What are you talking about?"

"Rock art."

The Indian was standing so close that Father John could smell the sour mix of sweat and tobacco about the man. He'd read the article in this morning's *Gazette,* below the black headline, "Rock Art Stolen." The petroglyph had stood at the entrance to Red Cliff Canyon for two thousand years. The article said it was worth a quarter of a million dollars. Father John wondered if this was the thief who'd chiseled the image out of a boulder and hauled it away. And for what? To sell it? The irony in the man's tone still hung in the air. The Indian intended to sell the petroglyph back to the tribes. *What rightfully belongs to them.*

"You have the petroglyph?"

"Me?" The Indian shook his head so hard that his shoulders swung back and forth. "I'm just deliverin' the message."

"The man you work for has the petroglyph."

"Hey, Father, you ever get close to warm, I'll let you know. The man knows his way around art and artifacts, all that stuff. You know what I mean? People that, let's say, come into possession of stuff know how to find him. He arranges things, that's all."

"So the thief wants the tribes to ransom their own petroglyph."

"The tribes, yeah, that's right." The black head nodded. "Doin' 'em a favor, you ask me. Givin' 'em first shot at it before . . ." He hesitated, glancing around again.

"Before what?"

"Hey, could be lots of rich folks out there wouldn't mind showin' off rock art on their big patios. Maybe they'd like to put it on the walls of their great big fancy living rooms. How do I know? I'm just tellin' you that, if the tribes want their art back, they better move fast."

"How much?"

"How much?" The Indian reared back and blinked at him. "Them rich people are gonna pay what that art's worth, and the newspaper says it's worth a quarter mil. Only fair, don't you think, that the tribes come up with the same amount? The man's not gonna take less than the fair amount. So you gonna deliver the message or what? Sho-Raps are gonna have to make up their minds real fast. The man's got rich people bangin' on his door, know what I mean?"

"What if the tribes can't raise that kind of money?"

"Now that would be a shame, wouldn't it? That rock art hangin' on some rich guy's wall. Decoratin' his big yard. A stinkin' shame, I'd call it. You know what I think? I think the tribes are gonna get the money 'cause the rock art is sacred and they want it back, and they'll do whatever it takes to get it. Thing is, something sacred like that, they're gonna want it right here on the reservation. Put it in a park someplace. Maybe some museum. There's museums around here, right?"

"What's your name?" Keep him talking, Father John was thinking. Get more information. All he knew about the Indian was that he drove a dirty Ford sedan with

Colorado plates and he was big and determined.

"Sitting Bull. Any friggin' name you like." A strangled laugh came out of the man's throat.

"Let's say I deliver the message. How will I get back to you?"

"You don't need to worry none about that." The Indian lifted one fist and knocked it in the air toward Father John's chest. "I'll be hangin' close, keepin' an eye on you. You'll be drivin' down the road, and there I'll be, right behind you. Next time, do me a favor and pull over, instead of draggin' me miles and miles through nothing. Jesus, there's a lot of nothing around here." He jabbed the fist out toward the road. "So we got a deal?"

"How do I know you aren't just a con artist?" Father John said. "Maybe you read about the petroglyph and you're trying to cash in. You want me to convince the tribes you can deliver the petroglyph, and you're hoping they'll be stupid enough to give you a lot of money."

"Yeah, maybe you got it all figured. Maybe you heard so many sins in that confessional of yours, you know all about con artists. You wanna give the tribes the chance to get their sacred art back? It's your choice."

"If I turn you down, you'll find somebody else," Father John said. "Your man wants the message delivered. I don't think he has any rich people lined up, or he wouldn't bother trying to sell it back to the tribes."

"Wrong, Father. Maybe I'll just tell the man the tribes ain't interested, so go ahead and sell the friggin' rock. Maybe I'll do that." The Indian turned back toward the Ford. He kicked at a pebble, sending it spiraling over the pavement.

"I want to talk to him," Father John said.

"What?" The Indian looked back.

"You heard me. I want proof he has the petroglyph. I want to make sure you aren't trying to scam the people here."

"Maybe the man don't want to talk to you."

"His choice," Father John said. "St. Francis Mission is in the telephone book." He stepped off the curb, got into the Toyota, and started the engine. As he backed out, he could see the Indian folding himself behind the sedan's steering wheel and pulling the door shut behind him.

Father John turned onto the road and fit the pickup between two SUVs. He checked his watch: 5:42. The tribal offices were already closed. The Indian could have gone to the offices earlier, asked to see one of the councilmen, delivered his own message. But he hadn't. *This Indian walks into one of them tribal offices, they're gonna slap me in jail.* He hadn't gone to the tribal offices because somebody might have recognized him. It was making sense now, the logic falling into place. Somebody on the reservation knew who he was, and that explained something else. He'd tried to pull him over on Blue Sky Highway where there wasn't much traffic. He could have delivered his message and been on his way. The Indian hadn't wanted to talk to him at the mission. He hadn't wanted to talk to him in the parking lot of a gas station and convenience store. He hadn't wanted to be where people were about.

Father John drove past the vacant dirt parking area in front of the tribal building. He'd been bluffing back at the gas station, but it might work. There was always the chance a bluff would work. If the Indian thought he was serious, he'd get hold of his boss, whoever he was. And the man would call. He would call — Father John was sure of it — because the quickest, easiest shot at making money on the petroglyph was to sell it back to the tribes.

Father John reached over and fumbled for

his cell phone in the glove compartment, which, for no reason he had ever figured out, Arapahos called the jockey box, finally dragging it past the crumpled maps and papers. He pressed the keys for information and got the number for Mickey Wolf. He had to slow down while he tapped it out. He jammed the cell against his ear and listened to the intermittent buzzing noise, followed by the sound of Mickey's voice over the wails of an infant.

"Hello?"

Father John said that something had come up. Could he take a rain check?

"No problem, Father," Mickey said. "We're not going anywhere."

Father John promised to stop by before the new baby went off to school.

A little rumble of laughter came down the line. "I'll tell him. See ya, Father," Mickey said before the line went dead.

Father John slowed the pickup and pulled the wheel to the right. He bumped over the barrow ditch and across a weed-patched field, then came out onto a narrow dirt road that wound past the backyards of two houses before plunging into the front yard of a small frame house with what looked like a new coat of gray paint. He stopped close to the wood stoop that jutted from the front door, turned off the engine, and waited. If Norman Yellow Hawk, one of the councilmen on the Arapaho Business Council, was home and wanted a visitor, he'd let Father John know in a couple of minutes.

2

Norman Yellow Hawk straddled the straight-backed kitchen chair like a child. He wrapped mitt-sized hands around the coffee mug on the table and regarded Father John with half-closed eyes, as if he were chasing an idea somewhere in his head. Father John could hear the water boiling on the stove behind them. The kitchen was attached to the back of the house like an afterthought, filled with the odors of hot tomato sauce and basil. There was the sound of children playing outside, and every once in a while, one of Norman's boys darted past the window next to the kitchen table.

"You ever seen the Indian before?" the councilman asked.

Father John shook his head. He took a sip of the hot coffee that Norman's wife, Lea, had set before him. *Stay for supper, Father?* she'd wanted to know. He'd thanked her and explained that he had to get back to the mission. AA meeting tonight, and Elena, who had managed the residence, prepared the meals, and looked after the priests at St. Francis Mission for more years than she or anyone else could remember, would have kept his foil-wrapped dinner warm in the oven.

"It's possible that someone here knows him," Father John said. "He didn't want to go to the tribal offices."

Lea moved away from the counter where she'd been tearing lettuce into little pieces and dropping them into a bowl. She was a pretty woman with blue-black hair smoothed around her head into a ponytail, a soft-looking face, and dark eyes that shone with worry. She wiped her hands on a towel, tossed it over to the counter, and set one hand on her husband's shoulder. "Remember what happened last time, Norman," she said.

"Yeah, I remember." Norman didn't move away from his wife's grasp. He stared at the window with a longing in his expression, eyes following the two boys tossing a baseball back and forth, shouting, laughing. Free. Beyond the dirt yard, the open plains stretched into the distances. "Last time a petroglyph was stolen, one of our Arapaho boys ended up shot to death," he said. "The other is still locked up down in Rawlins."

"An Indian came to the office to see you then." Lea tapped an index finger on her husband's shoulder. "Said he could get the petroglyph back."

"Two hundred thousand dollars." Norman rolled his head and glanced up at his wife. "Looks like the price went up. Now he wants two hundred and fifty for the Drowning Man. Bastard thinks we have that kind of money lying around in a slush fund someplace."

Father John took another drink of coffee and pushed the mug back. He set his forearms on the table and leaned toward the man across from him. "Who is he?" he said.

"Middleman, the fed called him. SOB probably doing the dirty work for some artifact dealer those Arapaho cowboys got hooked up with. You remember them, don't you, Father? Raymond Trublood and Travis Birdsong? Birdsong kept insisting he was innocent, never killed anybody. The way I figured it, they sold the glyph to some dealer that passed it on to rich folks for a lot of money. Lots of people looking for Indian art, you know. Don't care that buying stolen artifacts is illegal as hell. Before the dealer went to a lot of trouble, I figured he sent his middleman to see if we wanted to buy back our own petroglyph!"

He shook his head and glanced about the kitchen. Lea had moved back to the counter and was energetically chopping a tomato. The scrape of the knife on the wood block mixed with the muffled voices of the kids outside. "Wouldn't that have been something," Norman said. "Bastard might've gotten less money than some rich folks would've paid, but he could have turned the glyph faster without much risk. *Don't call the fed, or the deal's off.* That's what the Indian said. His boss figured we'd want that glyph back so bad we'd do whatever he said, and you know what? He was right."

Norman turned his head toward the window again, the same longing working beneath the surface of the tightened muscles in his face. "Indian told us we'd be contacted about making the exchange," he said. "Then Trublood was shot. Last we heard about the petroglyph."

"We'd better let Gianelli know the Indian could be back," Father John said. He'd known Ted Gianelli, the local FBI agent, for five or six years now. He was a good investigator. Like a dog with a bone, Gianelli didn't give up.

"No fed." The councilman took another gulp of coffee. "After Trublood's murder, there were feds, sheriff's deputies, police swarming all over the rez. Newspaper stories every day. It was all over the TV. That Indian vanished into thin air, and so did the petroglyph. Probably propped against a wall in Tokyo now, wouldn't surprise me none. Same thing's going to happen to the Drowning Man if we go to the fed. News will be all over the moccasin telegraph tomorrow."

"Look, Norman," Father John said, trying to fit together a logical argument. "It's a different situation now. Nobody's been murdered." He paused. *Lord, let that be true.* "There probably won't be a lot of publicity. The article in today's newspaper could be the extent of it."

"The gossip will start up, I'm telling you. We tried to keep it quiet about the Drowning Man, and what happened? Big article in the *Gazette.* Problem is, stealing a petroglyph is a federal crime, so last week, soon's that ranch hand came to the tribal offices and said the glyph was gone, we had to notify the fed. Two days later, a reporter started nosing around, asking questions. How many glyphs in the canyon? What're they worth? That white man out at the antiques place on the highway — Duncan Barnes, you know him? — gave the reporter what she was looking for. Glyph's worth a quarter mil, he tells her. Next thing I know, *Gazette*'s screaming how thieves stole an ancient petroglyph worth a fortune."

Norman raised one hand in a kind of salute before Father John could say anything. "We notify the fed about the Indian, that'll be all over the papers, too. How there's a big investigation, and the fed's looking high and low for the stolen glyph. The Indian will get nervous and disappear like last time, and we'll never see the Drowning Man again."

The councilman went back to his coffee, eyes watching the window over the rim of his mug. The late-afternoon sun glowed in the glass like a neon light. Outside, the kids looked like blurred, dark figures darting for the ball that flew between them.

Father John sipped at his own coffee. He had the sense that came over him sometimes in the confessional. There was more, something else that Norman hadn't told him. He waited, giving the Indian as much time as he needed.

After a long moment, Norman said, "Truth is, Father, petroglyphs aren't the only artifacts missing. Thieves have been robbing us for some time. Digging in the mounds beneath the glyphs, taking bones and ancient tools. We try to keep it quiet, but news gets out. Probably brought the thieves here looking for a petroglyph, the idea of making some big money. Right now, we have enough problems with the logging that's gonna start up in the Shoshone Forest. Lumber companies want to widen the road through Red Cliff Canyon so they can drive their trucks up and down. It'll destroy the canyon."

The Arapaho set his coffee mug down hard on the table, and Lea moved back and set her hands on his shoulders again. "We want this glyph back with the people where it belongs," Norman said. "Can't put it back in its proper place in the canyon, but we can protect it. Protect the spirit. Keep it in a safe place."

"Let Gianelli help you."

Norman was already shaking his head, as if he'd anticipated the suggestion. "Bottom line, Father. No more publicity and no outsiders trampling over the mountainside. Tribes've gotta handle this."

Father John finished his coffee. Lea had turned back to the counter and was rinsing dishes under the faucet. The sounds of the kids blurred into the noise of rushing water and clinking glass. After a moment, he said, "There could be more publicity . . ."

"There'll be publicity, all right, if we call in the fed."

"Either way, it doesn't matter. The story in the paper didn't come from Gianelli. He wouldn't have gone to the newspaper. The reporter must have come to him, and he'd had to confirm that the petroglyph was missing."

"You're saying somebody tipped off the reporter?"

"How many people knew the Drowning Man was gone?"

The councilman shifted sideways away from the window and stared at the doorway that led into the small living room at the front of the house. Patterns of light played over the braided carpet on the vinyl floor. The shadow of a sofa hugged the far wall. Finally, he said, "Joint Business Council. That's six Arapahos and six Shoshones. Couple of people in the tribal offices." He shrugged. "Could be more."

"The news made it onto the moccasin telegraph," Father John said. "The *Gazette* reporter must have heard the gossip and contacted Gianelli. How long will it be before word gets out that the thief wants a quarter-million-dollar ransom? There'll be another front-page article. Gianelli will read about the Indian in the newspaper."

Norman gripped the edge of the table and hauled himself to his feet. He stood still for a moment, black, unseeing eyes moving over the kitchen, chasing a new and unwanted idea in his head now. Then he exchanged a quick, almost imperceptible glance with his wife and stepped around the table. He flung open the back door. A gust of warm air, filled with the scents of dust and sage, floated into the kitchen.

"Hey," he called. "Time for supper." He leaned sideways, pushing the door against the wall with the weight of one shoulder, and waited as the two boys filed past, brown arms swinging at their sides, the knees of their blue jeans gray with smudged dirt.

"Hi, Father." It was a duet that cracked between soprano and baritone. Rows of white teeth flashed in the almost identical brown faces.

"You seen me catch that fastball?" one of the boys asked.

"Nice glove work," Father John said.

"Yeah." The boy grinned.

"Me, too." The other boy punched his brother on the arm.

"You're both looking good."

"You two Babe Ruths get washed up for supper." Norman closed the door and waited until the boys had disappeared through the living room, the thud of their sneakers receding into some other part of the house, before he said, "You might have something."

"Maybe the fed will help us get the glyph back without paying all that money." This from Lea who stood at the counter, threading the towel through her hands. "Maybe you oughtta call him."

Norman was already reaching for the phone on the wall. He grabbed the receiver and began jabbing at the buttons. Then he handed the receiver to Father John. "You tell the fed what happened," he said.

Father John pressed the plastic against his ear and waited through the automatic message: "Federal Bureau of Investigation. Leave your name and number and we'll get back to you."

"Father John," he said. He felt his voice swallowed in a vacuum. "An Indian stopped me at Ethete with a message for the tribes. Said they can get the Drowning Man back for a quarter million. It could be the same man who tried to ransom the other petroglyph seven years ago. I'll be at the mission in about an hour."

He pressed a key, then handed the receiver back to the councilman, who studied the keypad as if he were debating making another call. After a moment, Norman started tapping out a number. "I'm gonna have to inform the rest of the Joint Council about this tomorrow," he said, "but I oughtta let the natural resources director know right now that the Indian's around trying to sell us our petroglyph." He stared across the kitchen, clamping the black receiver against his ear. "Could mean the petroglyph's still around." The faintest note of hope sounded in his voice. "You know the new director? Mona Ledger?"

Father John nodded. He'd met her once at the tribal offices.

Norman slammed the receiver back into its cradle. "She's not answering. Took some of her staff up to the canyon to photograph the glyphs, check the records of where they're located on the slopes." He hesitated. "Check to see if any more are missing and keep an eye on things for a while. Construction gets started, they'll have to clear out. Joint Council's asked Vicky and Adam to come up with some plan to persuade the BLM that the logging companies oughtta take an alternate route into the forest."

Father John tried to focus on the rest of

what the man was saying: how he'd keep trying to reach the natural resources director, how he'd call Herbert Stockham, chairman of the Shoshone Business Council, and tell him something had come up. It was like trying to concentrate on the rest of the aria after the tenor had hit a flat note. The other notes faded into the background, leaving the flat note to clash and bang around in your head. Vicky Holden and Adam Lone Eagle. They were law partners. It was only natural for their names to be linked together in the same breath, the way their lives were linked. It was good, he told himself, struggling to shake off the familiar sense of loss that washed over him. *You can't lose what was never yours,* he told himself. *You can only lose the possibility.* He knew from years of counseling others that sometimes that was the greater loss.

He heard himself saying he would drive up to the canyon tomorrow and tell the resources director, as if his own voice could override his thoughts. It surprised him, the sudden need to drive across the open, flat spaces and into the wilderness of Red Cliff Canyon, a sacred place.

The councilman grasped at the offer. "That'd be great, Father," he said. "Mona'll be glad to hear we might get the glyph back."

3

The sun was riding over the peaks of the Wind River Range, the brightness fractured in the pickup's rearview mirror as Father John turned into the grounds of St. Francis Mission. He headed through the tunnel of cottonwoods that emptied into Circle Drive, then started around the drive past the mission buildings rooted in the dry earth with the wild grasses and shrubs. Looming on the left was the flat-faced, stucco administration building. Across the narrow alley that led to Eagle Hall and the guesthouse in back was the small white church decorated in blue and red Arapaho symbols, the steeple rising among the branches of an ancient cottonwood that tilted toward the roof. The stone-block school building that was now the Arapaho museum stood straight ahead. About thirty yards farther around the drive was the two-story red brick residence.

Familiar, Father John thought, as he came around the drive. The buildings, and the wind ruffling the grasses, the light shimmering through the cottonwood branches. He could have found his way about St. Francis Mission by the sound of the wind, the feel of the earth beneath his boots. It was home.

A Boston Irishman at home at an Indian mission on a reservation in the middle of Wyoming! He'd arrived nine years ago, fresh out of rehab at Grace House, filled with gratitude that Father Peter, the pastor, was willing to take a chance on an assistant still getting accustomed to sobriety. He could picture the old priest striding across the grounds that first day, a small man with a craggy face, a head of thick white hair, and the energy of a bull. "You'll like it here," he'd said. "Place gets to you. People get to you. Day will come when you won't be able to imagine yourself anywhere else."

He'd doubted that would be true, but he hadn't contradicted the old man. He was glad to be out of rehab, glad for a job and the chance to prove himself. He'd stay at St. Francis Mission a year or so, he'd told himself, long enough to prove to the provincial that he could be trusted to resume his old academic track. He would return to teaching American history at one of the Jesuit prep schools and continue work on his doctorate. The road ahead had been clear and steady. He'd tried not to think about whether he would be steady enough to follow it.

Then something had happened. He wasn't sure when it had happened. A gradual settling in, like a tree putting down roots. He'd become part of the mission and the reservation and the lives of the Arapahos. When Father Peter's heart started to give out and the old man went to a Jesuit retirement home, Father John became the pastor. It had seemed right, a normal progression, as if his entire career had been heading toward a small Arapaho mission in the middle of nowhere. *We go by the way we know not . . .* The words of St. John of the Cross struck Father John as truer than he could have ever believed. Still, he'd started to dread the phone call from the provincial that would send him somewhere else.

Dinner at six. Expect you'll be on time. He could hear the housekeeper's voice in his head as he drove toward the residence. He'd assured her he'd be home for dinner today, but that was before he'd known there was an Indian in a gray Ford sedan waiting to pull him over. Father Ian McCauley, his assistant, had probably been on time. Ian seemed to be doing everything right these days, and Father John was happy about that. Of course, he was happy. It was about time the mission had two priests who wanted to stay.

Except that Father John was on borrowed time. That was a fact. Six years was the usual length of an assignment, and each time the phone rang, he half expected the provincial to be at the other end with news of his next job. Sometimes in the middle of the night, he'd stare into the smudged darkness and wonder where he might be sent, what sort of place. But it was as if a curtain would draw itself over the images stuttering into his mind, and try as he might, he could never picture himself in another life.

As he parked next to Father Ian's blue sedan, he caught sight of a white SUV plunging through the tunnel of cottonwoods. He got out and waited until the vehicle pulled in beside him. Ted Gianelli jumped out and pushed the door shut. The sharp clack reverberated through the stillness. They shook hands. The fed's palm was dry and firm: his grip strong.

"Got the good news," Gianelli said. He

was over six feet tall with trimmed black hair flecked with gray and the broad shoulders and thick pectorals of the Patriots linebacker he'd once been. He wore blue jeans, a white shirt that took on a pinkish cast in the setting sun, a brown leather vest, and cowboy boots.

"Good?"

"Initial contact about the missing petroglyph? I'd say that's good. It means the petroglyph's in play. Thieves want to unload it. Where can we talk?"

Father John ushered the fed up the sidewalk and into the entry of the residence. The air was warm and thick with the odors of fried chicken. Walks-On, the golden retriever he'd found in the ditch on Seventeen-Mile Road a few years ago — nearly driving by, glimpsing what he'd thought was a bag of trash — bounded down the hallway and skidded to a stop on the wood floor. Father John reached down and scratched the dog's ears. He'd pulled over — thank God, he'd pulled over — picked up the injured animal and taken him to Riverton, where the vet had removed his left hind leg and saved his life. Father John had brought him home then and named him Walks-on-Three-Legs, Walks-On for short.

48

"We can talk in my study," he told Gianelli, but before the agent could step
through the door on the left, Walks-On leapt
ahead and made for the matted spot in the
carpet where he liked to sleep, next to the
worn leather chair behind the desk.

Gianelli dropped onto one of the side
chairs that Father John kept for visitors,
reached inside the front of his vest, and
extracted a small notepad and pen. "Start
at the beginning," he said, holding the pad
in one hand, the pen poised a few inches
away. "Where were you exactly and what
happened?"

Father John had to step over the dog to
get to his own chair. He sat down and, patting the dog's head, told the agent about
the Indian in the gray Ford sedan who had
followed him to the gas station at Ethete
and delivered a message that, he'd said, was
for the tribes. He hurried on, staring across
the study, trying to relate the exact words
that the Indian had used.

"Who was he?" Gianelli said.

"Nobody I'd ever seen."

"Wyoming plates?"

"Colorado."

"You get the number?"

Father John could see the license plate
emblazoned on the back of his eyelids. He

49

told the fed: the letters *MAS*, the three numbers.

"We'll pick him up."

"The tribes don't want him picked up."

The agent's head snapped back. "It's not their call."

"They want the petroglyph returned, Ted," Father John said. "The Indian is only the messenger boy. Somebody else has the glyph. If you arrest the Indian, whoever has the glyph could disappear, and the tribes will never see it again. It happened seven years ago."

"Yeah, I read the reports." Gianelli jabbed the pen into the air. "The agent here then solved the case. Two thieves, Raymond Trublood and Travis Birdsong, had a disagreement over the money and Birdsong shot his partner. Why waste the taxpayer's money charging Birdsong for theft of an Indian artifact on public lands, which might have put him away for two or three years, when the man was going to prison for voluntary manslaughter? The case went inactive."

"Could be that the Indian who delivered the message seven years ago stopped me today." Father John leaned forward and clasped his hands on the desk. "After Trublood was killed, contact was broken off and the tribes lost the glyph. They don't want to lose the Drowning Man."

"You want the truth, John?" The pen was poking the air again. "It's probably already lost. Sold to some art dealer who doesn't care about the pedigree of his merchandise. Everything's already ratcheted up to another level. First thing the dealer needs is proof of the petroglyph's value. The *Gazette* gets an anonymous phone call that the glyph has been stolen. A large rock with a picture carved on it? Who cares? They send out a reporter to confirm the theft and find out how important it might be. The reporter contacts a local antiques dealer and learns that the glyph is worth a quarter of a million dollars. The story makes the front page of the *Gazette.* See where I'm going?"

Father John nodded. "The dealer uses the newspaper article to get the price he wants."

"Exactly. Sure, he'll try the tribes first on the chance they can raise that much money fast. If they don't come up with the money, he has the newspaper article to prove the petroglyph's value. You can bet he already has buyers lined up. He's probably telling them he's got somebody else interested, meaning the tribes, which only whets their appetite. They may even top the quarter million and walk off with the glyph before the tribes can pay the ransom money."

"These buyers . . ." Father John reached down and ran his fingers over the dog's back. There were footsteps in the hall, the thump of the front door closing: Ian on his way to the social committee meeting. ". . . don't care that the petroglyph is a stolen sacred object?"

The agent gave a little laugh and shook his head. "That's what they like. It makes the glyph even more desirable. We're talking about people who already have all the Picassos and Renoirs they want. They're looking for something different, something none of their friends has. Gives them status, the way they see it, to have an ancient sacred object on their patio or displayed on a living room wall where they can show it off. There's a lot of rich people who'd like to get their hands on a petroglyph. It's even possible . . ."

The agent broke off and stared into space a moment, considering something, turning it over in his head. Finally, he said, "We've got a theory that some folks might actually order what they want. Tell a dealer about a petroglyph, and leave it to the dealer to arrange for some locals to cut it out. We think that's what happened seven years ago. A dealer hired Trublood and Birdsong to get a beautiful glyph, paid them a chunk of money, nothing close to what the dealer intended to collect, of course. There was no reason for the dealer to contact the tribes. He already had the buyer. Most likely, the buyer balked at the price, wanting a bargain. So the dealer put the pressure on by having the Indian contact the tribes. He was just haggling over price. It was a done deal. Could be the same scenario now. Our best chance will be to pick up the Indian and see what he knows and who he's working for."

Father John got to his feet and stepped over to the window. The sun had set, and the sky was beginning to fade into silver. Lines of blue shadows had started to trace the mission grounds. If the Indian refused to talk, the Drowning Man would be lost forever, like the last glyph. But there was still a chance — a small chance — that the tribes could reclaim this glyph. He walked back to the desk. The agent was scribbling on the notepad. "What about the man who might call me?" Father John said.

Gianelli didn't look up, just kept writing. "That'll be the dealer."

"Suppose I let him think the tribes have the money and are willing to pay."

In a swift, hard motion, the agent drew a long black line under whatever he had written. He glanced up. "You know what you're saying? We could be dealing with Rambo, ready to take out anybody who gets in his way or tries to pull something."

"I could set up a meeting . . ."

"Not going to happen."

"We can stall for time, Ted, keep him from selling the glyph to somebody else. If he thinks he can get the money fast, he'll agree to a meeting."

The agent pushed himself to his feet and crossed to the window. He stood quietly for a long moment, staring outside, framed in the silver light of evening. Finally he turned around. "You'll do it my way, understand? This will be between us. I don't want Norman or anybody else involved. I don't want anybody else at risk. We can't take any more chances than necessary. When the guy calls . . ."

"You think he'll call?" There it was, the doubt that he'd been trying to hold at bay, intruding itself in the conversation. The man had to call, Father John was thinking. Everything depended on the man with the petroglyph calling.

"He'll call. When he does, you play him along. Make him want to stay in the game.

Say you need the proof that he didn't read about the glyph in the newspaper and decide to shake down the tribes. Tell him that if he delivers the proof, you'll arrange for the quarter-million payment. You sure you want to do this?"

"It's the only chance, Ted."

"We take it one step at a time, okay? You call me the minute you hang up. I'm going to be involved in the meeting. You understand? Maybe we don't know who we're dealing with, but we do know one thing: Folks that trade in illegal Indian artifacts aren't nice people. They operate with their own set of rules, and they have one goal in mind — money. They'll do anything for money. There was a gang working in Nevada that . . ." He went back to his chair and sat down. "Forget it," he said.

"What happened, Ted?"

The fed stared at him a moment, then waved his hand, as if he would've liked to wave away his own reluctance. "Gang was stealing artifacts over two or three years. Digging archeological sites, taking ancient tools, arrowheads, corncobs, hammerstones, clay figurines, baskets, that kind of thing. Looting everything they could get their hands on and destroying the sites while they did it. Even helped themselves to several rare petroglyphs. Somebody in the gang contacted the Paiutes, offered to sell them the glyphs and some of the other artifacts."

"An Indian?"

Gianelli nodded. "Stranger to the area. Never was identified. One of the tribal councilmen got a phone call ordering him to put a hundred thousand dollars in a piece of luggage, leave it in a locker at the Reno airport, and mail the key to a post office box. The artifacts would be returned. The councilman followed instructions exactly, except for one detail. He called the BLM agent in the area, and the agent called in the FBI. Agents were watching the post office, but nobody ever showed up. Two days later, the councilman was shot to death. Not nice people, like I said."

Gianelli slipped the notepad into his shirt pocket, then got to his feet. "So you'll follow the rules," he said, and Father John wasn't sure whether it was a question or a command.

He followed the agent back into the entry and let him out the front door. Across the mission, he could see the dark hulks of pickups parked in front of the administration building. Headlights of other pickups were bouncing through the cottonwoods. He glanced at his watch. Almost eight o'clock. The social committee meeting was about to start, and AA would get under way in Eagle Hall in a few minutes.

Gianelli was halfway down the sidewalk when he turned back. "Call me the minute you hear from the dealer," he said.

Father John nodded, then closed the door and started down the hallway to the kitchen, Walks-On skittering ahead. He would feed the dog, and maybe grab a couple of bites himself before he headed over to the AA meeting.

4

"You read this?"

Amos Walking Bear filled up the doorway. One hand gripped the handle of the walking stick planted in the carpet to balance his bulky frame; the other waved a folded newspaper into the office.

"Nice to see you, Grandfather," Vicky Holden said, using the term of respect for the Arapaho elder. She got to her feet and came around the desk. The old man had burst through the door just as Annie had pressed the intercom key and told her that Amos wanted to see her. Vicky took hold of his arm and started to guide him forward while, at the same time, shoving the door closed against the clack of computer keys and the bleat of the ringing phone. The sounds retreated into the distance as they crossed the office, Amos following the walking stick that jabbed at the carpet. The old man had a musty odor about him, a mixture of sage and dust, like the landscape of the Wind River Reservation. Beneath the sleeve of his rough plaid shirt, Vicky could feel the tenseness in his muscles.

Amos settled himself into one of the twin upholstered chairs in front of the desk and let out a sharp exhalation of breath. He flapped the newspaper against one thigh.

"How can I help you, Grandfather?" Vicky walked around the desk, sat down, and stole a quick glance at the small clock at the corner of the desk blotter. Only about ten minutes before she would have to leave for the meeting with the Joint Arapaho and Shoshone Business Council in Fort Washakie. On the agenda was the Bureau of Land Management's plan to widen the road in Red Cliff Canyon. The Forest Service had recently opened parts of the Shoshone Forest to logging, and the timber companies had convinced the BLM that the best route was through a sacred canyon. The tribes wanted the road stopped. Last week, the Joint Council had asked Holden and Lone Eagle to look into the matter. Adam, her law partner — *more than just that,* she thought — had left early. Some other business to take care of, he'd said. He'd meet her at the council chambers.

Adam wouldn't like her to be late.

"They did it again." The elder leaned forward and slapped the newspaper against the edge of the desk. Threads of silvery perspiration glistened in the lines of his brown face. His hair was still black with strands of gray that looked as if they had been painted on, the way warriors in the Old Time had painted their hair. He had deep-set eyes beneath the cliff of his forehead, which made it seem as if he were staring out of the shadows at the newspaper folded to the article with the black half-inch headline: "Rock Art Stolen."

"I saw the article," Vicky said, not wanting to read it again, wishing that she hadn't already read it, as if the reading itself had made it real. Yesterday morning, alone in her apartment after Adam had left — still in her robe, the sun slanting through the kitchen window — she'd been sipping at a cup of coffee, eating a piece of buttered toast when she'd opened the paper and read the headline. She could still taste the mixture of coffee, toast, and acid that had risen in her throat. Who could have done such a thing! Chiseled out a petroglyph that had been in Red Cliff Canyon for who knew how long? A thousand years? Two thousand years? So long ago that time had not counted, time had not yet begun.

"It's terrible," she said.

"Terrible," Amos repeated, nodding his massive head — a slow lifting and dropping over his chest. She could see the white scalp in the pencil-wide part through his dark hair. The walking stick tapped out a steady rhythm on the carpet. "The monster that killed Raymond Trublood up at the Taylor Ranch seven years ago is back. Still doing his evil, taking another one of our glyphs. Wouldn't surprise me if he up and shoots somebody else, like he shot Raymond, and puts the blame on some innocent man like my grandson, Travis."

Vicky nodded. She was beginning to understand what had brought Amos Walking Bear the thirty or forty miles from his house on the reservation to the law offices of Holden and Lone Eagle on the Main Street of Lander. It wasn't just the petroglyph. She felt as if she'd put on a pair of glasses that brought the blurred world into focus. She'd been working at the law firm in Denver seven years ago. She'd heard about the stolen petroglyph — a brief mention in the *Denver Post,* maybe an inch or two, pushed by more important events to the bottom of a column of news briefs.

After she'd returned to the reservation,

she heard the gossip about Travis Birdsong. How he'd been seen running out of a barn after Raymond Trublood was shot to death. The two Arapahos, barely into their twenties, had been working at the Taylor Ranch when one of the petroglyphs in Red Cliff Canyon was chiseled out of a rock. Dust and chips from the rock had coated the bed of Raymond's pickup. A novice detective could have put the case together: Travis and Raymond had stolen the petroglyph, sold it on the black market, and argued over whatever money they'd gotten.

Except that Amos Walking Bear had never accepted his grandson's guilt. The old man had gone into seclusion for more than a year, not attending any of the tribal celebrations or ceremonies, not seeing anyone who came to check on him. People had left food at the front door.

They were still leaving food almost six years ago, when Vicky had come home and opened her own law office in the vague hope that her people would trust her with the issues that mattered — protecting the reservation's oil and gas, water, timber, and other natural resources that outsiders were always trying to get their hands on. Instead, she'd slowly built a practice handling divorces and DUIs and adoptions, and writing leases and

62

wills, while the tribe sent the important cases to lawyers in Casper and Cheyenne. It wasn't until she'd teamed up with Adam Lone Eagle, a Lakota, that the tribal council, which her people called the business council, had begun sending important cases their way.

"This here's proof." Amos slapped the newspaper onto the desk. The blotter skittered sideways. "This is what we need to help Travis."

Vicky was quiet a moment. It was strange. When she'd first learned of Raymond Trublood's death, she'd thought of his grandmother, Missy, who had raised him. She remembered the old woman making fry bread at the powwows, the gnarled hands kneading the thick dough. How hard it must have been for her, Raymond's death. And here was an old man still grieving over his grandson in prison.

"I'm not sure I'm following, Grandfather," she said finally, afraid that she was following, that the old man really believed another stolen petroglyph proved Travis was not the thief who had stolen the glyph seven years ago. Not the man who had killed Raymond.

"Same thing like before." The elder settled back and propped the walking stick against one leg. A door slammed somewhere in the office, sending a ripple of disturbance through the walls. An engine backfired on the street two stories below. "The killer goes up to Red Cliff Canyon 'cause he knows that's where the spirits carved their images. Dozens of images up there, some of 'em easy enough to chisel out. He can take his pick. Made himself a pile of dough seven years ago, so now he's back wantin' more money. Look at that." He pulled his body from side to side, working his way to the edge of the chair, and thrust a tightened fist toward the newspaper. "Took the Drowning Man this time. Some dealer says that petroglyph's worth a quarter million dollars. Enough to take the chance on gettin' it out of the canyon without anybody seein', that's what the thief figured. He done it soon's the snow started to melt and before the tourists started goin' to that dude ranch."

"Grandfather," Vicky began, searching for the words. There was the muffled sound of the phone ringing in the outer office. "There's no proof the same person took both petroglyphs."

"What're you talkin' about? Read that article. They was both stolen the same way. Chiseled around the edges. Pried outta the rock with a crowbar."

"But anybody could have done that."

"He done it! The monster that killed Raymond and sent my grandson to prison. He could've taken some other glyph. There's lots of 'em in the canyon. Some of 'em so small, he could've taken the whole boulder, hoisted it onto a flatbed. No! He wanted a petroglyph just like the last one. Two thousand years old, and the picture still sharp, like the spirits had carved it yesterday. Hear what I'm sayin', Vicky?"

The old man gripped the edges of the armrests, as if he might propel himself out of the chair. The walking stick slid sideways and made a thudding noise on the carpet. "You gotta get my grandson's conviction overturned. Get the governor to pardon him. You gotta do whatever it takes to get Travis out of prison. He's gonna die there, Vicky. I'm tellin' you, it's killin' him bein' in a cage. Every time he calls, I hear the sadness in his voice. He ain't the same, Vicky. He's lost hope. Now he's gonna get some hope."

The buzzer sounded. Vicky stretched out her hand and pressed the button on the intercom. "Yes?" she said.

"Joint Council meeting's gonna start in twenty minutes." Annie's voice was sharp, businesslike. "Adam's on the line, wondering where you are."

Vicky told the secretary to let Adam know that one of the tribal elders had stopped in. Then she pushed the button again.

"You gotta help Travis," Amos said, as if there hadn't been an interruption, as if nothing else mattered. He hadn't taken his eyes from her. "You can see him down at the state prison. He already seen his counselor and filled out the form sayin' you're gonna be his lawyer now, so you got the right to visit him."

In Rawlins, Vicky was thinking. A good two-hour drive. Travis might have listed her as a visitor, but she would have to file another prison form agreeing to be on Travis's list. And that was *if* she decided to talk to him.

She held the old man's gaze. His eyes were rheumy and red rimmed, mixed with worry and determination. He would not give up, she realized. He'd latched onto the new theft as the proof he needed to clear his grandson. How could she turn him down? It was Amos and the other elders who had stood behind her, encouraging her, telling her not to be discouraged when the Arapaho Business Council and the Joint Council reached out to other lawyers — white and male, as if they couldn't trust her, an Arapaho woman — telling her to be patient, that eventually her own people would come to her. It had been a thin strand of hope she'd held onto, even when the grandmothers had clucked and called her *Hi sei ci nihi,* Woman Alone, and gossiped about how she had stepped out ahead of the men, become a lawyer, tried to make herself a chief.

"Did Travis's attorney file an appeal?" she asked.

The old man didn't take his eyes away. For a long moment, he sat perfectly still, turned to stone. Finally he said, "Harry Gruenwald was the bastard's name. Said he was gonna appeal. Said no way was Travis guilty. Then he up and disappears. Some defense attorney, lettin' Travis rot in prison."

No appeal? Vicky was thinking. Travis's lawyer should have filed an appeal. And after seven years it would be too late, but she might be able to file a petition for post-conviction relief. The judge might reverse Travis's conviction and grant a new trial if there were new evidence. The theft of another petroglyph hardly met that criteria.

"Before I talk to Travis," she heard herself saying, "I'll have to see the trial transcript." If Gruenwald had mentioned an appeal, it was possible that he might have ordered a printed copy of the transcript before he dropped the idea. "It might contain some-thing that would give us grounds to reopen the case." She doubted that was true.

"You got the grounds right here," Amos said, thrusting his fist again at the newspa-per.

"I'll call you, Grandfather."

Amos stared at her a moment. Finally he gave a little nod. He leaned over and picked up the walking stick. Balancing both hands on the knob, he levered himself out of the chair and started toward the door.

Vicky jumped to her feet and, hurrying around the old man, opened the door and ushered him ahead. She followed him across the outer office, past Annie, who looked up from the computer monitor and nodded toward Amos. Vicky opened the outer door and waited as Amos moved into the cor-ridor. He turned back, rheumy eyes study-ing her again. "I knew you was gonna help Travis," he said.

Vicky didn't say anything. She tried for a smile — *a half smile,* she thought. She felt as if her face were cracking as she watched the old man thrust his weight around and start down the corridor in the direction of the elevator, his shadow broken along the railings that edged the stairway. She didn't know how she could help Travis Birdsong. The fact that another petroglyph had been stolen meant nothing. It certainly didn't prove that the same thief had shot Raymond Trublood seven years ago. It wasn't the type of evidence she could use to file a petition. She should have explained that to Amos, been more forceful. Why hadn't she been more forceful?

She closed the door and started back toward her own office. Past the opened door on the left, she could see Roger Hurst hunched over his desk. Two years out of law school, eager and smart, Roger was the assistant that she and Adam had hired to handle cases like Travis Birdsong's. She should have suggested that Amos Walking Bear talk to the new assistant, but she could never turn away one of the elders. That was the truth of it, and it clung to her like a heavy blanket on her shoulders as she walked to her own desk and pulled out a legal pad. She scribbled Travis Birdsong and District Court trial transcript on the top sheet, then took her briefcase out of the bottom desk drawer and went back into the outer office. She tore off the sheet and handed it across Annie's desk.

"Amos wants you to get his grandson out

of prison, right?" The secretary was staring at the scribbled words. "Poor man. Never could face the fact that Travis is a murderer. What're you gonna do, Vicky?" She looked up, curiosity flickering in her brown eyes.

"I'm not sure," Vicky said. "See if you can get the transcript." She slipped the slim briefcase under her arm and started for the door. Then she turned back. "Were you on the rez when Raymond Trublood was shot?"

The secretary nodded. "Oh, yeah. I'll never forget it. Moccasin telegraph was so full, it's a wonder it didn't break down. Everybody had an opinion about why Travis Birdsong went and killed his best friend. Didn't help Amos any, with everybody saying Travis was guilty even before he was tried. It was like the trial was just some kind of formality. They could've just dumped Travis in prison without bothering to wait for the jury to find him guilty, and nobody would've cared. Everybody was so upset about Raymond Trublood getting killed. It was just Amos that kept saying Travis didn't do it. And Travis, I guess. He kept saying he was innocent; somebody set him up."

Annie paused. The hint of a smile tugged at the corners of her mouth. "Guess they all say that, don't they? Murderers, I mean. They all say they're innocent."

"I guess so," Vicky said. She turned back to the door and let herself out into the corridor, pulling the door shut behind her, the secretary's words ringing in her head. *They all say they're innocent. And so do the people who love them,* she thought.

5

"There you are." Adam Lone Eagle jumped up from the chair at the table near the front of the tribal chambers the instant that Vicky stepped through the door. The table faced the raised dais where the members of the Joint Arapaho and Shoshone Business Council sat behind a long table — Arapahos on the right, Shoshones on the left. An executive session, Vicky knew. Called to discuss sensitive matters. There was no one else in the chambers. The brown eyes of the councilmen followed her as she made her way past the empty rows of spectator chairs to the table where Adam had pulled out the chair next to him.

"Sorry I'm late," Vicky said, directing the apology to Norman Yellow Hawk, seated at the center of the table on the dais, which meant that it was the Arapaho chairman's turn to conduct a joint meeting. She nodded to the others, letting them know they were included in the apology. Next to Norman was Herbert Stockham, who headed the Shoshone Business Council. The other council members — men, all of them — looked older, with gray-tipped black hair, unreadable expressions in their brown, leathery faces, and steady gazes no longer capable of surprise. Vicky knew them all. Members of families she'd known all her life. She'd gone to school with their kids and younger sisters and brothers. She'd watched them dance at the powwows, ride the broncos in the rodeos. They were her people, the leaders of the two tribes on the Wind River Reservation.

Both chairmen were younger. Norman, an Arapaho with rounded, powerful-looking shoulders, who probably tipped the scales at 200, and Herbert, a Shoshone, rail thin with black hair slicked behind his ears. They dressed nearly the same in light-colored plaid short-sleeve shirts with bolo ties that hung below opened collars, one with what looked like the silver head of a bull, the other with a silver bronco. She sat down, squared the legal pad in front of her, and extracted a pen from her briefcase. Light from the ceiling fixtures glistened like streams of water running across the polished table.

Adam was still on his feet, the sleeves of his blue shirt rolled almost to his elbows, the way he always rolled his sleeves, as if cuffs were too confining, too bothersome. So many things were familiar about him now that he was part of her life, Vicky thought. They'd been law partners for three months, lovers for even longer. When he left her apartment this morning with sleeves down, cuffs buttoned, she knew that by the time he got to the office, the sleeves would be rolled up. She watched the muscles flex in his forearm as he flipped the pages of the large white tablet propped on an easel at the corner of the table. His long, brown fingers flattened the cushion of papers beneath a map of the Wind River Range on the western border of the reservation. The Shoshone Forest was a splash of green and bronze.

"Just to bring you up to speed," Adam said, tossing an impatient glance her way. The meeting had been scheduled for four o'clock, and Adam liked to start on time. A white habit, he called it, that he'd picked up in law school and at white firms in Denver and Casper. It made no difference that everyone in the chambers was Indian, and the Indian way was to start when the time was ready, which meant when everybody had arrived. Yet the Joint Council had voted to go into executive session, and they had started without her.

"I'd appreciate it." Vicky scribbled the date across the top of the yellow pad. She wondered if Adam, eager to hurry the meeting along, hadn't assured the council members that it was fine to start without her.

"The Forest Service has opened this area to logging," Adam was saying, and Vicky looked up. His black hair was combed back, close to his head, which gave his handsome, sculptured features an austere look that emphasized the small red scar on his cheek. The hint of impatience was still there in the way that he ran an index finger along the spine of green mountains.

A guffaw erupted from Norman Yellow Hawk, as if he'd found it necessary to clear his throat. "They want to clear out the underbrush and the dead trees to prevent fires, that's what the Forest Service says. What they're really up to is giving those lumber companies what they've been after for years — rights to cut down the big ponderosas."

"We fought the decision." This from a Shoshone councilman, who had leaned forward and was clasping and unclasping rough-looking rancher's hands. "Shoshones and Arapahos got together, told the BLM director we didn't want trucks and heavy equipment traveling across the rez to get to Red Cliff Canyon. Didn't do any good. BLM's gonna let all them trucks up into the canyon, right through *poha kahni.* The house of power. A sacred place."

One of the Arapaho councilmen leaned over the table and cleared his throat. The others drew back, giving him all the space and time he needed. "Problem is," he said, "canyon's on BLM land, leads right into the national forest, so they can run trucks there if they want. They said they did an environmental study. What it was, was a bunch of their scientists saying no problem. They had a public meeting, and we were the only ones that showed up to comment. Bottom line is, logging companies had already made up their minds to widen the road so they can haul heavy equipment and timber. Better road will also bring in a lot more outsiders than the handful of tourists that drive up to the dude ranch every summer." He paused, as if to allow time for a new thought forming in his mind. "Now we got another petroglyph stolen, and that fool Duncan Barnes runs the antiques place out on the highway told the newspaper it's worth a quarter of a million dollars. Lots of folks could get the idea to come into the canyon and help themselves to the rock art."

Norman set his elbows on the table and clasped his hands. "Couldn't come at a worse time," he said, peering over the bulging knobs of his knuckles. "Archeologist and some students been working in the canyon the last couple summers, trying to date the petroglyphs. They were planning to finish the project this summer, but there won't be enough time if road construction starts."

He paused. Behind the gripped hands, Norman's lips were set in a tight line. "They've been doing radiocarbon dating of the patina on the rocks," he said. "Also excavated a couple of mounds beneath the images. Found all kinds of artifacts — arrowheads, bones, carved tools used for chipping rocks. Said that by dating the artifacts, they could corroborate the radiocarbon dating." He drew in a long breath and shook his head. "Construction is gonna stir up big clouds of dust and create a lot of noise. Vibrations might damage the rock art images, and the dust . . . well, the dust could pollute the patina and throw off the radiocarbon dating by hundreds of years."

"The spirits will abandon the canyon," Stockham said, his voice low and steady, cutting through the emotional charge in the room. He had turned slightly in his chair and was staring at the small window that interrupted the wall running the length of the chambers, as if he were witnessing the exodus of the spirits. The late-afternoon sun was intense; an oblong splash of orange-red light lay across the gray carpet. "They'll go where there's peace and quiet. The images will disappear. Maybe the spirits will carve new images of themselves in some other place; maybe not."

No one spoke. A sense of hopelessness, unseen, yet as real as a spirit, moved through the quiet. This was what it was about, Vicky was thinking. The total lack of respect for the beliefs of her people, the beliefs of everyone in the room. The engineers and surveyors who came to widen the road, the truckers who would haul the equipment into the forest and haul out the logs — they would scoff at the idea that the petroglyphs were more than ancient pictures carved into rocks. Scoff at the idea they were the spirits themselves who dwelled in the canyon, the spirits who *showed* their images. The canyon was a sacred place. They had to protect it.

"Adam and I have been discussing the options," Vicky said. They'd spent part of the morning going over them. It had been comfortable talking with Adam. He was Lakota. He hadn't scoffed when she'd said they had to find a way to protect the spirits. She glanced up at him now, expecting him to explain.

Instead, he lifted one hand, another impatient gesture, and motioned her to her feet. Then he stepped back and folded his arms across his chest. Vicky went over to the map. It was a moment before her index finger found the tiny red line, almost invisible, that marked the dirt road running from Highway 287 into the mountains of the Shoshone National Forest. The road was about two miles south of Red Cliff Canyon. "We suggest that the tribes propose an alternate road to the BLM," she said, glancing along the row of brown faces on the dais above her.

Stockham was shaking his head. "Shoshones won't go for it," he said. "We got a couple families living up there off that road."

"But the homes aren't right on the road," Adam said, and Vicky felt a wave of gratitude that he'd jumped in on her side. *We're a good team, Vicky.* She could hear his voice in her head. He was right. They were stronger together than either had been alone. Then another voice in her head — her own. *Maybe I am kidding myself. Maybe I am the one who is stronger with Adam at my side.*

"You've thought about everything." Norman gave Adam a look of approval. "The homes and barns are a mile or so south of the road." Glancing sideways at the Shoshones, he said, "That a fact?"

Stockham shrugged and lifted his eyebrows, a gesture that said, "Could be." The other Shoshone councilmen gave almost imperceptible nods. Stockham went on, "Why would the BLM go for a road that's not much more than two tracks through the brush?"

"The logging companies will have to improve either road," Vicky said. "There are advantages to the alternate road. It leaves the highway and crosses a mile and a half of flats before starting the climb into the mountains. And it's a gentler climb with fewer curves than Red Cliff Canyon, which would make it easier for the trucks hauling heavy equipment and logs to negotiate. We can make a strong case that it would be in the best interests of the logging companies to use this road."

The room was quiet a moment; then Stockham said, "That fails, we can always go to the *Gazette.* Looks like that hotshot young reporter — what's her name? Aileen Harrison? — is real interested in petroglyphs. Couldn't wait to write the article about the Drowning Man, tell the world where the glyphs are. Well, maybe she'd like to tell the world about how the logging companies are going to destroy them. Get public opinion riled up enough, it'll force the BLM to use the other road."

"Too big a risk," Adam said. It was an option she had brought up this morning, Vicky was thinking, but Adam had waved it away. "The petroglyphs are too vulnerable," he went on. "Even the article about the stolen glyph is bound to bring more people into the canyon. People who'd never even heard about the petroglyphs will be hiking all over the mountain looking for rock art."

Adam stepped over to the map. "Looks to me like we're walking a fine line here," he continued. "We want people to appreciate the art carved into rocks a thousand, two thousand years ago. What we don't want are curiosity seekers tromping over the mountain, thinking, 'Gee, rock art is valuable,' and wondering how they might steal it."

The two tribal chairmen exchanged a quick glance. Then Norman said, "Natural resources director for the tribes, Mona Ledger, is going to be in the canyon for a while with some of her staff. They're photographing and cataloging the rest of the glyphs. They know to keep their eyes open for anybody looking suspicious. But they can't stay there forever. We have to count on the public having a memory of about five minutes and forgetting the glyphs are there. No sense in stirring up the newspapers about the dangers of a new road. Only calls attention to the petroglyphs."

"I'm not sure I agree." Vicky tossed a glance at Adam. "I think you have a good point, Herb," she said to the Shoshone. "If the BLM thought the public was on our side, they might back off." She'd made the same point to Adam this morning, a point that he'd ignored. She hurried on, looking past the irritation in Adam's expression, directing her comments now to the men on the dais. "I don't think the BLM wants to be perceived as an agency that destroys sacred places."

Norman shrugged. "Couple of other things," he said, making a tipi with his hands. "Not for publication, you understand?"

"We're your lawyers, Norman," Adam said.

"Herb and me" — a glance at the Shoshone next to him — "rest of the Joint Councilmen, the fed, and Father John, we're the only ones know what's coming down."

"Father John," Vicky said, his name escaping her lips as if it had been there all the time, on the tip of her tongue. Of course he would be involved in whatever Norman was about to tell her. He'd become part of the lives of her people, just as he'd become part of hers.

"The thief sent a message to Father John," Norman said. "We come up with the money, we might get the Drowning Man back."

"How much money?" Vicky heard herself asking.

"Same as what the newspaper says. Quarter million. Last time a glyph was stolen, the thief wanted two hundred thousand."

"Wait a minute." Vicky took her seat and locked eyes with the Arapaho chairman. "You were contacted seven years ago?"

"Thought we had a deal," Norman said. "Then Travis Birdsong went crazy, killed his partner. There was all kinds of publicity, and the contact went away. We don't want that to happen again, ruin our chance to get the glyph back."

Vicky took a moment. She stared past Adam and the easel with the map of the Red Cliff Canyon area, a new thought forming in her head. "How was Father John contacted?" she said.

"Indian stopped him over in Ethete." This from Norman. "Didn't want to come to the tribal offices himself . . ."

"It could be the same contact." Vicky could feel her heart speeding up. Amos Walking Bear could be right. Whoever had taken the first glyph had come back for another one, and sent the same man to try to collect a ransom. Which could mean that Amos's grandson could be in prison for a murder he didn't commit.

"Another reason not to bring on a lot of publicity," Adam said, glancing at Vicky as he stepped back to the table. "The Indian'll disappear, just like last time."

"Another problem." Norman said. He was bouncing his tipied hands off each other. "Newspaper reporter keeps poking around, she'll find out that the petroglyphs aren't all that's been stolen up in the canyon. Thieves've been taking small artifacts for some time now. Mona and her staff came across several mounds that were dug up recently."

"Artifacts are also missing?" Vicky said.

The tribal councilmen were nodding in unison, heads bobbing over the long table. "Ancient tools, bones, who knows what else was taken," Norman said. "Probably sold on the black market, same place the Drowning Man will disappear into if we don't get it back." The corners of the man's mouth pulled downward. His eyebrows folded into the deep crease above his nose. "You'd be surprised at how much money people are willing to pay for old bones. Anything that's Indian, they don't care, they lay out their money. Don't have any respect. We don't need the newspapers telling folks about artifacts and even more valuable petroglyphs."

"The alternate road will speak for itself," Adam said. "Fewer curves, easier grade. We don't need to involve the press."

"How soon can you write up a proposal for the BLM?" Norman said.

"Right away," Adam told the chairman.

Norman nodded. "We made real progress here. You two . . ." Norman glanced from Adam to Vicky. "I'd say you know what you're doing. We're gonna go into regular session, take a vote on going forward with this. We'll get back to you."

Adam thanked the councilman, then walked over and held the door open, waiting. Vicky picked up her briefcase and walked past him. "Annie said one of the elders came in," he said, closing the door behind them.

"If you knew that, Adam, then you knew

why I was late." Vicky started down the corridor ahead of him.

"This was an important meeting." Adam's footsteps clacked alongside her on the tiled floor; his shoulder brushed hers.

Vicky didn't say anything for a moment. She should not have to explain to Adam Lone Eagle that it would have been impolite to refuse to see Amos Walking Bear. It was what had made their partnership possible, the fact that Adam understood the Arapaho Way. Finally she told him the old man was convinced that his grandson had been convicted seven years ago of a crime he didn't commit.

They were outside now, walking across the gravel to her Jeep. She opened the door and faced him. He'd stopped a few feet behind her, staring across the lot, squinting against the sun that gave his face a reddish cast, his own briefcase hanging next to the leg of his khaki trousers. This had nothing to do with her arriving late for the meeting, nothing to do with Amos Walking Bear's unexpected visit. "What's going on, Adam?" she said.

When he turned toward her, Vicky saw the absent look in his black eyes, as if they hadn't just suggested a possible recourse to the BLM's decision, as if they weren't in the parking lot in front of the stone building that housed the tribal offices, the life-size metal sculpture of Chief Washakie guarding the front door. He had gone somewhere else.

Adam said, "We'll have dinner tonight, Vicky. We can talk about it then."

6

The pickup's engine gave off an intermittent belching noise that punctuated the music of "Perchè tarda la luna" as Father John drove north across the reservation. The vastness of the area was monumental — the reservation itself melting into the plains, a flat, empty landscape with plateaus that rose out of nowhere, arroyos that cut unexpectedly through the earth, and thin roads that snaked into the brush. In the west was the gray smudge of the foothills of the Wind River Range. The sky was cloudless, the color of cobalt, pressing down everywhere. He'd gotten used to the emptiness of the plains, the sense of timelessness. It was familiar and comfortable. He passed the small sign at the edge of the road — *Leaving the Wind River Reservation* — and drove on.

It had been past noon before he'd gotten away from his desk and walked down the corridor of the administration building to tell Ian that he'd be gone a few hours. Parishioners had been dropping by all morning; the phone had rung nonstop. *Not good, Father, another petroglyph gone. Spirits gonna be upset. We gotta get the Drowning Man back.* He'd tried to reassure the callers, but all the time, he'd sensed that he was only trying to reassure himself. And each time he'd reached for the receiver, he'd wondered if this was the call, if this was the dealer. But the man hadn't called. Not last night, not this morning.

Outside his window, the foothills began moving closer, patches of scrub brush and stunted pines crawling over the slopes. On the other side of the road ahead, the line of high bluffs came into view, jagged red slopes shining in the afternoon sun. Now and then a pickup or sedan had shimmered in the oncoming lane a moment before sweeping past. He let up on the accelerator. It was easy to miss the turnoff into Red Cliff Canyon, nothing more than a dirt road on the left that meandered into the foothills before beginning the climb into the mountains. There was a ranch directly across from the turnoff, he remembered — the Taylor Ranch. He could see the house and barn and outbuildings rising out of the earth now, an uneven collection of log walls and metal roofs stacked against the red slopes of the bluffs.

He slowed for the turnoff ahead, the interruption of dirt at the side of the road. The pickup bounced past the sagebrush that lapped at the doors and the tape skipped across the opening notes of "Signore, ascolta!" The pickup started winding upward, spitting out clouds of dust that sprinkled the windshield with a fine, gray film. Then he was in the canyon, climbing along the mountainside. Past the edge of the road on the left, the slope dropped into a creek that looked like a silver ribbon flung over the rocks. He kept one eye on the slope rising on the other side for the flat-faced boulders with the carved images. They were hard to spot, he knew. There were people who drove through the canyon and had no idea the petroglyphs were there.

He kept the pickup at about fifteen miles an hour, he guessed — the odometer had stopped working a few years ago — switching his gaze between the road and the rocky, tree-studded slope, looking for remnants of the rock that had held the Drowning Man. Odd, he thought. It was the one petroglyph easy to spot, if you knew where to look, but now that it was gone, it was as if the rock itself had faded into the mountain.

The pickup banked into another curve. As he came out of it, he spotted the line of pickups parked ahead, tilting sideways toward the barrow ditch. On the other side, a camper stood in a wide, bare-dirt area that jutted over the drop-off into the creek below. Beyond the camper, close to the edge of the drop-off, were a pair of green canvas tents, the walls dented in the breeze.

Father John stopped behind the row of pickups and got out. The sounds of *Turandot* floated outside with him. He slammed the door, leaving the tape playing, and scanned the slope. The natural resources director and some of her staff were probably up there somewhere, hidden by the rocks and scrub brush, the mountain itself, just like the petroglyphs. The sun was hot, and the warm breeze plucked at his shirt sleeves. He lifted one hand and pulled his cowboy hat forward to shade his eyes.

Then he saw it: about a hundred feet up the slope, the broken sandstone boulder where the petroglyph had been. The face looked empty and gray with jagged ridges left by chisels and hammers. A sharp sense of loss stabbed at him, the loss of something beautiful that should have stayed. He was only half aware of the sound of a door banging shut.

"Disgusting, isn't it?" A woman's voice cut into the silence.

Father John swung around. She was walking across the road from the improvised campsite, a tall, slim woman, probably in her thirties, wearing blue jeans and a red tee shirt, with long black hair that emphasized the intense dark eyes of the Arapaho.

"Hi, Mona," he said, shaking her hand. "Father O'Malley from St. Francis."

"I remember you." The woman nodded, as if that were the extent of the polite preliminaries that were required. "I take it that you read about the stolen petroglyph and wanted to see for yourself," she said. "We've had people up here all yesterday looking for the place where the petroglyph used to be. Most of them had never noticed it when it was here."

"I saw it. It was beautiful."

That seemed to please her. She looked past him up the slope, her eyes resting, he knew, on the jagged, gray scar. He said, "The thief sent a message to the tribes. Norman Yellow Hawk thought you'd want to know."

As she brought her eyes back to his, her

features settled into a look of acceptance, as if the news didn't surprise her. "We can talk over there," she said, tilting her head toward the campground.

Father John followed the woman across the road to the camper, where she pulled the door open and, one boot on the metal step, looked over her shoulder. "Something to drink? Coke?"

He said a Coke would be fine, and she lifted herself into the camper, leaving the door hanging open. In the shadows inside, he could see her rummaging inside a cooler that stood on the floor. There was the sound of swishing water and clinking ice cubes. Finally she came back outside carrying two cans of soda. She kicked the door shut behind her.

"We can sit in the shade," she said, handing him one of the Cokes and starting around the camper. He popped the tab, took a long drink of the sweet, syrupy liquid that dropped like a cold rope inside his chest, then followed her. She'd already pulled a webbed folding chair open in a square of shade and was in the process of opening another, her Coke on the ground in front of other chairs that leaned against the white wall of the camper.

"All the comforts of home." She gestured

for him to take a chair, scooped up her Coke, and sat down in the other one. "Even got a shower in there," she said, lifting the can toward the camper. "I'm staying here for a few days to keep an eye on the canyon — you know, after that newspaper article. Couple of my staff are here. We're taking new photographs of the glyphs, cataloging and updating our records. I guess Norman told you we found out the glyphs aren't the only artifacts that have been looted. Some of the mounds in front of the glyphs have been disturbed. Tools, bones, that kind of thing, probably gone. Now the logging companies are making noise about widening the road. You heard about that?"

Father John nodded, and she hurried on: "The lawyers think they're gonna stop it; I say, good luck. We want to get as much data as we can before construction gets started." She stopped, took a long drink from her Coke, and swiped at her lips with the back of one hand. She was pretty in a natural, disarming way, as if that were something she didn't know. A fine web of tiny lines fanned from the corners of her dark, intense eyes. "What's this about a message?" she said.

He told her about the Indian and the ransom message. She rolled her eyes to the sky when he mentioned the 250,000 dollars, and he continued, filling her in on his conversation yesterday evening with Norman. "We're hoping that the man the Indian works for will call."

"Why you?" she asked.

Father John shook his head. "The Indian didn't want to be recognized," he said finally. Then he told her his theory that the Indian might be the same man who had contacted the tribes about the stolen glyph seven years ago.

"I heard about that." Mona Ledger lifted her face toward the mountain across the road. "A pair of losers cut out the glyph and got into a fight about the money. One of them ended up dead, and the Indian messenger took off. It was the last the Arapahos and Shoshones heard about the glyph."

"Norman doesn't want it to happen again."

She tipped her head back and drained the last of her Coke, then squeezed the can until the sides cracked together, and got to her feet. "Hang on a minute," she said, darting around the corner of the camper.

Father John finished his own Coke and waited. He could hear the woman moving about inside: an object clanked against a hard surface, a cabinet door slammed shut. Then she was back, carrying a large photograph album. She pulled the folding chair forward, sat down, and opened the album between them. The cellophane pages fell back naturally, as if they were the usual pages consulted.

Mona shifted the album sideways until it was resting on Father John's thigh. "These photographs were taken seven years ago. This is the Drowning Man." She pointed to one of the photographs pressed under the cellophane.

He stared at the familiar image: the elongated, rectangular body, the squared head, and the truncated arms sticking out to the sides, the small, squared feet that jutted from the truncated legs. Surrounding the figure were wavy lines, like ripples of water. He felt again the sharp sting of loss.

"The elders say that petroglyphs are images of the spirits that live in the rocks," Mona said. "They say the spirits themselves carved their images. The spirits have guarded this canyon from the beginning of time. So when an image is taken, the spirit leaves the canyon. The other spirits will leave, too, if all the trucks and heavy equipment move in here and start widening the road." She closed the album, slowly, reverently, he thought, as if the paper images themselves were sacred. "Would you like to climb up and see some of the other petroglyphs?"

He'd forgotten how steep the slope was. It had been two or three years since he'd been in Red Cliff Canyon to view the petroglyphs. From the road, the slope looked like an easy uphill stroll, but he could feel the hard pull in his calf muscles. Mona Ledger was about ten feet ahead, long legs zigzagging around the boulders, brush, and clumps of stunted trees. He tried to stay in her path, stopping from time to time to catch his breath and look down. The highway slithered across the brown plains like a large, silver snake. At the foot of the canyon, the buildings of the Taylor Ranch looked like the painted image on a canvas.

He took in another gulp of air and hurried to catch up. Mona had pushed away the branch of a pine and was standing inside the other branches that dipped around her. Next to her legs, he could see the small, bullet-shaped boulder with the image carved into the face.

"A glyph like this is especially vulnerable to thieves," she said when he'd reached her. "It stands alone and it's small. The only protection is this tree. Chances are most people who hike up here have never noticed it. And over there" — the branch swung back into place as she stepped away from the tree and nodded toward a place farther along the slope — "those glyphs are clustered on massive sandstone outcroppings. Much more difficult to extricate a carving."

Mona started walking toward the outcroppings, and Father John stayed in step, their boots drumming an irregular rhythm on the underbrush and the hard earth. Coming toward them was a tall man in a tan, wide-brim hat with a string of brown leather that dangled under his chin and flopped against his yellow shirt. A few yards above, a young woman crouched at the base of a clump of rocks, peering upward at a carved image through the lens of a camera.

"We've got a visitor," Mona called out.

The man stopped and waited next to the dead branch of a pine tree that straddled the slope. "This is Father O'Malley from the mission," Mona said, tilting her head backward. "Father, meet my assistant, Cliff Fast Horse. Been taking care of these glyphs for the last several years."

"Didn't do a good enough job." The Arapaho ran his gaze across the slope. His black eyes were flecked with sadness.

"You're only one person," Mona said. "Couldn't check the canyon every day." She turned back to Father John. "That's the problem, not enough personnel. This is BLM land. They have one preservation agent working this whole region. We're talking hundreds of miles of empty land. The tribes have Cliff here, trying to oversee the sacred sites in the area."

"Have a look." Fast Horse pivoted about and headed toward the outcroppings. Father John waved Mona ahead, then fell in behind.

"We've been trying to learn all we can about the glyphs." Fast Horse tossed the information over his shoulder. "Last couple of summers, an archeologist and some students from the university were working up here trying to date them. Started with radiocarbon techniques. From the patina on the rocks, they proved some carvings are a thousand years old, but they also found two or three that date back two thousand years. The Drowning Man was one of them. We were hoping that the team could continue the studies this summer, uncover a few mounds at the base of the glyphs and locate the tools used to carve the images. They can date tools, bones, and other objects and corroborate the radiocarbon dating."

Mona turned and faced Father John. "But now we know looters have been after the mounds," she said, her voice tight with anger. "And if construction gets started, the patina buildup on the glyphs could be affected, which will skew the radiocarbon results. It's a disaster."

They stopped in front of a series of images carved into the walls of the rock outcropping. No one spoke for a moment. Father John was struck by the silent majesty of the images: a procession of figures — humans, birds, animals — moving across the gray expanse of boulders that shouldered against one another.

Fast Horse swept a hand toward the images. "Every glyph is more beautiful and interesting than the next," he said, elements of excitement and awe working in his voice. "The most dominant figures here are birds, or, if you like, anthropomorphic figures with wings for arms and bird-claw feet. These spirits inhabit the sky realm above the earth."

Father John followed the man's hand. Carved into the rock faces were images of large, lumbering birds and small, delicate birds, all primitive and fantastic, yet filled with a sense of motion and life.

"We know the old stories about the spirits

carving the images," the man said, shooting a glance at Mona, "but archeologists say the images were carved by shamans. Holy men who put themselves into hallucinogenic trances to obtain spiritual knowledge and power to help the people. Maybe they ingested peyote, or some other seeds or herbs that produced the desired effect. Then they traveled through the three realms of the world, middle earth, or the legged realm, above the earth in the sky and below the earth in the waters. Different creatures dwell in each realm. Humans, of course, live in the middle earth. Once out of a trance, the shamans chiseled the images of their experiences. The birdlike images reflect the experience of flying, of being above the earth, among the birds."

Fast Horse stepped closer to the end of the outcroppings. "Image like this," he said, one hand stretched toward a small petroglyph, "looks like a turtle. There are similar images that reflect frogs or lizards, the kind of creatures that move among all three realms, as the shaman must have done in his trance. The Drowning Man" — he nodded across the slope in the direction from which they'd come — "was unique. The shaman had obviously traveled into the world below, the world of water. He carved out wavy lines around the figure to give the sense of waves and ripples and the sense of drowning that he must have experienced."

"Before he emerged into the middle earth," Father John said.

A look of appreciation came into the dark eyes of the two Arapahos. Fast Horse nodded. "The drowning image is a symbol of life," he said. "Of coming into the world. Of being born." He glanced across the slope. "Over there about a mile is the boulder that the glyph was taken from seven years ago. We have photos of that glyph. It had the same motif of drowning. It's possible both stolen glyphs were carved by the same shaman. He was a great artist. The images were clear, chiseled deep into the rock. Had fine proportions. You looked at them, and you felt like you were moving underwater. The archeologists said they were the most accomplished glyphs in the canyon, the best executed pieces of art. Whoever took them knew exactly what he wanted."

"Do you really believe the same thief took both glyphs?" There was a note of astonishment in Mona's voice. "Those Arapaho cowboys working down at the Taylor Ranch stole the first glyph and sold it. One of them was shot to death. The other's in prison."

"I'm not saying the same thief came up

here and took both glyphs." The man shook his head. "But the more I think about it, the more convinced I am that somebody wanted the two images carved by the same artist."

"That implies that whoever is behind the thefts is familiar with the petroglyphs in this canyon," Father John said.

"You got it, Father," the Arapaho said.

Father John led the way back across the mountain, Mona's boots crunching the brush behind him. Before they reached the boulder where the Drowning Man had been, he veered right and started zigzagging down the steep slope, not wanting to see again the gray, defaced rock. A juniper rose out of a clump of rocks and obstructed the path. He pushed aside one of the branches and waited until Mona had gone ahead before he went after her, conscious of the branch swishing into place behind him.

When they reached the road, Mona turned around and looked at him. The color of her eyes was almost black in the bright sunshine. He could see the fear in them. "There's something he didn't tell you," she said. "There are other glyphs similar to the Drowning Man up there. The same shaman chiseled four or five other images."

He had the picture. If the same person was behind two of the thefts, he could come after the others. No wonder the natural resources director was camping here, guarding the canyon. But she couldn't guard it forever.

"How accessible are the other images?" he said.

"They're all accessible when it comes down to it, aren't they? If somebody wants them enough." She paused and looked away, watching the road, as if the thief might materialize out of the brightness. "What do we do now?"

Father John took a moment before he said, "We wait."

7

The evening was warm with a pale light bathing the façades and shining in the windows of the two-story brick buildings along Main Street. "How does an ice cream cone sound?" Adam said when they had finished dinner in the small restaurant with plank wood floors and stuccoed walls. Ice cream sounded good, Vicky told him, and he guided her out of the restaurant and down half a block to the ice cream parlor.

And there they were, she thought, strolling along the sidewalk past the red, yellow, and white flowers that sprouted from planters at the curb, licking double scoops of chocolate ice cream, the endless feeling of summer in the air. That was how dinner had gone, as if Adam's mood had lifted; they had no worries, no disagreements, nothing but time to enjoy each other's company, and for long moments Vicky had allowed herself to believe it was true. The law firm had faded away, no longer the three-hundred-pound monster that at times seemed to wedge itself between them. Whatever it was that Adam had wanted to talk about, he hadn't brought it up, and neither had she.

They crossed the street and veered into the small park that ran along the banks of the Popo Agie River. Vicky climbed onto the top of a redwood picnic table, and Adam perched next to her. At a nearby table, a family was clearing away the remains of a picnic. A blond, pretty woman who looked about seven months pregnant was folding a red and white checkered tablecloth while a tall, slim man, a black baseball cap turned backwards on his head, hoisted a cooler and started toward the brown van parked at the side of the road. A boy about eight and a little girl who looked about two years younger, both blond and white-skinned with reddish sun stripes across their cheeks, skipped back and forth, hauling wads of paper plates and napkins to the trash container.

In that moment, unbidden, as if she'd turned a page in an old, forgotten album, the photograph had sprung before her eyes, and Vicky saw her own kids: Lucas and Susan, black-haired with brown faces and skinny brown arms and knowing black eyes.

They'd gone on picnics, she and Ben and the children. Picnics right here in this little park. She pulled her eyes over to the river rippling over the rocks, streaked with light. There had been good times with Ben, before the drinking and the whoring, before he'd ever hit her. Those were the times she tried to remember, and yet the memories always had a way of plunging down into the dark tunnel of the bad times.

"I have to go to Casper for a few days." Adam's voice was quiet beside her. She was aware that he was also looking at the river. "I'm sorry, Vicky, but I'm afraid you'll have to handle the details on the BLM proposal," he said. The secretary of the Joint Council had called just before they'd left the office to say that the council wanted them to proceed. "Handle the negotiations," Adam was saying. "That's if you can get the BLM to agree to negotiate. We'll work together, of course. We can talk by phone."

Vicky glanced at the man beside her. She felt a little catch in her throat at the hard set of his jaw, the way he kept his eyes straight ahead, as if it was the river he was talking to. He'd practiced law in Casper for several years; he owned rental houses there. Every few weeks he had to drive the 120 miles to take care of business — broken lease, new tenant, damaged roof, plumbing that had stopped working. But this was different somehow. She could sense the difference in the silent gulf that had opened between them.

She asked the same question she'd asked earlier: "What's going on?"

"It's not important." Adam took a moment before giving her a sideways glance. "You know there's always something with rental property." He shrugged, then went on. Renters up and gone, no notice, trash left behind. He'd have to have the place renovated. Too bad his properties were in Casper. He should think about selling them and investing in Lander.

Vicky didn't take her eyes away as he talked, conscious of the gulf widening, as if Adam Lone Eagle were receding on the opposite shore of the river. He was lying.

Vicky got off the table and made herself walk over to the trash bin, taking her time, placing one foot in front of the other. *Relax, relax,* she told herself. After all, she was an expert on lies; she'd heard them all from Ben, the master of lies. *Don't wait up. Got some business to attend to tonight. Trust me, trust me.* She tossed the remainder of her cone into the trash and watched the chocolate ice cream dribble into a pile of paper cups and plates.

She could feel Adam's eyes boring into her back. After a moment, she turned and walked back to the table. It was starting to get dark, as if a blue curtain were falling over the park. The family had left. Their picnic table had a deserted look; there were tire tracks in the dirt where the van had parked. She slid her bag off the bench. "Don't worry," she said, keeping her voice steady, empty of concern, as if she were addressing a stranger. "I'll take care of the proposal."

"Vicky, Vicky." Adam reached out and took her hand. "Sit down," he said, leading her back up onto the table beside him. "I'm not going to lie to you anymore."

Anymore! Vicky kept her gaze on the pickups and sedans crawling along Main Street, faint headlights flickering into the dusk. She felt something hard forming inside her, like a wall growing around her heart. She gripped the edge of the table, trying to fight off the urge to jump down and walk away.

"It's Julie," he said.

Vicky didn't say anything. Her mouth had gone dry; she was conscious of her tongue pushing against the back of her teeth. Adam's ex-wife lived in Casper. Why hadn't she put it together? All those trips to Casper on business, when it had been Julie.

"She's been having a rough time, Vicky, and . . ." Adam paused. She could hear the quick intakes of breath. "She doesn't have anybody else."

"You're not married to her anymore," Vicky heard herself saying.

"She's the mother of my son. I can't turn her down when she needs help. She lost her job a couple of months ago, so I moved her into one of the rental houses. She maxed out her credit cards, so I paid them off and gave her some money to carry her through until she found another job. Now the IRS is after her. Seems that she's neglected or forgot to file her income taxes the last five years, so I have to help her get it straightened out."

"So all the business trips to Casper . . ."

"I didn't think you'd understand."

Vicky started to slide off the table. She felt the warm pressure of his hand on her arm and jerked away. "This is what I can't understand, Adam. I can't understand why you lied."

She swung around, dodging past his hand before he could take her arm again, and strode across the park. She darted through the traffic on Main and kept going past the storefronts, dodging the flowerpots and the lampposts and the occasional pedestrians strolling along, only half aware of her own image following like a shadow in the plate glass windows. A lazy line of traffic moved down the street, a tan sedan, a couple of trucks, a pickup with hip-hop blaring through the opened windows. She could make out the shape of the tan brick building on the corner ahead, the law offices of Lone Eagle and Holden on the second floor.

She was running now, across the pavement of the parking lot next to the building, weaving around the few vehicles still in the lot, toward her Jeep parked in a puddle of light from the street lamp. Another moment and she was driving out of the lot, barely conscious of the squealing tires and the honking horn as she pulled in front of a pickup, her own thoughts beating like a drum in her head: She did not need Adam Lone Eagle.

Father John wedged the pickup between Father Ian's blue sedan and a sleek, black sedan with Wisconsin license plates that stood in front of the residence. He hurried up the sidewalk and let himself in the front door. Walks-On was there to meet him as always. He patted the dog's head, trying to ignore the hard knot twisting in his stomach. Headquarters of the Wisconsin Province of the Society of Jesus were in Milwaukee, and St. Francis Mission fell within the province, which meant that the visitor was from the provincial's office. And he knew — maybe he'd always known — that the day the provincial decided to assign him somewhere else, he would send a messenger to deliver the news.

Father John glanced through the doorway to the living room on the right, expecting to find Father Ian and the visitor. No one was there. The hot odors of grease and fried meat — chicken or hamburgers — wafted down the hallway from the kitchen. There was the noise of a running faucet, the sound of metal clanking against metal. He could see the stout figure of Elena, white apron tied over a blue dress, bustling past the doorway. No one knew how old the house-keeper was. Every time the subject had come up, she'd told him that she was sixty-eight. It always made him smile. The woman had been sixty-eight for nine years.

He walked around the foot of the stairs and knocked on the closed door to his study, certain now that Ian had ushered the visitor out of the housekeeper's earshot. No sense in sending the news over the moccasin telegraph before the pastor had been told. Walks-On brushed against the leg of his jeans.

He knocked again, then pushed the door open into the small room. It was vacant, everything in place. Desk with papers sprawled over the top, bookcases along the walls, slants of late-afternoon sun spilling through the half-opened blinds.

He closed the door and went down the hall to the kitchen, Walks-On at his heels. "I see we have a visitor," he said trying for a matter-of-fact tone, as if visitors from Wisconsin routinely showed up at St. Francis Mission.

Elena turned away from the sink, brown hands smoothing the front of her apron. She tilted her chin up and gave him an exasperated look. She was a mixed blood, with tightly curled gray hair that framed the smooth, round face of the Cheyenne and accentuated the dark, knowing eyes of the Arapaho. "Just waitin' for the pastor to show up for dinner. I got the table set in the dining room. Been tryin' to keep everything hot . . ."

"You know I was racing to get back." He cut in, smiling at the old woman. They'd been over this before. She reminded him of his mother, always admonishing him to be home in time for dinner, and he, always assuring her of his good intentions. They both knew he was usually late. "Broke all the speed records," he said.

"Don't give me your Irish blarney." She brushed at the space between them with one hand. A smile wrinkled the corners of her mouth.

It was all so familiar, he was thinking. Familiar and comfortable, his life at St. Francis. He shook some dry food into the dog's dish and set it on the floor. This was the place where he could be the priest he wanted to be. The knot in his stomach pulled tighter. He would miss all of this: the mission, the people, all the little routines that had filled up the days.

"Where have you hidden our visitor?" he said.

Elena gestured with her head toward the door that led to the back porch. "Out on the patio. You want some iced tea?"

Father John waved away the offer and headed for the door. He crossed the porch, opened the outside door, and started down the wooden steps toward the two men seated on the webbed, metal chairs, facing the foothills that glowed gold in the distance, gripping half-full glasses of iced tea.

"Here's John now." Father Ian jumped up, a tall, slightly built man with sandy hair and the nervous energy of a runner tensed for the starting pistol. He set his glass down hard on the table. The brown liquid shimmered in the light. "We've been waiting for you," he said.

Bill Rutherford, the provincial himself, was getting to his feet, a slow unfolding upward, one hand depositing the glass on the table, the other gripping the back of the chair. They'd been in the seminary together, and Rutherford would have been voted the man most likely to succeed, if such a survey had been taken. Energetic and witty, the center of attention in every room he entered. They'd taught at the same prep school for two years, until their careers had diverged. A doctorate for Rutherford, a teaching position at Marquette, and finally the fast track into the top echelons of the Society, administering one of the largest Jesuit provinces, while Father John had stalled out, muffling the noise of loneliness in whiskey in the evening and blurring his way through classes in the day, on the fast track to rehab. It had been three or four years since he'd seen Bill Rutherford. The man looked thirty pounds heavier, with puffy eyes and a tiredness in the slope of his shoulders, as if he were carrying a heavy burden that he'd like to put down.

"John, how are you?" The provincial held out a fleshy hand. His grip was quick and routine. Father John was struck by the way the energy of the seminary student had leaked out of the man.

"This is a surprise." Father John swung a metal chair from its perch against the back of the house and sat down at an angle to the other men, who had already resumed their own seats. So Rutherford himself, his old classmate, had come to deliver the bad news. He was aware of the oddest things: the sunlight stippling the grass, the breeze ruffling the leaves of the old cottonwood at the corner of the house, the cool air in the shade of the patio.

"What brings you to our neck of the woods?" He pushed on, as if he didn't know, and he wondered who he was kidding. Not the provincial, and certainly not Father Ian, who was perfectly capable of assuming the job of pastor. Which, he realized, was why he could be reassigned. The provincial had been waiting for a capable man to put in his place.

"Just a road trip," Rutherford said. He did a half turn on his seat, lifted his glass, and sipped at the tea a moment. "Frankly, I needed time away from the office. Drove out to Denver to see how things are going, and decided on a side trip to the reservation. Haven't been here in a while, you know."

Father John nodded. He was wondering when the provincial had last visited St. Francis Mission — not since he'd been here. They'd talked on the telephone, and once or twice Rutherford had sent one of his assistants to check on how things were going, usually after Father John's photo had been plastered over the television and newspapers in connection with some crime that had occurred on the reservation. The assistants had warned him about getting involved in unsavory matters, and he had told them he had no intention of turning away someone who needed help, no matter where it might lead. They'd both known where he stood. They'd also known that it was only a matter of time before he would be reassigned.

"Stay in the guesthouse for a while," Father John said. "You can get a little rest."

Father Ian shifted forward and stared past the provincial. "I've been telling him the same thing. Give him the chance to see what a great place this is, meet some of the

117

people." He slapped the palm of his hand against his thigh and turned to Rutherford. "Never know. You might decide to take an assignment here yourself."

The provincial emitted a strangled laugh. "Tell you the truth, sometimes the idea of serving at an Indian mission sounds pretty good. Peaceful. Quiet. Surrounded by miles and miles of nothing. Yes, there are times, John" — he gave Father John a sideways look — "when I've thought about changing jobs with you. Put you in charge back in Milwaukee and I'll come out here and say Mass, teach religion classes, and organize volunteers to do the rest."

Father John caught Ian's eye. So that's what the powers-that-be thought they did. No wonder a procession of assistants had left after a few months. Mission work had not been what they'd been led to believe. Except for Ian, who was like him, arriving at St. Francis fresh out of rehab and finding something unexpected to be sure, but something that had made him want to stay.

"Dinner's on." Elena's voice burst over the sound of the door cracking open at the top of the stairs. Then the door slammed shut.

Father Rutherford carried a mug of coffee

into the living room and dropped his bulky weight onto the worn upholstered chair across from the sofa. He leaned back, emitted a long sigh, then crossed his legs and swung a polished black shoe toward the coffee table. "What a pleasant surprise," he said. He'd had no idea the priests at St. Francis were living so well. "Excellent cook. Excellent food."

"What can I say?" Father John took the end cushion on the sofa and sipped at his own coffee. "We eat like this every day," he said after a moment. They'd had fried hamburger, mashed potatoes, and peas, and Elena had made a delicious rhubarb cobbler, and the coffee was strong and good. There was comfort in the old house, settling into evening. The faintest daylight glowed in the front window, the clock on the mantle ticked in the quiet. Elena had left an hour ago, her grandson honking for her in front, and Father Ian had gulped down a serving of cobbler and left for the religious education meeting.

"So you took a little side trip, Bill?" Father John reached around and flipped on the table lamp. A circle of yellow light flooded over the sofa and coffee table and lapped at the edge of the provincial's chair. "What, about four hundred miles out of the way?"

Four hundred miles out of the way, he was thinking, to deliver the news that the pastor would be leaving for a new assignment.

Rutherford gave him a half smile over the top of his coffee mug. "How's Ian working out?"

Ian McCauley was working out fine, Father John told the man. It was the truth. He didn't take his eyes away from the provincial's. The mission and his new assistant were a good fit, the first assistant who seemed to belong, who wanted to stay.

"The drinking?"

"He's staying on the wagon."

The provincial planted his polished shoes on the carpet, leaned forward, and set his mug on the coffee table. It made a dull thud. "You've been a good mentor for the man, John, a good superior. No doubt you've set a fine example."

"The man made his own choice."

Rutherford nodded. "As we all must. Tell me, have you thought about going back to teaching?"

There it was, the windup for the curveball. But he'd seen it coming, hadn't he? He'd had time to adjust his stance. "Have you?" Father John asked.

The other priest drew back into his chair and recrossed his legs. "Every day problems arise that I have no solution for. Problems I never anticipated and couldn't even imagine." He shrugged. "I have positions I can't fill. Priests getting older, retiring, and there aren't enough young men to take their place. Sometimes I think the Society's dying out, John, after five hundred years. To be honest, there are days when I wish I had nothing to worry about except preparing the next lecture for a philosophy class." He shifted toward Father John. "What about you? Don't tell me there aren't days you wish you were in front of a class again. You had a real gift for teaching, John. We all have an obligation to use the unique gifts God gave us, for the good of everyone else."

"Where's this going, Bill?"

"Not where you might think." The provincial turned away. He placed his elbows on his thighs and clasped his hands between his knees. "I've left you here longer than usual." *Three years longer,* Father John thought. "There are four or five other positions that I could place you in, but for the time being, I'd like you to stay here. I wouldn't want to put Ian in charge until I'm sure he's going to stay steady, and there's no one else at the moment begging for an assignment here."

Father John could feel the tension inside him draining away. The future opened up ahead, the future he envisioned for himself at the mission. *The hardest part for you, son, is going to be that vow of obedience.* He could hear his father's voice in his head when he'd told his parents he intended to become a priest. *It's gonna be the killer. You think you're up to it?* He was up to it, he'd said. Of course, he was up to it. He wanted to be a priest, and obedience came with the territory. He would do whatever he was asked. But that was before St. Francis, before he'd come *home.* And now, sometimes in the middle of the night, he wondered how he'd ever be able to obey the order to leave.

"You won't be here forever," Rutherford said, as if the man had seen into his thoughts.

"You drove four hundred miles to remind me?"

"To ask you a favor." The massive head bobbed up and down, the puffy eyes slitted. "There's an elderly priest at the retirement house in Denver that I'd like to send here for a while. A couple of months, maybe. He can make a retreat here. I figure he could stay at the guesthouse."

"You don't need my permission."

"He's not in good health, John. Eighty-two years old. Two, three heart attacks in the last couple of years, several surgeries. They've taken their toll. Bottom line is, the man's dying. Nevertheless, he manages to get around. He needs a lot of rest, but he's not an invalid. Perhaps he could even help out a little. I imagine you could find a few easy tasks to keep him busy."

"Who is he?"

"Lloyd Elsner. Know him?"

Father John shook his head. It had been years since he'd attended meetings or been in large groups of Jesuits. There were a lot of fellow Jesuits he didn't know.

Rutherford gripped the armrests and pushed himself to his feet. "I'll call the retirement home and have them arrange to fly Lloyd to Riverton. If you don't mind, think I'll turn in. It's a long, boring drive up here. Not much to see."

"You don't like driving through the wide-open spaces?"

Rutherford moved toward the doorway, then turned back. "I'm glad you do," he said.

8

State of Wyoming v. Travis Birdsong. *Charge: Murder, first degree. The Honorable Mason Harding presiding. Michael Deaver, prosecutor. Harry Gruenwald, defense.*

Vicky flipped through the court transcript, glancing down the pages to get the gist of what had happened. The defense attorney, Harry Gruenwald, had intended to file an appeal. Otherwise, he wouldn't have ordered the copy of the transcript. Yet Amos said that no appeal had been filed.

It had surprised her how thin the transcript was when Annie dropped it on her desk this morning. Now she saw the brief statements, the few witnesses, and the hurried examinations. Murder trials were usually more complicated — witness after witness, a methodical introduction of evidence. But Travis Birdsong's trial had lasted only a day and a half. The jury reached the verdict in two hours. The evidence must not have been strong enough for a murder conviction, so Travis was convicted of voluntary manslaughter, a crime of passion. There was a hurried sense, almost like an odor, lifting off the pages, as if Travis had certainly been guilty of *something.*

The phone was ringing again in the outer office. It had been ringing all day. Routine matters that probably went to Roger Hurst, the new associate. Important matters, like the proposal for the BLM that would protect Red Cliff Canyon — those were the matters that she and Adam handled. They were building the kind of practice Adam wanted. They both wanted, she reminded herself. She'd finished the proposal a few minutes ago and e-mailed the copy to members of the Joint Council.

Now she thumbed backward through the transcript of Travis Birdsong's trial until she came to the prosecutor's opening statements. Michael Deaver, assistant prosecuting attorney seven years ago, elected county and prosecuting attorney last fall. She'd faced the man in court numerous times. He was tenacious and confident. And he could be brutal, like a predator waiting to tear to pieces the testimony of any witness who gave any hint of stumbling. In the cases she'd defended against Deaver — burglary, assault, fraud — she'd sat on the edge of her chair, ready to jump to her feet and object to his tactics. She'd won a number of cases, and Deaver was not the kind of prosecutor who appreciated losing. She could imagine the way he had commanded the space between the prosecutor's table and the bench at Travis's trial, shooting pointed glances at the jury, the spectators, the defendant, everything in his tone and manner affirming that Travis Birdsong was guilty of murder, no question.

Members of the jury, the state will show beyond a reasonable doubt, indeed beyond any doubt whatsoever, that the defendant pointed a shotgun at the victim, Raymond Trublood, a man who had been his friend, a man who had trusted him. The defendant pulled the trigger, firing the shot that ended his friend's life. We will produce the evidence, ladies and gentlemen of the jury . . .

Vicky paged through the rest of it. She could almost hear his voice, rising at certain points — *beyond any doubt whatsoever* — and lowering to a whisper at just the right moment — *a man who had trusted him.* Oh, he was good, Deaver.

She read through the testimony of Deaver's first witness, Mrs. Marjorie Taylor, owner of the Taylor Ranch.

Deaver: Mrs. Taylor, please tell the court of your association with Travis Birdsong and the victim.

Taylor: I hired them. They worked for me, both those Indians. They came around in the fall, said they were looking for cowboying work. Well, they looked sturdy enough and they had some okay references, so we decided to take them on, give them a chance, you know. We're always trying to help out the Indians around here, those that want to work.

Deaver: When you say, "we," who do you mean?

Taylor: Andy Lyle, my foreman. Been with me for going on ten years now, ever since my husband died. Couldn't run the ranch without Andy. About the time the Indians showed up, we'd bought a Hereford bull since we were looking to increase our herd. So we figured a couple extra hands could help out.

Deaver: Was it unusual for two men to

apply together for work on the ranch?

Taylor: We didn't make anything of it. They were friends, they said. Worked on a ranch south of Lander the year before. Guess they liked working together.

Deaver: Birdsong and Trublood didn't get along very well, did they?

Taylor: Well, they got in a big fight day before the murder. Raymond was beating the you-know-what out of Travis. I yelled for Andy and he broke them up. I told them, any more of that and they were going to be off the ranch.

Vicky pulled a yellow highlighter out of the desk drawer and made a long, yellow smear across the question. "Leading question," she said out loud. Where was Harry Gruenwald? He should have objected; then the judge would have asked Deaver to rephrase.

Deaver: What were they fighting about?

"Object, Gruenwald." Out loud again, as if the defense attorney were in the office.

Taylor: About money, what else? They

128

stole that petroglyph, and they got into a fight over the money they got.

Gruenwald: Objection. This is hearsay and conjecture, Your Honor.

Judge: Sustained. The jury will disregard. Mr. Deaver, you're on a fishing expedition. You will confine your questions to the matter before this court.

Deaver: Your Honor, it is a fact that a petroglyph was recently stolen from Red Cliff Canyon. Chips and rocks identified as having come from the rock of the petroglyph were found in the victim's pickup. The theft goes to the defendant's motive for shooting Mr. Trublood.

Judge: The defendant was not charged, Mr. Deaver. Stay on track.

Deaver: Mrs. Taylor, please tell the court what you saw the following day.

Taylor: Yeah, that day I'll never forget. I was working in the office up by the house when I heard a gunshot. "Jesus," I said to myself. "One of those Indians went and shot the other." So I ran out of the office

129

down the road to the barn because I knew Raymond had been shoeing horses in the corral right next to the barn. I saw Andy running ahead. He was already in the barn when I got there. Right inside the door, there was Raymond on the ground, a big hole in his stomach. I've seen enough varmints get hit with a shotgun. I knew the Indian was dead. Laying next to him was the shotgun that we kept in the barn. Andy says, "I seen the bastard. I'll get him," and he takes off running. I ran back to the office and called the sheriff. Next thing I know, here comes Andy with Travis. I mean he's got that Indian by the arm and there wasn't any way he was going to run off again.

Deaver: Your witness, Mr. Gruenwald.

Gruenwald: No questions.

No questions? Vicky ran the highlighter over the words, pressing so hard that the print turned orange. She skipped past the next few lines: Andy Lyle called to the stand. Sworn in. States his name and says he is the foreman at the Taylor Ranch.

Deaver: Mr. Lyle, please tell the court

what you witnessed on the day of the murder.

Lyle: Well, it's just like Marjorie, Mrs. Taylor, says. I was bringing a couple of horses to the corral when I heard the gunshot. I jumped off my horse and went running for the barn. Just as I got to the door, Travis there comes running out, and he's going, I mean, a hundred miles an hour, like he can't get away fast enough.

Gruenwald: Objection.

Judge: Stick to the facts, Mr. Lyle.

Lyle: Okay. Fact is, I seen him running out of the barn fast. So I went after him and brought him back. Sheriff's deputies were there. They arrested him.

Deaver: Your witness.

Gruenwald: No questions, Your Honor.

Vicky could feel the frustration bubbling inside her. She skipped through the testimony of other witnesses: the deputy who took Travis into custody, the man from the Wyoming Crime Unit who said the fingerprints found on the gun stock matched those of Travis Birdsong. It was like watching planks set into place until, finally, the side of a barn loomed in front of her.

Now it was Gruenwald's turn to present the defense. She'd met the man on only one occasion, shortly after she'd left the firm in Denver and moved to Lander to open a one-woman law office. She'd made a point of visiting other lawyers in Lander and Riverton, introducing herself, chatting a little, saying she'd just stopped by to meet them, and all of them knowing she was angling for a referral now and then. Gruenwald was a year beyond Travis Birdsong's case then, a large, shambling man, she remembered, in rumpled slacks and shirt, the miniature silver buffalo head of his bolo tie bobbing on his chest. He had moist hands that gripped both of hers, and he'd told her he was glad to meet her. Should she ever need advice on how to handle a case, she shouldn't hesitate to call. He'd had . . . what was it? Thirty-five, forty years' experience? Knew all the judges in the county, knew the prosecutors, too, knew his way around. Knew how to get things done in these parts. Shortly afterward, she'd heard that he'd left town.

Gruenwald: Ladies and gentlemen of the jury, my client, Travis Birdsong, is an honest and hardworking Indian, never been in trouble in his life. I intend to offer evidence which will prove that Mr. Birdsong is an upright citizen and an ethical man. The evidence will show that Mr. Birdsong would never have committed such a heinous act.

Vicky stared at the typed words, forcing herself to believe what she was reading. Why didn't he focus on the fact that the prosecution would be unable to prove the charge beyond a reasonable doubt? He could raise some significant issues: How much time had elapsed before Lyle had reached the barn after hearing the shotgun blast? Any blood spatter in the barn? Blood spatter on Travis? Where was a ballistics test on Travis? Where was the evidence that he'd recently fired the gun? How was it that Lyle had seen Travis exit the barn, but Marjorie Taylor did not see him?

But Gruenwald hadn't raised any of those issues. Instead, he'd said: *I would like to begin by calling Mr. Amos Walking Bear, my client's grandfather.*

Walking Bear. God, the elder had been carrying a heavy burden for seven years.

He'd testified on behalf of his grandson, sure that he was helping him.

Gruenwald: Mr. Walking Bear, tell the court the nature of your relationship with Travis Birdsong.

Walking Bear: Travis is my grandson, my daughter's boy.

Gruenwald: Will you describe his character?

Deaver: Your Honor!

Gruenwald: If it pleases the court, my defense of Mr. Birdsong rests upon the man's proven character, and his grandfather is in a position to testify about this from his own experience.

Deaver: Mr. Walking Bear was not present on the day in question.

Judge: I'm inclined to go along with you, Mr. Gruenwald, but don't step out of bounds.

Walking Bear: I've known Travis since the day he was born. His mother, that's my Emma, had him right there in the living room. My wife and two friends took care of everything. Emma and the baby stayed on with us. After my wife died and Emma was killed in a car accident, there was just me and the boy. He was ten years old. I always taught him the Arapaho Way best I could. That boy knew right from wrong. He had good character. No way could Travis shoot Raymond. No way. Travis had a hard time even pulling the trigger on varmints, even though sometimes he had to.

Gruenwald: Nothing further, Your Honor.

Judge: Mr. Deaver?

Deaver: You taught Travis the Arapaho Way.

Walking Bear: Yes, sir.

Deaver: And what might that be?

Walking Bear: To live with honor so he can walk upright like a man that don't have any heavy loads weighing him down. Think about what he was doing. Be thoughtful in everything. Don't hurt nobody. Don't kill nobody. Make the people proud.

Deaver: I see. And when did Travis leave your home?

Walking Bear: After he got out of high school, he went out and started cowboying. Worked at a couple of ranches around the area before he hired on with Mrs. Taylor.

Deaver: After high school. So that would be about four years ago, would it not? Travis left your home four years ago, so you don't know if he continued to follow the Arapaho Way.

Walking Bear: I know.

Deaver: When was the last time you saw your grandson?

Walking Bear: I'm seeing him right now. I seen him yesterday in the jail.

Deaver: And before that?

Walking Bear: Week before the murder, he come to the house.

Deaver: Did he tell you how things were going at the ranch?

Walking Bear: He didn't say much.

Deaver: Was that unusual? Your grand-son whom you raised like your own child not wanting to talk? Was it because some-thing had happened between him and his friend, Raymond?

Walking Bear: He didn't say.

Deaver: Didn't say anything? Anything at all?

Walking Bear: Said he might be looking for another job in the summer.

Deaver: I see. He was planning to leave the ranch, which might suggest, would it not, that there was some trouble, some reason that he wanted to get away.

Gruenwald: Objection. Calls for opinion.

Vicky smeared the last lines with yellow highlighter. "Where have you been, Gruen-wald?" she said. Out loud again, as if he had come through her door and were sham-bling across her office. "Asleep?"

Deaver: Mr. Walking Bear, you stated

that Travis didn't even like killing varmints, even though there were times he had to do so. What might those times be?

Walking Bear: Coyotes or fox getting after the calves. Sometimes he had to shoot them, but he didn't like doing it.

Deaver: But he did it anyway, isn't that true? Why, Mr. Walking Bear? Because they represented a threat, and Travis Birdsong thought he was justified in eliminating any creature that he perceived to be a threat.

Gruenwald: Your Honor, this is outrageous.

Judge: Yes, it is. The jury will ignore Mr. Deaver's remarks.

Deaver: No further questions for this witness.

Gruenwald: Your Honor, the defense has no further witnesses.

Vicky stared across the office. The image of the lawyer was clear as a colored poster that might have appeared on the wall. The man had called Amos Walking Bear without any idea of what the old man might say. Deaver had moved in for the kill and turned Travis's grandfather into a witness for the prosecution. But Deaver had also given the defense an opening: He'd shown that Travis could have used the weapon earlier to kill coyotes. Gruenwald could have recalled Andy Lyle to the stand. He could have asked if Travis had ever used the shotgun to shoot coyotes and fox. He could have hammered home the point that Travis's fingerprints on the shotgun did not prove he had killed Raymond. He could have planted more than reasonable doubt in the minds of the jury.

But he didn't do any of it.

Vicky slapped the transcript on top of the pile of papers growing on her desk. She knew the rest of it. The reiteration of the evidence by Deaver, and Gruenwald's pitiful defense summation that didn't address any of Deaver's arguments. She tapped her fingers on the cover of the transcript. What was she missing? Everything was in place for a conviction, except . . .

Except for the motive. Where was the motive? The stolen petroglyph? Neither one had been charged with the theft. Travis and Raymond got into a fight two days before the murder? So what? People got into fights; cowboys got into fights. It didn't mean someone ended up shot to death. They'd grown up together. They were friends. Chances were, they'd gotten into fights in the past, and nobody had been killed.

But Deaver had supplied the motive. The man was clever, she had to give him that. He'd gotten Mrs. Taylor to mention the stolen petroglyph; he'd managed to reinforce what everyone on the jury was probably already thinking: Travis had shot Raymond over whatever money they'd gotten for the petroglyph. There was a climate in the courtroom — it lifted off the pages of the transcript like dry dust — that they were both guilty, which made it easy to assume that Travis was also guilty of shooting his friend. True, the judge had instructed the jury to disregard the prosecutor's comment, but the words had been spoken, they existed. They had lived in the jurors' minds.

And it explained why the jurors had brought in the verdict that they did. They had assumed that Travis and Raymond had gotten into another fight, probably over money, and that Travis had grabbed the shotgun and pulled the trigger. A crime of passion: voluntary manslaughter.

Still — and this was the part she couldn't

get around — there was no evidence to link a seven-year-old theft to the petroglyph stolen last week. Amos Walking Bear was grasping at straws. An old man, longing to see his grandson free again before he himself died.

Vicky had pulled her bag out of the bottom drawer of the desk and gotten to her feet when the phone rang. She picked up the receiver. "Norman's on the line," Annie said.

"Put him through."

The line went dead a moment, and Vicky dropped back into her chair. Then, a clicking noise. The chairman's voice boomed in her ear: "Vicky, what's going on?"

She waited a beat before she said, "I e-mailed the proposal an hour ago, Norman. Didn't you get it?"

"We're looking it over. That's not what I'm calling about. Gossip around here says you're taking up Travis Birdsong's case, gonna get that SOB out of prison."

"Amos Walking Bear came to see me."

"You and every other lawyer in the county. Nobody else has been foolish enough to get involved. Birdsong's a murderer, Vicky. Nobody wants him back on the rez, except Amos. Best leave Travis where he belongs."

"I don't believe he got a fair trial, Norman."

"Him and every other murderer at Rawlins."

"I promised Amos I'd look into the case. I think that's what you'd want me to do, if Travis were your grandson."

"Travis Birdsong was my grandson, I would've sat him down a long time ago and explained the facts of life. He's Arapaho, not some crazy guy. Amos, he was always looking the other way. Couldn't see anything but good in that boy, and where'd that get Travis? Behind bars, that's where. Bad enough the Drowning Man's gone. We don't need to dredge up the fact that those two Arapahos stole that glyph seven years ago. I tell you, Vicky, you bring up that old case, you're gonna lose a lot of friends."

And what was that? Vicky leaned into the back of her chair. A veiled threat? If she pursued Travis's case, Lone Eagle and Holden shouldn't expect any more work from the Arapaho tribe? "No one was charged with stealing that petroglyph," she said.

"They were guilty." The certainty in his voice was thick enough to slice. "Maybe we could've gotten that glyph back, if Travis hadn't gone crazy and killed Raymond."

"I understand, Norman."

"Listen to me, Vicky. I'm asking you personally not to drag up that old murder case. Let it be. It's no way for you to be helping people around here."

She told the councilman that she would think about it. Then she replaced the receiver, picked up her bag and briefcase, and went into the outer office.

"Get Michael Deaver's office on the phone," she said to Annie as she headed to the door, barely aware of the secretary swiveling from the computer across to the desk. "Tell them I'm on the way over. I need to talk to Deaver. Then call the Wyoming Department of Corrections and arrange for me to visit Travis Birdsong on Friday." Vicky yanked open the door and glanced back. "One more thing. See if you can locate an attorney who used to practice in Lander. His name is Harry Gruenwald."

Annie lifted her chin. Her hand was suspended above the phone. She shot Vicky a look of incredulity. "You're gonna get involved with Birdsong?" she said, as if she hadn't heard anything else. "You sure, Vicky? People around here won't like that much."

"So I've heard," Vicky said. "Just make the arrangements." She stepped into the corridor and pulled the door shut behind her.

9

Father John stood at the wide window overlooking the runway at the Riverton Regional Airport. A few minutes earlier, the turboprop had taxied to a point about fifty feet from the terminal. A metal staircase rolled to the door, and a short line of passengers began filing down the steps. Father Lloyd Elsner was easy to spot, a small man in dark slacks and shirt, standing on the landing, blinking into the sunshine. Other passengers bunched in the doorway behind him, impatience printed in their expressions. Finally the man started down, balancing himself on each step before venturing to the next. He walked around the cluster of bags that several airport workers had extracted from the plane's belly, selected one, and moved into the line of passengers heading across the tarmac, shoulders stooped, gray, balding head thrust forward, the black luggage with a red belt around the middle bouncing behind.

Father John stepped toward the man when he emerged through the door. "Father Elsner," he said, stretching out his hand. "Welcome to Wyoming."

"You must be Father John." The other priest grasped his hand as if it were a rope guide across unfamiliar territory. The firmness in his grip lasted only a second before it seemed to drain away. He had a weathered face, with a deep cleft that divided his chin, and watery blue eyes that blinked around the terminal now, as if he were trying to get his bearings.

"Good of you to come for me," he said, blinking up at Father John.

"Pickup's this way." Father John motioned toward the double doors on the other side of the terminal. "Let me get this." He reached around, took the luggage handle out of the old man's grip, and led the way outside.

They walked to the parking lot under a blinding sun. The sky descended all around them, as clear as a crystal blue mountain lake. There was the sound of tires crunching gravel as a car drove out of the lot, then only the noise of the flag flapping in the hot breeze on top of a metal pole. Father John helped the old man into the pickup, hoisted

146

the luggage into the back, and got in behind the wheel.

He was a psychologist, Lloyd Elsner said as Father John drove along Highway 26, curving down from the flat rise where the airport was located. Not the kind of psychologist most people think of, you understand, not *Freudian*, but, of course, he'd finished his doctorate in psychology. But that was many years ago, oh, many years ago when there weren't that many people interested in the stuff. Always interested him, though, trying to figure out how people worked. So the Society had made him a counselor. Yes, that had been his career, years of counseling troubled students at various Jesuit schools. Well, they weren't all troubled, of course, but searching, looking for their way.

The midday traffic was light through the outskirts of Riverton until Father John caught up with a truck belching black exhaust. He crawled through the center of town behind the truck, past the flat-faced brick buildings with store windows winking in the sun and people strolling along the sidewalks, while Father Lloyd talked on. The man was like a windup top that couldn't stop spinning until the spring had finally released. Or was it that he was lonely, Father John was thinking. Unaccustomed to someone listening?

The truck lumbered across an intersection, and Father John turned right and kept going through the southern part of town, past garages and warehouses and drive-through liquor stores and the bare lots that wrapped across the fronts of trailer parks. They'd retired him — the old priest was saying — yes, retired him when he was still young, still a lot to do. He'd been sixty-five then, it was true, and maybe somebody like Father John didn't think that was so young, but he should just wait. He'd see. Sixty-five didn't mean you should be put out to pasture, like an old horse, people just waiting for you to die. He'd tried to keep his hand in, offer his services, but living in retirement homes, well, it wasn't as if there were a lot of opportunities. Maybe he wasn't in such great shape anymore. Doctors didn't want to tell him outright, of course, but he could hear what they didn't say. He was a psychologist, after all. They thought he was dying, but he had his heart medication. Working just fine. He could help out at the mission. Yes, he was looking forward to being useful while he was at St. Francis.

Father John took his eyes away from the

asphalt rolling ahead and glanced at the man. "The provincial said you were looking for a quiet place to make a retreat."

"Retreat." The other priest dropped the word between them, as if it were a rock that might sink out of sight. "John. I may call you John, right? I've been on retreat for the last seventeen years. What else would you call retirement homes? Retreat from life. I'd rather you put me to work. Anything at all. I was a good counselor."

"We have a lot of people who want to talk to a priest." Father John slowed down for another right turn, and they were on the reservation. The landscape opened up, a house here and there set back from the road, surrounded by wide areas of prairie with nothing but sagebrush and clusters of gnarled cottonwoods.

"There's a small office across the hall from mine," Father John said. "We can clear it out for you."

"Sounds like we have a perfect fit, John. So that's home." The old priest gestured past the windshield toward the sign looming just ahead over Seventeen-Mile Road. *St. Francis Mission.*

"It's home," Father John said. He turned into the mission grounds, drove past the flat-roofed school with the tipi-shaped entry, and slowed onto Circle Drive, pointing out the buildings: the administration building and church, the Arapaho Museum, the residence. Behind the residence was the baseball diamond that he and the kids had made out of a grassy field that first summer at St. Francis, when he'd started the Eagles. The kids had needed a baseball team, he'd told himself, and he'd needed a team to coach.

"Baseball practice every afternoon," he said. "You might want to come over and watch."

"Good. Good."

Out of the corner of his eye, Father John could see the old man nodding. Nodding and smiling, a kind of half smile, as if the mission brought back fond memories. "You'll have the guesthouse," he told the other priest. They were bumping down the dirt driveway that ran between the church and the administration building. Directly behind the building was Eagle Hall and, another thirty feet beyond, the square house with the board siding and the scuffed white paint.

He helped the old man out of the pickup, then lifted the luggage out of the back and showed him into the house. Living room with a worn sofa and chair, bookcase with paperbacks neatly stacked on the shelves, lamp with a faded gold shade that might have been shielding lightbulbs for fifty years. "Bedroom's in the back," he said, leading the way into the small alcove with barely enough room for a nightstand between the bed and the old highboy that served as a closet. He set the luggage on the bed and went back into the living room. "Kitchen's there." Nodding to another alcove off the living room. "In case you want to make yourself a cup of coffee. Meals are at the residence. Breakfast at seven."

"Never liked getting up early. One advantage to being retired, I don't have to do it anymore."

"Come over to the house anytime you like. Lunch is usually around noon — sandwich, soup. Dinner at six." He didn't have the heart to tell the old man that Elena expected the priests to be on time. A bit like boot camp, he sometimes thought. He was seldom on time, and it looked as if Lloyd Elsner might also fail to live up to the housekeeper's expectations.

He left the old man heading into the bedroom to unpack — "Get settled in," he'd said — and followed the fresh tire tracks back down the alley. He parked in front of the administration building and let himself through the heavy wood door into the corridor lined with the framed photos of past Jesuits staring through rimless glasses, keeping watch over the place, he always thought. The plank floor, streaked with sunlight from the front window and worn into little pathways by more than a century of footsteps, stretched past his office on the right to Father Ian's office in back. He went into his office, checked the answering machine — no messages — and headed down the corridor.

Ian McCauley was at his desk, bent toward the columns of numbers moving down the computer monitor. "Everything go okay?" he said, not looking up. A bald spot, the diameter of a quarter, interrupted the man's sandy hair on the crown of his head.

Father John told him that he'd left Lloyd Elsner at the guesthouse. "He's a counselor," he said. "Sounds like he's had a lot of experience. Says he'd like to be useful. He can use the office across the hall."

The other priest rolled his chair back, and, behind his eyes, Father John could see him shifting the gears in his head. "Rachel Roanhorse came in this morning," he said after a moment. "Having trouble with her son. Fourteen-year-old hanging out with a fast crowd. She's afraid he'll get involved with drugs. I talked to her awhile. I think she has reason to worry, John, so I suggested she bring the boy over for a talk. It'll be good to have a trained psychologist around. By the way," he went on, riffling through the papers scattered next to the computer, the gears shifting again, "call came while you were out. I jotted down the information somewhere."

"Who was it?" The dealer, or whoever had the petroglyph, Father John thought, watching the other priest glance at a sheet of paper and toss it aside.

"Here we go." Ian yanked a paper out of the stack and handed it across the desk. "Reporter from the *Gazette.* Wants to stop by and ask you a few questions. Should be here any minute," he said, glancing at his watch.

"Did he say what it was about?"

"She, John. Aileen M. Harrison is a woman."

She leaned into the upholstered cushion of the chair that stood at an angle to Father John's desk, a beautiful young woman in her early twenties, he thought, probably not long out of college, with deep blue, watchful eyes suffused with an intensity that made her seem older than her years, blond hair that brushed the shoulders of her white blouse, and long legs crossed one over the other. She opened a small notebook, smoothed the pages, and produced a pen from somewhere in the bag she'd hung off the arm of the chair. She smiled at him. "I'm sure you know what this is about," she said.

She had been coming through the door as he'd started back down the corridor to his office, and she'd been a tornado of words. She was Aileen M. Harrison, and he would be Father O'Malley, she guessed. He'd told her that she guessed right and ushered her into his office. She liked the *M,* she told him, although he hadn't asked why she used her middle initial. It implied professionalism, she said, and she was proud to be a professional journalist. She would always use her middle initial. She'd been hearing about him forever, well, ever since she'd started at the *Gazette* three months ago.

When she drew a breath, Father John said, "I'm afraid you have me at a disadvantage. You could be here about any number of things."

"The stolen petroglyph, Father." There was a slight edge to her tone, as if she'd thought he was teasing and she didn't appreciate teasing. "You must know my paper broke the story."

"I read the article." He was thinking that he'd read past the byline, which had probably been Aileen M. Harrison.

"It wasn't an easy story to get." She glanced around the room a moment, the memory bringing a tiny smile to the corners of her mouth. "No one wanted to admit that a two-thousand-year-old piece of art had been stolen from Red Cliff Canyon. I had to request the theft report that the tribes had made to the BLM. Director there said they'd had to call in the FBI agent to handle the investigation; they're short staffed, you know. Only one officer to investigate thefts on hundreds of square miles of BLM land. Of course Ted Gianelli — he's the fed that's taken over the case — said he couldn't comment except to confirm that the petroglyph was missing. Ongoing investigation, and all that. But Duncan Barnes, an antiques dealer who knows what he's talking about, valued the petroglyph at a quarter million. And get this" — she had warmed up to the subject — "when I confronted the tribal officials they actually requested that we hold the story. Imagine! A valuable petroglyph stolen! We're hardly in the business of *hold-*

ing important stories the public has a right to know about."

She looked down and began scribbling something in the notebook. "After all," she said, as if it were an afterthought, "the petroglyphs don't belong only to the tribes. They're on public land. They belong to all of us."

"How did you hear about the theft?"

"What?" Her head snapped up and the blue eyes blinked at him. Then she smiled again, but the intensity in her eyes made them look darker. "We're in the same kind of business, Father. We both keep secrets and protect sources. You must gather all sorts of information in the confessional, but I'm sure you'd never divulge the source. Confidentiality is part of our business."

"Not quite the same, Ms. Harrison."

"You may call me Aileen."

"Priests don't publicize what they learn in confidence."

"Well, we reporters protect our sources." She moved forward slightly and jabbed the pen toward him, as if to emphasize the point. "My source wished to remain anonymous. Naturally I verified the information after I got the tip. I wouldn't be doing my job if I ignored the tip."

She waited a moment, as if she expected

him to argue the point, and when he didn't say anything, she hurried on: "Frankly, I see my job as the opportunity to educate people. I was astonished that a tribal leader asked me not to run the story. I can't identify him, of course, but he even tried to convince me that the story would bring curiosity seekers to the canyon and endanger other petroglyphs, which is absurd. The fact that the canyon is so remote and deserted most of the year" — she paused, punctuating the air with the pen — "is what endangers the petroglyphs. The more people know about the petroglyphs, the less likely someone will attempt to steal one. When people hereabouts realize how old and valuable the rock art is, they'll want to protect it. As you can see, I'm passionate about my profession."

"I can see that," he said. She was so young, he was thinking. Like his students in prep school, idealistic, convinced the world would change, if only they worked hard enough.

"I'm here to verify other information I've received . . ."

"From an anonymous source?"

". . . that you were recently contacted by the people who may have stolen the petroglyph and have it in their possession."

"Have you thought about the possibility

that your anonymous source may be the thief?"

The girl — she wasn't much more than a girl — lowered her eyes and went back to scribbling in the notebook, but there was something about the way she kept her eyes lowered, even when she'd finished writing, that suggested she had considered the possibility and that it had bothered her — a conundrum she hadn't quite known how to solve, and so she had decided to push on.

She glanced up. "Is my information correct?"

"Sorry." Father John shook his head. "I don't have any comment."

"No comment? Am I to understand that it *is* correct? That the thief initiated contact with you as someone the Arapahos and Shoshones can trust? Did you relay the message, Father?"

"Whoa! Hold on." Father John got to his feet and walked around the desk. "What I said was, I don't have any comment."

Aileen M. Harrison hesitated a moment, as if she were trying to wrap her mind around the notion that he expected her to leave. She began lifting herself out of the chair. There was so much disappointment in her expression, it bordered on grief. She turned past him and walked ahead into the corridor. Sliding to a stop at the front door, as if it were a barrier that had risen unexpectedly before her, she looked back. "I have other ways to verify the information, you know."

"I suggest you take them." Father John reached around and opened the door for her. A rush of hot air shot into the coolness of the building.

She stepped onto the concrete landing at the top of the steps and gave another backward look. "I'll have to write that you refused comment," she said. "Some readers could conclude you're unwilling to help the tribes retrieve their treasure. Everyone here . . ." She hesitated a moment, as if she'd lumbered down a road she wasn't certain she should follow; then she said: "I've done my homework, Father, and everyone in the area thinks that you're a friend to the Arapahos. The Shoshones, too. They call you the Indian priest. My article will probably change their opinion."

"I'll have to take my chances, won't I?" He tried to keep his tone friendly. She was so young.

"All right, then," she said, squaring her shoulders in an attempt, he thought, to make him think she was older, an experienced reporter, hardly someone venturing into uncharted territory. "I'll be in touch again, I'm sure," she said, before she swung around and hurried down the steps toward the small green sedan parked next to his pickup.

Father John watched the sedan back into Circle Drive, then start forward, gravel shooting from beneath the tires. He thought about the sources the girl had quoted in the article: Ted Gianelli, who confirmed that the petroglyph had been stolen, and the antiques dealer . . . what was his name? Duncan Barnes. Duncan Barnes, the man who happened to know how much the petroglyph was worth.

He waited until the sedan had disappeared into the tunnel of cottonwoods, then went back into the office. There were things to take care of — phone calls to return, mail to answer. Then he intended to drive over to Duncan's Antiques and see what else the man might know about the stolen petroglyph.

10

Michael Deaver, a good 250 pounds of muscle, with a massive head set on a thick neck and sleeves of a blue shirt rolled up over clublike forearms, took up most of the doorway between the entry and the inner sanctum of the Fremont County and Prosecuting Attorney's Office.

"This is a pleasant surprise," he said.

Vicky doubted that was true. There was a harried, annoyed look in the man's gray eyes. "Do you have a few minutes?" she said. She'd been pacing the small entry, carving a little circle past the plastic chairs pushed against the wall, the front door, the counter below the glass partition that divided the entry from the rest of the office, the metal communicator next to the door. She'd taken a chance that Deaver would be in, and that the phone call from her secretary would hold him for a few moments if he was on the way out. The blond woman on the other side of the partition had warned that the prosecuting attorney was very busy. Vicky had ignored the annoyed expression on the woman's face and continued pacing.

"Come on back," Deaver said, leading the way down the corridor past rows of closed doors. "All I have is a few minutes." He tossed the words into the empty corridor ahead. They were on the lower level of the new brick courthouse with light streaming through the windows and the faint odor of fresh paint permeating the air. Their footsteps made a hushed noise against the carpet. Somewhere in the building, a phone was ringing. The buzz of conversation floated through a closed door.

"Appointments all day. Here we go."

Vicky followed the man into a spacious office twice as large as her own, with a bank of windows that framed the branches of cottonwoods. Past the branches, she could see the tan walls of the Fremont County Jail and the top of a pickup moving down Railroad Street.

"So what's this all about?" Deaver nodded toward one of the wood-framed, upholstered chairs arranged in front of the desk. He walked around and dropped into a swivel chair that emitted a sound like air escaping from a punctured tire.

White people, Vicky was thinking, were so quick to get right to the point. No time for the exchange of pleasantries, no time to move onto common ground, to connect — one human being with another — before launching into business.

She took her time sitting down; then she said, "I've been reading the transcript of Travis Birdsong's trial. You were the prosecuting attorney."

Michael Deaver stared at her with an expression as blank as the polished surface of his desk. "Refresh my memory," he said after a moment, clasping his hands together and leaning over the desk. "I've tried a couple hundred cases in my career. Indian, I take it?"

"Arapaho. Convicted of the shotgun slaying of his friend, Raymond Trublood."

"Okay." Deaver drew out the word so it sounded like *Youuuu Kay.* "Don't hear any bells ringing."

Vicky had to swallow back the sense of indignation. "Seven years ago, you put Travis Birdsong in prison for fifteen years," she said. "It was after the first petroglyph was stolen in Red Cliff Canyon."

The district attorney blinked a couple of times. He pushed his bulk into the chair, which rocked backward against the window frame. "Got it," he said. "Tall, skinny Indian with hair smoothed back like it was glued on his head. Attitude. Man, did that Indian have an attitude. By the way, the U.S. attorney never got around to charging him with theft in the missing petroglyph case. Most Birdsong could've gotten for that offense was five years, and that's if the judge was in a real bad mood and gave him the maximum. We had him for twelve to fifteen on voluntary manslaughter, so the U.S. attorney saved a lot of time and trouble, not to mention taxpayer money, by filing the case away under 'unsolved.'" Deaver rolled his head back. "Birdsong and Trublood," he went on, his gaze somewhere on the ceiling. "What a couple of princes. Cut out the sacred art of their own people and sold it. Tell you what kind of guys they were?"

"I'm trying to understand Harry Gruenwald's defense strategy," Vicky said, working to keep the indignation out of her tone. "It was a lousy defense."

"Old Harry had himself a lousy case, Vicky. You read the transcript. We had all the evidence we needed. Shotgun with Birdsong's fingerprints all over it. We had the motive. Birdsong and Trublood had gotten into a fight two days before. They got into another fight in the barn, and Birdsong went for the shotgun. Had all the markings of a crime of passion. Jury was right about that. Witness saw Birdsong running from the murder scene. Cases don't come much tighter."

"That's just it," Vicky said. "It was a little too tight. Gruenwald could have made your job a lot more difficult, Michael. He could have thrown doubt on every piece of evidence. Fingerprints on the shotgun? Travis may have used the same gun to kill coyotes. Ballistics test, where was it? Motive? It was a joke."

"Joke? The victim still had the bruises when he was shot."

Vicky ignored the interruption and pushed on: "They grew up together. They'd probably gotten into fights before. So what if Travis found the body and ran? He was scared. He probably figured he'd be a suspect, and he wasn't thinking straight. Gruenwald could have cross-examined Marjorie Taylor and her foreman. Confirmed that it was normal for Travis's prints to be on the shotgun. He could have made the point that Travis wasn't the only one at the ranch when Raymond was shot. He could have thrown doubt on all of your so-called evidence."

Deaver crossed his arms over his chest and smiled at her, swiveling the chair from side to side a little. "So I should be grateful you weren't defending the guy, trotting out a lot of alternative scenarios and explanations, right? Some little old lady on the jury might've started thinking maybe that poor Indian was innocent as a newborn baby. Wasn't that what his grandpa testified? Travis couldn't've killed anybody. That Indian could still be walking around, instead of sitting behind bars where he belongs."

"Why didn't Gruenwald go ahead with an appeal? He'd filed a notice of intent and ordered the trial transcript."

"Why don't you ask him?"

"Come on, Michael. We both know he should have appealed Travis's conviction. There were grounds for appeal in the trial. I would ask him, if I knew where to find him. I thought he'd left the state."

"Last I heard, he's living on a little ranch south of town. The case was tight. Maybe he figured an appeal would've been a waste of time and money."

Vicky glanced away. There was a neatness about the office, books aligned by height in the long, mahogany bookcase against the wall, drawers tightly shut in the filing cabinets against the other wall, everything in order as it should be. Snatches of conversation sounded from the corridor. She could feel the atmosphere begin to change, the impatience leaking across the desk.

"If the case against Travis was so tight," she said, "I'm surprised Gruenwald didn't try for a deal. Agree to an involuntary manslaughter plea, argue for a shorter sentence."

"We tried to cut a deal, if I recall. Yeah. We were working with the fed, you know, quietly. Travis Birdsong gives up the location of the stolen petroglyph, the names of whoever he sold it to, helps the Indians get their sacred art back, and lets the fed dump that case into the closed files, and we let him take a plea and save the taxpayers of Fremont County a lot of money, and me and my staff a lot of trouble. Didn't fly, Vicky. Gruenwald took it to his client, who turned it down flat. Kept saying he was innocent. Wasn't gonna cop to any murder he didn't do."

"Maybe Travis is innocent," Vicky said. The idea was beginning to take hold, settle into her mind, and she knew it wouldn't be easy to dislodge. A guilty man would've grabbed at the chance of a plea bargain. He would have seen himself walking out of prison after a shorter sentence. It would have been a light shining at the end of a long, dark tunnel. But Travis had turned down the chance, which could also mean — this was the rest of it — that he didn't have anything to trade. Not only hadn't he killed Raymond; he hadn't stolen the petroglyph and didn't know where it was. And Deaver had realized that. She could feel the warm flush of anger working through her.

"What brought up all this old history?" the prosecutor said, lifting himself to his feet, a signal that he'd run out of time. "Oh, I get it," he went on. "The glyph that was just stolen from the same canyon. No connection, Vicky, if that's what you're thinking. How could there be? One thief's dead; the other's down at Rawlins. The old man got to you, right?"

Deaver came around the desk, and Vicky stood up, fixed the strap of her bag over one shoulder, and faced him. "You didn't believe Travis had taken the petroglyph seven years ago, did you?"

The man walked around the desk and yanked open the door. He held it open. "You got information to trade to save even a little bit of your skin, you're gonna trade it. Travis wasn't trading. You led the jury to believe that Travis and Raymond had stolen the petroglyph and fought over the money."

Vicky ignored the outstretched hand ushering her into the corridor.

"We proved the motive, Vicky. Those Indians had been in a violent fight. Over what? Who knows. Maybe a bottle of whiskey, some woman. Doesn't matter. They had a beef. Travis had a grudge. That's all that mattered."

"The stolen petroglyph was in that courtroom. You introduced it as evidence toward motive . . ."

"Wrong, counselor." The fleshy hand was waving in the corridor. "The judge instructed the jury not to consider the theft. No way was it part of the trial."

"We both know how that works, Michael," Vicky said, her voice a barely controlled whisper. "I'm going to file a petition for post-conviction relief." She stepped past the man.

"On what grounds?" There was the faintest hint of alarm in his tone. "Don't tell me you have new evidence."

"How about ineffective assistance of counsel? Prejudicial statement on the part of the prosecuting attorney?"

"I heard you and Adam were only taking on big civil cases, advising the tribes on natural resources, that sort of stuff. What's Adam think about you getting involved with a convicted felon?"

"If the petition is denied . . ." Vicky said, louder now, firmer. A secretary walking past them in the corridor gave her a quick, startled look.

"Which it will be after seven years."

"I'll ask the parole board to reduce his sentence to time served."

"Oh, Vicky, Vicky," Deaver began, a placating tone now, but she'd already turned and started down the corridor, anger burning like coals in her face.

"You'll hear from me, Deaver," she said, halfway down the corridor now, not caring whether he'd heard.

Vicky pulled the cell phone out of her bag as she hurried along the sidewalk past the sedans and trucks parked at the curb. Two messages showed in the display window: Adam Lone Eagle. Lone Eagle and Holden. She slid behind the steering wheel of the Jeep, started the engine, and rolled down the windows. There was a hint of coolness in the breeze that wafted across the front seat.

She played the first message: "Hi, Vicky. Looks like I'll have to stay here another day or so. Trust everything's going okay with the BLM proposal. I've been thinking a lot about us. Call me when you get this."

Vicky deleted the message, then played the next. Annie's voice, saying Adam had been calling the office, wanting to know when she was expected. Probably wanted to know where she'd gone, the secretary added — she couldn't resist, Vicky thought — but she hadn't told him, just that Vicky was out on business.

Another delete. Vicky tapped the key for the office. The sound of a ringing phone buzzed in her ear, then Annie's voice, as close as if the secretary were in the passenger seat. "Lone Eagle and Holden."

"It's me."

"Adam's real anxious to talk to you." Annie's voice sounded breathless, as if she'd been running. "I told him you got the BLM proposal finished. He felt better about that."

Vicky tried to ignore the comment, but it was like ignoring the prick of a cactus. Adam felt better? He should have trusted her.

"Just got off the phone with Norman," Annie was saying. "He wants you to call him right away. Says it's important."

Vicky said she'd take care of it. "Any luck in finding Gruenwald?"

The secretary said that she was still working on it.

Vicky told her that the man could be living on a ranch somewhere south of town. Then she pressed the end button and tapped out the number to the tribal offices. The sun bounced and glittered off the hood of the Jeep. There was the thrum of tires on pavement as a truck drove past.

Finally a woman's voice came on the line: "Arapaho Business Office." Vicky gave her name and started to say she was returning Norman Yellow Hawk's call when the woman interrupted. "Hold on, Norman's been waiting to hear from you."

"Vicky?" A defeated note in the chairman's voice. "He's not going for the alternate route."

"Who?"

"Bud Ladd, over at the BLM. Notified the Joint Council an hour ago. Said the logging company's all set to widen Red Cliff, and it's too late to consider some other route." The man waited a couple of beats, and Vicky could hear the labored sound of his breathing. "They don't care they're gonna tear up one of our sacred places. Council voted on moving forward. We notified Ladd that we want a meeting between him and our lawyers. It's set for eleven tomorrow."

Vicky told the man that she'd be there. "We can't give up, Norman," she said, but she could sense that the man had already given up. It was still with them, the century-old futility of trying to protect what was theirs while watching it being taken away. It clung to her people like a stain that couldn't be removed.

The line had gone quiet, and for a moment, Vicky thought she'd lost the signal. Finally, Norman's voice again. "Maybe you can change his mind," he said, the faintest hint of hope in his voice now. She wondered if she had imagined it, if her own people were finally beginning to believe in her. And yet, back at the office, Norman had warned her not to get mixed up with Travis Birdsong.

She stopped herself from bringing up the subject again, trying to convince the chairman that Travis had deserved a better defense. *Better defense?* The thought made her want to weep with frustration. Travis Birdsong had deserved a defense.

She told the councilman she'd do her best, then pressed the end button again. For the briefest moment, she considered calling Annie back and asking her to set up an appointment with Marjorie Taylor. She decided against it. Suppose the woman refused to see her? Refused to talk to a lawyer with questions about the man convicted of killing one of her employees? Sometimes it was better to catch people unaware, before they had time to summon up any objections.

Vicky tossed the cell on top of her bag in the passenger seat. Then she turned onto Main Street and drove west toward the reservation.

11

Highway 287 ran through open spaces luminous in the sunshine. A sense of peace pervaded the plains, Vicky thought. The way the land dissolved into the sky always called her back to herself. She was different here than in the white world. Part of something larger than herself, part of the stories that had shaped her life: women in the villages, preparing food, tanning hides; children playing about; warriors riding out for buffalo. And always the old stories of Chief Black Coal and her own great-great-grandfather, Chief Sharp Nose, leading the people onto the reservation — the reserved lands cut from a corner of the vast lands that had once belonged to the Arapaho. Time collapsed into the present on the reservation, a circle encompassing the past and the future, not like the ribbon of asphalt shooting straight into the horizon.

It struck her with the sharpness of a whip

how terrible it must be for Travis Birdsong, locked up in a cell so far away — a million miles away — from the endless sweep of the plains. She gripped the steering wheel hard and tried to fight back the nearly physical sense of pain. Deaver had deliberately linked Travis to the stolen petroglyph, even though he didn't believe Travis was guilty. Who could guess how Marjorie Taylor's comment had influenced the jury?

Another several miles, and the bluffs outside the passenger window took on the look of a fortress with steep walls carved out of various hues of red and pink stone. Below the bluffs stood a cluster of ranch buildings. She slowed and turned right onto a dirt road.

The Jeep skittered across the pebbles for a few seconds before the tires began to dig in.

Horses grazed in the pastures on either side. The Taylor Ranch could be a picture on a postcard, she thought. Two-story log house pushed up against the looming red walls of the bluffs, an apron of grass in front and rows of cottonwoods along the sides, branches swaying in the breeze. In the field beyond the house was a collection of pick-ups, tractors, and other vehicles. The road curved past the house and a cabin, then ran down a hill into a valley where the log fence of a corral stretched between a brown, sturdy-looking barn and a collection of outbuildings with corrugated metal roofs that glinted in the sun.

Vicky parked close to the house and walked up the stone steps to the porch that ran along the front. The plank floor creaked under her footsteps. She knocked on the door and glanced around. No one was about, no sign of life apart from the horses nodding lazily in the pastures. The wind whispered in the cottonwoods, and a stray branch tapped against the side of the house. She knocked again. The house was silent.

She stepped off the porch and took the dirt path to the small, one-story log cabin. Someone had walked here not long before. She could see the boot prints, the pattern of the soles. The cabin looked newer than the house: The chinks were still solid between the logs, and the logs themselves exuded the odor of freshly cut pine. There was no porch, only a small concrete stoop. She knocked at the door, then knocked again. Through the rectangular window next to the door, she peered into the dimness inside: A desk jutted into the middle of a neatly arranged room with a bank of filing cabinets against the far wall and several wooden chairs set at angles to one another.

She went back to the Jeep and drove down the dirt road past the log fence that ran along the pasture. Two sorrel horses watched the Jeep approach out of almond-shaped brown eyes. One of the horses whinnied as she parked in front of the barn and got out.

"Hello!" she called, pushing her hair back against the wind. Her voice sounded muffled, lost in the emptiness. She let the Jeep's door slam into the quiet.

The double door of the barn was open, and she walked over and looked inside. "Hello?" she called again. A wedge of sunlight lay over the center of the dirt floor, but the rest of the barn was in shadow. She stepped inside and glanced about. Harnesses and tack hung from nails along either side of a narrow, closed door on the far wall; tools and other metal equipment winked in the shadows on the left. On the right were the dark hulks of blankets and saddles thrown over benches and the outlines of stalls. Everything neat and orderly, in its place. Above the saddles, in a rack on the wall, was a shotgun.

This was where Raymond Trublood died, she thought. She ran her eyes over the floor from the center where tiny particles of dirt flashed silver in the sunlight to the gray, dead shadows near the walls. There was a clacking noise overhead, and she felt herself tense until she spotted the small bird fluttering in the rafters. She was aware of being alone — Woman Alone, *Hi sei ci nihi,* the grandmothers called her. She should have told Annie — she should have told someone — where she was going. She tried to shake off the feeling of unease. There was no reason to be so jumpy, she told herself. Yet the atmosphere in the barn, a place of death, felt heavy and dark, like an invisible shroud.

"What do you want?" A shadow moved into the patch of sunshine on the floor.

Vicky whirled about. Standing in the doorway was the dark figure of a woman, backlit by the light. She was slender, dressed in blue jeans and a light-colored shirt that looked faded in the brightness. Sunshine shone through her long, blond hair.

"You must be Marjorie Taylor." Vicky started toward the doorway.

"Who are you?" The woman barred the way. She looked trim and fit, with the compact body of a woman accustomed to hard work. Probably in her forties, Vicky guessed, close to her own age.

"Vicky Holden. I'm an attor . . ."

179

"I've heard of you."

"I'm here about Travis Birdsong." Vicky could hear the sound of her own voice flapping like the bird's wings in the rafters. "I'd like to speak with you."

The woman seemed to consider this. "What'd Travis do? Kill somebody in prison?" She began backing out of the doorway, and Vicky stepped outside after her, feeling a sense of relief washing over her in the hot wind. In the distance, she could see two cowboys galloping across the pasture.

She said, "Travis's grandfather thinks he was wrongly convicted. I've read the trial transcript, and I tend to agree. I'm considering taking his case. Before I see him in the prison Friday, I wanted to talk to you."

Marjorie Taylor studied her a moment. There was the slightest flicker of interest in the woman's gray eyes. "On what possible grounds could you reopen that killer's case?"

"I'm not sure," Vicky said. "Ineffective counsel, for starters. Trumped-up evidence. I'm wondering what other evidence the detective . . ."

"Lou Hamblin. He knew what he was doing. Too bad he's not around anymore. Moved to California, last I heard. Damn good investigator."

"It's possible he missed something while he was investigating Trublood's murder," Vicky said. A dun-colored pickup was coming down the road, trailing a cloud of dust.

"Missed something?"

The pickup skidded to a stop, and the woman looked around. She hooked her thumbs into the pockets of her jeans and waited as a tall, muscular man in blue jeans and a blue plaid shirt with a black Stetson shading his face hauled himself out from behind the steering wheel and came toward them.

"Who's our visitor?" he said, stopping beside Marjorie. He seemed to speak out of the corner of his mouth, lips tightly drawn. He looked younger than Marjorie Taylor, late thirties, perhaps, with eyes like blue slits in a sunburned, handsome face. Traces of brown hair poked from the rim of his Stetson and nearly obscured the squint lines that fanned across his temples.

"The Arapaho lawyer, Vicky Holden," Marjorie said. "Here about that ranch hand's murder seven years ago."

"Andy Lyle, foreman," the man said, lips still not moving. For a moment, Vicky thought he might extend his hand, but instead he hooked his thumbs in his jeans

181

pockets and turned his attention to the pair of cowboys galloping toward the corral.

"You testified you saw Travis run out of the barn," Vicky said.

"We'll talk in the office." Marjorie's gaze had followed the foreman's. The sound of the horses' hooves vibrated in the ground. The woman swung about and started back up the road.

Vicky walked past the Jeep and headed up the incline, holding her hair back in the wind with one hand. She could hear the foreman's boots scraping the earth behind her. Then his shadow elongated next to hers. His boots kicked at small rocks that spun out ahead. She could almost feel his breath on the back of her neck as Marjorie pushed open the door to the cabin and led the way into the small office.

"Yeah, I saw Travis leave the barn after he shot Raymond," Andy Lyle said. He kicked the door shut, then nudged a straight-backed wooden chair away from the wall with one boot and nodded for Vicky to sit down. "Travis took off and I went after him."

"She knows all that." Marjorie sat down behind the desk and began straightening the already straightened piles of papers, as if the desk and the papers somehow con-

182

firmed her authority. From this small office, from behind this solid wood desk, Vicky thought, Marjorie Taylor gave orders to her employees.

"She's read the transcript," she went on, as if Vicky weren't sitting in front of her. "She thinks the detective missed something."

"So what d'ya think he missed?" Lyle said.

Vicky had to shift around to see the man leaning against the closed door — blocking the exit, she thought — arms folded across the front of his plaid shirt. He looked relaxed, as if they had all the time in the world to sit inside this cabin. No one would leave until he said so.

Vicky took a moment before she said, "Who else was around?"

When neither Marjorie nor the foreman said anything, Vicky pushed on: "What about the other wranglers? What did they see?"

"Raymond and Travis, they were the wranglers," Marjorie said, and Vicky had to turn back to face the woman. "Ollie had already left."

"Ollie?" Vicky heard the surprise in her voice. There hadn't been anyone by the name of Ollie in the transcript.

"Ollie Goodman," Marjorie said. "Cowboy artist likes to paint at the ranch sometimes."

A loud snort erupted behind her, as if the foreman were clearing his throat and stifling a laugh at the same time. "Goodman roams over the countryside like a goddamn gypsy, painting pictures of petroglyphs mostly." Something hard had come into the foreman's voice, as if the conversation had lurched into familiar territory, and he was repeating already sharpened arguments. "You ask me, he don't have any business using the ranch for his pictures. He's no cowboy, goddamn cripple. *Paints* horses, that's what he does, the only way he knows the front end from the back. Paints barns and pastures. Sells his pictures back East where everybody thinks they're the real McCoy, genuine cowboy art."

"Ollie's been painting at the ranch for a long time," Marjorie said, her voice even and defiant. "Let's not get on that subject again."

Vicky stood up and scooted her chair sideways so that she had a view of both the foreman and the woman behind the desk. Then she dropped back onto the edge of her chair. "You're saying Ollie Goodman was painting here the day of the murder?"

"He likes the ranch. Can't blame him, can you?" She had stacked all the papers into a single pile that listed to one side and threatened to spill over the desk. "Old log house up against the red bluffs, the barn and pasture. There's probably a dozen pictures of the Taylor Ranch hanging in rich people's houses around the country." She shrugged. "Ollie likes to paint in the mornings. Best light, he says. He'd left a couple of hours before Raymond got shot."

"Did the detective talk to Ollie?" Vicky said. She had the answer in the guffaw that came from the foreman.

"How the hell do we know who that detective talked to?" he said. "We weren't privy to his investigations. You're the one that's got the records. You tell us."

"I have no idea," Vicky said. That wasn't true, she was thinking. She was beginning to get the idea that everyone — prosecutor, defense attorney, even the chief investigator — had decided that Travis was guilty. She could feel the knot of frustration tightening in her stomach. It was an old story, wasn't it? Indian's guilty. Toss him in prison.

"Look, Ms. Holden," Andy Lyle said. "The killer's where he belongs. You want my advice, stay out of it. Go back to the rez and ask the Indians. They're gonna tell you the same thing. Nobody in these parts wants Travis Birdsong walking around free."

"How did you happen to hire Travis and Raymond?" Vicky said, turning toward Marjorie Taylor, whose eyes were still fixed on the foreman. Gradually, she shifted her gaze to Vicky. "They showed up here, wanting jobs wrangling. Lyle happened to need a couple of extra hands, and they had experience. Hands come and go in this business. Most times when you're the busiest — take calving season — that's when they go. Dad used to say the hardest part of ranching was keeping good hands. Probably different, back when his grandpa started the ranch. Lots of Indians around then, all of 'em looking for honest work."

The woman stood up and came around the desk. "Wasn't til after the murder, I saw what Travis and Raymond were all about. They weren't looking for honest work. They were looking for a place to hide out from the law."

Vicky remained seated. If she got to her feet, she knew, the woman would usher her to the door. Andy Lyle had already moved to the side, one hand gripping the knob, ready to fling the door open. "What makes you think that?" she said.

"Why else would they show up here, out

of the blue? We're not exactly on the beaten track. They could hang out here for a long time before anybody knew where they were."

"Travis's grandfather said that Travis came to the rez to see him."

Marjorie Taylor tossed her blond hair back and looked over at the foreman, who yanked the door open. "The old man said what he thought was gonna help Travis."

"What Marjorie's saying," the foreman put in, "is those two Indian cowboys stole the petroglyph. Who knows what else they'd been up to? They came here 'cause they had something to hide."

Vicky got up. She thanked Marjorie Taylor for her time and, brushing past the foreman, stepped outside. She started walking down the road, then turned back. The woman stood on the stoop, a head shorter than the man behind her in the doorway, both of them watching her. "Where can I find Ollie Goodman?" Vicky said.

Marjorie tossed her head in the direction of Dubois, another three miles north. "Got a gallery over in town."

The man rolled his eyes and shook his head. His mouth was set in a tight line, but Vicky could almost hear the words bunching behind his lips: "Stubborn woman, doesn't take advice."

Vicky swung around and hurried toward the Jeep.

12

Dubois branched from Highway 287 like a flag stretched from a pole. Another eighty miles, and the highway crossed into Yellowstone National Park, a fact that brought countless tourists through town every summer day. Vicky followed the traffic down Mercantile Street, looking for a vacant place along the curb. It was a town straight out of the Old West. Except for the SUVs and pickups crawling along a street wide enough in which to turn a wagon train, you could picture the gunslingers facing each other, revolvers drawn, and ladies with long skirts and parasols parading along the wooden sidewalks under the roofs that jutted from flat-fronted buildings. Behind the windows blinking in the sun were restaurants, gift shops, bars, Western-wear shops, a bookstore, local museums and art galleries, offering everything tourists, or even the locals, could want. It was hard to tell the two groups apart. Everybody was dressed the same, in jeans, boots, and cowboy hats.

There were no vacant spaces, and Vicky drove on, hunting the signs over the shops and galleries for some hint of Ollie Goodman. She reached the end of the commercial district and turned into a street lined with small bungalows. As she made a U-turn, intending to retrace her route down Mercantile, she spotted the small sign propped on a single post in front of a Victorian house painted the light green color of new grass. *Goodman Galleries Western Art.* She left the Jeep in the driveway and followed a brick-paved sidewalk to the wooden porch with a swing on one side and a small, white, wrought-iron table and two chairs on the other. Through the oblong beveled glass window in the door, the paintings on the walls inside collided into different colors and shapes, like the glass pieces of a kaleidoscope. She opened the door and stepped into what had once been a living room. A bell continued jangling into the quiet for a moment after she shut the door.

The room was filled with paintings hung in uneven rows, stacked in corners and against the Victorian loveseat, the scattered chairs, and the desk on the far side of the room. Mountains and pastures, horses, barns. The paintings captured the sweep of the plains in the sunshine and the reflection of the sky in the mountain streams. There was a musty odor in the room, a combination of oil and turpentine and dust, yet the paintings seemed alive, as if the actual landscapes had been transferred to the canvases.

Several paintings on the left, above the loveseat, depicted the Taylor Ranch: the old house, gray against the sun-washed vermilion walls of the bluff. But it was the collection on the right wall that drew her. Six paintings of the petroglyphs in Red Cliff Canyon, arranged in two rows that extended from the ceiling molding almost to the gray carpet. Vicky moved closer. She was aware of her heart jumping. The spirits themselves might have been in the room, the images were so clear and intense. Gray lines of figures carved into sand-colored rocks striped with shadow and light, sheltering under branches of pines.

"Can I help you?"

Vicky swung around, startled by a female voice erupting into the silence. A small, middle-aged woman emerged through the door next to the desk. Her dark, gray-flecked hair pulled back into a bun fastened with two black lacquered sticks that stuck out above her head, she wore a red dress with a skirt that flowed over the tops of her black cowboy boots and a belt of silver medallions that draped around her slim hips. Through the door, Vicky could see the clutter of papers and cartons that covered the surfaces of a desk and a sagging yellow sofa with rose-colored flowers.

"I'm looking for Ollie Goodman," Vicky said.

"And you are?" The woman had green eyes narrowed into slits, as if she were staring into the sun.

"Vicky Holden. I'm an attorney. Is Ollie available?"

"An attorney?" The green eyes flew wide open. "Whatever has Ollie been up to?"

Vicky tried for a smile that might set the woman at ease. "I have a few questions he may be able to help me with. It will only take a few moments." She glanced at the opened door, half expecting a man to materialize.

"Ollie's not here," the woman said. "What makes you think Ollie can help?"

"He's familiar with a murder case I'm looking into," Vicky said. "When could I see him?"

"Murder! I can't imagine that Ollie could

be of any help." The woman tucked a little strand of hair into place. "He's busy painting. Spends the summer working in his cabin. I'm afraid you'll have to look elsewhere for your answers."

Vicky extracted a business card from her bag and held it out to the woman. "Please give him my card and ask him to call me." When the woman made no movement toward the card, Vicky walked over and set it on the edge of the desk. Then she dug a pen out of her bag and wrote "Travis Birdsong's case" in the quarter inch of white space above the black letters of her name.

She stepped back to the woman. "Tell him that it's about the shooting death seven years ago at the Taylor Ranch."

The woman seemed to freeze, breathing halted, features hard set, as if Vicky had thrown ice water in her face. "Ollie has nothing more to say about that," she said.

"It's important," Vicky said. "It's possible the wrong man was convicted."

"That Indian? Travis whatever his name was?"

"Birdsong."

"He's guilty as hell. He tried to run away after he pulled the trigger. What more do you want? Read the newspapers. It was bad enough after it happened, reporters and a lawyer coming around, asking a lot of questions. Ollie wasn't there."

"Lawyer?"

"You know, the prosecutor that sent that murderer to prison where he belongs."

"What about the defense attorney, Harry Gruenwald?"

"I don't remember. Ollie had a belly full of that murder." She was moving backwards now, reaching around for the door handle. "Do us a favor," she said, yanking open the door. "Forget about Ollie. Don't bother him."

Vicky held the woman's gaze a moment, then stepped through the opened door. She got into the Jeep and pulled the key out of her bag, then the cell phone, aware of the dark head moving at the edge of the window in the front of the house. Michael Deaver had questioned Ollie Goodman; the man was a dogged prosecutor. But what about Travis's defense attorney? Why hadn't he bothered to find out what Goodman might have seen before he left the ranch? For that matter, why hadn't he bothered to confirm that Goodman had, in fact, left the ranch?

Vicky jammed the key into the ignition, rolled down the windows, and checked her phone calls. A hot breeze swept through the Jeep. The dark head had moved to the center of the window now, impatience and defiance radiating from the woman's rigid shoulders. Adam had called twice.

She tapped the cell against the rim of the steering wheel. She'd been putting off calling Adam; that was the truth. She hadn't wanted to hear his voice, to be lulled again into a sense of well-being, of business as usual. She hadn't wanted to be put off her guard.

And yet that was silly. They were law partners; they had business together that had nothing to do with any personal relationship. *Personal relationship.* Well, that was a laugh. She'd thought she was in a personal relationship. She had no idea what Adam thought, and it didn't matter, she realized. It no longer mattered. They were just law partners.

She tapped in the number to Adam's cell. It rang once, and he was at the other end. "Vicky? I've been trying to reach you all day."

"I've been busy," Vicky said.

"What about the proposal?"

"The BLM turned it down."

"Turned it down?" A note of incredulity sounded in Adam's voice, and Vicky felt the slight sensation of another prick, as if the

BLM wouldn't have turned down the proposal had he been the one who wrote it.

A door slammed. The woman stepped off the porch and started down the brick sidewalk. Her hair had come loose and was blowing back like dirty straw.

"I'm going to meet with the BLM director tomorrow." Vicky watched the woman coming closer, fists clenched at her side.

"Tomorrow? That doesn't give me much leeway, Vicky. I'm pretty tied down here for another day or two. Julie's affairs are in a bigger mess than I'd suspected."

"I'll handle it, Adam."

The woman was at the passenger door, waving her hands. "Get out of here," she shouted. "I told you, Ollie's not here. You can't see him!"

"What's going on?" Adam's voice loud in her ear.

"I said, I'll handle the BLM. There's no need for you to be here." Vicky pressed the button on the door. The passenger window began to rise. The woman took a step back, still flinging her hands about.

"You're trespassing." She was shouting, the words becoming more muffled as the window rose higher. "I want you out of here. I'm going to call the police." The trapped air inside the Jeep was instantly hot and stuffy.

"You okay, Vicky?" Adam said.

"Hang on a minute." Vicky put the vehicle into reverse and backed out of the driveway, one eye on the woman throwing her arms toward the Jeep as if she could push it into the street.

She shifted into forward and drove toward the stop sign, jiggling the buttons on the air conditioner until she felt a stream of cool air rushing over her, pressing the cell to her ear. "You still there?"

"What's going on?"

"Everything's okay. I'll let you know how the meeting comes out."

"Where are you?"

"Dubois," Vicky heard herself say. She watched the traffic on the right, then the left, waiting for an opening.

"You're in Dubois? What are you doing in Dubois?" A beat passed, and Vicky turned left onto Mercantile and fit the Jeep into the slow-moving parade of traffic in the central part of town. "Oh, I get it," Adam went on. "You're following up on the old man's crazy claim that his grandson was wrongly convicted of shooting somebody. Right? You're going to handle the case, aren't you? Despite everything we've talked about."

"Listen, Adam . . ."

"No, you listen. You don't have time to do everything. We hired Roger to take on cases like that. I thought we had an agreement, Vicky. I trusted you."

Vicky steered the Jeep into a right turn onto the highway. She could feel the hot rush of anger in her cheeks, despite the cool air floating about her. "Travis Birdsong did not get a fair trial."

"The man is probably guilty."

"He didn't get a fair trial, Adam." Vicky pressed down on the accelerator. A blur of wild grasses and sagebrush passed outside the window. "I'm on the highway," she said. "I have to go."

She took the cell from her ear, ignoring Adam's voice, the garbled words coming through the hot plastic in her hand, her fingers searching for the feel of the end key. She pushed the cell into her bag and gripped the steering wheel hard, the blur moving faster outside the windows. She drove for the reservation.

13

Duncan's Antiques turned out to be a low-slung brown building that resembled a double garage set back from the highway at the end of a graveled drive. *BARGAINS* loomed in large white letters shimmering in the sun below the peaked roof. It was close to 2:30 in the afternoon, the heat radiating off the gravel, when Father John parked in front of the stall on the right. The overhead door was open. He stepped inside and made his way across the dirt floor, past the metal wagon wheels, farm tools, sleds, and parts of old trucks that loomed through the shadows. It was probably ten degrees cooler inside, the air oily and redolent of odors from the past.

He'd intended to get away from the mission earlier, but Father Ian had left to visit parishioners at Riverton Memorial, and the phone had rung almost nonstop. He'd grabbed the receiver on the first ring, hoping this was the call — this was the man with the petroglyph. He'd had to fight to keep the disappointment out of his voice. Parishioners wanting to arrange baptisms for new babies, register kids for the next session of the summer education classes, inquire about the Friday-night socials for teenagers that he planned to start next week to give the kids someplace to go and something to do. After each call, he'd stared at the silent phone, willing it to ring again, willing an unfamiliar voice on the other end. Then he'd gone back to the piles of papers in front of him — letters to answer, the summer budget to pull together.

Budget, that was a laugh. Donations rose and fell in the summer. Parishioners traveled to Oklahoma or Montana to see relatives, or went to the powwows around the West. Some Sundays there were only a handful of people in the pews; other Sundays were standing room only, depending upon the number of tourists wanting to attend Mass at an Indian church.

The mission lurched from week to week, he and Father Ian shuffling the bills, paying the most pressing ones, setting aside others for later, and he, at least, counting on what he called the little miracles, the donations that fell out of envelopes with postmarks from obscure towns he'd never heard of and notes saying, "This is for the Arapahos." Strange, the way the little miracles arrived when he most needed them. About the time he was ready to concede that they should cut back on programs, the miracles arrived. Which still astounded his assistant, always certain that the most recent check would be the last, wondering how responsible, sane men could run a mission on miracles.

When Father Ian had gotten back from visiting Joe Moon and Marian Pretty Horse in the hospital, Father John had pushed the papers still awaiting his attention to the corner of the desk and headed across the grounds for the pickup. Eagles practice started at four, and the antique dealer's gallery was a good forty minutes away. He would have to push the speed limit to make it back to the mission on time.

He let himself through a door to the other half of the garage and stepped into a cavernous room that emptied into a series of other rooms stretching into the shadows. He had the odd sense that he had stepped into a past containing personal items of individuals, but not the individuals themselves. Display cases stood haphazardly around the concrete floor, as if they'd taken root wherever they'd been shoved. He threaded his way around the cases, studying the array of Indian artifacts laid out on the dusty glass shelves: pipes, beaded vests, moccasins and necklaces, bows and arrows, rattles, leather quirts, amulets, fans, feathered staffs and headdresses, beaded breastplates. On the side wall beyond the display cases were beaded ceremonial dresses hung between the painted skulls of cattle and buffalo.

Paintings of Western scenes covered a half wall that jutted between two rooms — mountains and bluffs silhouetted against a vast blue sky, fishermen wading in a stream, cowboys lounging against the porch railing in front of a gray building bleached in the sun, *SALOON* tattooed in black letters on a board hanging from the roof. The paintings looked old, colors dark and faded, scenes enclosed in bronze frames that had turned to shades of brown.

Next to the oblong window that looked out onto the parking lot were four large paintings of petroglyphs. The white carved figures leapt out from the background of reddish gray rocks, dark green pines, and blue sky. Father John walked around the display case to get a closer look at the painting on the right. He recognized the human-like figure with the square head and the truncated arms and legs that seemed to be in frantic motion, and the curved lines that looked like waves enveloping a drowning man. The petroglyph had stood at the mouth of Red Cliff Canyon until someone had chopped it out of the rock and taken it away.

"Like 'em?"

Father John turned around. The voice had materialized out of nowhere. For the first time, he noticed the counter in the shadows beyond the half wall. He could make out the shiny bald head of the man seated on the other side. Looming out of the papers and boxes piled on top of the counter was an old cash register with designs embossed in the metal sides. The bald head began slowly rising until the black eyebrows and the fleshy face appeared over the cash register. A short, square-set man leaned over the counter and gripped the edge. Then he started forward, lurching from display case to display case, holding on to the edges as if they were railings. His boots made a scuffing noise on the concrete floor.

"Are you Duncan?" Father John felt as if he were calling out across time.

"That's me. Local artist painted them glyphs." The man pushed out the words between gasps of breath. His face was flushed, and his eyes so bright, Father John wondered if he had a fever.

"You heard of Ollie Goodman? Lives in Dubois," the dealer went on. "Gettin' real famous, Ollie is. Big galleries in Santa Fe and Tucson sell his stuff nowadays, but me and Ollie, we go back seven, eight years now. I was sellin' Ollie's paintings when nobody else'd give him the time of day. That's how come he still shows some paintings here. Best price you'll get anywhere. Down in Santa Fe, you'll pay ten times what I'm askin', especially for a painting of that petroglyph on the right that I seen you lookin' at. You heard about the petroglyph that got stolen last week? Well, that's the one," he said. His breath came in rapid bursts, as if he were struggling up a steep mountainside. "Lot of interest in it, I can tell you that. People stoppin' in every day wantin' to see what that petroglyph looked like. I already got three people wantin' to buy it, but I always say, first come, first served, you know what I mean? First guy puts his money down is gonna be the one walks out of here a lucky SOB."

The man held out a wide hand with stubby fingers and a diamond the size of a marble glittering on a gold ring. "Don't believe I got your name."

"Father O'Malley from St. Francis Mission." Father John was surprised at the strength in the man's grip.

"You the Indian priest?" The man reared back. The bright eyes shot across Father John like a laser: plaid shirt, blue jeans, boots. "Guess everybody in these parts has heard of you workin' with them Indians like you do," he said. "Me, I like them Indians. Never had any trouble with 'em. Come in and sell their stuff. I give 'em a good price. Always treat 'em fair."

Father John didn't say anything, and the man took a step backward and swung his upper body toward a display case. "Take this stuff here." The gold ring tapped the glass above a breastplate, the design of beads and porcupine quills broken in places, the leather gray and curled at the edges. "Old Indian come in here and said that beaded breastplate was his grandfather's. Needed some cash, he said, or he wouldn't be sellin' it. So I give him a good price, better'n anybody around here would've give him. Might take me awhile to sell it. Not like I can sell it real quick to a museum somewhere. Museums nowadays are real particular. Want proof where the artifact comes from. Just 'cause some Indian says it was his grandfather's, well, that don't mean anything. They think the Indian could've dug up a grave somewhere and stole the stuff. But me, I'm more trusting. I know the families around here. Indian says it's been in the family, I believe him. Sooner or later, the right buyer comes along, somebody appreciates old Indian things. Now you, bein' the Indian priest, might . . ."

Father John shook his head, his eyes still on the breastplate. It was old, very old, once owned by a warrior riding into . . . which battle? There had been hundreds on the plains. Confident that the thin piece of leather, the mix of beads and porcupine quills, would stop an arrow or a bullet.

"You have quite a collection." Father John gestured toward the rows of display cases. "Ever have any petroglyphs?"

"Petroglyphs!" The dealer let out a howl almost of pain. "I'm runnin' a legit business here, Father. Somebody brings me a petroglyph, I'm gonna be like a museum. I'm gonna want a lot of proof where it come from. Federal law against takin' artifacts off public lands and sellin' 'em. I'm not lookin' for any trouble with the law. Truth is," the man began, leaning forward, his voice lowered to a confidential tone, as if he were about to confess. "I had a small petroglyph in here two, three years ago. Chopped out of the rock a hundred years ago by some rancher clearin' his land. In the family ever since. They had photos goin' back a long time of that old petroglyph propped up next to a barn. So I said okay. Sold that sucker in three days. Should've held on to it longer. Could've gotten a lot more."

Father John nodded toward the painting of the stolen petroglyph. "Is that how you knew the Drowning Man is worth a quarter million?"

"Minimum." The dealer was shaking his head. "Reporter comes around wantin' numbers. Makes a better story, I guess. Nobody cares if some picture on a rock gets stolen, but lots of people get interested when it's worth big money. So I give her the minimum value, based on my experience and . . ." He glanced up at the ceiling a moment. "Dealers talk, you know. I hear how much some of those glyphs go for."

"You mean, from dealers who sell them?"

The man hesitated a moment, as if he'd lost his way and wasn't certain that the path he'd found himself on was where he wanted to be. He shifted his gaze toward the painting. "Don't know 'em personally," he said. "I hear the gossip, that's all. We got our own antiquities telegraph, just like them Indians got their moccasin telegraph."

He jerked his gaze back to Father John. "You want to know the truth? There's lots of crooks in this business. The fed came around here askin' a lot of questions. Who do you know? Who's gonna handle a stolen petroglyph? I tol' him, crooked dealers are around, but I don't know 'em personally. I stay away from all that. I run a legitimate business. It's like I tell my customers, you better know the dealer you're buyin' from, or you could be layin' out a whole lot of money for a stolen artifact, and that could get you in a whole lot of trouble."

The man shrugged and drew in a raspy breath. His chest heaved against the sweat-blotched yellow shirt. "Thing is, lots of rich people are willin' to take the chance. I mean, what are the odds that some federal agent is gonna knock on your door and demand that you turn over the stolen petro-glyph you bought from some crooked dealer? I say the odds are all in the rich people's favor, and they know it. So they don't ask questions, you know what I mean? They want an Indian pipe that's been dug up from an old grave or a petroglyph that's been chopped off a rock, they buy it."

"What have you heard about the stolen petroglyph?" He was pushing, Father John knew, but Duncan was talking, and when people started talking, they often kept going, saying things they hadn't intended to say.

"Nothing." The dealer lifted his shoulders and let them drop in a forced shrug. "It's like that glyph fell into a black hole."

"The tribes would like to get it back," Father John said.

"What for? They can't put it back up in Red Cliff Canyon."

"They can protect it and keep it with the people. Petroglyphs are sacred."

"You ask me, whoever took that sucker's gonna make a whole lot of money. He ain't givin' it back to the tribes, not after all the trouble he went to."

"Maybe the tribes would pay to get it back. I was thinking," Father John hurried on, pushing against his own hope now, "that you could put the word out on the antiquities telegraph that the tribes are interested in making a deal."

"What's in it for you?" The dealer cocked his head back, and Father John had the feeling that he was being appraised, as if he were some type of Indian artifact.

"I'd like to see the petroglyph back where it belongs."

"You want my opinion, you're too late.

That sucker went to the same place that other stolen glyph went to some years back. They're both sittin' in the gardens of mansions out in California or maybe New York. Maybe Aspen or Santa Fe. Fact is, they're gone. Rich folks sittin' around, sippin' cocktails, sayin', 'My dear, wherever did you find *that?*' " He'd switched into a falsetto and lifted an invisible cocktail glass in a mock toast. " 'Oh, just something I picked up,' " he went on, still in the falsetto. " 'Nothing, really.' Yeah, nothin'," he said, his usual voice now. "A little quarter-million, maybe half-million nothin'."

Father John was quiet. *Don't let it be true,* he was thinking. And yet the logic was there. Logic was relentless. Why would the thief hang around and wait? There were too many uncertainties, too many maybes. Maybe the tribes would agree to buy back the petroglyph. Maybe the tribes could raise the money. Maybe the thief could hand over the petroglyph and collect the ransom without getting caught. Maybe. Maybe. And all the time, there were buyers with the money and the desire for something different, something unlike all the other things they owned, something with a hint of scandal and danger that made the petroglyph all the more attractive.

"I'd appreciate it if you put the word out anyway," Father John said. He could hear the note of hope sounding in his voice, like the last note of an aria before the curtain drops.

"Yeah, whatever." The dealer lifted his shoulders in another shrug, and Father John thanked the man and made his way back through the rows of display cases and the motes of dust floating in the columns of sunshine. He glanced at his watch as he crossed the dirt floor of the garage. Almost three thirty. He was going to have to break a few speed limits to get back in time for baseball practice.

The kids were already on the diamond when Father John drove into the mission. Helmets and gloves milling about, a couple of bats swinging, a ball sailing out of sight behind the residence. He parked next to Del Baxter's brown pickup. Del's son, Cody, had pitched a winning game against the Riverton Cowboys last Saturday, and afterwards, the parents had taken up a collection in the bleachers and everyone had come back to the mission for a pizza party on the grass in the middle of Circle Drive.

"Busy afternoon, John?" The voice came out of nowhere. Father John glanced around as he got out of the pickup. Standing near the tailgate was Father Lloyd, like a ghost that had suddenly materialized. Father John hadn't seen the old man on the grounds. Maybe he'd come out of the church and walked across the grass while Father John had been parking. He just hadn't noticed. Earlier, when he'd driven out of the mission, he'd spotted Father Lloyd strolling in the cluster of cottonwoods, stooping to examine something on the ground, nearly disappearing behind a trunk, then starting out again, head and shoulders bent. *A solitary, lonely old man,* Father John had thought. It might be good for him to have a little work.

"I believe the office will work just fine." Father Lloyd moved along the side of the pickup until he was a couple of feet away. The cleft in his chin looked like an ink mark. "Your maintenance man — Leonard, I believe he said his name was — has been most helpful. He's already started clearing out the space. Just as you predicted, there was a desk under the cartons. Leonard assured me he'll find a chair and lamp and maybe even an extra telephone in the attic.

We should be up and rolling in two or three days. I see no reason why you couldn't begin to schedule counseling sessions."

"You're sure, Lloyd? Why not take a little time, get acquainted with the place? You don't have to go to work right away."

"Ah, but there's always the need, is there not? Always people in need of help."

Father John nodded. The fact was, there were always calls, always people stopping by to talk to one of the priests. There were days when he and Ian did nothing other than counsel people who had dropped by. Everything else — preparing agendas for upcoming meetings, writing next Sunday's homily, visiting parishioners in the hospital, stopping by the senior center — came to a stop. There was no doubt that this old man, a trained psychologist, could be a big help.

"You like baseball?" Father John started toward the curb, then waited for the other priest to catch up. The voices of the kids shouting to one another reverberated around the mission grounds.

"Followed the game a bit in my time," Father Lloyd said.

"We have a good team."

"With much enthusiasm. I watched the boys running out to the diamond a few moments ago."

"We don't mind visitors at practice."

The old man gave a hesitant nod, Father John thought. Finally, he said, "That might be fine. Yes, quite possibly I would find it entertaining, if you're sure you don't mind."

"Come on." Father John took hold of the man's arm and steered him toward the path across the field to the diamond. He was surprised at how frail he seemed, his arm as light and fragile as a twig beneath the thin fabric of his shirtsleeve.

14

The residence seemed unnaturally quiet even for nighttime. No ringing phones or footsteps in the corridor. *Turandot* had ended some time ago, and Father John had allowed the quiet to settle over the study rather than swivel around and insert another opera into the tape player on the shelf next to his desk. Then Walks-On had wandered off. The click of the dog's nails in the hallway was the last sound to break the quiet.

Father John finished writing a thank-you note and stuffed it into an envelope. Another donor to St. Francis. No one he knew or would probably ever meet, just someone who had heard of the mission and had written one of the checks that kept the place afloat. He was about to start another thank-you note when the phone rang. There was something unsettling about the sound, erupting as it did into the quiet. He glanced at the black oblong box beyond the puddle of light from the desk lamp. Green numbers blinked on the little clock next to the phone: 11:46. Emergency calls came in the night. Someone in trouble. Automobile accident, heart attack. Someone arrested on a DUI or assault charge. But even as he reached for the receiver, he had the sense that this was not an emergency. It was the call he'd been waiting for.

"Father O'Malley," he said.

"You deliver the message?" A man's voice, low and raspy, like the sound of leaves crunched under a boot. The words were clipped and impatient.

"Who is this?"

"Answer the question."

"The tribes have your message."

"Don't play games with me, Father. I don't have time for games. Do they want the petroglyph or not?"

"They'd like to have the petroglyph returned. Maybe you don't know what it means."

A guffaw floated over the line. "Why do you think buyers are lining up? There's not a lot of two-thousand-year-old artifacts with spiritual meaning on the market. The petroglyph's holy, and that makes it real valuable." There was the rumbling sound of a cough on the other end. "The price is a quarter mil. The Indians got the money?"

"They're trying to raise it."

"Not good enough. I have buyers at my door with cash in hand. Cash, you hear that? Indians have to match it."

"How do I know you have the petroglyph?"

"What?" The man waited, and when Father John didn't say anything, he said, "What the hell do you think?"

"I think you could have read about the stolen petroglyph in the newspaper and decided to try and collect a lot of money."

"I don't have time for bullshit." The voice was heavy with warning. The man coughed again. "Tell the tribes to get the money. They have twenty-four hours."

Father John pushed on, Gianelli's voice ringing in his head: *Play him along. Make him want to stay in the game.* "The Arapahos and Shoshones want proof you have the petroglyph. When they see the proof, they'll make a deal. You'll get the money."

"You put them up to this? Jesuit priest thinks he can outsmart everybody? Buy some time while you bring in the cops? That what this is all about?" The man stopped. A hissing noise floated down the line now. "No cops," he said. "You bring in cops or feds and the petroglyph goes away. You got that? The tribes'll never see it again. They can say bye-bye to their sacred spirit."

"I told you, we'll have a deal as soon as we see the proof."

A second passed. Father John could hear the hissing noise at the other end again, as if the man were blowing through clenched teeth. Finally, he said, "I'll be in touch." The line went dead.

Father John set the receiver in the cradle. He kept his gaze on the phone. Gianelli was already involved, a fact that the man obviously didn't know. How long before word reached him? Sooner or later news that the Indian had made contact would leak through the tribal offices and onto the moccasin telegraph. There was bound to be speculation about Gianelli getting involved; people would assume the fed was on the trail of the Indian and the petroglyph.

And something else. He glanced across the study at the shadows striping the walls and bookcase, trying to grasp the idea forming in his mind, fit it into a logical sequence. The man understood that Arapahos and Shoshones considered the petroglyph sacred. He knew they would want it returned and would do whatever they could to raise the money. Chances were, the man was local.

There was more. The logic propelled itself to another conclusion. If the man were local, he could have someone watching the mission to make certain Gianelli's SUV didn't drive onto the grounds.

He would have to be careful, Father John realized. Gianelli had already come to the mission. They had to watch their steps. The man could disappear, just as he'd disappeared seven years ago. *If* he had been involved in the theft of the first petroglyph. *If* the Indian was the same messenger. *If. If. If.* There were so many ifs, so many conjectures. Where was the evidence to link the two thefts? A local would have known about the first petroglyph. He could have copied the theft, down to sending an Indian messenger, hoping to frighten the tribes into raising the money quickly — no questions, no cops — before they lost another petroglyph.

But that left another problem. Suppose the tribes refused to pay the ransom? Then what? What kind of local had buyers around the country lining up to give him a quarter of a million dollars? The proprietor of Duncan's Antiques? A converted warehouse with a layer of dust on the display cases and paintings askew on the walls? Father John could picture a few tourists plunking quarters in the Coke machine out front, maybe buying a few souvenirs. But serious collectors willing to spend a lot of money? It was hard to imagine anyone like that buying from Duncan Barnes.

Who, then?

Father John rolled his chair back and got to his feet. In two strides, he was around the desk and in the entry. He let himself out the front door and crossed the mission. A field of stars blinked against the black sky. He took the steps in front of the administration building two at a time. He had to bend over to fit his key into the lock lost in the shadows. He let himself into the old building and headed for his office, past the photographs of former Jesuit pastors. He flipped on the ceiling light in his office, walked around the desk, and pushed the chair over to the small table with the used computer that the owner of a tire store in Riverton had brought over one day. "Just got us some new equipment," he'd said. "Any chance you can use this?" There was every chance, Father John had told the man.

He perched on the chair, turned on the

computer, and watched the gray monitor shimmer into life. Another couple of minutes, and he was surfing the Web for articles on stolen Indian artifacts. There were dozens of sites. It was impossible to read them all. Most were tied to the West: Nevada, Arizona, New Mexico, Utah, Colorado, Montana. He skimmed the pages for some mention of Wyoming, then did another search: "Theft Indian Artifacts Wyoming." Nothing came up. Nothing.

He scrolled back to an article on Colorado. The Indian drove a pickup with Colorado plates. The headline crossed the top of the monitor: "Museums Acknowledge Dark Past." He skimmed down the text: *Museums across the country concede that in the red-hot art market of the twentieth century, they had purchased prized Indian artifacts from third parties who did not or could not substantiate the provenance of the artifacts. Many artifacts include burial and other ceremonial objects of great cultural significance. Under NAGPRA, federal legislation passed in 1990, museums must return certain items to tribal owners. Curators have been combing museum records, reviewing documents in efforts to repatriate cultural artifacts. Museums now adhere to strict rules of provenance for any artifacts offered to their collections. Prospective sellers must be able to prove that the artifacts were obtained through legitimate . . .*

Father John clicked on the next article and watched another headline take shape: "Collectors Play Role in Looting."

The Indian carving on stone that is the centerpiece of your neighbor's art collection may have emerged from a dark secret of the art world only now beginning to come to light. Authorities say that the willingness of wealthy collectors and art investors to look the other way and not question how their latest prize art was acquired has contributed to looting. "People with a lot of money to throw around like to impress their friends," said Evan Holwell, owner of Holwell Galleries in Santa Fe. "They'll thumb their noses at pieces of Indian art and sculpture with provenance in favor of a petroglyph or other unusual artifact that was most likely looted and shouldn't be on the market. What they're interested in is 'wall power,' owning the kind of piece that nobody else has. The fact that the artifact may have been illegally obtained only adds to the mystique. The element of danger makes the piece even more desirable."

Other gallery owners and museum curators

agree that the willingness of wealthy clients to invest in illegal artifacts drives the illegal market. One curator, who asked not to be identified, estimates that collectors have bought up millions of dollars in illegal artifacts in the last two or three years. The curator bases that figure on the value of artifacts offered to the museum. "Collectors looking for large tax write-offs will approach us with offers to donate artifacts," she explained. "They back away quickly as soon as they read our procedures for proving provenance, because, of course, they cannot prove where the artifacts came from or whether they were legitimately obtained."

Lucianne Newport, owner of Newport's Gallery in Scottsdale, pointed out that wealthy collectors are looking for ever more unusual objects. "The market is red hot," she said. "When clients say they want to purchase an ancient petroglyph or an unusual Indian funerary relic, I always explain that very few such objects come on the market. There must be evidence that the objects have been in a family for generations and that the seller has the right to put the objects on the market. Absent the evidence, you can conclude the objects have been looted. It is illegal to purchase or *own them. I've had clients shrug off the warning. Next thing I know, they're bragging about the ancient petroglyph they happened to find. I used to believe they didn't know what was going on, but now I'm convinced that some collectors simply don't care. As long as they are buying, looters are looting not only the Indian cultural heritage, but part of our national heritage."*

Father John skimmed through several other articles. More of the same, from various art centers: Santa Fe, Scottsdale, Aspen, all lamenting the market that encourages theft and looting. Another headline came up: "Gang Suspected in Artifact Thefts."

This was it then, the article he'd been looking for. He read through the text, hoping to pry out of the words some sense of the way a local man might connect with "lines of buyers" looking for something even more unusual than what they already had, willing to write a check for a quarter of a million dollars.

A gang of thieves is suspected of pilfering Indian artifacts across Nevada, authorities said. The artifacts are believed to include tools, pottery, fiber sandals, bracelets and pendants, breastplates, and carved stone knives, as well as ancient petroglyphs cut out of rocks.

"The gang appears to be well organized," said David Hane, Assistant U.S. Attorney in Las Vegas. "They research the locations of grave sites and other areas, uncover the sites, and loot the artifacts, which are sold on the illegal market." Hane said that the gang also seems to target specific artifacts. "We believe they may be pilfering certain objects ordered by dealers for their clients. There are any number of dealers willing to buy and sell below the radar," he said.

Father John exited the site and turned off the computer. He picked up a pencil and began tapping at the edge of the table, working through the information, his eyes fixed on the monitor settling into a blank grayness. A theft ring could be operating locally. What was it the article had said? *Certain objects ordered by dealers for their clients.* It was possible that the man on the phone was an outsider — a dealer. But it was locals who would know about the ancient petroglyphs in a remote canyon that nobody traveled to most of the year. Locals that the dealer had counted on seven years ago to get a petroglyph for one of his clients. And when another client wanted a petroglyph, he'd gone to the same locals . . .

Except that Raymond Trublood was dead and Travis Birdsong was in prison, which meant that either they were not involved in the theft of the earlier petroglyph or they were not the only ones involved. Other locals could have been in on it, and the dealer had called upon them again.

Father John flicked the pencil across the table and got to his feet. He turned off the light on his way out and retraced his route across the grounds. The man on the phone — he could still hear the impatience leaking through the raspy voice — probably had people lined up waiting to buy. At the first hint that anything was wrong — that Gianelli was involved — the man and the Indian and everybody else who knew about the Drowning Man would sink out of sight, like a rock sinking beneath the surface of a lake. They would take the petroglyph with them.

He had to be careful.

15

Bud Ladd, director of the BLM in Lander, peered at the papers on his desk through thick glasses that rode partway down his nose. He was a big man with clublike arms that lay on top of the papers. Behind the desk, a window framed the narrow view of a red-tinged butte, and a length of sunshine fell like a column on the vinyl floor. Vicky was about to rap on the door frame when the man glanced up over the rim of his glasses. He had small eyes, like dull pebbles, embedded in his fleshy face. The lenses of his glasses magnified the pockmarks along the rim of his cheeks.

"Come in. Sit down," he said, waving her toward a blue plastic chair and lifting his bulky frame a few inches over the desk before dropping back into his own chair. She could see the pink scalp through the man's light-colored, thinning hair. "Tribal councilmen insisted I talk to their lawyers.

Sorry you had to take time out for this. Where's your partner?"

Vicky settled herself on the hard plastic. She had the sense that the man was sorry *he* had to take time out to see her. "Out of town," she said.

Ladd shrugged. "I notified the Joint Council of the situation," he said, shuffling some papers into a stack, which he then set crossways on an existing stack. A cleared space appeared in front of him, and he laid his hands in the space and laced his fingers together.

"What exactly is the situation?" Vicky said.

"We've already surveyed Red Cliff Canyon . . ."

"We?"

"We've been working with the three major logging companies that have permits to take timber from Shoshone Forest. That's our charge, protect the public lands. We'd be negligent if we didn't work with the parties involved."

"What about the tribes?"

"This isn't reservation land, as you well know. Red Cliff Canyon is BLM land. Construction is slated to get under way in two weeks."

"You're telling me it's a done deal. You and the logging companies have already made the decision." Vicky let her black bag fall at her feet. It made a soft thud on the vinyl floor.

"Based on our environmental study. I assure you that we do not make such decisions lightly. We looked at four or five other routes into the logging area, including the route you proposed. They all have problems. Grades too steep, curves too sharp. The tribes're gonna have to trust our judgment on this. We're trying to work out the best solution for all the users."

Vicky didn't say anything for a moment. "Red Cliff Canyon is a sacred area," she said.

"And one of the other routes we looked at crosses a wetlands. The bird lovers would be out in force. Another route cuts off a corner of a ranch, so we'd have to go to court to condemn the section we'd need for the road." The man pulled his hands apart. He drilled an elbow into a stack of papers and began combing his fingers through wisps of blond hair. "Believe me, headaches like that I don't need. We have the fewest problems with Red Cliff Canyon. There's been a road there for a hundred years, Vicky. We're not constructing in virgin territory."

"There's not a lot of traffic there now, and most of it is seasonal — tourists going to the dude ranch. You know that every time a road into the wilderness is improved, it brings more traffic. There'll be a demand for campgrounds and hiking trails." And that was all right with the BLM director. Vicky could see the truth of it in the man's expression, the way he began nudging his glasses up his nose with his knuckle. "There'll be a steady flow of traffic through the canyon five months of the year," she heard herself saying, as if her own voice were disembodied, a tape player running on regardless of whether anyone was listening. She had to fight back the wave of revulsion at the images flashing in her head — streams of trucks and equipment and campers and SUVs all flowing through the canyon.

"We have to accommodate multiuse, Vicky. Let me remind you, we're talking about public lands."

"What about the public comments?"

"What?"

"Public hearings, discussions about widening a road through a sacred area."

"Comment period is over. You know how public meetings go. Only people that turn out have their own ax to grind. Tribal officials showed up at the meeting we scheduled, said they didn't want the new road constructed. So what else is new? Nobody else bothered to make a comment."

"Maybe people didn't know about the meetings, Bud. Maybe they didn't realize what was riding on the decision. Some of the petroglyphs in the canyon are several hundred years old. Others are a thousand years old. A few date back two thousand years. That's how long the spirits have dwelled there, two thousand years. Two sacred petroglyphs have already been stolen. I don't think people around here want the others exposed to theft."

"Nothing we can do about that."

"You said it was your job to protect public lands."

"For Chrissake, Vicky. We've got one man in the field. He can't be everywhere, watching everything."

"You and the logging companies had already made the decision before the public comment period. Isn't that true?"

"I'm sorry you don't approve." Bud Ladd gripped the armrests and pushed himself to his feet. "Wouldn't matter which route we decided on, there'd be some lawyer like you sitting in my office complaining. There's no pleasing everybody; that's a fact. I'm afraid you're gonna have to go back to the Arapahos and Shoshones and explain that we're doing the best job we can in the best interest of the most people."

Vicky stood up and faced the man across the desk. "We'd like you to extend the public comment period," she said. It was the last weapon in her arsenal. Leave the public out of it, Norman had said. Adam had agreed.

She pushed on: "The *Gazette* is already following the story about the latest petroglyph theft. I think the reporter will be interested in follow-up stories about the sacredness of the canyon. Once the public realizes what's at stake, I imagine you'll have quite a crowd at the public hearings."

The man let out a loud guffaw, as if she'd landed a punch in his solar plexus. "Don't make me laugh. You want a crowd at the hearings? You want newspaper reporters writing about the glyphs in the canyon? You'd have so many people flocking up there to see what all the fuss is about, it'd look like a stampede. People that never heard of rock carvings, stomping around the mountainside, climbing over the rocks. Taking potshots at the carvings with their BB guns. You'd have nothing but destruction. That what you want in your sacred place? I don't think so."

"I don't want your trucks and all your

construction equipment. I don't want the noise and pollution, and I don't want campers and SUVs traveling the canyon summer after summer. Is any place sacred in your multiuse agenda? Any place that can be protected?"

The man looked like a boulder embedded in place behind the desk. "Matter's settled," he said.

"Not yet, it isn't." Vicky started for the door, then remembered her bag. She could feel the pebbly eyes crawling over her as she scooped the bag from the floor. Her hands were shaking. She kneaded them into the bag's soft leather and walked out of the office.

Annie was seated at her desk, gazing up with the attention of a teenager at Roger Hurst, perched on the corner. The new associate jumped to his feet as Vicky shut the door. A faint redness rose like a rash on the man's bony neck and into his cheeks. He emitted a little cough. "Just got back from tribal court," he said. "Judge gave Debbie a warning. Next time she's arrested on a disturbance charge, she's gonna see some jail time."

It took Vicky a couple of beats to catch up, and she gave the associate a nod meant to be encouraging and congratulatory. Debbie Loneman had been arrested a few days ago for taking a baseball bat to her ex-boyfriend's truck. Annie had routed the call from Debbie's father to Roger. The new associate would handle the routine cases, Vicky and Adam had instructed. Reserve the important matters for us! They would prevent the construction of a new road through Red Cliff Canyon . . .

God, the meeting with Ladd had gone badly. She felt weak with futility, flailing about, swimming against the current, unable to get control of the important matters, unable to convince the BLM director of the importance of saving a sacred place, reduced to threatening . . . what? Publicity?

Blustering was all it was, and who was she kidding? Bud Ladd? She had to stifle a laugh. The man had given the green light to the logging companies. The construction equipment was probably already on the way into the area.

Annie was on her feet. She nearly collided with Roger heading toward the door to his office. There was a mutual exchange of *pardon-me*s and *sorry*s, amid a flurry of gestures, and in the way that Roger's hand brushed the secretary's shoulder, Vicky caught an image of the rest of it: They were personally involved. Well, that was just great. Another personal relationship to complicate matters in the office.

"Get me the reporter at the *Gazette* who's covering the petroglyph story," she told the secretary. Then she took the pad of telephone messages that Annie thrust toward her and walked into her own office. She flipped through the pages. Adam had called — once, twice, three times. *Eager to talk to you. Wants to talk to you. Call him.*

And on the last sheet, another name: Ollie Goodman. Below the artist's name was the telephone number.

The phone rang. She reached across the desk for the receiver. "Aileen Harrison's on the line," Annie said. There was a click, then a woman's voice: "How can I help you?"

Vicky dropped onto her chair and told the reporter about the BLM's intention to construct a major road through a sacred canyon. She could hear the excitement in the questions the reporter shot down the line: "When do they intend to start construction?" "What will happen to the petroglyphs?" "Why would they do that?"

Vicky gave the reporter Bud Ladd's name and number and suggested she contact him. She ended the call and stared at the phone a moment, wondering how she would explain the publicity to Norman Yellow Hawk and the rest of the Joint Council. To Adam.

She rifled through the messages again, then pressed the numbers for Ollie Goodman. The rhythmic buzzing noise was interrupted by a man's voice: "This is Ollie."

For a moment, she thought she'd reached an answering machine, and she was waiting for the rest of the message when the voice said: "Who's this?"

"Vicky Holden. I'd like to talk to you, Mr. Goodman."

"So I heard. You want to come up to the studio, we can talk." Then he gave her the directions: *Ten miles up Red Cliff Canyon. Follow the dirt road past the dude ranch. Log cabin by the lake. You can't miss it.*

Vicky said that she was on the way and replaced the receiver. She checked her bag, making sure she had a notepad with blank pages. Then she retraced her route through the outer office, telling Annie as she went that she'd be back later.

Annie's voice trailed after her: "Where shall I tell Adam you've gone, if he calls?" Vicky let herself through the door and slammed it shut without answering.

Silence pervaded the canyon, the silence of

236

outer space, Vicky thought. Nothing but the narrow dirt road climbing away from the highway and the Taylor Ranch below and winding out of sight ahead. Outside her window, the mountain sloped downward into the silvery ribbon of the creek. The glass-clear blue sky pressed down upon the rocky, tree-studded mountains ahead and the slope rising on the right. Hidden among the rock outcroppings, Vicky knew, sheltering in the shadow of the wild brush and the limber pines, were the sacred petroglyphs. Everything about the canyon was sacred. She'd sensed the sacredness the minute she'd started up the road. It was like entering a great cathedral.

She was accustomed to seeing the Drowning Man as she came out of the first curve, and she found herself subconsciously looking for it, as if it might materialize out of the rocks or the sky. A small image, she reminded herself, not more than two by three feet, yet it had seemed to fill up the entire slope. She leaned over the steering wheel and glanced upward through the windshield, hoping to catch sight of one of the other petroglyphs. They remained hidden in the dense expanse of brush and rocks, as if they knew what was to come and refused to allow their images to be seen.

They knew. The words drummed in her mind in rhythm with the thrum of the tires.

Vicky took another curve, then another, the road still winding upward, and the creek narrowing below, water glistening in the willows along the banks. The sky seemed to drop around her, and the canyon began to widen. There were a few horses grazing on the green-gray grass in the valley that opened ahead. She could see the buildings of the dude ranch — small cabins scattered about, a barn and empty corral, a large, peak-roofed cabin. It looked like a lake shimmering nearby, but as she got closer, the mirage dissolved into the air.

She drove past the turnoff to the dude ranch, the road flattening into not much more than a two-track across the valley. On the far side was the cabin, like a meteor that had fallen from the sky, and beyond the cabin, a turquoise lake that reflected crescents of white and pink light on the surface. Vicky turned left and bumped across a bridge with parallel planks laid lengthwise over the logs. She could see a stream trickling beneath the logs. The metal gate on the other side hung open against a barbed wire fence that zigzagged through the brush. She had to gear down to negotiate the two-track trail that snaked over the scraggly brush and rocks to the log cabin perched on a little hill jutting out of the valley.

She parked next to the cabin and made her way up the sawed-log steps to a porch that ran along one side of the cabin and wrapped around the corner. Little pieces of gray chinking lay on the plank floor. She followed the porch around to the door that faced the lake, even more beautiful from there, concentric rings of light dissolving and reforming, the colors deepening into magenta and bronze against the turquoise surface. She could see the images of pines along the shore, even the image of the cabin, reflected in the water.

She was about to knock at the door when a man's voice said, "Come in." It was the voice on the phone, muffled by the logs and cracked strips of concrete.

She should have mentioned to Annie where she was going, Vicky thought, but it was a fleeting thought, like the glimpse of something from the corner of her eye. The doorknob turned in her hand, and she stepped inside.

16

Vicky stared at the man hunched toward an easel in front of a window that overlooked the lake and the valley crawling into the sky. The picture he was painting looked like a half-formed image of the view. He dabbed his brush at the canvas, and the edge of the lake pushed forward. He had on a white shirt that stretched across thick shoulders, dotted by little circles of gray perspiration. His hair was the color of straw that dipped down his neck into the collar of his shirt. She could see the red tips of his ears poking through strands of hair.

"I'm Vicky Holden," she said, taking in the small room: wood-framed sofa with faded plaid cushions pushed against the log wall next to the door, Navajo blanket draped over the top, matching chair, and rectangular table, its surface hidden under the slopes of magazines. Perpendicular to the easel was what looked like a bookcase, but instead of books, small cans of paint and an assortment of boxes that probably contained brushes and other supplies sat askew on the shelves. A metal crutch lay on the floor along the bookcase.

"Figured it was you that drove up." He studied the tray that contained various cans of colored paints at the base of the easel before dabbing the brush into one and making another slice of turquoise on the canvas. Then — slow motion, like a dream — he worked the brush into a tan cloth for a moment before setting it next to other brushes in the tray. Beneath the thin cliff of light-colored hair was a high forehead, a prominent nose and chin. He had the profile of the Marlboro Man. She could picture him sitting on a fence, looking out over a pasture, face and hands weathered by the sun and wind.

At the periphery of her vision, Vicky saw a slight, dark-haired man in blue jeans and a black tee shirt rise out of the wing-backed chair facing toward the fireplace. "Guess I'll be taking off, Ollie," he said. His hair was black and smoothed back above his ears, shiny looking. He cleared his throat and came around the chair, trailing one hand along the top of the back. A large diamond sparkled on his pinky.

"Looks like you have other business." The man stared at Vicky. There were mica glints in his gray eyes, and she had the acute sense of being appraised, of some value being determined.

"Sorry to interrupt." Vicky looked back at the artist. She hadn't seen any vehicles, but the two-track ran around the cabin. Other vehicles were probably parked in back.

"You were expected." Ollie Goodman swung around on his stool, and that was when she saw the wrinkled scar of burned skin stretched across the other side of his face. It had the deep red color of a dying ember. His eye was stretched into a tiny slit.

"Does it bother you?"

"I'm sorry," Vicky said. She must have flinched. She realized that she'd stepped backward.

"Don't let him put you off," the other man said. "He likes the reaction."

"Thank you for that bit of analysis." Goodman gave a slight nod in the other man's direction. "Justin Barone, one of my associates," he said, keeping his one good eye on Vicky. "You met Diana, I believe, at the gallery. They handle the business end of things. I prefer to spend my days in the quiet and solitude of the canyon. With the other spirits of what used to be."

Barone was still appraising her. Vicky could feel the gray eyes boring into her back like a laser. She turned to him. "Vicky Holden," she said. "I'm an attorney."

"Attorney?" The man coughed out the word. He seemed to find this interesting. There was the faintest hint of a smile at the corners of his mouth. "Well, as much as I enjoy the company of beautiful women," he said, "I shall leave you and Ollie to speak in private." He lifted one hand in the artist's direction, then let himself out the door. There was the clack of footsteps along the porch, then quiet.

"You're here about the murder of that Indian cowboy on the Taylor Ranch." Goodman turned back to the easel. "When was that, exactly?"

"Seven years ago."

"Ah. Seven years. Who would have thought that much time could pass in what feels like a snap of your fingers. You might as well sit down. You will pardon me for continuing my work. I have a client waiting for this painting of the high meadow." He dipped his head toward the tray, picked up another brush, and took his time twirling it through a can of green paint.

Vicky found a wood, high-backed chair wedged between another case of paints and a small table. She scooted the chair forward and sat down. From outside came the sound of a motor turning over, then the noise of tires digging into the two-track. "What can you tell me about the day of the shooting?" she said.

The man laughed, a strangled sound that emerged from half of his mouth. The eye in the burned skin drooped almost closed. "Shooting took place after I left the ranch. I'd been working there that morning, in my usual place. Sun shining on the face of the bluffs, blue shadow on the log cabin. Sold that painting right away. As for the shooting, what I can tell you is nothing. Nothing. Exactly what I told the investigator who camped out here for two hours, asking a lot of inane questions. Did I know Raymond whatever his name was?" He waved a hand between them. "Did I know Travis Birdsnest?"

"Birdsong."

"No, I did not know them personally. A couple of cowboys that worked on the ranch. Cowboys came and went around there, still do as far as I know. But I saw what those two were up to. Oh, I saw that, all right."

Vicky leaned forward and waited.

The man pulled half of his mouth into a

smile. "I saw them here in the canyon, scraping the ground in front of a petroglyph. I didn't have to be a genius to know they were looking for artifacts. Found 'em, too. That's why they kept coming back. I must've seen them three, four times."

"How did you happen to see them, Mr. Goodman?"

"Mr. Goodman? Please. Let's dispense with the formalities. We both know why you're here. You're hoping I'm going to hand you the means of getting that killer out of prison. But what you're gonna get is this: He belongs in prison. He's a thief, just like his buddy. They were stealing artifacts . . ."

"Where were you when you saw them?"

Goodman turned his head sideways, displaying the handsome profile and looking at her out of the corner of his eye. "I have a perch in the rocks with an unobstructed view of the petroglyphs above. I can make my way upslope quite well, thank you very much, with the help of my old friend here." He tipped his head toward the metal crutch on the floor. "Painting images of the spirits is how I make most of my living. I sit for hours with the spirits, and they tell me many things. Oh, back then before the murder, the spirits told me how those two cowboy

Indians had discovered their tools. Yes, even their buried bones. They're very valuable today. Rich people pay a lot of money for old Indian bones and chisels and knives carved out of stone."

"You saw Travis and Raymond plundering the sites . . ."

"The spirits and I watched them, but they didn't know we were watching. Next time I saw those two Indians, they were working on the ranch. I put it together. I got the image, all right, and I understood what it meant." He leaned back. Half of his face broke into a smile; the other side remained as impassive as an image carved in rock. "Sure those Indians went looking for work on the Taylor Ranch. You drive out of the canyon, you're at the ranch. Perfect place for them to hide out. Spend all day up in the high pastures. Who's gonna go looking for them? Anybody report them digging up artifacts, they'd be back at the ranch before the cops got their ass up the canyon."

"Did you report what you saw?"

"Yeah." He hesitated. "I reported two clowns desecrating holy ground. Sheriff said wasn't his territory. I should take my story to the feds. Well, I got more to do than chase around trying to find the proper authorities. A couple weeks later, those Indians got a bigger idea. Instead of looking for bones and bits of tools, they'd steal a petroglyph and hit the big bucks. Took one of the best pieces of art in the canyon. Whoever chiseled that petroglyph — spirit, shaman, take your pick — knew what he was doing. He was a great artist. Produced two masterpieces. First one was stolen seven years ago. Now the second one's gone, the one the Indians call the Drowning Man."

"Travis couldn't have taken the Drowning Man. Maybe he didn't have anything to do with the first theft, either."

Goodman turned away, giving Vicky another sideways smile. "You ask me, some other Indian — yeah, one of your own people — got the idea for making off with another masterpiece. Figured he'd make some big bucks, the kind of money that pair of cowboy Indians pulled in. You seen the oils I did of those petroglyphs?"

Vicky gave a little nod. "Nothing's making sense," she said, trying to bring the subject back to Travis. "Everybody seemed certain that Travis and Raymond had stolen the petroglyph, sold it, and got into a fight over the money. Yet somebody had tried to sell the petroglyph to the tribes. Contact wasn't broken off until after Raymond was killed. That would suggest, wouldn't it, that the petroglyph hadn't yet been disposed of? Travis was arrested immediately. How would he have had time to sell it?"

"Duncan's Antiques," the man said.

"Excuse me?"

"Out on Highway 789. Duncan has an oil of the Drowning Man for sale right now. I've got a few petroglyph paintings left at the gallery in Dubois. Guess you seen those. Petroglyphs sell great in Santa Fe, too. Course those Easterners that go there like my Western landscapes, too. They're willing to pay the kind of money that supports the arts. Supports my art, that's for sure."

Vicky studied the man holding himself upright against the narrow back of his stool, blue jeans clinging to bony thighs. "There's something else that doesn't make sense," Vicky pushed on. "How would two Indian cowboys know where to unload a valuable petroglyph?"

"What?" Ollie Goodman blinked at her, a look of comprehension gradually invading the unscarred half of his face. "Same place he and that other cowboy sold the tools and bones. There's a lot of . . ." he glanced across the room, taking time to reconsider, she thought, to plot his way. "Let's just say there are some less than honest dealers in the art world. Couple Indians selling bones and tools in some flea market, and all of a sudden, a dealer finds them. Probably gave them the idea to go for the real art. 'Get me a petroglyph' " — Goodman dropped his voice and took on a conspiratorial tone — " 'I'll make it damn worth the effort.' "

He tried another tentative smile. "What? You don't agree?"

"I'm thinking that an artist like you, with connections in Santa Fe, could have run into a few dishonest dealers."

This seemed to halt whatever line of thought the artist had been pursuing. The emerging smile on his lips dissolved into a crimped, thin line. "Now why would you think that? Because I'm an artist? I make my living selling my work to people who value true art? Quite a leap from selling art in the legitimate marketplace to cavorting with criminals. But I understand. Oh, I see the picture. You're an attorney whose main interest is springing a thief and a murderer from prison, and you're willing to do whatever it might take to accomplish your mission. Should that involve casting a little dirt on the reputation of a legitimate artist such as myself, well . . ." He shrugged. "That, I suppose, is what you will do, but I warn you. I won't hesitate to sue you if you make any slanderous statements."

Vicky got to her feet. "I appreciate your time," she said, starting toward the door.

"I don't doubt that you'll be very well paid."

"What?" She turned back.

"Sooner you get that Indian out of prison, sooner he'll be reunited with his money. I expect he'll spread a little of it your way. You ask me, he was damn lucky to get a manslaughter conviction. That lawyer of his did him the biggest favor of his life."

Vicky didn't say anything. She crossed the room, let herself out the door, and took a deep breath of the warm mountain air. It had the faintest taste of sage. She hurried around the porch and down the steps, aware of the fast beat of her footsteps in the silence, as if she were running from something . . . something unholy.

She negotiated the curves down the canyon and turned south onto the highway, heading back through the reservation to Lander, Ollie Goodman's voice ringing in her head. *He'll be reunited with his money.* It was almost comical. There she was, jeopardizing the law firm, ignoring the agreement she'd made with Adam, and for what? A man who technically wasn't even her client. A man who could have stolen a sacred petroglyph, maybe even murdered his friend. *Damn lucky to get a manslaughter conviction.*

And yet she couldn't shake the image of Amos Walking Bear, the fear and grief in the old man's eyes. "You gotta help Travis," he'd said.

Vicky swung left onto Highway 26, taking the shorter route across the top of the reservation to St. Francis Mission. She had to talk to John O'Malley.

Vicky tapped the brake as she drove around Circle Drive. Boys of various sizes, ten to twelve years old, with brown faces and black hair falling over their foreheads and white teeth flashing in wide grins, jostled one another across the grass in the center of the mission. She stopped as they tumbled out into the drive. Two of the boys hoisted large bags with bulges in the sides and bats protruding from the end. The smaller kid, with a round face and a cowlick shooting from the back of his head, let his bag drop into the field. He stared at it a moment before fitting the strap onto one shoulder and staggering off, the bag bumping along behind.

Father John walked with the kids, an even larger bag slung over his shoulder. Behind him was Del Baxter. She'd gone to school at St. Francis Mission with Del. He'd played first base on the baseball team. An odd memory to pull out of the past; it had been so many years ago. She didn't recognize the elderly man loping along with the kids. Reddish face and a slight stoop, talking as he walked, waving both hands in front, his white head swiveling between Del and the kids.

Father John broke ahead and hurried toward the boy with the cowlick, wobbling under the bulky bag. He reached down, grabbed the strap, and lifted the bag. Together they stepped off the curb, swinging the bag between them. She wasn't sure he'd seen the Jeep until he veered over.

"This will just take a few minutes," Father John said, leaning toward Vicky's window. He might have been expecting her, she thought, as if he'd guessed that sooner or later she would show up and want to talk about the stolen petroglyph. The boy grinned at her before looking up at Father John, and she was struck by the trust in the boy's eyes. These were his kids.

"There's coffee in the office." Father John nodded toward the administration building. "No guarantees on the taste."

In the side-view mirror, she could see the

line of pickups and cars building up —
parents coming to pick up the kids. The
late-afternoon sunlight fell through the cottonwoods, and there were great globs of
shade that lay over the patch of grass in
front of the administration building and the
paved alley that led past the church to the
Little Wind River. "Think I'll take a walk to
the river," she said.

17

It was quiet in the cottonwoods. Vicky could hear the water lapping at the banks before she spotted the river flashing silver through the brush. This was where her people camped when they first came to the reservation, a straggly lot, Grandfather used to say, more dead than alive, exhausted from the years of fleeing across the plains ahead of the soldiers and their rifles. The children were sick and hungry, most of the warriors were dead, and finally, those who were left — survivors, all of them — gathered on the riverbank. The spirits of the ancestors were still here. She could sense their presence. She found herself returning again and again when she needed their strength.

She reached the river, picked up a pebble, and skipped it over the surface. She watched it bounce until it dipped below the current. It was then that she heard the footsteps and the crack of branches. She spun around.

John O'Malley ducked around a branch and came down the path toward her.

"Looks like you have a guest," she said, although she wasn't sure why she had blurted it. There had been times when she had stayed at the guesthouse. The mission was a sanctuary. It was silly to think she was the only one who might come here to regain some equanimity.

Father John stopped beside her. "Retired priest," he said. "Father Lloyd Elsner. He'll be with us awhile. How have you been?"

Vicky shrugged. It was startling how blue his eyes were, and the way he had of seeing more than she wanted to reveal. She turned away from his gaze and told him that Amos Walking Bear had asked her to file an appeal for his grandson, Travis Birdsong. She hurried on, saying that she knew nothing about Travis, except that he'd been convicted of manslaughter. She'd never met him.

But as she talked, other thoughts tumbled across her mind: Maybe Travis had been one of the kids at a powwow or rodeo, as anonymous as the kids running across the mission after baseball practice. She'd been away so long — ten years in Denver going to college and law school and working at a Seventeenth Street law firm, ten years of another life on another planet. The reservation had changed when she'd returned; so many people had come and gone and grown up. Her own children, Susan and Lucas, grown up, on their own. She had changed, too, of course, but there were times . . . there were times when she still felt like the scared Arapaho girl she'd once been on the reservation.

Father John walked over and picked up a pebble, taking his time, considering. He sent the pebble skipping over the water. The river bent out of sight around a cluster of trees. He threw another pebble, then said, "The jury found Travis guilty."

"Everybody assumed Travis and Raymond Trublood had taken the petroglyph and that Travis had shot his friend. The thing is, neither one was charged with the theft. What did you think?" Vicky held herself very still, scarcely breathing.

After a moment, John O'Malley turned to her. "I visited Travis in jail before the trial. Travis swore he didn't know anything about Raymond's murder. He was certain he'd be acquitted."

"Did you believe him?"

"He didn't act like an innocent man."

"How do innocent men act?"

"Don't tell me all your clients are guilty."

A flash of amusement came into the blue eyes. "They're eager, Vicky. They want to tell everything they know. They want to help the police find the real killer so the police will get off their backs. Travis clammed up. I told him he should do everything he could to help himself. He told me to save my advice. He had complete trust that his lawyer would prove the whole thing was some regrettable mistake. I don't think he comprehended the danger he was in."

"He had a lousy lawyer."

Father John took a couple of steps farther along the riverbank. "I knew Raymond," he said. "He came around from time to time and helped coach the Eagles. He'd been a pretty good ballplayer in high school, but he was a cowboy at heart. Loved working with horses, working in the outdoors. I remember the day he showed up for practice and said he'd gotten his chance. After knocking around a lot of ranching jobs that went nowhere, he'd hired on with the Taylor Ranch. 'Beautiful spread,' he told me. 'Fine herd of cattle that I'm gonna help build and some of the prettiest horses in the county.' "

Father John looked back. "I remember thinking that a part of him was already on the ranch. Raymond had been in his share of trouble, probably got fired a few times.

He'd had a tough life. Father killed in a bar fight when he was about six, older brother Hugh in prison for assault. Raymond was accused of robbing a gas station once, but the charges were dropped. The station attendant couldn't identify him. When it came right down to it, the attendant admitted that all Indians looked alike to him. The job at the Taylor Ranch was Raymond's chance, and I remember telling him not to mess up. He said he was through messing up. He was going to be strong. The kids hated to lose him. They followed him out to his pickup. They were still waving after he drove out of the mission. A couple of months later, he was dead."

"I'm sorry, John," Vicky said.

"It was stupid and senseless."

"Murder always is." Vicky waited a moment before she told him that she'd talked to Marjorie Taylor and the ranch foreman, as well as an artist named Ollie Goodman who had been at the ranch the day Raymond was shot. "Everybody's convinced Travis is guilty."

"But you don't agree," he said.

Vicky could feel the calmness in John O'Malley's voice flowing through her. She began to feel steadier. "I don't know what to think," she said. "Goodman says he saw

Travis and Raymond digging in the mounds below the petroglyphs. If they were stealing other artifacts, they might have taken the petroglyph."

"Even if it's true, it doesn't make Travis guilty of killing Raymond."

"But that was the only motive the prosecutor had. He managed to let the jury think that Travis had shot Raymond over the money they'd gotten for the glyph."

Vicky was dimly aware that she'd started pacing, carving out a small circle in the stubby grasses, trying to carve a path through the tangle of thoughts. "If Travis was part of the theft, why didn't he try to help himself? He could have cooperated. Named the other people involved and helped the tribe recover the petroglyph. He was charged with first-degree murder. He could have gone to prison for life. As it turned out, the jury convicted him of voluntary manslaughter. Fifteen years in prison! That's eternity for an Arapaho. A big black hole that stretched in front of him, and he was dropped into it. Yet he kept maintaining that he was innocent."

Vicky stopped pacing and stared at the tall, redheaded man watching her from the riverbank. "I'm going to Rawlins to talk to Travis. I'm thinking about representing him, filing a petition for post-conviction relief, getting the judge to grant a new trial."

"What's bothering you, Vicky?"

My God, how well John O'Malley knew her. She felt the blue eyes fix her in place. It was a moment before she said, "Norman asked me on behalf of the tribe — an unofficial request — to stay out of the case. Let Travis serve the rest of his time in prison. If I continue — he didn't say so, but I heard it loud and strong — the tribe won't be sending any more business to the firm."

Vicky walked over and dropped onto a fallen log. "The thing is, John, I can't shake the notion that Travis Birdsong was convicted of a crime he didn't commit. I keep thinking the prosecutor could be partly right. Maybe Raymond was involved in the theft, and someone wanted him dead. It just wasn't Travis. Whoever shot Raymond got as far away from the reservation as possible and took the petroglyph. That would explain why the tribes were never contacted again. Now another petroglyph's been stolen. Probably the same Indian that contacted the tribes seven years ago delivered the ransom message to you. I think the same people took both petroglyphs, and one of them is a murderer who's been walking around free for seven years while Travis

Birdsong's been in prison."

That's when John O'Malley told her that he'd gotten a call the previous night from a man who wanted to make a deal with the tribes. A quarter of a million dollars for the petroglyph. "I told him we need proof that he actually has the glyph. He said he'd call back."

"Then it hasn't been sold yet." Vicky felt a surge of hope, like a jolt of electricity that immediately dissolved into a new worry. The thief was still hoping to collect from the tribes without the risk of selling the petroglyph on the illegal market. But what about the risk of collecting the ransom? Everything would have to go smoothly, quietly. No police or FBI agent, no newspaper articles and interviews that might link the two stolen petroglyphs, no television anchor blathering on about a lawyer trying to reopen the case of an Indian shot to death after the first petroglyph was stolen, no newspaper reporter writing front-page stories. Nothing that might lead to a new investigation of Raymond Trublood's death. Nothing that might scare off the real killer.

"You may not hear from the man again," she said.

"Why do you say that?" Father John sat down on the log beside her.

"The moccasin telegraph already knows I might try to help Travis. If the news gets to the Indian or the man who called you, they'll leave the area."

"You can't turn away from a man who might be innocent."

"Travis deserves another chance. He deserves a good defense." She hesitated a moment, then got to her feet and started back along the path toward the center of the mission, aware of the reluctance seeping through her. There was tranquility in this place. The sky was turning into shades of blue and purple; a strip of sunlight hovered over the mountains in the distance. The feeling of evening had begun to settle in ahead of the evening itself. John O'Malley would have people waiting for him, things to do. She was aware of the sound of his footsteps behind her.

"Promise me you'll be careful, Vicky," he said as they crossed Circle Drive toward the Jeep. "We don't know why Raymond was shot, but if your theory is right, he must have posed some kind of threat. Whoever shot him got away with it. There's nothing to stop the killer from killing again if he feels threatened."

Vicky gave him a smile meant to be reassuring, but she had the limp feeling that she was only trying to reassure herself. She got behind the steering wheel and started the engine. John O'Malley stepped away as she pulled out onto the drive, but he remained in the rearview mirror, looking after her, until she turned onto the road shaded by rows of cottonwoods.

She passed the school and was about to turn onto Seventeen-Mile Road when she pulled the cell phone out of her bag and punched in the office number. The secretary picked up on the first ring. "Vicky? Thank God. I've been trying to get ahold of you."

"What's going on?" Vicky said, trying to focus on the office, the ordinary problems that might arise.

The hum of a passing pickup cut through the sound of Annie's voice: A man had come to the office this afternoon. Arapaho, but she didn't know him; well, maybe she'd seen him somewhere on the rez, but she couldn't place him and he wouldn't give his name. He'd walked out, and thirty minutes later he was back.

"What did he want?"

"You, Vicky. He wanted to see you. He made me nervous, the way he kept pacing around."

"Did he say what it was about?"

" 'When's she gonna be back,' that's all

he kept asking. I said he should make an appointment, but he walked out again. Slammed the door, too." She was hurrying on, notes of alarm sounding in her voice. "I don't like him, Vicky."

"Is Roger still in the office?" The Indian could be in some kind of trouble and needed a lawyer — the kind of case Roger handled.

"Roger? Roger went over to the jail to see the guy that got arrested on a DUI last night. He's not back yet. I'm here alone. I've been waiting for you to call."

"Okay," Vicky said. Someone in trouble. DUI, divorce, job discrimination. "Lock up and go on home. If he comes back tomorrow, Roger can see him."

She was about to punch the end key when Annie said: "Wait, Vicky. I forgot to tell you, it's all set. You can see Travis Birdsong at the prison tomorrow, first thing after lunch."

The sky had turned to slate, and dusk was closing in when Vicky slowed along Main Street in Lander. Traffic consisted of a few cars and trucks straggling home. An occasional pedestrian hurried along the sidewalk, past storefront windows that had darkened. A man was locking up one of the shops. Vicky turned into the lot next to the flat-faced yellow brick building where the office of Lone Eagle and Holden took up a corner of the second floor. She parked in her reserved slot, turned off the motor, and considered calling Adam on her cell, then thought better of it. She'd check the messages at the office first, see if there was any word from Bud Ladd. Adam would want an update. She'd call him later.

She let herself in through the outside door, crossed the tiled entry past the upholstered chairs arranged around a small glass table, and started up the stairs that curved along the wall on the left, her footsteps echoing around her. The air conditioner hummed overhead, and as she climbed, she moved in and out of columns of cool air. Below were the rows of doors to the first-floor offices. They looked as if they'd been sealed. Every other tenant in the building had probably left for the day.

She walked along the railing that overlooked the first floor, digging in her bag for the key. The doors across from the railing were closed and mute. White letters on the placard next to the first door glinted in the light that streamed from the fluorescent fixture at the top of the stairs: *Lone Eagle and Holden, Attorneys at Law.* She crossed the corridor and started to insert the key.

"About time you showed up." A man's voice boomed into the quiet.

Vicky spun around. Stepping out of the shadows of an alcove that led to the elevator was a heavy-set man with black hair pulled back from a broad forehead that loomed like an arch over his shadowy eyes. Then he was coming toward her — thick shoulders and enormous chest, silver belt buckle lodged between his blue jeans and the folds of his red plaid shirt.

"What do you want?" Vicky took a couple of steps backward toward the railing, out of the man's path. She could guess who he was: the long nose and flared nostrils, the way his mouth curved up at the corners in a kind of perpetual sneer. Everyone in the Trublood family shared the same traits. She tried to remember what John O'Malley had said about Raymond's older brother: Hugh had spent time in prison on an assault charge.

"You remember my little brother, Raymond?" The man was close now, no more than two feet away. Little pricks of sweat stood out on his forehead.

"I remember him."

"Went to the powwows, Raymond did. Rode in some rodeos."

"Why are you here?" Vicky stepped back

into the railing.

"You know what I did when that jury said Travis Birdsong was guilty of killin' my little brother? I took my shotgun and went out on the prairie and started pullin' the trigger. I shot up the ground and I shot up the air. If that no good sonofabitch had been around, I would've shot him to pieces. He deserved to be dead for what he did to Raymond, but instead he was gonna be sittin' in prison for fifteen years. And you know what?" He was shaking a fist in her face, and Vicky moved backwards, the top rail digging into her hip. "That didn't make me feel much better. Travis Birdsong should rot there like the stinkin' shit he is."

Vicky threw a glance at the row of closed doors. The building was vacant. There was no one else here. She slid the key along her palm, until it protruded between her fingers, and locked eyes with the Indian leaning toward her. His breath reeked of tobacco and something else, something spicy. "What makes you so certain Travis killed your brother?" she said.

"You gotta be kiddin' me." He glanced around the building — the corridor, the stairs, the entry below. "Everybody knows Travis killed him. That's why he's gonna stay in prison, you understand?" His jaw was clenched now, the words forced past tight lips.

"I think you'd better go," Vicky said. Her fingers were clasped so hard around the key that it felt like part of her hand.

His arm shot around her. He grabbed the railing, blocking the way to the stairs, enclosing her in a little circle. "You ain't told me what I want to hear," he said.

Vicky was aware of the intermittent hum and thrust of traffic on Main Street, the screech of a truck grinding down. It was as if the noise came across a far distance. She locked eyes with the man leaning over her. "I remember Grandmother Missy," she said.

"What?" Hugh Trublood jerked his head backward. "What're you talkin' about?"

"I remember Grandmother at the pow-wows. She used to make delicious fry bread. She raised you and Raymond, didn't she?"

The man was staring at her, the mixture of disbelief and questions moving through his black eyes. "Broke her heart when Raymond got killed," he said.

Vicky nodded. "It must have also broken her heart when you went to prison for assault. That wasn't what she had hoped for you."

A long moment passed before Vicky sensed his grip on the railing begin to relax.

Hugh Trublood stepped back. It was a long moment before he said, "We got an understanding, all right?"

Vicky started around the man, conscious of the warm feel of the key jammed between her fingers, almost expecting him to grab her. He didn't move. She crossed the corridor to her door, jammed the key into the lock, and looked back. Hugh Trublood was still watching her, and she realized he was waiting for her answer.

"I'm going to Rawlins tomorrow to talk to Travis," she said. "I'll know then what I have to do."

"That Indian gets out of prison," he said, "I'm holdin' you responsible." He left his gaze on her a moment, then turned and started down the stairs, taking his time, thick arms rigid as logs at his side. Then he was out of sight, his boots thudding across the tiled entry below. The door slammed shut, sending a little vibration through the floor.

Vicky let herself into the office, shut the door, and leaned against it, giving herself a moment to quiet the trembling that had taken hold of her. It was a potent combination, she was thinking. Grief. Frustration. Anger. A man like Hugh Trublood could be dangerous.

18

"First time I heard the stories of the petro-glyphs . . ." Ellie Nighthorse paused, and Father John watched the black eyes dart among the other members of the liturgy committee. She was a large woman, leaning back against her chair, the dark flesh of her arms crossed over a white blouse. The stories weren't for everyone, he knew, and for a moment he wondered if he should leave, make some excuse about having to finish some work this evening. The meeting had gotten under way an hour ago. Nobody had even looked at the agenda. Nobody was interested in anything other than the fact that another sacred petroglyph had been taken.

Amos Walking Bear shifted in the chair beside him. "It's okay," the elder assured the woman. "Nobody here but us."

Us. The word fell like a soft blanket over everyone at the table. He was one of them, the Indian priest. Ellie cleared her throat and went on with her story: How Grandfather was still a boy when he went up to Red Cliff Canyon. Rode his pony there by himself in the winter, 'cause he wanted to be with the spirits. Wanted to ask the spirits to show him the road he oughtta follow. There was snow everywhere, Grandfather said. Snow covering the ground and pushing down the branches of the pines, and it was real quiet. That was what he remembered about the canyon, how quiet it was, like the world had stopped.

Ellie Nighthorse hesitated again. She tilted her head back so that her black hair folded like a scarf below her head, her eyes gazing upward, as if there were an image on the ceiling of the boy riding into the white silence. She went on: Turned the pony up the mountain, and the snow was so deep, that pony got to be a high trotter. Grandfather couldn't see the petroglyphs and he was getting worried, he said, like he wasn't worthy to see the images of the spirits. So he closed his eyes and hung on to the pony, and he prayed. He said, "If I am worthy, please show yourselves." When he opened his eyes, he seen them. Up the slope, straight ahead, and it made him laugh, he said, he was so happy. So he laughed into the silence, and the sound of him laughing kept coming back at him.

That was when he heard the sounds of the village, he said. That was the special part, the sounds of drums and singing, the horses neighing and dogs barking. He heard the clinking sounds of the warriors making tools. The village was right in front of him, spread in a circle all around the petroglyphs, the white tipis lifting up like snowdrifts, little campfires burning in front, and people coming and going, women tending the cooking pots over the fires with babies strapped on their backs. He seen all of it, he said, before the village and the ancestors vanished into the boulders, and all that was left was the pictures they'd carved in the rocks, so we'd remember. That's what the ancestors want, Grandfather said, for us to remember who we are.

The room went as quiet, Father John thought, as that winter day. The boy had most likely fallen asleep on his pony and had seen the village in a dream, except for the note of certainty that rang in the woman's story. *That logic of yours,* Amos had told him when he'd first come to St. Francis, *it don't account for everything.*

Amos cleared his throat, and the dark

heads above the table swiveled in the elder's direction. "Thank you for that story, Ellie," he said. "We gotta get the petroglyph back for the people. That's what Travis wants, too." The old man held his shoulders in a straight line, like a bulwark against the sudden coldness in the atmosphere. "That's a fact," he said. "Travis has got respect for the ancestors. He didn't take the Drowning Man. Didn't take our other petroglyph seven years ago. Didn't kill nobody, either." He turned to Father John, the deep-set black eyes of an old warrior sending out an appeal for backup. "That's the truth, ain't it, Father?"

"If anyone can find out what happened, it'll be Vicky," Father John said, trying to meet the elder's expectations. He was aware of the way the other pairs of eyes had begun scouring the surface of the table. Respect for an elder invaded the room like the memory of a melody. No one would contradict Amos, yet everyone at the table, Father John realized, had decided seven years ago what had happened.

Ellie reached across the table and coaxed the agendas that she'd distributed earlier back in her direction. "Maybe we better set up another meeting," she said, arranging the papers into a neat stack. "That okay, Father?"

Father John said that was okay. There was only one thing that mattered, one thing on everyone's mind. He waited until the committee members had filed out of the hall, Amos first, the others marking the same halting pace behind the old man, ready to leap forward should he falter. Then Father John folded the chairs and stacked them against the wall. He turned out the lights and headed across the mission.

Red taillights flickered through the cottonwoods toward Seventeen-Mile Road. The growl of engines reverberated across the mission. The only vehicles left on Circle Drive were the old Toyota and Father Ian's blue sedan in front of the residence. The religious education meeting must have also let out early. No one could talk about anything but another lost petroglyph. A deserted feeling fell over the mission, like that of an Arapaho village that had been abandoned. The people made the village; they made the mission.

Father John heard the high-pitched notes of a ringing phone, like the sound of a train in the middle of the night. He hurried up the sidewalk to the residence. The front door swung open before he could reach for the knob. Father Ian stood in the doorway, backlit by the light in the entry.

"Call for you," his assistant said, thrusting the cordless phone toward him.

Father John took the cool plastic object and, shouldering past the other priest, crossed the entry into his study. He knew who was on the other end; he could sense the malevolent presence. He dropped into his chair behind the desk and pressed the receiver hard against his ear. "Father O'Malley," he said.

"You get your proof tonight." The same raspy voice, the slow intakes of breath, as if the man were struggling to draw enough oxygen into his lungs. "You listening?"

"I'm listening."

"Drive north on Federal. You'll see the gray sedan. No feds and no police. You listening?"

"Where will I find the sedan?" Federal would be a long stretch of shadows bunched around the dark, faceless buildings behind arcs of streetlights. There would be a small procession of vehicles stopping at the red lights, jumping forward to close the space left by the vehicles ahead.

"It'll find you." The line went dead.

"Emergency?" Father Ian's voice cut through the quiet.

Father John set the receiver into the cradle and glanced up at his assistant standing in the doorway. "I have to go out for a while," he said.

"This about the stolen petroglyph?" Disapproval rang in the other priest's voice.

Father John nodded. He got to his feet and headed into the entry. The other priest had to step back to give him room — disapproval even in that. He'd told Ian about the ransom message after the Indian had stopped him in Ethete. *A mistake,* he thought now. "Stay out of it," his assistant had warned. "It really isn't our business, John. We've got the mission to run. Isn't that right? We need to concentrate on increasing attendance at Sunday Mass. Get more people involved in the programs. Be an influence for good here, help the people with their problems. Isn't that our mission? Be reasonable, John. Let the FBI handle the petroglyph business."

He started to explain, then glanced at Ian's hard-set face. It would be like talking to a rock. The other priest was shaking his head, mouth drawn into a tight line.

And yet — here was the thing that had nagged Father John in the middle of the night — Ian could be right. The stolen petroglyph wasn't his business — their business. Their business was to run the mission, and Father Ian McCauley — oh, there was no doubt about it — intended to run St. Francis Mission the way it should be run, on a sound financial basis, raising money from corporate donors — his latest suggestion — and tailoring the programs to fit the budget. Well, that would be a different approach. There was no doubt about it. Ian McCauley would be the perfect replacement when the provincial sent the pastor somewhere else.

But other voices had cut through the nighttime wilderness. Amos Walking Bear's. Norman Yellow Hawk's. *We gotta get our petroglyph back.* He knew that when he closed his eyes again, he'd see the grief and fear in the black eyes arranged around the table this evening. The Drowning Man could become part of everything else that had been lost.

Father John headed outside, conscious of his assistant standing in the entry, the sense of disapproval blowing like a gust of wind down the sidewalk after him.

In ten minutes he was in Riverton, driving north on Federal, scanning the parking lots in front of the stores and restaurants and office buildings. He'd waited until he'd turned off Seventeen-Mile Road before he called Gianelli and told him the meeting was set. The gray sedan would be somewhere on Federal. The Indian would probably be the one who handed over the proof that they had the petroglyph. The caller had said no police, no feds.

"We're on this, John," Gianelli had said and clicked off.

Where was the sedan? He thought he'd spotted it a block back, sunk in the shadows of a parking lot, but as he slowed down, searching the vehicle for some sense of familiarity, he'd seen that it was a Chevy. The Indian had driven a Ford.

A horn blared behind him. Father John glanced up, expecting the sedan to materialize in the rearview mirror. A light-colored pickup crowded his bumper. He pushed down on the accelerator and went back to checking both sides of the street. The supermarket lights blazed through the plate glass windows, glass doors sliding away for people moving in and out. Cars and pickups were scattered in irregular rows around the parking lot. The redbrick façade of the city hall and the police department looked black against the gray night sky. Three police vehicles were parked on the side. And across the street, empty parking lots stretched in front of darkened, flat-faced shops. Gas station, restaurant, lights still blinking in the windows, a few vehicles outside. On the corner ahead, a large, block-shaped motel.

He saw the gray sedan then — in the corner of the motel's parking lot, pointed toward Federal, the dark shape of the Indian behind the steering wheel. Father John flipped on the blinker, but before he could swing into the lot, the car shot out into his lane and continued north.

So this was the game. The Indian leading him somewhere else to give him the proof. Speeding off somewhere, two taillights bobbing in the darkness, then veering into the oncoming lane and jumping ahead of another vehicle. Father John pressed down on the accelerator and caught up to a truck. He waited for an oncoming vehicle to swoosh past, then pulled out — the accelerator tight against the floor, the Toyota shimmying and bucking. The truck's headlights swung right and extinguished themselves; the lights of Riverton fell back. He had the sense of plunging into a black pool after the blurry red lights that kept getting smaller and smaller.

Then the lights started to grow. This is where the Indian would give him the proof,

Father John thought, on a deserted highway. But the sedan kept going. Ahead, on the left, the dark shape of a building came into view.

This would be it. Except that the Indian didn't pull over. A package of some sort flew out of the car's window and skidded over the highway in the rim of the Toyota's headlights. Father John lost sight of it for a second before it jumped back into the light, then lay still and deserted in the middle of the road. The Indian's taillights were dissolving into a single red glow.

Father John hit the brake pedal and skidded to a stop. The package was behind him now. He could make out the light-colored shape, but maybe he was only remembering where it had landed. He started backing up, hugging the side of the road to make certain that he didn't run it over.

He stopped next to the package, got out, and picked it up. An oversized white envelope, the contents firm, as if whatever was inside was solid and true. He slid back behind the steering wheel. Leaving the door open, he worked in the dim overhead light until his finger had loosened the flap. A warm gust blew into the cab and sent a dust cloud rolling through the yellow headlights.

An animal somewhere was making a chirping noise.

He had the sense that someone was watching from the darkness, staring into the light that flooded out around the Toyota, like a peeping Tom staring through a lighted window. He tore back the flap and glanced around. On the other side of the road was an old log cabin that looked abandoned, slivers of starlight filtering through the gaping doors and windows. The porch sloped across the front, and part of the roof was missing.

He turned his attention back to the envelope and pulled out the contents. Two pieces of cardboard. Flattened between them, an eight-by-ten photograph of the Drowning Man. He held the photograph up in the light flaring from the ceiling. It was either the petroglyph or a good imitation. The carved gray image loomed out of the pinkish stone: a human figure, truncated arms and legs flailing through the rippling water. He could make out the chisel marks along the edges of the stone. To the right, propped up against something, was the front page of this morning's *Gazette.*

Father John slid the photograph back into the envelope between the pieces of cardboard. As he shut the door and pulled into a U-turn, he saw the headlights coming toward him. Beyond was the faint glow of lights from Riverton. The headlights started flashing — on off, on off. A horn blared, and Father John realized that the white SUV behind the headlights was Gianelli's.

He stopped at the side of the road and waited as the SUV swung across the lane, the headlights blinding him for an instant, until the vehicle pulled in ahead. A door slammed, and the agent walked back through the stream of lights to his passenger window.

"The caller said no feds, no cops," Father John said.

"You get the evidence?"

"Someone could have been watching." Father John gestured with his head in the direction of the old log cabin.

"The evidence, John. I asked the Riverton PD to keep an eye on you. We know you followed the Indian's car from the motel." He held out one hand. "What do you have?"

"A photograph of the petroglyph with today's *Gazette*. Listen to me, Ted. The caller could have been waiting inside that old cabin. He told the Indian to toss this" — Father John tapped the envelope against the steering wheel, then handed it to the agent — "on the highway in front of the cabin. He picked a place where there wasn't anyone around."

"Okay. We've got unmarked cars watching for the Indian. Maybe we're finally catching a break here. We ran into a wall on the license plates. They were lifted off a car in Denver two weeks ago. We find out where the Indian's staying, it'll lead us to whoever's behind this."

"You arrest the Indian, it'll be all over."

"I'm aware of the risks. Don't tell me my job." Gianelli held up the white envelope. "Go on back to the mission."

In the rearview mirror a dark shape, like a gathering force, was coming up from behind. Gianelli cocked his head sideways and stepped back, a reflex motion, Father John realized, as if the agent expected the force to collide with the pickup. In a rush of noise — whirring tires, straining engine — a dark truck with headlights off swept past, plunging toward the glow of Riverton and leaving in its wake watery images of metal and red taillights.

"The caller," Father John said, but he was talking to himself. The agent had already snapped open his cell and was pressing it against his ear. "We have what looks like a brown pickup heading into town. No headlights. See if you can pick it up."

Gianelli snapped the cell closed. It disappeared inside the pocket of his vest. "Go back to the mission, John," he said again.

"Listen to me, Ted. The petroglyph . . ."

But the agent had swung around and was already lowering himself behind the steering wheel of his SUV.

19

A handful of people were scattered about the church for the early Mass, Ida Morning Star in her usual place in the front pew, Luke White half sitting, half kneeling behind her, a few other elders. Seated in the back were four or five of the younger generation — younger than the elders by a decade or so — who had started coming to daily Mass. But where were the other familiar faces? Connie Buckman and JoAnn Postings? Where was Norman Yellow Hawk?

"Let us pray together," Father John said. There was the scrape of kneelers pushed back into place as the congregation shuffled to their feet amid the murmur of voices: "I confess to Almighty God and to you, my brothers and sisters, that I have sinned . . ."

It was never routine, never automatic, moving through the prayers. Each time he said Mass, Father John thought, was like the first. And yet the sense of peace and quiet that drifted over him with the murmured prayers was familiar, as if he had stepped again into the quiet center of things away from the noise and confusion.

He'd been awake most of the night. Tossing about in the stuffy bedroom with the window thrown open and not a whiff of air moving, the bedclothes tangled on the floor somewhere, unable to stop the images moving through his head, like a DVD on automatic replay. The white envelope flying through the air and skidding over the highway, the photo of the Drowning Man. And the dark pickup speeding past after Gianelli had stopped him on the highway.

"No police," the caller had said.

"I believe in God, the Father Almighty . . ." Father John could hear the sound of his own voice — half a word ahead — leading the congregation. His thoughts were still on last night. If the caller had been in the pickup, if he had seen him — how could he not have seen him talking to the fed? — he and the Indian would disappear, just like seven years ago.

"Dear Lord," he prayed. Silently now, breaking the bread for the offertory. "Don't let the people lose any more than has already been lost."

■ ■ ■ ■

He crossed the grounds in the first daylight, the sun already warm on his shoulders and the peace of the Mass settling like fine rain over the mission. The house was quiet, too. No sounds floating down the hall of water running, spoons clacking against pans, cabinets shutting. He found Father Ian seated at the kitchen table in a pool of light, working at a mug of coffee, the *Gazette* opened in front of him.

"Where's Elena?" he said.

The other priest shrugged, his gaze still on the paper. "Looks like the BLM is going to allow the logging companies to widen the road in Red Cliff Canyon. Vicky Holden is quoted as saying that the BLM has refused to extend the period for public comment. 'The government agency demonstrates its willingness to allow the destruction of what is sacred to native people,' she says."

Father Ian snapped the paper shut. "Surprised me Elena wasn't here when I came down for breakfast. I made the coffee." He pulled a face. "Sorry. Never was very good at getting the ratio of water to coffee quite right. There's a little dry cereal left."

Father John poured the bronze-colored liquid into a mug. He was thinking that Vicky must have decided that the only way to stop the road through Red Cliff Canyon was by appealing to the public. He shook some cereal into a bowl, tipped in the milk, then carried the mug and the bowl over to the table. "Did Elena call?"

The other priest shook his head and got to his feet. "I called her house, but nobody answered. She's probably on the way."

Father John took a bite of cereal, listening to Ian's boots thud down the hallway and up the stairs. He couldn't remember Elena ever being late. She usually let herself in through the front door while he or his assistant was at Mass. When he got to the kitchen, coffee was brewing and the oatmeal was ready. There was a pile of hot toast on a plate. He glanced at his watch. If Elena wasn't here in thirty minutes, he'd drive to her house to make sure she was okay.

He pulled the *Gazette* across the table and scanned the front page as he finished the cereal, aware at some point of Ian pounding down the stairs. The front door slammed shut. He was still sipping at the coffee and reading through the article when the door opened. There was the sound of footsteps in the hallway again, hurried this time, as if his assistant were running.

Father John glanced around.

The other priest was gripping the door-jamb, his head bobbing into the kitchen. "You'd better come, John," he said.

Father John jumped to his feet and followed the other priest back down the hall and out the front door. He saw the crowd gathered in front of the administration building, cowboy hats and black heads floating above the tightening circle. Several other people were hurrying over from the pickups and trucks that had pulled into Circle Drive. A couple of pickups had driven onto the grass in the center of the drive, and still more vehicles were turning into the mission, metal bumpers flashing through the stand of cottonwoods.

Father John burst ahead of Ian and started running across the grass, around the parked pickups. He spotted Elena huddled with a group of grandmothers. Norman Yellow Hawk stood at the edge of the crowd, his dark eyes following Father John.

"What's going on?" Father John said when he reached the man. The circle started to break up. People began drifting around, closing in — his parishioners, he thought, his people. He was aware of Ian elbowing his way through the crowd and of the silence that seemed to freeze everyone in place.

"You seen this?" Norman held out a piece of paper the color of the sky folded in half, and Father John realized that the others were also holding blue sheets of paper.

He took the paper and, not looking away from Norman, began unfolding it. He glanced down. The thick, black letters bolted off the paper like sand blowing into his face, burning and stinging his eyes.

BEWARE
PEDOPHILE PRIEST ON RESERVATION

Below was the photograph of a man in his forties, dark haired and handsome with the deep cleft in his chin, dressed in a black suit with a white Roman collar, smiling frankly into the camera, white teeth contrasting with his tanned skin. And the eyes — something about Lloyd Elsner's eyes, open and unflinching, yet veiled.

Father Lloyd Elsner is now at St. Francis Mission. He has sexually abused many children. Do not allow your children near the mission. He will ruin their lives.
This man is dangerous.

I know because I am one of his victims.

Typed at the bottom of the page was the name David Caldwell.

Father John stared at the photo of Lloyd Elsner taken at least thirty years ago. He was aware of the barely perceptible intakes and exhalations of breath around him, the way in which everything seemed suspended in a void — the circle of people, the mission grounds stretching away — and the rage rising inside him like molten lava erupting from the center of the earth. His heart was thumping in his temples.

It was a long moment before he managed to lift his eyes from the sheet of paper. He made himself take another moment, draw in a long breath, before he said, "This is a very serious accusation." His voice sounded tight and choked. His saliva was hot. He tried to relax his jaw muscles. "I promise you I'll find out if there is any truth in it." Then he turned and worked his way through the crowd, shouldering past Norman, past Elena, past the others who had trusted him. Trusted him. My God, this was their mission, their place, and they had trusted him.

"I assure you" — Ian's voice breaking through the quiet — "that neither Father John nor I would ever allow . . ."

Father John broke into a run, his boots pounding the loose gravel across Circle Drive, down the alley, the church and the administration building blurring on either side. He crunched the sheet of paper in his fist. He was near the guesthouse when he heard footsteps running behind him, and Ian's voice again: "Hold up, John."

Then the other priest was running alongside him, the man's hand grabbing at his shoulder. He veered away and ran onto the stoop in front of the guesthouse and drove his fist against the door.

"Take it easy," Ian said. "You said yourself, it's an accusation. Let's hear what Father Lloyd has to say."

Oh, that was sensible. Logical and sensible, Father John thought, and yet his heart was pounding in his ears. It could not be the truth — not here, not at his mission, among his people, his kids. There had to be some explanation. Lloyd Elsner would have to explain.

He knocked again on the door, aware that his assistant had crowded onto the narrow stoop beside him and was trying to shove him away. He pounded again and again. "Where is he?" Father John heard himself shouting.

"He's around here someplace, John." Ian's

grip was tight on his arm. "Priests have been falsely accused. It wouldn't be the first time a false accusation has been made."

"Where'd he go?" Father John stepped off the stoop and started running again along the path toward the river. He knew where the old priest had gone. On a walk to the river, through the trees, circling the mission, then emerging out of nowhere. Out of the shadow world?

Father Ian was still at his side, the man's boots clomping in rhythm with his own, and Ian was out of breath; he could tell by the sounds of the man gasping for air as they ran, and that struck him as funny because, he was thinking, he could run forever. He could run and run until he found Lloyd Elsner.

And then the old priest was in front of them, winding through the brush, around the trunks of the cottonwoods, finally stepping out onto the narrow dirt path. The sun shone through his white hair like a halo. He stood still, surprise fixed in his expression.

Father John was struck by the odd sense of pity for the old man that started through his anger. He felt Ian's hand gripping his shoulder and heard the other priest's voice saying again, "We don't know if it's true."

"I'll talk to him," Father John told his assistant, not taking his eyes away from the old priest.

"My, my," Father Lloyd said as Father John shook off Ian's grip and walked over. "What's happened?"

Father John handed him the crumpled blue sheet of paper. "This happened," he said.

The old priest took a long moment, flattening the sheet, peering down at it, lifting it closer to his face. And as he read, Father John had the sinking feeling that the words on the blue sheet were true. An old man needing a place to stay, somewhere out of the way, somewhere that David Caldwell didn't know about.

Except that David Caldwell had found him.

Ian moved in closer. He might have been a bodyguard, ready to inject himself between the old priest and the pastor of St. Francis Mission. And yet that wasn't necessary, Father John thought, watching the expressionless look on Lloyd's face as he continued studying the flyer, the sagging jowls and the sallow, pockmarked skin, the brown liver spots on his hands. Not necessary at all. Lloyd Elsner was old and pitiful. Pitiful.

"He's a lunatic." Father Lloyd shoved the blue flyer back toward him. "A stalker. He follows me wherever I go."

"Is he the reason you had to leave Denver?" Father John said.

"Flyers all over the neighborhood." The old priest made a halfhearted attempt at a shrug. "Went to the *Denver Post,* told them a big story. Looking for his fifteen minutes of fame, I suppose. He's really quite mad."

"What happened?" Father John heard the tightness in his voice. He could feel his jaws clenching again. The man was lying, and he'd heard so many lies. Lies in the confessional, lies in counseling sessions, and after a while, they all had the same hollow sound. *Nah, I never did that. It wasn't me. Must've been somebody else, some misunderstanding. That's not what happened at all.*

"I beg your pardon?"

"Take it easy, John." Ian again, moving closer to the old priest. "He says the man's a stalker. Remember, other priests have been unjustly accused . . ."

"A lot of guilty priests have been accused." Father John kept his gaze on the old priest. "Tell me the truth, Lloyd," he said.

"The truth?" Father Lloyd gave a shiver of laughter. "The truth is that I have no memory of anyone named David Caldwell."

"One of the students you counseled, Lloyd? How many others were there?"

"That's unfair, John," Ian said. "We don't know the real story."

"How many others, Lloyd? How many boys who came to talk to a counselor, the priest they trusted?" Father John could feel the heat of anger in his face. The office was almost ready. A drawer in the desk needed to be repaired, that was all. He'd already told a couple of parishioners that an experienced psychologist would be available to counsel their kids. He'd invited Father Lloyd to watch the Eagles practice. He'd planned on taking him to the game in Riverton this afternoon. Get the old priest out. Give him a change of scenery. God. God. God.

"I do not have to stand here and be badgered."

Father Lloyd started to move past, and Father John blocked his way. "You will stay close to the guesthouse the rest of the time that you're here."

"Am I to be a prisoner?"

"You will have no contact with any of my parishioners." *My people,* he thought. "You will not go near any child. Not the Eagles, not any child. Do you understand?"

"I have no choice but to leave this dreadful place."

"That's right," Father John said, moving out of the old priest's way. "You'll leave as soon as I can arrange it with the provincial."

Father Lloyd hesitated a moment, then started walking in the direction of the guesthouse, listing sideways a little, as if he were walking into the wind.

"Suppose he's innocent," Ian said, his gaze on the old man's back. "What you just did is very unfair, unjust. At least you could have waited until you spoke with the provincial. Surely you don't think he would have sent a pedophile here . . ."

"It's exactly what I think." Father John spun around and started after the priest. He passed him on the path and broke into a trot, retracing his route down the alley and across Circle Drive. The pickups and cars had vanished, leaving the mission empty, deserted, with nothing but the faint traces of footprints in the dirt and gravel around the drive. He bounded up the steps to the administration building, headed into his office, and grabbed the phone. Then he was punching in the provincial's number and tracing out a circle from the desk to the side chair and the window, then around the circle again, barely conscious of the front door slamming and Ian's footsteps in the corridor, his mind focused like a laser beam on the intermittent noise of a phone ringing thirteen hundred miles away.

A low, calm voice interrupted the buzzing noise: "Jesuit provincial's office."

"This is Father O'Malley," he said, still circling, catching sight of Ian planted in the doorway. "Get me Bill Rutherford."

"I'm sorry, Father, the provincial . . ."

"Get him on the phone now."

"This isn't the way, John." Ian was a blur at the corner of his eye as he made another turn around the desk.

"Father, please be good enough to let me speak. Father Rutherford is not in the office."

"Where is he?"

"I'm not at liberty . . ."

"John, for heaven's sakes . . ."

"I want to talk to him now."

"I can take a message and have him get back to you the moment he comes in."

Father John stopped pacing. He locked eyes with his assistant a moment; then he said, "You do that. You have him get back to me right away."

"What shall I tell him this is about?"

"He knows what it's about," Father John said before he slammed down the phone.

"John, do you really think . . . ?" His assistant had a defeated look about him, shoulders sagging, blond head hanging forward.

"What do you think, Ian? Somebody named David Caldwell follows Lloyd Elsner to Denver, distributes flyers around the neighborhood, goes to the *Denver Post.* Then Rutherford shows up here and says an elderly priest needs a place to rest and recuperate, and three days after Elsner arrives, David Caldwell is distributing flyers around the reservation. What do you think?"

The other priest ran the palm of his hand across his cheeks, then cupped his chin and stared at the floor. "I don't want to believe it's true."

Father John walked over to the window. The Eagles would be arriving in another couple of hours, pickups and cars gathering in Circle Drive before everyone headed to the Riverton ballpark, a procession of vehicles moving from the mission to town. Would they come, these kids? His kids to protect. Walks-On came walking around the residence, crouched down on a shady patch of lawn, and surveyed the grounds, rolling his head between the entrance to the church and the museum, a sentinel on alert, and

yet the harm was already here. It had arrived unannounced and hidden.

"Believe it," he said.

20

The Wyoming State Penitentiary sprawled in the west, a collection of squat, dun-colored buildings that shimmered on the brown plains like a mirage that could dissolve with the blink of an eye. To the north was Rawlins, a Western town of wide streets and sand blowing in the wind. The last remnants of the town — warehouses, gas stations, truck stops — had trickled down the highway and stopped a couple of miles back. Vicky exited the highway and took a left onto the paved two-lane road that shot like an arrow toward the penitentiary. Next to the road was a slab of pink concrete with gold lettering carved into the face, like the carved images on a petroglyph: *Department of Corrections. Wyoming State Penitentiary.*

The road dead-ended at a metal gate that extended from the administration building, a blocklike structure of beige stucco that crept out from the other buildings. Vicky could see the smudge of a corrections officer's dark blue uniform moving behind the window next to the gate. She pulled into the visitors' lot and walked back to the building through cones of heat lifting off the pavement. Her own reflection moved across the black-tinted glass on the double doors at the front.

The entry was small, with walls of white concrete blocks and closed doors on either end. There was an oblong window in the wall that divided the entry from an office area where a woman with a mass of blond hair sat hunched over a desk. Vicky bent toward the opening at the base of the window, gave her name, and said that she was there to see Travis Birdsong.

The blond head bobbed from the papers sprawled over the desk to a clipboard holding a sheet with a list of names. She ran an index finger down the list, then looked up and gave a little nod of acknowledgment. Leaning toward an invisible microphone, she said, "Vicky Holden here."

A couple of seconds passed before an electronic whirring noise cut through the air. "You can go in there." The woman nodded toward the door on Vicky's right.

Vicky gripped the metal knob and pushed the door inward. It moved slowly on its hinges, like a slab of steel. She stepped into a large room with the same concrete-block walls, vinyl floor, and faint odor of antiseptic. Rows of lockers lined the wall on the left. Seated at a desk on the right was a security officer in a pressed navy blue uniform. He might be native, she thought, with dark complexion and black hair that shone under the fluorescent ceiling lights. He pushed an opened book across the desk, his face a mask. Columns of signatures and dates ran down the pages. "Sign there," he said, handing her a ballpoint pen, then pointing to the first vacant line. His tone was as flat as his expression.

After she'd dashed off her signature and the date, the officer said he needed a picture ID. Vicky dug through her bag and handed him her driver's license, which he stared at for several seconds — glancing up at her, then scrutinizing the postage-stamp photo. Finally he slipped the license into one of the slots on a board next to the desk and removed a badge with the number 365 in black letters. He wrote the number next to her name, then pushed the badge and a key across the desk. "Leave your bag in the locker," he said, dipping his head in the direction of the wall behind her.

Vicky stuffed her purse into the locker and

handed the key back to the officer as the door from the entry opened. Another blue-uniformed officer — a woman in her thirties, sandy hair pulled back from a scrubbed face with a band of freckles on her nose and cheeks — came toward her, right arm extended. "Officer Mary Connor," she said. Her hand was slender, her grip firm. "I'll be your escort. We go this way." She ushered Vicky toward the X-ray screener across the room where the other officer had already stationed himself. The peeping noise startled her as she walked through the security frame.

The dark eyes in the masklike face rested on her for a moment before the man came around and picked up a wand. Vicky stood with her arms out — she knew the drill — while the officer ran the wand up and down about two inches from her body. "Belt buckle," he announced. She unbuckled her belt and handed it to him. He nodded toward the door beyond the security station.

They were outside then, she and Officer Connor, standing on the hot pavement on the other side of the metal gate, the blue uniform still visible behind the window. A white van pulled up with another officer at the wheel and Vicky climbed inside. "Take any seat," the woman said behind her. They were the only passengers.

The van made a U-turn and rumbled down the road toward a complex of buildings, moving farther and farther into the empty vastness of the plains, away from her Jeep and the highway she'd sped along, away from the town of Rawlins with sedans and pickups crawling through the streets and people going about their business, away from normalcy.

The van bumped to a stop in front of a smaller version of the administration building, and Vicky followed Officer Connor through the front door to another security checkpoint. A bulky officer with squared creases in his blue uniform shirt waited until she had cleared the security frame. Then he walked around and planted himself in front of the door beyond the checkpoint.

"Where's she gonna see the inmate?" This was directed to Officer Connor.

"Interview booth," Connor said.

"I'd like to talk to my client in a private room," Vicky said.

"This the first time you've seen him?" The officer knew that was true; it was obvious in the tone of her voice.

"I know his grandfather."

"We suggest you conduct the first interview in a booth with a partition between you. You can see your client through the Plexiglas. You'll communicate by a telephone. It's for your own safety."

"I prefer a private room," Vicky said again. There was so much you could tell about a person, so much you could sense, when you sat across from him without a glass barrier to smooth the impression.

"Your choice. You'll wear a PMT." The bulky officer with the creased shirt moved sideways toward a cabinet with rows of cubicles. He pulled out a black, rectangular object the size of a pack of cigarettes and handed it to Connor. It was the same as the objects clipped in both officers' shirt pockets.

"Personal Monitor Transmitter," Connor said. "You'll keep this on you at all times. If you need assistance, you push the red button." She held out the rectangle and pointed to the red button on top. "Any emergency, you pull this string," she said, pointing now at the two-inch-long string that dangled from the bottom. "Responders will arrive within seconds."

Vicky clipped the monitor to the waistband of her slacks and followed the officer outside and across a paved lot, surrounded by concrete walls and high metal fences topped with rolls of concertina wire. They stopped at the door to another building. There was a clicking noise. "They see us," Connor said, glancing up at the small camera in the wall overhead. "The control room. Doors stay locked until they push a button."

The officer opened the door and ushered Vicky into an empty, concrete-block room with a wide sweep of gray vinyl floor. They walked across the room to another door at the far end, waited for the clicking noise, then entered the visitors' area. There was furniture here, round white tables and neon blue plastic chairs scattered about, a day-time drama flashing on the television that hung from a frame under the ceiling. Two men dressed in loose white shirts and baggy pants, like hospital scrubs, lounged on chairs, staring at the screen. Stacked against the wall on the right were boxes of toys and games and two infant seats. Connor must have been following her gaze, because she said, "This is where families come to visit."

An officer seated at the desk just inside the door handed Vicky another book with columns of scribbled names and dates. Vicky added her name to the last column.

"Birdsong, your lawyer's here." The other officer shouted over the television noise.

A tall, angular man in white unfolded himself out of a chair, his eyes on the TV screen a moment before he swung around and worked his way past the tables toward them. Travis Birdsong was about thirty, she knew, but he seemed older, slightly stooped, with shadows of anger and defeat in the deep-set black eyes, a long face with a prominent nose and black hair that fell along the nape of his neck. He wore soft-soled white shoes that made a shushing noise on the vinyl.

"I'm Vicky Holden," she said, holding out her hand.

The black eyes narrowed on her hand a moment, as if he were weighing the consequences of touching her. He glanced at Officer Connor before he finally shook Vicky's hand. She was surprised at the cool smoothness of his palm.

"You can talk here." Connor called over her shoulder. The officer had already started walking past the windows and doors that ran down the left side of the visitors' rooms. "Number six," she said, yanking open one of the doors.

Vicky started after the officer, conscious of the shush of Travis's soft shoes on the floor behind her. She let Travis duck past, then followed him into a room the size of a large closet with chairs facing each other across a table that took up most of the space.

"You sit there." Connor ushered Vicky toward the chair next to the large red button on the wall. "Any trouble, hit that button. I'll be outside."

Travis had already dropped into the other chair, as if he knew the routine. He'd had other visitors. He clasped his hands, set them on the table, and waited while Vicky sat down. Still waiting, with the patience of a man who had nothing but time, as Officer Connor backed out of the room and closed the door. The television noise disappeared, leaving the silence of a vacuum. The faintest odor of soap permeated the air.

"Your grandfather came to see me," Vicky said.

For the first time, the hint of a smile started at the corners of the man's mouth. "Grandfather's been tryin' to get a lawyer to take up my case for seven years. They're all too busy, they say. Nothin' to go on. No new evidence to reopen the case. But he don't give up. Calls me every week and says, 'Travis, don't give up. Some lawyer's gonna help us out.' In the meantime, I just do my time, keep my nose clean. So I tell him, 'Don't worry about it. Three more years and

I'm walkin' out of here,' but he says, 'I ain't gonna be here that long, Travis. I wanna see you walkin' out.' "

Vicky leaned over the table. She could feel the PMT's hard plastic bite into her waist. "What happened the day Raymond was killed?"

"You gonna take my case?"

"I need your story, Travis."

He shrugged. "That day was like every other day on the ranch. I herded some horses to the upper pasture to graze. Took most of the day. Started back for the ranch in the afternoon. That's when I heard the gunshot . . ."

Vicky put up a hand. "You were riding back when you heard the gunshot?" That hadn't come out in the trial.

"Yeah. I know a shotgun when I hear it. Out there, you can hear noise like that all over the place. Everybody heard it."

"Andy Lyle, the foreman, heard it," Vicky said. "That's what brought him to the barn."

"Well, I got there first; that was the problem. Didn't see nothin' when I rode into the corral, so I left the mare and went into the barn. That's when I seen Raymond on the ground. Then I seen the blood. He was layin' in a puddle of blood, and I seen the shotgun beside him. Should've been in the rack on the wall, but it was on the ground. I got outta there fast. Started runnin'. I didn't know where I was goin'. All I knew was I had to get as far away as I could, 'cause everybody was gonna think I shot him."

"Because you and Raymond had gotten into a fight the day before?"

"We got into lots of fights, me and him." Travis unclasped his hands and began drumming his long fingers on the table, making a slow, rhythmic noise like the tick-tock of a clock. "Raymond had a big mouth. Always blowin' hot air, tellin' me how to do the job, like he knew so much. I told him to lay off and he threw a punch. So we got into it. Didn't mean nothin'."

Vicky didn't take her eyes from the man. An uneasy feeling had come over her, like a chill moving across her shoulders. The same feeling that gripped her in the courtroom when a witness was lying.

"Tell you the truth" — fingers drumming harder now — "I used that shotgun couple days before Raymond got shot. Andy told me to get the coyote that was botherin' the cattle. I knew my fingerprints were all over that gun."

"What's the rest of the story?"

Travis hooked an arm over the back of his chair and surveyed the visitation area be-

311

yond the windows. Vicky followed his gaze: a white-clad inmate talking across a table to a young woman with black hair that fell down her slim back. "The rest of the story . . ." Travis shook his head and brought his eyes back. "I was runnin' full out, but Andy came after me in a pickup. I could see the highway — some cars and trucks whizzin' by. If I could've gotten out there, I could've hitched a ride to the rez. I could hear the pickup's engine screamin' behind me. I started zigzaggin', but Andy kept comin', like he was runnin' down a coyote. Drove up alongside me; he was grinnin' like a fool, keepin' that pickup right beside me. I'd swerve away, and that damn pickup was right on me."

"You're telling me he ran into you?"

"I seen him grinnin'. I seen him jerk on the steerin' wheel. I jumped sideways and the front bumper caught me in the leg. Next thing I know, I'm rollin' on the ground and Andy's on top of me. Poundin' me with everything's he got. Finally, he gets enough and pulls me up. Man, everything was spinnin' around. My leg was hurtin' like hell. He pushed me into the pickup and drove back to the ranch. I don't know how long it was before a sheriff's deputy showed up. Andy pulls me outta the pickup. 'Here's your killer,' he tells the deputy."

"Was anyone else around?"

"Whole bunch of sheriff's cars came racin' down the road. I think there was an ambulance, some other cars. Deputies was struttin' around, in and out of the barn, all puffed up 'cause they got the killer so fast. I was tryin' to hold on, you know. I didn't wanna pass out. If they was gonna shoot me right then, I wanted to be lookin' 'em in the eye when they did it."

Vicky looked away. It was hard to tell which was more depressing: the visitation area with the young couple holding hands, another inmate seated on the floor rolling a ball to a small boy while a young woman cuddled a baby nearby, the images moving soundlessly across the television screen. That, or the interview room and Travis Birdsong, with the white clothes and the dead-looking eyes, convicted before he ever set foot in the courtroom.

She made herself turn back to the Indian. "Did you see anyone as you rode back to the barn?" she said. "The foreman bringing horses to the corral? Marjorie Taylor?"

He was shaking his head. "I seen Lyle's pickup up at the house when I rode in, but I didn't see him anywhere around. Must've been somewhere close, though. He got down to the barn same time as I run off. Mrs. Taylor . . ." He shrugged. "Didn't see her. I figure she was in the office like usual that time of day."

"What about the artist, Ollie Goodman?"

Travis studied the surface of the table a moment before he said, "I'm pretty sure he was around when I rode out that mornin'. He set up that whatchamacallit — easel — over in the pasture in front of the house. Paintin' another one of them pictures of his. He wasn't there when I got back."

"You're telling me you didn't see anyone running from the barn after you heard the shot?"

"Maybe the guy that shot Raymond ran out the back door. How do I know? I didn't see nobody. 'Trust me,' Gruenwald said. 'They're never gonna convict you. All they got is Andy Lyle's word, and that don't prove nothin'. We're just gonna let 'em hang themselves. You're walking outta court a free man, my man,' he says." Travis retrieved his arm from the back of the chair and leaned over the table, so close that the sour smell of his breath lay trapped between them. It was then that something changed, some disturbance in the atmosphere, and someone else seemed to emerge from behind the black, angry eyes, some stranger rising out of a dark abyss. Vicky was conscious of the weight of the PMT at her waist and the large red button blossoming on the wall.

"Makes me wanna puke. Wasn't for Gruenwald," he went on, "I wouldn't've spent the last seven years in this hellhole. He tells me I should be grateful the jury went for voluntary manslaughter. Grateful! Grateful to go to prison for something I never done."

"Why didn't he file an appeal?" Vicky sat back, away from the intensity and the electrical charge in the air.

"Sat right there in that chair" — Travis let his eyes rest on her a moment, as if he were seeing someone else in her place — "said I wasn't to worry; he was gonna get an appeal and the judge was gonna throw out my conviction. I never seen him again. He went away, dropped off the face of the earth. Just as well, 'cause if he ever come back, if I ever got in the interview room with him again . . ."

"What, Travis?" Vicky crossed her arms over her waist. The tips of her fingers touched the PMT.

"You figure it out."

"The guards would come in seconds."

"First responders? I had 'em timed. They wouldn't've gotten here in time."

315

"You'd be in prison the rest of your life."

"You don't get it." He shook his head and glanced away. When he looked back, Travis was there again behind the dead eyes. "He was nothing but a damn drunk. I could smell the whiskey on him in court."

An incompetent defense mounted by a drunk. That would be helpful, Vicky thought, if she could prove it. She looked back at the window. The table was vacant where the couple had sat holding hands. The woman and the two babies were gone; the last inmate, a skinny guy with a flattened look to the back of his head, stood at the door across the room, waiting to return to the population.

"The prosecutor let the jury think you and Raymond took the petroglyph," she said, looking back at Travis.

"That was a stinkin' lie." For a moment, Vicky feared the stranger would return.

"There were chips of rock and dust that could have been from the petroglyph in the bed of Raymond's pickup."

"How do I know what Raymond did? He was a know-it-all hothead, like I told you. He could've done anything."

Beyond the window, Vicky saw the door open across the visitation room and the prisoner step through. The room was vacant now, the TV images flashing for an audience that was no longer there, the blue ball abandoned on the floor. Out of sight, just seconds away, she knew, were Officer Connor and the officer at the desk.

And across from her, a man who didn't deny the debris from a stolen petroglyph in his friend's pickup, a man who could be lying. What had Norman said? *Best leave Travis where he belongs.* And Hugh Trublood? *He killed my brother.* She should get up and walk out. And yet, guilty or innocent, Travis Birdsong had deserved a fair trial.

"I'm going to take your case," she heard herself say. Her voice was almost a whisper. "I can't make any promises. I may not be able to help you. Do you understand?"

Travis got to his feet. "Don't make me no promises you can't keep." He opened the door and headed across the room toward the door through which the other prisoner had disappeared.

Vicky walked back to the desk. "All set?" Officer Connor asked, satisfaction in her voice, as if she'd been responsible for a reunion between Vicky and an old friend.

Vicky nodded and followed the woman through the steel doors, across empty rooms and hot sand blowing through concertina wire. Then she was in the Jeep, heading down the arrow-straight road into the vastness and freedom of the plains.

21

She would take his case, Vicky had told
Travis Birdsong, the grandson of Amos
Walking Bear, who believed him innocent,
incapable of shooting a man. It was Travis's
case, not the case of the stranger who had
invaded the interview room for a moment,
that she would try to get the district court
to reopen. Travis's conviction that she would
try to get the judge to overturn.

She watched the asphalt fling itself across
the plains ahead, vanishing into the haze of
heat. A truck swooshed past in a cloud of
dust, a pickup that she'd passed some time
ago that had blurred into the landscape
framed in the rearview mirror. Clumps of
gray sagebrush, wilting in the sun, passed
outside the windows, and in the distance
red-tinged bluffs rose out of the expanse of
brown earth. The only signs of life were the
sleek herds of antelope that appeared from
nowhere and loped alongside the Jeep

before veering away and blending back into the plains.

An innocent man, Travis. A man who had just threatened to kill his first defense counsel.

Well, that wasn't exactly true. He hadn't actually voiced a threat, but the innuendo, the implied intention, the stranger behind the eyes, and the charged atmosphere, she had *sensed* the threat. And yet, if he hadn't shot Raymond, it was Gruenwald's incompetence — the incompetence of a drunk — that had sent him to prison.

Vicky drummed her fingers on the steering wheel. Reba McIntyre was on the radio, and the music mixed with the hum of the air conditioner and the steady hum of the tires on the asphalt. This was what she kept coming back to: She had agreed to take the case of a man who could change, and the man he changed into might be capable of shooting another human being. And maybe the changed man was the one Norman and Raymond's brother and a lot of other people had seen, the man nobody wanted back on the reservation.

But there was something else: There were holes in the stories of the witnesses, holes that Gruenwald had made no effort to fill.

The foreman had heard the gunshot and run to the barn. Well, so had Travis, if what he'd said was true, and there was always the possibility that it was not. "Are all your clients guilty?" John O'Malley had asked. She wanted to believe them innocent, give them the benefit of the doubt. But there was always the possibility . . .

In any case, there were other people on the ranch: the foreman, the owner. And who knew when Ollie Goodman had packed up his easel and paints and driven away? Others who could have been in the vicinity of the barn. And here was the irony: It was her own client, the man she had agreed to help, who corroborated their alibis. Andy Lyle? *I seen Lyle's pickup at the house.* Marjorie Taylor, the owner? *In the office like usual.* Ollie Goodman? No sign of him when Travis had gotten back to the barn.

Her fingernails drummed faster on the warm plastic. There was no new evidence, nothing that she could introduce that wouldn't strengthen the prosecutor's case. But there was this: The defense attorney was a drunk. He had come to the trial inebriated.

And it was also possible that Raymond Trublood had been involved in the theft of the first petroglyph, which meant that the prosecutor's theory about motive could be right. It was just that he had the wrong accomplice. Which meant that someone else might have had a motive to want Raymond dead. Maybe Raymond wanted a bigger cut. Or maybe he'd had an attack of remorse over taking a sacred carving from Red Cliff Canyon, and the other thief had gotten worried he might go to the police. There could be any number of reasons — any number of motives — for one thief to kill another and . . .

And kill anyone else who got in the way of the profits.

Vicky wasn't sure when the brown truck took shape in the rearview mirror. She was still trying to work it all out, picking up all the strands, trying to weave them together into some kind of coherent possibility. Follow the logic. She could hear John O'Malley's voice in her head. Whoever took the first petroglyph came back seven years later for the Drowning Man. The thief had already killed once. A man capable of killing someone who was in his way had gotten away with it.

Oh, it was logical, all right. Whoever had helped Raymond cut out the first petroglyph had shot him and made it look as if Travis

Birdsong had pulled the trigger. Which brought it back to Andy Lyle, the only witness, the man who swore he'd seen Travis running out of the barn right after he'd heard the gunshot.

Andy Lyle, whose truck had been at the house, according to her own client.

Vicky glanced in the rearview mirror again. The brown truck was gaining on her, a Chevy coming up fast. She watched it grow out of a dark blur and take shape, metal bumpers and trim flashing in the brightness. The sound of the engine bearing down was like the roar of the wind. She could see the figure of a man hunched over the steering wheel, cowboy hat pulled low. There was another cowboy hat bobbing in the windshield on the passenger side. She slowed to about sixty-five. The truck would pass her.

But the truck wasn't pulling out into the other lane; it was looming in the mirror, bearing down on her, and beneath the brim of the driver's cowboy hat, she could see the white-toothed flash of a grin. She pushed down on the accelerator and sped ahead, putting the distance of two vehicles between them, but her advantage was momentary. The truck was speeding up, engine howling. Then came the crash of metal against metal, and she felt herself jerked backward, like a dog on a leash. The Jeep jumped ahead before it started shimmying back and forth across the road. She gripped the wheel hard and tried to steer the vehicle in a straight line, conscious of the truck looming closer in the rearview mirror. The speedometer trembled at eighty, eighty-three, eighty-eight. There was nowhere to go, nothing but the highway uncoiling into the haze ahead. She was trapped in a vast emptiness, like an animal flailing inside an invisible cage.

The highway started climbing. She could feel the Jeep straining with this new effort. The brown truck couldn't have been more than two feet behind. And ahead, at the top of the incline — oh, she remembered now — the plains dropped away on both sides of the road. The cowboys were waiting. They would ram her again when they reached the top. An image of the Jeep hurtling off the road, plunging downslope, flashed in her mind.

And then she saw it: In the blur of asphalt and brown earth outside the passenger window the ditch was beginning to flatten out, so that the edge of pavement ran into the plains without any separation. There was already a slope developing, but it looked like a gradual drop down the hill. There was a chance . . .

Keeping an eye on the truck, she pushed hard on the accelerator to gain a few feet of safety, then pulled the steering wheel to the right and headed onto the plains, barely aware of the truck also swerving right. There was the loud thump as the truck clipped the rear of the Jeep and sent it fishtailing over the dusty ground, barreling faster and faster down the slight slope. She was barely aware of the blur of the truck speeding past. She took her foot off the accelerator and concentrated on steering the Jeep over the ruts and ridges. Stalks of sagebrush gripped the undercarriage and clouds of dust churned around her. A curtain of dust fell over the windshield. She was driving blind, trying to keep the vehicle upright, tapping on the brake pedal.

Then she came to an abrupt stop, and something white and hard crashed around her. She heard the air rush from her lungs, like air rushing from a balloon. She was pinned to the seat, unable to move, and the darkness, when it came, descended like the blackest night.

"We have the Indian." Ted Gianelli pushed back in the chair and swiveled from one corner of the desk to the other. The window behind him framed a rectangular view of the flat-roofed buildings across Main Street in Lander. Flowing from the CD player on the bookcase against the wall were the soft notes of *La Gioconda.* The agent was the only one Father John knew who loved opera as much as he did.

He didn't take his eyes from the man on the other side of the desk, forcing himself to concentrate on the implications of what he'd just said, his mind still racing with thoughts of Lloyd Elsner. After the pickups and sedans had driven out of the mission, no one else had come. The kids hadn't shown up for the baseball game, and he'd called the Riverton coach and forfeited. The mission was deserted. The phone hadn't rung all day. Then, with the afternoon wearing on, the sound of the phone ringing had burst into the quiet of his study. He had sprung for the receiver, shouted the provincial's name into the mouthpiece, and kept going on — "What have you done?" — when Gianelli's voice had cut over his own. "John, it's me, Ted. We need to talk."

Now, locking eyes with the agent, Father John said, "What do you mean, you have the Indian? You arrested him? We'll lose the petroglyph."

"Take it easy, John." Gianelli stopped swiveling and jerked one thumb in the air. "We know where he's staying. Riverton PD spotted the sedan and followed it to a motel on the east side of town. He parked in the back for all the obvious reasons. Only way the police could have seen the vehicle earlier would have been from the alley. Manager says he checked in Monday evening and handed over cash for a week. Spends most of his time in the room. Keeps the drapes closed, TV going day and night. Manager heard him drive off a couple of times. Saw the Indian carrying bags of fast food into the room. No calls in or out, which means he has a cell. Lives like a hermit. A hermit with a cell." Gianelli gave a little laugh and swung sideways.

"He's waiting for the next instructions." The boss, whoever he was, was calling the shots, Father John was thinking. The Indian was just the messenger. But the Indian knew who he was working for. He knew where the petroglyph was.

"Police got the vehicle identification number," Gianelli said. "Dead end, like the license plates. The sedan was last sold five years ago. I suspect that car's changed hands — legally and illegally — more times than a twenty-dollar bill."

The agent turned back to the center of the desk, dragged over a file folder from the stack at one side, and flipped it open. He picked up a sheet of paper with a small photo at the top and pushed it forward. "We might have something. Recognize this guy?"

Father John studied the photo a moment, aware of the plaintive melody of "Voce di donna" washing the air. The black hair hung in braids, not slicked back; the face looked beefier, the eyes harder, and the shoulders more muscular. But it was the Indian all right — a younger, surlier version of the man who had pulled in behind him at Ethete and delivered the message. In small black print beneath the photo was the name Benito Behan.

Father John handed the paper back. "It's the Indian. How'd you get this?"

"Sent out a memo to other FBI offices in the region." Gianelli tossed one hand in the direction of the computer on the side table next to the desk. "Requested information on investigations into stolen Indian artifacts in the last three years. Responses have been coming in all week. You know how many of these investigations are ongoing? New Mexico, Arizona, Nevada, Utah, Colorado — agents are chasing after clowns digging up Indian burial sites, walking out of small-town museums with Indian artifacts tucked under their shirts, drilling petroglyphs out of rocks." The man was shaking his head. "We're talking about thousands of miles of prairie and desert and mountains with nobody around. By the time an agent gets a report of looting, the looters are hundreds of miles away hitting another area. And the artifacts have been sold. So long as there's a market . . ." He shrugged. "It's not going to stop."

Gianelli picked up the sheet of paper and stared at it a moment. "Came in this morning from Nevada. Benito Behan, Navajo, thirty-eight years old, wanted in connection with the plundering of Indian graves on public land. Investigating agent believes he's part of a gang that has been looting sites for years. Behan here was last seen in Denver," he said, tapping at the photo. "Agents have gotten close to him, but they've always been about five minutes too late in picking him up. Seems that the man has an uncanny sense of survival. He knows when it's time to move on."

"It's not time, not until he thinks he and his boss can collect the ransom."

"His job is to handle the locals. He's native. Fits himself into a reservation without drawing a lot of attention. That's the way he worked in Nevada. Makes contact with locals who know where artifacts are located, sets everything up, arranges for the artifacts to be delivered to his boss. Goes away, and the locals disappear into the landscape. So far the Indian and the masterminds have managed to avoid arrest."

"You're saying that locals stole the petroglyphs in Red Cliff Canyon?"

"Who else knows where the oldest and most beautiful petroglyphs are located? This is a big area, John. Hundreds of square miles of wilderness, petroglyphs in a lot of places. That's Behan's pattern."

Father John leaned into the back of his chair and stared at the stack of components on the bookshelf. The aria was nearing the end. Pattern — there was always logic in a pattern. He didn't like the conclusion. After a moment, he said, "You're saying that Travis Birdsong and Raymond Trublood were the locals. After Raymond was killed, Behan fled the area."

"With the information we now have, that's what it comes down to. Behan's going to stay around until his job is done or until something goes wrong and he has to hightail it out of here. For the moment, he's lying low in the motel. Sedan's parked in the alley. The police have a surveillance crew across the street."

Gianelli picked up the photo and stared at it, as if he wanted to memorize every part of the Indian's face as a kind of insurance that the man wouldn't get away again. "He leaves the motel, an unmarked car will be right behind him. Sooner or later he's going to take us to the petroglyph. We'll get it back, John." He slipped the sheet of paper inside the folder.

Father John didn't say anything for a moment. It was a good sign, the fact that the Indian hadn't yet bolted. It meant that whoever was running things hadn't spotted Gianelli's car parked next to his pickup on the highway last night, even though he'd had the sense that, in the dark blankness of the log cabin across the highway, someone had been watching when the Indian had tossed out the envelope. He'd been sure that whoever was watching had driven past when he was stopped with Gianelli. He'd been wrong. It wasn't the first time, he thought.

He said, "If the Indian spots a police car tailing him, he'll notify his boss. He won't lead you anywhere near the petroglyph."

"We're gonna have to take our chances." Gianelli shifted his bulky frame forward and extracted another folder from the stack on the desk. He pulled out the large photograph of the petroglyph taken with yesterday's *Gazette.* "Look at this," he said, flicking his fingers at the edge and sending the photo skimming across the desk. "Anything seem familiar?"

Father John picked up the photograph. It looked pale, washed out, as if it were fading into the white background, disappearing the way the petroglyph had disappeared from the face of the boulder. The Drowning Man was positioned in the center, the newspaper propped up somehow next to it so that the date, headlines, photos, and columns of text from the front page were clearly visible. Behind the petroglyph and the newspaper was what looked like an unfinished wall with horizontal boards fixed at intervals against vertical studs.

"It could have been taken in a warehouse or a barn," he said, conscious of the agent watching him, expecting him to see something . . .

There was a small, dark splotch on the floor in front of the petroglyph. "Maybe a garage," he said.

Gianelli clasped his hands on the desk. "So we've narrowed the location to several hundred places. It would take a year to check out all the garages, barns, and warehouses in Fremont County. Point is, I think the petroglyph is still in the area. Out there somewhere," he said, tossing his head back toward the window, "in an old barn on a ranch, in a warehouse or garage in Riverton or Lander. Hell, it could be in a shed on the reservation. The boss hasn't taken it to Colorado or New Mexico or some other place to sell it. It's still right here, and he's salivating at the prospect of collecting a lot of cash for very little worry. He's sure now the tribes want that petroglyph back. He took the bait we threw him. He'll be in touch."

"I hope you're right."

"Do you?" The agent was shaking his head. "I think at this point, John, I'm going to move this away from you. It's too dangerous. The boss is running the operation. He and the Indian and even the locals have a lot riding on the outcome. They don't want any trouble. From now on, you're out of this, John. Understand?"

"I'm the one he'll call, if he calls again."

"Oh, he'll call, all right, and that will be the extent of your involvement. He's delivered the proof and he'll want to set up the exchange. You'll tell him the tribes will only allow a tribal member to carry the money. There's an undercover officer with the Wind

River police who will go in for the exchange. We need a trained officer handling this."

"And then what?" Father John had a sinking feeling, as if the petroglyph itself were floating beyond his grasp.

"The officer will be wired. We'll know where he is at every minute. As soon as the exchange is made, we'll move in and make the arrest."

"He'll never go for that, Ted, and you know it." The aria had ended, leaving a sense of vacancy in the office.

"It's that or nothing. It's bad enough you drove out on the highway alone to get the photograph. Anything could have gone wrong if the Indian had figured out that we were watching your back."

"You didn't have to watch my back."

"This is my call. We're playing this my way."

"I tell the caller that the tribes are sending somebody else, he'll call everything off. The Arapahos and Shoshones want that petroglyph back."

"Well, your job is to convince him." Gianelli swiveled his chair from one side to the other and beat out a rhythm against the edge of the desk with a pen. "Play him along; keep him on the hook. Don't forget that he's salivating at the idea of all that cash. Say you'll vouch for the money man and the tribes are anxious to get the petroglyph. Make him believe, John." Gianelli did a drum roll with the pen. "Give him faith. Call me the minute you hang up."

Father John leaned forward. He braced his elbows on his thighs and clasped his hands between his knees. "I have to be the one who makes the exchange." That was the logical thing. He hurried on. "They're going to expect me to be there. The guy could get a feeling that things aren't right. It's too risky to substitute somebody else. We can't take the chance."

Gianelli let a second pass before he said, "My way, John. Don't even think about anything else."

The phone rang through the silence that dropped over the office. Gianelli took his eyes away and stared at the black object a moment, as if it were an intruder that had burst through the door. He watched as it rang again. Finally he reached over and picked up the receiver.

"Special Agent Gianelli," he said, studying the top of the desk now, fingers flipping the edges of the folder. "Yeah, he's here." Looking up, he held the receiver over the desk. "You better take this."

Father John was already on his feet, reaching for the phone, the familiar knot starting to tighten in his stomach. Another emergency. Someone hurting, someone in need of a priest, and yet Father Ian was at the mission. He could have taken the call.

"This is Father John," he said, pressing the receiver against his ear, realizing that whoever had tracked him to the FBI office in Lander was in need of him.

"There's been an accident, John." It was Ian's voice, low and soft with concern, coming down the line. "Lander hospital just called. I thought you'd want to know."

"What is it?" The knot turned into a piece of lead inside him.

"It's Vicky."

22

Father John turned into the drive in front of the Lander Valley Medical Center on a bluff at the southern edge of town. The white façade gleamed in the fierce afternoon sun that lay over the parking lots. He'd raced out of Gianelli's office and down the steps onto the sidewalk, only vaguely aware of getting into the pickup and making a U-turn across Main Street, horns blaring around him. He'd driven through the intersection on a yellow that turned red, and kept going, traffic, storefronts, and parking lots flashing past. He could still hear Ian's voice in his head: *It's Vicky. It's Vicky.*

He left the pickup in the space with the sign in front that said *Clergy* and sprinted across the drive, through the entry, and down a corridor to the emergency waiting room. He could have found his way blindfolded. So many emergencies, so many calls:

Father, can you come?

The woman behind the counter looked up as he burst through the door. "How'd you get here so fast, Father?" she said.

"How is she?" Father John strode across the small room and gripped the edge of the counter.

"It was a pretty bad accident. They brought her in about two hours ago."

"I want to see her."

"The doctors are still with her." The woman stood very still for a moment, the ballpoint in her hand poised over a stack of papers attached to a clipboard. Then she dropped the ballpoint and turned toward the opened door behind her. "I'll get someone," she said over her shoulder.

Father John slammed a fist into the top of the counter, making a dull thud that sent a ripple of motion through the Formica. He turned around. The green plastic chairs looked worn and tired, the seats rubbed to a shiny gray. The magazines on the side tables were puffy and wrinkled. A white ambulance rolled past the window that framed part of the parking lot. He squared himself toward the door across the room. Vicky was in one of the warren of cubicles that opened off the corridor beyond the door. He struggled against the impulse to go looking for her. A madman, shouting up and down the corridor, "Vicky? Where are you?"

God, this was crazy. He was crazy. The doctor would come and take him to her. If . . .

Please, God, let her be okay. Let her be . . . alive.

The door swung open. A short, stocky man in green scrubs balanced his weight against the frame and held onto the knob. "Father O'Malley?" he said. "I'm Doctor Mora. Come with me."

Father John followed him into the corridor. He was absurdly aware of the way the fluorescent ceiling light gleamed in the bald circle on the man's scalp. "How bad is it?" he heard himself ask. His lips were so tight he could barely form the words.

The doctor waited a pace for Father John to fall in beside him before he said, "She was in shock. Has some nasty bruises, but no broken bones. I'm waiting for the results of the CAT scan on her brain before I rule out a concussion. I'd say she was pretty lucky."

Father John realized that he'd stopped walking and was staring after the doctor who had gone on. *Thank God,* he thought. He could feel the energy draining from him, leaving him weak with gratitude.

The doctor glanced back. "I told her you're here," he said, motioning him forward. "She's waiting to see you."

The figure under the white sheet on the gurney looked so small that, for a moment, Father John thought the doctor had ushered him into the wrong examining room. The nurse standing at the counter threw him a smile, then went back to writing something on a clipboard. He moved closer to the gurney. A tube ran from Vicky's arm to the bag of clear liquid hanging on a metal pole. Her black hair fanned over the small white pillow. Her eyes were shut, but he could see the fluttering beneath her eyelids. He leaned close and placed his hand over hers. It felt like a lump of ice, and instinctively he started massaging her fingers and knuckles and the small tendons that stretched beneath her skin, aware now that she was looking up at him.

"You're going to be okay," he said. With his other hand, he pushed her hair back, then bent over and kissed her forehead. Odd. Her hand was so cold, yet her forehead felt warm and clammy.

"They tried to kill me." It was a whisper. The nurse stopped writing and looked around. "The state patrol is investigating," she said. "Someone reported the accident. A patrolman was there in twenty minutes."

"It wasn't an accident," Vicky said, a hint of her usual energy in her voice.

"Well, as I say, they're investigating . . ."

"What happened?" Father John wrapped his hand around Vicky's.

"I went to the prison to see Travis." Vicky hesitated, and he could see that her gaze had gone somewhere else. She went on. "I was on the way back when a brown Chevy truck came up behind me. Full size, could have been a four-door. Two cowboys. I expected them to pass. Next thing I knew, they rammed my rear bumper. They wanted to run me off the road. I sped ahead, but they kept after me, so I . . ."

She hesitated again. The tears were coming now, thin threads of moisture glistening on her cheeks. Father John smoothed the moisture away with the palm of his hand. "You're okay," he said.

Vicky gulped at a sob.

"Try not to upset her," the nurse said, and Father John realized that she had spun around again, her eyes full of warning.

"I saw a flat place ahead," Vicky said, "so I ran off the road. There was nothing but sagebrush and dust. It was so bumpy, and then . . ." She started sobbing again. It was a moment before she said, "I must have hit something and everything went black. The next thing I heard was a loud wailing noise, and I realized I was in an ambulance."

"Did you see the men in the truck?"

Vicky lifted her hand against his in a gesture of futility. "All I could see were the black cowboy hats."

Father John was aware of the door opening behind him. Doctor Mora moved alongside the gurney, clutching a large brown envelope. He stopped next to the nurse. "Good news," he said, looking down at Vicky. "No sign of a concussion. When you feel strong enough, there's no reason you can't go home. You should take it easy a few days. You've had quite a shock."

"I'll take you," Father John said.

There was the sound of footsteps, and Father John glanced around. Another nurse stood in the doorway, her white uniform cinched tightly around a bulky waist. "Someone else to see . . ."

Adam Lone Eagle shouldered past the nurse, filling up the space between the door and the gurney. Father John had forgotten how tall and broad shouldered the Lakota was. He seemed to suck the oxygen out of the room.

"Vicky," he said, his gaze fixed on her, as if they were the only two people there. "Are you all right? What can I do? What do you want me to do?"

Vicky's lips were moving, but there was no sound. Finally, she said, "Why are you here, Adam?"

"Annie called me. I came as fast as I could. Probably broke a few speed limits between here and Casper." He threw a glance around, as if searching for approval. He locked eyes with Father John. "Obviously I wasn't the first to get here."

"You didn't have to come," Vicky said.

"What're you talking about? You're my law partner. You're my . . ." He glanced around again. "Of course I had to come. What's more important?"

He turned to the doctor. "How bad is it?"

Doctor Mora repeated what he'd said earlier, as if he were describing a specimen in a lab. Bruises, shock, no concussion. The patient was lucky. She might have been killed. She could go home.

"I'll take her home," Adam said.

This, Father John knew, was directed at him. He squeezed Vicky's hand, then let it go. "We'll talk later," he said. "Go home and get some rest." He backed along the gurney, stepped past Adam Lone Eagle, and started down the corridor.

Back through the waiting room, down the other corridor, and out into a wall of heat. He let himself into the pickup that felt like a blast furnace, rolled down the windows, and drove back through town, sucking at the hot air. It was as it should be, he told himself. Adam would take care of her. They loved each other. But that was the problem. That was the thing that made his heart ache.

Then he was on Rendezvous Road crossing the reservation, replaying in his mind what Vicky had said. She had gone to see Travis Birdsong, and on the way back, two cowboys had tried to run her off the road. Whoever they were, they had known where to find her. But that wasn't really a surprise. The news had probably surfaced on the moccasin telegraph. The tribe didn't want her to take Travis's case, Vicky had said. Norman Yellow Hawk had tried to warn her away. People were waiting to see what she'd do, and Vicky's secretary could have dropped a casual comment that Vicky intended to visit Travis today.

Still, it didn't make sense. Why would anyone want to kill her? Where was the pattern, the thread of logic beneath the surface of things? It was like trying to make out the picture carved into a rock from a distance.

The picture was there, if only he could bring it into focus.

The sun was dropping behind the mountains as Father John drove into the mission. Shadows were beginning to move across the plains, narrow blue columns of darkness creeping up the sides of the buildings. There would be no pickups around Circle Drive this evening, he knew. No one heading into Eagle Hall for a meeting. The social committee had canceled the monthly carry-in supper. The windows were gray, like the gaping holes in the abandoned houses of a ghost town.

It was a ghost mission, he thought.

Sounds of the TV floated out of the living room when Father John walked into the entry of the residence. Walks-On stood in the doorway to the kitchen, expectancy in the thud of his tail against the frame. Father John tossed his hat on the bench in the entry, went into the kitchen, and fed the dog. Then he walked back down the hall to the living room. The TV light flickered over Father Ian slumped on the sofa, legs stretched out on the coffee table.

"Any calls?" Father John said.

The other priest jerked his legs off the table, knocking a stack of magazines to the floor. "Must've been dozing," he said, shifting toward the doorway. "Calls? No. It's pretty quiet around here. Elena made dinner."

"Elena came back?" That was good, Father John thought. He'd wondered if she would ever come back.

"Said she didn't want the starvation of two priests on her conscience."

"It's her place," Father John said. The truth was, St. Francis belonged to the Arapahos. Better the priests should leave than the Arapahos.

"A plate's in the oven for you," Ian said. "I took a plate over to Father Lloyd. He said he wasn't hungry, but I left it anyway. The man should eat."

Father John backed away from the door and glanced down the hall at the shadows gathering in the kitchen. He could hear the dog pushing the dish around the corner. There was a feeling of emptiness to the old house. He crossed the entry to his study, sank into the chair behind the desk, and flipped on the lamp. A circle of light fell over the papers and folders that flowed across the surface. He set his elbows on the edge and dropped his head against his clasped hands, trying to swallow back the familiar thirst that came over him when he didn't want it, when he wasn't prepared, wasn't strong. Whiskey had made him strong. It was amazing, now that he thought about it, how strong he had felt with two fingers of whiskey inside him. One drink — one sip would make all the difference — and he would be strong and confident.

"God help me," he whispered, yet his voice seemed to boom around him. It had been almost ten years since he'd had a drink. Ten years, and there wasn't a day — if he was honest, there wasn't a day — that he didn't want one.

The noise of the ringing phone came at him through the fog of his own thoughts, and he stared at the black rectangle of plastic a moment, trying to clear his head, before he lifted the receiver.

"Father O'Malley."

"I understand you called earlier." It was the voice of the provincial. They used to go drinking together, he and Bill Rutherford, on vacations from the seminary. A few beers at a bar, two, three, four shots of whiskey. A little relaxation. What difference did it make? No difference for Rutherford. He could stop.

Father John leaned over the desk. The rage that he'd been trying to tamp down all day was like a fire flaring up inside him again. "You sent a pedophile to the mission," he said. "To the mission!"

"I can explain. Take it easy, John."

"Take it easy? You lied to me about Lloyd Elsner. An old man, recovering from a heart attack. That's the story you told me."

"I told you the truth," Rutherford said. The words were clipped and cold.

"I want all of the truth, Bill. I want the whole story. The number of men who have come forward and accused Lloyd Elsner of molesting them when they were kids. How many did you settle with? How many free counseling sessions and apologies have you handed out? What happened? Couldn't you buy off David Caldwell?"

"You're not in a position to understand any of this, John." Now the provincial's voice was heavy with disappointment. "Perhaps we should talk tomorrow when you're calmer and have a clearer head, when you're. . . ."

Father John was on his feet. "You think I'm drunk?" He could hear himself shouting. Lord, he was providing the provincial with the kind of evidence he was looking for. "We're talking about the pedophile you sent to my mission," he said, the words measured.

"Your mission?"

"I'm the pastor here. These are my people.

You had the moral obligation to tell me the truth."

"Let me ask you, John. Had I told you the truth, would you have taken Father Lloyd?"

"No."

"Well, there it is. We have a sick man among us. Should I put him on the streets? Where do you suggest I place him?"

"There's a school on the grounds. We have a baseball team. There are kids coming and going all day long. I was going to let him do some counseling."

"What? I told you Father Lloyd needed rest. A few routine tasks, maybe. He needs to pray and reflect. You had no right to let him resume counseling. The guesthouse was the perfect place. He could live quietly there. No one needed to know that he was at the mission."

"David Caldwell knew."

A sigh of fatigue floated down the line. "The man started hounding Lloyd three years ago. He finds out where he is and launches a campaign to get rid of him. I've moved Lloyd four times now. Obviously Caldwell discovered his location again. He's like a ferret that can find anything."

"I want Lloyd Elsner out of here tomorrow."

"He's an old man, John, with a bad heart.

He's not going to live long."

"You find him a home where there are no schools, no baseball teams, no kids." He thought, *We have become jailors.*

"Caldwell will come after him, cause the same ruckus, drive him out of wherever I send him. You don't understand, John. He's like a stalker."

"There were others, weren't there?" Father John said. "How did you deal with them?"

The line seemed to go dead. A second passed before the provincial said, "We made financial settlements, paid for counseling, offered our apologies. We did what we could. But Caldwell has refused all offers. He wants revenge. He wants to see Lloyd suffer. The abuse happened in Denver thirty years ago. We've turned the complaints over to the police there, but the statute of limitations on abuse has expired. Sometimes I think . . ." He hesitated, then hurried on. "Caldwell won't rest until Lloyd Elsner is dead."

"You have to move him, Bill," Father John said.

"I'll need some time to make the arrangements."

"There's no time. The people have left the mission. They won't come back until Lloyd Elsner is gone."

"Give me the weekend."

"I'm putting him on a plane Monday," Father John said. Then he dropped the receiver into the cradle. *Two more days,* he was thinking. *Two more days in a deserted mission.*

23

A bell was clanging somewhere. Vicky felt herself swimming against the dark undertow toward the insistent noise. Then the noise stopped. She realized that she was in her own bed with bright streaks of light outlining the edge of the blinds and that the phone had been ringing. On the nightstand, the red numbers on the clock shimmered through the glass of water that Adam had brought last night: 9:33.

They had driven to her apartment in silence, she and Adam. What was there to talk about? The fact that she'd visited Travis Birdsong in prison? That would have brought another lecture on how they had agreed to restrict the law practice to important matters. Then what would she have told him? That two men in cowboy hats driving a brown truck had tried to kill her? She gave a little laugh, muffled in the pillow. The effort sent a ripple of pain through her rib cage. She could almost hear Adam's voice: *Let the criminal lawyers handle clients like Travis Birdsong. They love cases like that — hopeless cases of unjustly convicted murderers. They live for such cases. They make their reputations by winning reprieves.*

She had heard it all before. Silence was preferable. And there had been something else: She knew Adam Lone Eagle well enough to sense when he was angry. He had already guessed where she'd been.

She remembered leaning back against the headrest, conscious of the rhythm of her own heart beating and the hum of the tires on the asphalt. She'd felt drained. She'd hurt all over; she'd hurt with each breath. She'd wanted to crawl into bed and sleep. And fix in her memory the feeling of John O'Malley's lips on her forehead.

Then, somehow, they were walking into the apartment building, Adam's hand warm on her arm. She remembered the weightless sensation as the elevator rose to the second floor, and she was standing in her living room, clutching her bag, statuelike in the space between the front door and the counter that wrapped around the kitchen. Adam was at her side, his arm around her, holding her lightly, carefully. She remembered that. "What can I do?" he'd said. "What can I get you?" He'd led her down the hall to the bedroom. "I'll get you a glass of water," he'd said.

She'd managed to undress, pull on a nightgown, and crawl into bed. Needles of pain pricked at her back, her hips, her ribs, working through the exhaustion that coursed through her. She was half asleep, vaguely aware of the warmth of a hand on her shoulder, and she was back in the hospital and John O'Malley was standing beside her.

"Sleep." It was Adam's voice that had punched through the dream. "I'm going to stay with you tonight. Call me if you need anything. I'll be on the sofa."

Now she threw back the sheet. It was warm and clammy; the flimsy nightgown stuck to her skin. She started to get up, but it was as if her body had stiffened like a fallen tree, and she had to lift herself out of bed piece by piece, leg, other leg, arms, shoulders, back. She stood up and started to stretch, trying to work out the worst of the stiffness. The odor of fresh coffee floated past the half-closed door. From the kitchen came the sound of a cabinet door snapping shut, paper rustling.

She gathered a pile of clean clothes and

made her way into the bathroom where she stood in the hot shower for a long while, leaning against the tiled wall, the hot water and steam soaking into her muscles. Then she toweled herself off, dressed in a tee shirt and blue jeans, and, smoothing back her wet hair, went down the hall to the kitchen.

Adam sat at the counter, the *Gazette* opened in front of him, a mug of coffee at the edge of the paper. She felt his eyes following her as she poured herself some coffee and slid onto the stool next to him. "Good morning," he said.

"I didn't intend to sleep so long." She hadn't slept through half of the morning since she was a teenager. "You should have wakened me."

"No way." He smiled at her. "I checked on you. You were breathing. I figured you needed to sleep." He got to his feet and pulled a set of keys out of the pocket of his khakis. "You are now driving a red Firebird," he said, dropping the keys on the counter. "The Jeep will probably be at Mickey's Garage for a week, but Mickey assures me he'll have it in tip-top condition."

"Thanks, Adam." Vicky reached for his hand, but he pulled away and walked around the counter. It struck her that he had wanted to avoid her touch.

"Bagel?" he said, pulling an oversized bagel out of the brown bag next to the stove and setting it on a plate. "Cream cheese? Orange juice? I did a little shopping this morning." He set the plate next to her coffee mug, then opened the refrigerator. In another moment, a tin of cream cheese and a glass of orange juice were in front of her.

"Maybe we ought to talk about it," Adam said. He remained standing on the other side of the counter, facing her, and there was something in his voice that made her look away. She pulled the bagel apart, spread a glob of the cream cheese on a piece, and took a bite. When she swallowed, it was as if the food had dropped into a hollow space. When had she last eaten? Sometime yesterday, when everything had seemed normal.

Vicky could feel Adam's eyes boring into her. She made herself meet his gaze. "I went to the prison to talk to Travis Birdsong."

Adam nodded, his gaze still fastened on her. For a moment, she felt like a child, trying to explain why she had misbehaved. The feeling went away, like a bat flapping past, leaving behind a spark of anger. "I'm going to take his case," she said.

"I know."

"You know?"

Adam swung around to the phone, picked up a pad of paper, and handed it to her. "You had a call this morning. He wouldn't give his name, but he said it was about Travis Birdsong's case."

Vicky glanced at the number scrawled across the top page. A local number, not one she recognized.

"Travis didn't get a fair trial," she said, locking eyes again with Adam.

"I see. A murderer who didn't get a fair trial. It'll be pro bono, right?"

"His lawyer was an incompetent drunk. He never filed an appeal, even though there were grounds."

Adam was shaking his head. "There are lawyers in Cheyenne, Denver, Billings — take your pick — who would love to take the case pro bono. Get a reprieve for some poor Indian deprived of his right to a fair trial, never mind that he killed a man. Get the poor guy out of prison, get into the newspapers, go on the talk shows, become an expert on TV, and then, what do you know, they've made their reputation as smart criminal lawyers, the kind that guilty people pay large fees to hire. Is that what you want, Vicky?"

"That's unfair, Adam." Vicky dropped the

piece of bagel onto the plate and pushed it away. She picked up the mug, then set it down. She would choke if she tried to take a drink.

"What is it you want?" Adam jammed his fists into his khaki pockets and stared at her. "I don't get it. We're establishing the kind of practice that we agreed upon. Everything's going our way. What is it with you? A raging need to get Arapahos out of prison?"

Vicky got to her feet. "What I have is a raging need to make sure that my people have the same rights as everybody else. If you can't handle that . . ."

"You're right about that. I can't handle it. We don't want the same practice; we don't want the same things. Julie's right . . ."

"Julie! You discussed *us* with Julie?"

"She's my former wife, Vicky. I've spent the last few days trying to straighten out her finances, get her to a better place. We have a son together. We have ties."

"You discussed our relationship with her?"

"Don't tell me you broke all the ties with Ben the day you divorced him. You hated him. You loved him. You told me you went back to him once. You had a history. You had Susan and Lucas. Ties like that can't be broken."

Vicky lifted herself off the stool and stepped backward — away from the counter, away from Adam. She struggled against the urge to run out of the apartment, down the corridor, down the stairs. Run until she was out on the plains with nothing but the sun on her face and the wind whipping through her hair. What he'd said was true, and the truth of it had slammed into her like a tornado, bringing memories that she didn't want. All those times she had tried to make things work with Ben because of the *ties,* the ties that couldn't be broken — kids, family, history — and always knowing that it could never work.

"This isn't about Travis Birdsong," she said. "This is about you and your ex-wife and whatever has happened while you've been in Casper."

"We'll discuss this later." Adam squared his shoulders and headed for the door.

"We need to discuss it now," Vicky said to his back.

He gripped the knob, then turned around. "You know that I love you, Vicky," he said.

"You love her."

"She needs me."

Vicky swung around, walked past the dining room table to the window, and stared down at a cream-colored sedan crawling along the street, a boy with black hair pedaling a bicycle toward some imaginary finishing line. The door opened and slammed shut behind her. She heard Adam's footsteps recede along the corridor, until there was only the vacant quiet settling over the apartment.

"Julie needs him," she said out loud, talking to herself now, like some crazy, lonely woman with no one else to talk to. An ex-husband who was dead. Lucas and Susan grown and gone, living their own lives in Denver and Los Angeles. When did they even talk on the phone? A couple of times a month, and then it was like talking to strangers, her own children, because there was so much to catch up on, so much they didn't know about one another. It was impossible. *Hi sei ci nihi,* the grandmothers called her. Woman Alone.

She watched Adam burst through the glass doors at the entrance below, head for his truck parked at the curb, and climb into the cab. A puff of gray smoke broke from the tailpipe; then the pickup jerked into the lane and accelerated until it had disappeared behind the bushes and trees halfway down the block.

She leaned closer, the window pane cool

against her cheek. She had wanted to need Adam Lone Eagle. She had wanted them to need each other. She had willed it to be true, but she had been fooling herself. It was not the true thing. "I'm sorry, Adam," she said. The fog of her own breath appeared on the glass.

It was a long moment before Vicky walked back to the counter and sat down. A profound weariness wrapped around her like a heavy blanket. She tried to sip at the coffee, but it had turned tepid and bitter. A dull ache coursed through her head, and the stiffness in her body made her aware of her joints and shoulder blades, the outlines of her ribs, as if all of her bones were pushing against her skin. She reached out and brushed her fingertips against the notepad, bringing it along the counter toward her, then studied the unfamiliar telephone number, trying to connect it to a name or a face. Nothing.

Finally, she got up and walked over to the phone at the end of the counter. She tapped in the numbers and listened to the whirring noise of a phone ringing somewhere in the area, her gaze on the window and the white clouds skimming the blue sky.

The noise gave way to a deadness, followed by a thud, as if the phone had been dropped. Finally, a man's voice, "Yes? Who's there?"

"Vicky Holden. I'm returning your call."

"Ah, Ms. Holden. I believe you have been trying to reach me. I'm Harry Gruenwald."

"Mr. Gruenwald." Vicky tried to mask the surprise that hit her. Her secretary had spent the last four days calling bar associations and law firms, trying to find the incompetent attorney that Travis had been stuck with, and had met with nothing but brick walls. Now the man was on the line. "I'd like to talk to you," Vicky said. "I represent one of your former clients, Travis Birdsong."

Vicky could hear the labored breathing at the other end, as if the man were sucking air through a tube. "So I understand," he said finally.

"I can come wherever you are."

"I'm thinking it over."

"It's important, Mr. Gruenwald. There's new evidence in Travis's case." She held her breath. There was new evidence, all right. Evidence that Travis's attorney had been an incompetent drunk.

A sigh floated down the line, like air escaping a balloon. "I knew this would happen someday," the man said. "You might as well come to my house."

"Tell me how to get there." Vicky found a pen next to the phone and began scribbling the directions: Highway 28 south. Popo Agie River. White house on right. "I'll be there in thirty minutes," she said.

She hung up, went back to the bedroom, and began pulling lawyer clothes from the closet: dark skirt, blue blouse, black pumps, trying to shake the sound of Adam's voice in her head. *What is it with you? A raging need to get Arapahos out of prison?* In ten minutes she was backing the red Firebird out of her parking space, her bag on the seat beside her next to the slim black leather folder with a notepad and pen inside. She shot a glance in the rearview mirror. Her hair was pulled back and clipped with a beaded barrette. She'd dabbed on a little makeup, a touch of lipstick. It would have to do.

Saturday morning traffic on Main was beginning to pick up, shops had come to life, people walking along the sidewalks, pushing baby strollers, pulling toddlers by the hand. It was already hot, and a dry, warm breeze brushed the sides of the Firebird. Vicky followed the traffic through an intersection. A couple more lights, and she was on the highway heading south, pressing down on the accelerator, open stretches of land whipping past the windows. There was no other traffic — just like yesterday — and she found herself checking the rearview mirror, almost expecting to see a brown truck coming up behind her.

She started to slow down, hunting for the white house. She spotted it ahead, set back in a clump of trees at the end of a dirt road, not much larger than a storage shed with a peaked roof and two oblong windows that looked black in the sun. There was a small porch that jutted from the front door.

Vicky swung right and drove down the dirt road to the porch. She grabbed her bag and notepad folder, went to the front door, and knocked. Even in the shade splashing the house, the air was hot. A gust of wind lifted little balls of dust in the air. Her throat felt as dry as the dust.

She knocked again. A couple of seconds passed before she heard the sound of footsteps shuffling on the other side of the door, then a woman's voice: "Who are you? What do you want?"

Vicky leaned toward the door. "Mr. Gruenwald's expecting me."

"It's all right, Helen." A man's voice, the voice on the phone.

The door swung open. Looming in the doorway was a large man with bulky shoulders and thick arms and chest, wearing a white shirt with a silver buffalo on his bolo tie and dark, pressed slacks, like a lawyer who still had an office to go to. His hair was gray and curly, his face almost square, with ruddy cheeks that drooped into his jaw. He stared at her through thick glasses that gave a startled look to his red-rimmed eyes. A small, gray-haired woman swayed in the shadows behind him.

"You'd better come in," Harry Gruenwald said.

24

Vicky stepped into the small living room. Drapes were pulled halfway across the front window, so that a vertical column of sunshine ran across the vinyl floor and folded around a sofa that sagged in the middle. Oblongs of light filtered past her through the door. She could see fragments of her own shadow splayed on the opposite wall. The air was close, the sharp smell of antiseptic cutting through the odors of stale food and burnt coffee and something else — something like the damp smell of a cave.

"Thanks for agreeing to see me," she said. She realized that Harry Gruenwald was holding on to the edge of the door, waiting for her to move deeper inside. There was a faint trembling in his other hand, and little beads of perspiration dotted his forehead.

Vicky stepped forward, and the door closed behind her. Her shadow melded into the dimness. A slight, elderly woman with matted gray hair and a loose-fitting dress was pacing between the corner of the sofa and a recliner that still bore the faint imprints of a body.

"We'll talk in the kitchen." The lawyer started toward the rear of the house. "Go to your room, Helen," he said, snapping his fingers toward the woman. She had stopped pacing and stood with arms dangling at her sides, like someone stranded on a street corner, uncertain of which direction to take.

"Hello," Vicky said. The woman stared at her out of blank eyes, and Vicky had the sense that, inside the frail body swaying from side to side, there was no one there.

"In here." Notes of irritation sounded in Gruenwald's voice. The man beckoned her toward the doorway across the room.

Vicky nodded at the woman as she walked past. My God, the old woman had once been there; she deserved respect. The lawyer was waiting in the center of the kitchen, little more than a hallway with cabinets, stove, and refrigerator across from a round table that had been cut in half and shoved under the small window.

"I'm sorry about your wife," Vicky said, gesturing with her head toward the living room.

"We don't need your pity." Gruenwald

dropped onto a small chair at the table.

Vicky took the other chair. Salt and pepper shakers and a napkin holder had been shoved to the edge of the table. A trail of salt zigzagged across the surface. She kept her bag in her lap, opened the leather folder, and withdrew the ballpoint from the slot.

"How did you hear I was looking for you?" she asked.

"I still got friends in this community." He gave a halfhearted shrug. "Figured it was about that Arapaho that killed his buddy. Another petroglyph's gone missing, so some hotshot lawyer was bound to start looking into the old case. Let me guess. Amos Walking Around . . ."

"Walking Bear."

"Yeah, whatever. That old man's still trying to get his grandson out of prison, and now there's an Arapaho lawyer in town just itching to right all the old wrongs. Get to the purpose of your visit."

"You could have filed an appeal immediately. Why didn't you?"

A door slammed somewhere in the house, as if a gust of wind had blown through. Dishes rattled next to the sink.

The man threw a glance toward the living room, then set both hands on the table. The trembling in his left hand seemed more pronounced. He covered it with the other hand, but the trembling only ran through both. A faint vibration started through the table.

"What good would it have done? Appellate courts grant one out of ten appeals. I got that Indian off on a manslaughter conviction. He was damned lucky. There wasn't the need for any appeal. Appeals cost money."

"Was that the reason? Money?"

Gruenwald looked at the window a moment. Finally he said, "We talked it over."

"Who?" At the top of the notepad paper, Vicky wrote Harry Gruenwald and the date.

"Travis and me. His grandfather had hired me, but Travis said the old man didn't have any more money. So he wanted me to handle the appeal. On contingency, he called it." Gruenwald shook his head and gave a forced laugh that sounded as if some hard object were stuck in his throat.

Vicky jotted down what the man was saying.

"Contingency. Like we'd be going for a big settlement and I'd get a share of the pot. Only that's not the way it works in a criminal appeal. There isn't any pot at the end of the rainbow. Travis kept saying he'd pay me soon's he got out of prison. I said no thanks. I had enough going on. I didn't have time for any appeal; I didn't want any more cases. I wanted out. Helen and me had plans. We moved up to Montana and worked on her brother's ranch. It was good, what I needed."

"To get sober?" Vicky heard herself say. It was the courtroom tone, the no-holds-barred tone she reserved for hostile witnesses.

"I'm not proud of it."

"I read the trial transcript."

"What do you want?"

"There's a lot I don't understand. Why didn't you call witnesses to rebut the prosecutor's witnesses?"

"I called his grandfather. Who else was gonna get up on the stand and say that Travis didn't shoot that guy?"

"Travis's other family. Friends. Teachers. They would have vouched for him. He'd never been in any kind of trouble. You could have brought out the fact that Travis had reached the barn ahead of Andy Lyle, that's all. You could have given the jury reasonable doubt. If Lyle had gotten there first, maybe he would have been charged." She paused, then pushed on. "We both know a white man would have received every benefit of doubt."

The man slumped against his chair. The table was shaking under his hands, and he pulled them into his lap. He ran his tongue over his lower lip before he said, "I could've put a whole lot of folks on the stand. What good would it have done? They weren't there; they didn't see it happen. I ran the defense the way I saw it."

"You assured Travis that he would be acquitted."

The lawyer licked at his lips again. He was clenching and unclenching his fist over his belly. "Lots of folks thought he'd be acquitted. Mrs. Taylor herself was on his side. Came to see him in jail. Besides, what was I gonna tell him? They're gonna slap his sorry ass in prison?"

"Marjorie Taylor visited him?" Vicky heard the surprise ringing in her voice. Travis hadn't said anything about his employer coming to the jail.

"Two or three times, I know of. I ran the defense the way I saw fit. You gonna file for a new trial? Good luck."

Vicky took a moment and scribbled a few more notes. She'd nearly filled up the page. She was getting nowhere — an incompetent attorney who'd convinced himself that he was competent. She wrote the word *incompetent* and drew a line underneath that nearly sliced through the paper. A client who hadn't leveled with her.

She locked eyes with the man at the opposite curve of the table. "I think you were inebriated during the trial," she said.

"That's a lie, a slanderous accusation, counselor." Gruenwald dropped his clasped hands on the table, which shuddered beneath the blow. "You utter that outside this room, and I'll sue you from here to kingdom come."

"I'm giving you an excuse, Mr. Gruenwald," Vicky said. "What else would explain the ineffective assistance of counsel? Just so you know, that's one of the points I intend to bring before the judge."

The man pulled back again, lifted his chin, and stared at the ceiling for a long moment. Ropes of blue veins pulsed beneath the folds of his neck. Finally, he brought his eyes back to hers. "I ran a respectable law practice in this area for years. I had a good reputation, and you're gonna blow that away, as if it was nothing. It's my life. Maybe I took a drink now and then during the trial. I don't remember. There was a lot more on my mind than keeping some murderer out of prison. Practice was going to hell, with a bunch of smart, new lawyers putting out their shingles all over the area. Helen there"

— He nodded toward the living room — "I could tell she wasn't the same, something was happening to her. We needed to get out of here, get away from all the stress. I wanted to be finished with Travis Birdsong so we could pack the pickup and head for Montana where she'd be okay again. That's all I was thinking."

Vicky flipped the page that was covered with black lines and stared at a blank page. How many people like Travis were in prison thanks to lawyers like Gruenwald? How many Arapahos?

Locking eyes with him again, she said, "Maybe you shouldn't have taken the case."

He let out a guffaw. His sour breath floated across the table. "You got so much money, you can turn clients away? Well, congratulations." He leaned toward her. "I needed the money so me and Helen could get the hell outta here. Only things didn't work out, did they? She started getting worse, her brother didn't want us around, so we came back here. She owns this place." He let his eyes roam around the small kitchen, taking it all in. "Father left it to her. All we got left. This house and my reputation. Get my drift? You come here thinking I'm gonna start crying and confessing how I was a no-good alkie that got a killer sent to prison, that I'm gonna sign you an affidavit saying I was ineffective so, please, judge, give that bastard another chance. Well, forget it. Comes right down to it, that's all I got left of what used to be my life. Reputation."

Vicky closed the folder and picked up her bag. "I've taken enough of your time."

Gruenwald was on his feet before she could stand up. "I'll see you out," he said, starting back through the house.

Vicky drove back down the dirt road, fingers lightly touching the steering wheel that burned like a hot iron. She turned onto the highway behind a semi. The noise of tires humming against the hot asphalt and the faint odor of diesel fumes wafted through the air conditioning. What had she been hoping for? That Harry Gruenwald would feel remorse for having let down a client who had spent the last seven years in prison? Sign an affidavit to the effect that he'd been drunk during the trial, all that was necessary for the district judge to grant a new trial that would give Travis the chance to clear his name?

But that wasn't the way it was going to be. Gruenwald felt about as much remorse as a clump of sagebrush. He was congratulating himself on getting Travis convicted for manslaughter, instead of getting him acquitted for a murder he didn't commit. An old man with an old and sick wife, living in a shack, clinging to the only thing he had left, the memory of better times when he had been a reputable attorney.

And she was going to have to take that away from him.

She would set out the facts in the petition for post-conviction relief. Gruenwald hadn't brought out all the pertinent facts in the case. He hadn't had Travis testify that he'd heard the gunshot and gone to the barn, just as Lyle did moments later. Travis hadn't testified that he'd seen the foreman's truck near the house and that, earlier, he'd seen Ollie Goodman on the ranch. There were no ballistics tests done on Travis.

But there was something else nipping at her like a dog at her heels. What was it the lawyer had said? Travis had offered to pay him for the appeal *after* he'd been acquitted. Contingency fee, Gruenwald had called it. After the lawyer had won the case.

Which meant that, not only had Travis failed to mention Marjorie Taylor's visit, but he hadn't mentioned that he intended to pay for the appeal later.

Vicky pounded the wheel again and stared

at the gray exhaust curling down the asphalt from the semi. How would Travis have paid Gruenwald, unless he had already collected a sum of money? Unless the prosecutor was right, and Travis and Raymond had both been involved in stealing the petroglyph?

And yet, if Travis had already collected the money, why had he let his grandfather pay Gruenwald's initial fees? He could have paid his own fees. It was only after Amos Walking Bear had run out of money that Travis had promised to pay Gruenwald for the appeal. And what did that mean? That Travis hadn't yet collected whatever payment he was expecting? That he had to get out of prison to collect?

Vicky made herself breathe slowly. One, two, three breaths. She had to stay focused. The smell of exhaust was working its way into the Firebird, and Vicky realized she was closing on the semi. She let up on the accelerator and started dropping back until the space of a couple of vehicles opened ahead.

It came down to Gruenwald. He should have made it clear that Travis and Lyle had heard the gunshot at the same time, but Travis had gotten to the barn first. He should have made it clear that there were other people at the ranch. Marjorie Taylor.

Andy Lyle. Maybe Ollie Goodman. They should have been asked about where they were when Raymond was shot. There was reasonable doubt leaking from the case, but Gruenwald had failed to convey that to the jury.

She was gripping the wheel hard now, the rim still warm against her palms. She would ask for a new trial on the basis of ineffective assistance of counsel. She would point out that Deaver had unfairly prejudiced the jury by suggesting there was evidence outside of the trial that proved Travis had a motive to kill Raymond. Gruenwald could have asked for a mistrial, but he hadn't. He hadn't been sober enough. It shouldn't be hard to convince the judge that Travis had been denied a fair trial.

She was barely aware of a dark object falling like a shadow over the rearview mirror. She glanced up. A brown truck was coming up fast. She felt her heart leap in her chest, and she pressed down on the accelerator and moved closer to the semi. The truck was right behind her now, riding on the rear bumper. They were like a parade of three floats speeding down the highway. The idea made her want to laugh. She swallowed hard and concentrated on driving. If she started laughing, she wouldn't be able to stop.

As far as she could see, the highway ahead looked clear. She started to pull out around the semi. The truck also pulled out and started accelerating. She jerked the steering wheel back as the truck sped past.

Her heart was still thumping, and she made herself take another couple of deep breaths. She was getting paranoid, she told herself. There were a thousand brown trucks in the area; everybody wore cowboy hats. Not every brown truck intended to run her off the road.

She followed the semi around the bend and into town, trying to focus on something else that Gruenwald had said: Marjorie Taylor had visited Travis in jail.

Vicky drove down Main Street past the office and kept going. Then she was heading north across the reservation on Highway 287 toward the Taylor Ranch.

25

Vicky turned off the highway onto the paved dirt road that ran between the log fences with the pasture rolling into the distance. She stopped in front of the two-story log house dozing among the cottonwoods, bluffs the color of dried blood looming in the background. The silence about the Taylor Ranch was so pervasive that she had the odd sense she had stepped into a painting. There were no vehicles about, no trucks or tractors. Nothing but the slow rustle of the cottonwoods in the breeze. She crossed the porch and knocked on the door.

She waited a moment before starting down the dirt path to Marjorie Taylor's office. The sound of her footsteps scuffing the hard-packed ground were magnified in the silence. She knocked again. Then, shielding her eyes from the sun, she peered through one of the narrow windows that flanked the door. In the dimness inside, she could make out the outlines of Marjorie's desk and chair, the glint of a metal lamp.

The neighing of a horse broke through the quiet. Vicky walked back to the Firebird and drove down the road to the barn. She could see a tan cowboy hat bobbing among the horses in the corral. She got out and followed the fence around to where Marjorie Taylor was brushing a brown mare.

"What can I do for you?" The woman didn't look up, just kept running the brush over the mare's flank. Vicky had the feeling that Marjorie Taylor had been watching the Firebird from the moment she had turned onto the ranch.

"I'd like to talk to you," Vicky said. The mare stepped closer to the fence and began tossing its head.

"Wouldn't get too close to Queenie, if I was you." The woman was pulling the brush along the horse's back now in what looked like a finishing gesture. "Doesn't take to strangers." She set the brush on top of a fence post, then stepped over to the corral gate and let herself through. There was a sprinkling of golden dust over her blue jeans and dark blouse. A layer of dust worked its way up the sides of her boots. She pulled the gate shut, looped a chain over the post, and, retrieving the brush, headed across the path to the barn.

Vicky followed her inside where the woman put the brush on a shelf and busied herself for a moment straightening an array of ropes and tackle. "Want a Coke? Water?" she asked, pushing the tan cowboy hat back on her head. A strand of blond hair fell forward, and she tucked it under the hat. "You look like you could use a drink. You been sick or something?" She walked over to a half-size refrigerator next to the closed door in the far wall.

"Water sounds good," Vicky said. The barn still had the cool, damp feel of a tomb. "I was in an accident," she went on. "My Jeep was forced off the road."

"Crazy people out there." Marjorie extracted two bottles with blue labels from the refrigerator and walked back. "We can talk outside," she said, tossing one of the bottles to Vicky. The plastic was cold and moist, as if it were sweating ice.

Vicky walked out and sat down on the wood bench along the wall. The roof overhang created a narrow island of shade. Even the breeze sweeping between the barn and the corral felt cooler. She sipped at the cold water, which only accentuated the hunger that had begun to gnaw at her. She hadn't had anything to eat except for a piece of a bagel and half a cup of coffee. She could still taste the bitterness of the argument with Adam.

Beyond the corral was a barely visible trail that cut through the pasture, then turned toward the bluffs and wound around the rocky base before disappearing. Most likely, the trail led upward to a high meadow — the high pasture, Travis had called it. Riding down the trail, he would have had a clear view of the front of the house and barn.

It was a long moment before Marjorie emerged from the barn and sat down on the end of the bench. She tilted her water bottle back and took a sip, keeping her gaze on the horses standing like sentinels in the corral. Finally she turned to Vicky. "So what is it this time?"

"I'm still trying to make sense out of what happened here the day of the murder. Travis told me that he heard the gunshot when he was coming back from the high pasture. Lyle said he had also heard the gunshot. That means Raymond was killed before either one had gotten there."

"You believe a cold-blooded murderer? Travis Birdsong is lyin' through his teeth."

"Is Lyle around?"

The woman lifted the water bottle to her mouth and took a drink; then she said,

"Lyle's in Riverton taking care of some business. He'd tell you the same as before. Travis was in the barn with Raymond. They had another argument. They were always arguing, them two. I was gettin' ready to fire 'em, interviewing other cowboys when Raymond got killed. Another day, and they would have both been outta here. Too bad, 'cause I didn't need all the trouble. Still don't need trouble, Ms. Holden. Why do you want to drag all that up again? Drag the Taylor Ranch through the manure? Bad enough seven years ago, deputies crawlin' all over the place. Now you keep comin' around, askin' questions. You get that Indian's case reopened, and there's gonna be more investigators and reporters pokin' their noses into my business. Why are you doin' this?"

"I told you . . ."

"Oh, yeah." The woman waved her water bottle between them. "Travis Birdsong didn't get a fair trial. Well, you know what? That's the way the deck cuts. You think life oughtta be fair?" She tossed her head back and gave a bark of laughter. "My grandfather came out here and started this ranch with nothing but his bare hands. Hitched up a wagon, went up Red Cliff Canyon, and spent the summer choppin' down trees.

Built the house with his bare hands, log by log. Did the same for the barn and the rest of the buildings. Fenced in the pasture and got a loan from the bank in Riverton so he could start a herd. Took my dad his whole damn life to pay off that loan. Last seventeen years, I been runnin' the place, and Lyle's been helpin' me keep it together, hirin' on hands when we had enough money, stayin' two feet ahead of the tax collectors who'd like nothing better than to throw us off of here. Last year, I had to scrape together everything I could get my hands on, go to Lander, and stand on the courthouse steps — the courthouse steps, you hear me? — and buy back my own goddamn ranch from the tax collectors. You think they wouldn't have been happy to sell it out from under me to some rich Easterner that wants to brag about his private spread out in Wyoming? You think that's fair, Ms. Holden?"

Vicky started to say that she was sorry, but Marjorie Taylor waved a hand and looked back at the corral. Vicky waited a moment before she said, "What time did Ollie Goodman leave the ranch the day Raymond was shot?"

"What did Ollie tell you?"

Vicky took another sip of water, giving

herself a moment. Obviously Ollie Goodman and Marjorie Taylor had talked. "He told me he'd left in the morning. I wonder if that's what you remembered."

"What I want to do is forget," the woman said. Then she added, "Ollie left when he said he left."

"There's something else." Vicky pushed on. "I've been wondering why you visited Travis when he was awaiting trial."

Marjorie Taylor shifted sideways on the bench and took another long drink, her eyes watching Vicky over the water bottle. Then she recapped the bottle and balanced it on top of one thigh. "He worked for me," she said.

"But you believe he killed another man who worked for you."

"Call it an act of mercy. You heard of that, haven't you? Visiting somebody in jail, one of the corporal acts of mercy the preacher used to talk about back in the days when Dad dragged us to church. Ask your priest friend."

Vicky stared at the other woman a moment. "How do you know who my friends are?" she said, making an effort to keep her voice steady.

"You come around here askin' questions. I figure I can ask my own questions. You and that priest over at the mission, you get yourselves involved in things that are none of your business, you ask me."

"We don't like seeing the wrong people convicted."

Marjorie Taylor got to her feet and started to walk away. Then she turned back. "The jury said Travis Birdsong was guilty. The judge sentenced him to fifteen years. You ask me, that bastard got off easy. He oughtta be looking at bars the rest of his useless life, but he's gonna be out in three years if he's paroled. You oughtta just leave it alone, Ms. Holden. From what I hear, your own tribe wants you to back off. And I hear Raymond's family sure as hell doesn't want Travis walkin' out of prison anytime soon. Hugh Trublood came around here couple days ago, wantin' to know what you were up to. I'd watch my step, if I was you."

"I intend to," Vicky said. "Thanks for your time."

"I don't see any reason for you to be comin' around again."

"Neither do I. I think I have what I need."

"Yeah, whatever." The woman shrugged and started walking up the road.

She was still heading toward the house,

looking straight ahead, when Vicky drove past.

Vicky turned south onto the highway, passing the turnoff into Red Cliff Canyon. The road winding upward looked like a trail. She shuddered at the idea of trucks lumbering through the boulders and pines, engines roaring and tires pounding. First thing Monday, she'd call Bud Ladd at the BLM. If he didn't agree to an alternate road, then she intended to continue following through on her threat. She'd ask the federal court to grant an injunction and to require the BLM to extend the public comment period. Then she'd call Aileen Harrison at the *Gazette* and inform her of the developments. And there were other reporters, other newspapers. There was television. People in these parts had a right to know.

Except that the tribes hadn't wanted the publicity. Adam hadn't wanted it, and he was the one they'd trust to handle the matter. The truth was, the matter would stay with Adam if she left the firm.

If she left the firm. The idea had been flitting like an unreal thing at the edge of her mind. This morning, after Adam had left, the idea had taken on substance. A true thing, she realized, truer than whatever had been between her and Adam — the firm, the relationship. She watched the gray asphalt unrolling into the haze of heat ahead and forced herself to look at this idea, turn it over in her head, examine it, as if it were a physical object that she'd just found and she had to find a place for it.

She tightened her grip on the steering wheel. There was no place in her life for it. She would not break up the firm. She would stay and do everything possible to protect Red Cliff Canyon. She owed it to her people. And no matter what Adam thought, she would not abandon Travis Birdsong. Tomorrow she would drive to Rawlins and have another talk with him, and this time, she would insist that he level with her about the stolen petroglyph.

The sun was streaming through the passenger window; the Firebird was an oven. Vicky started to turn up the air conditioning, and that was when she saw the brown truck in the rearview mirror. She felt her muscles start to spasm, her heart start galloping. Two men in black cowboy hats, the brims shadowing their faces. Then the passenger hunched forward; he might have been fiddling with something on the floor.

Vicky could see the indentation in the top of his hat.

The truck was speeding up, closing in, the left signal light flicking. It was getting ready to pass her. She gulped in some air, aware that she had been holding her breath. There were hundreds of brown trucks. My God, would she never get over the feeling that every brown truck intended to run her off the road?

She kept her own speed steady, waiting for the truck to pass. The gray smudge of an oncoming vehicle began to materialize out of the haze ahead, and as the truck drew alongside, Vicky let up on the accelerator, giving it more room to pull ahead. Except that it wasn't pulling ahead. They were like two racehorses, neck to neck, plunging down an asphalt track with a dark sedan looming in front.

Vicky took her foot off the accelerator and glanced over at the truck. The window was rolling down, and for the first time, she saw that, beneath the brim of the cowboy hat, was the type of knitted mask that hunters wore in the winter. Two egg-shaped cutouts exposed intense dark eyes fired with hatred and amusement. The long, silver barrel of a shotgun protruded across the lowered window. Vicky stomped on the accelerator and shot forward as the blast rocked the car. There was a shattering noise. Pebbles of glass showered over her, drove into her hair and stung her face and arms, wedged themselves between her blouse and skin. She was aware of silvery pebbles littering the top of the dashboard, sprinkling the passenger seat, piling onto her lap, and jabbing at her thighs.

The brown truck blurred past as the Firebird rocked sideways toward the ditch. She turned the steering wheel hard, but now she was swerving out into the other lane, the blue sedan rising in front of her. She pulled back on the wheel and veered out of the way as the sedan rocketed past. She tapped on the brake pedal, yawing and pitching across the lanes until she managed to roll to a stop next to the ditch in the oncoming lane. In the rearview mirror, she could see the crystals of glass clinging to the sills of both doors. The sound of her heart drummed in her ears, and she tried to fight back the waves of nausea coming over her. The gunshot had passed through the car — would've passed through her, she knew, except for that fraction of an instant that had saved her life.

She held on to the wheel, struggling to still the shaking that convulsed her. Her mouth had gone dry, but hot moisture had started running down her cheeks. Odd. She must have been shot after all. She should feel pain, but there was nothing but the numbness and the shaking. She lifted her hand, wiped at the moisture, and stared at her palm, unable to comprehend why her blood was as colorless as water. It was then that she ran her tongue over her lips and tasted the salt and realized that she was crying.

The sound of gravel sputtering under tires made her glance at the rearview mirror again. Somehow, the blue sedan was now heading in her direction, crossing the lane, and slowing behind her. The motor turned off, and a light-haired man — God, he was just a teenager — slammed out of the driver's side and ran up alongside her. "You okay? You okay?" he shouted.

Vicky tried to locate the button to roll down her window, but her hand was shaking. She gave it up. She could hear him through the blasted rear windows. Her door sprang open, and the young man's face came so close that she found herself concentrating on the marks of acne that dotted his cheeks, and oddly she began to feel steadier. "You hurt?" he said.

"I don't think so."

"I already called 911."

Vicky shifted her focus to the phone waving in his hand.

"I seen the whole thing," he said. "I seen the gun, I seen everything. You better stay in the car. Anybody you want me to call?"

Vicky felt the pressure of his hand on her shoulder and realized that she'd started to get out, but he was right. She shouldn't try to stand up.

She turned toward the windshield and studied the empty highway, the haze of heat blurring the asphalt in the distance. "Someone is trying to kill me," she said. Then she asked him to call the pastor at St. Francis Mission.

26

"You sure it's a photograph of the Drowning Man?" Norman Yellow Hawk balanced his elbows on his thighs, clasped his hands between his knees, and leaned forward. He kept his face unreadable, the set of his jaws, the sculptured look of his cheeks and forehead unchanged, despite the mixture of dread and hope alternating in his dark eyes.

"It's the petroglyph," Father John said. Warm air gusted through the open window of his study and rippled the papers on his desk. Outside, a motor coughed into life, followed by the sound of tires mashing the gravel. The only penitent who had come to confessions this afternoon. He and Father Ian alternated Saturday confessions, and this had been Ian's week. It had surprised Father John that even one vehicle had been parked in front of the church when he'd walked over to the office, hoping to make a dent in the messages and bills piled on his desk. It was as if St. Francis had become part of the cemetery out on Seventeen-Mile Road that pickups and cars rumbled past.

"Got a minute?" Norman had leaned around the doorjamb about thirty minutes ago.

Father John had waved the councilman toward the chair angled next to his desk. Then he'd gotten to his feet, gone over to the small table behind the door, and poured some coffee into Styrofoam cups stacked by the coffeepot. He'd handed a cup to the councilman before settling back behind the desk.

"Thanks for coming by," he'd told the councilman. "People have been avoiding the mission. I guess you know. Father Elsner will be leaving soon."

Norman had nodded. "That's not why I'm here," he'd said. Then he'd asked if there was any news about the petroglyph, and Father John had told him about the envelope tossed from the gray sedan out on the highway, and the photo of the petroglyph.

"Lot of glyphs look alike," Norman said now. There was a distant look in his eyes, as if he were carrying on an argument with himself. "That Indian could've gone up to Red Cliff Canyon and gotten a photograph of some other glyph."

"I saw the photograph," Father John said, trying to reassure the man. "Gianelli thinks that the petroglyph is still in the area. In a warehouse or barn someplace. The thief wants to make a deal."

"He called you back to make arrangements for the exchange?"

Father John shook his head. "He'll call, Norman."

The councilman held onto the coffee cup balanced on the armrest and sat very still, as if the heavy possibility of losing the petroglyph pressed him against the chair.

"It's been almost two days."

"He wants the money."

"It's ready. Arapaho and Shoshone business councils agreed we gotta get the glyph back. Took most of the week, but we pulled some cash out of the operating funds and borrowed the rest against the oil and gas royalties. We've got the cash. The minute you hear from the guy, I'll see you get it. You make the exchange."

"Listen, Norman," Father John began. Gianelli must not have told the councilman about the new plan. "The fed wants to send in an undercover police officer . . ."

"I know what he wants." Norman threw back his head. His eyes traced the ceiling a long moment. "You gotta make the exchange, John. That's what the guy's expecting. He's nervous as a bobcat. You start talking about how the Sho-Raps want to send in some Indian and you know what's gonna happen?"

Father John didn't reply. He knew exactly what would happen.

The councilman pushed on: "You're gonna be talking to yourself, because the guy's gonna hang up. Then you know what's gonna happen? He's gonna pack up the glyph and take off. How long you think it's gonna be before he sells that glyph? One day? One week?"

"Listen, Norman," Father John began again. "Gianelli's handling the investigation. He wants the petroglyph back, and he doesn't want the tribes to lose a quarter of a million dollars. He knows what he's doing."

Norman stood up, walked over to the table, and set down his cup. He turned back. "That's where you're wrong, John. The fed wasn't here seven years ago; he doesn't know what happened."

"He has the records."

"He doesn't have the instincts. Otherwise, he wouldn't be putting together this crazy plan that's gonna lose us another sacred glyph. We've lost too much already. Sites have been looted. No telling how many artifacts have been stolen. We're gonna find more disturbed sites, you can bet on it. Nobody but us gives a damn: not the fed, not the folks over at the BLM. Let the logging companies build a big road and run their trucks up and down Red Cliff Canyon. What difference does it make? Bring in more thieves, more diggers, run the spirits out of the place. How'd they like it if we was to build a highway through one of their cathedrals, start looting some of the art and other precious objects? We gotta protect what's holy, John, before there's nothing holy left on the earth. We want the Drowning Man returned. The people need that glyph."

The telephone rang. Father John reached across the desk, conscious of the stillness and sense of expectation that invaded the office and the way the Arapaho's eyes followed the receiver as Father John lifted it to his ear.

"Father O'Malley," he said.

"You the mission priest?" A man's voice, but not one that Father John recognized.

"That's right. How may I help you?"

"Oh, good. I wasn't sure I got the number right. You don't know me . . ." There was a shakiness in the voice, and it occurred to

Father John that the caller was young, a teenager who had found himself in an adult world. "A friend of yours gave me your number. Vicky Holden. She asked me to call you. She had some trouble . . ."

"Where is she?" Father John was on his feet.

"On her way home now. Said to tell you she'll be there in thirty minutes."

Father John thanked the caller and hung up. "Vicky's in some kind of trouble," he said to the Arapaho.

"Trouble? What kinda trouble?"

"I don't know." Father John walked around the desk.

"I told her not to get mixed up with that bum Travis Birdsong. What about the petroglyph?"

"We all want to get it back, Norman." Father John grabbed his cowboy hat from the coat tree. She would have called him herself, if she could have, he was thinking, half aware of the councilman behind him as he started down the corridor.

"You gonna call me soon as you hear from the guy?"

She was on the way home. That was a good sign. But she'd wanted him to know there was some kind of trouble; she'd asked someone to call for her. She expected him to meet her.

"We'll have to talk about this later." Father John held the front door for the other man. Then he passed the councilman on the steps and broke into a run across the grounds.

He was about to get into the pickup in front of the residence when, out of the corner of his eye, he saw Father Lloyd coming across the drive from the direction of the museum. There hadn't been anybody else around: Norman's truck in front of the administration building, Ian's sedan at the residence. No other sign of life. Then the elderly priest had appeared, like a shadow falling across the grounds without warning.

Father John called over the top of the pickup's door as he got behind the steering wheel: "Let Father Ian know that I had to go out, will you?"

The old priest lifted one hand into the air in acknowledgment, a gesture that Father John caught in the rear-view mirror as he backed the pickup onto Circle Drive.

Vicky drove into the lot behind the apartment building and parked in the space behind the sign that said, "Unit 205." She'd spent at least an hour parked alongside the ditch out on the highway, answering questions the state patrol officer had thrown at her. *You know the two men? Ever seen them before?*

No, she didn't know who they were. Yes, they had run her off the road yesterday.

Finally she'd convinced the officer that she was okay. She could drive home. She had to get away from that place.

She'd driven on automatic: across the reservation and into Lander, gripping the steering wheel, not wanting to check the rearview mirror, yet checking it all the time, expecting the brown truck to rise out of the asphalt. Carved in her mind was the image of the shotgun lifting over the windowsill, the barrel leveled at her, and the light flickering in the eyes behind the mask. The cowboy had wanted to kill her; he would have enjoyed killing her.

She let the engine run and closed her eyes against the nausea blowing over her like the hot wind gusting past the broken windows in the back. She sat very still. *Be still —* Grandmother's voice in her head — *like the quiet of the plains, the images of the spirits carved in the rocks. In the stillness, you can find your way.*

"Vicky?" The familiar voice cut through the fog swirling about her. Her eyes snapped open, and she peered through her window into the eyes of John O'Malley. He was leaning down, one forearm resting on the sill. She fumbled for the door handle, pushed it down, and watched the door swing open by itself, as if it had a will of its own, except that — and this was odd; it was as if everything had a counterexplanation — John O'Malley had yanked the door open.

She started to crawl out, aware of the pressure of his hand on her arm, steadying her. Then, he leaned into the car, turned off the ignition, and closed her fingers around the keys. "Are you all right?" he said.

She was hanging on to the car to keep the world from whirling away: the asphalt, the parked cars, the red bricks of the apartment building, the man beside her.

"Vicky!" John O'Malley said. Now the weight of his arm slipped around her shoulders.

"He tried to shoot me," she heard herself saying.

"What? Who, Vicky? The cowboys from yesterday?"

Vicky felt herself leaning into him, burying her face against his chest, unable to move. It was a moment before she realized that the front of his shirt was damp and that she was crying. She stepped back and ran the palm of her hand over her cheeks, mopping at the moisture, beginning to feel upright again, as if the world had regained its balance.

"Are you hurt?"

She shook her head. "I think I could use something to eat."

"Come on," he said, guiding her over to the Toyota pickup.

From the table in the corner of the restaurant, they could see the traffic crawling along Main Street. Vicky kept glancing out the window as she told John O'Malley about the brown truck, the two masked cowboys, the shotgun gleaming in the sun. Talking, talking, taking a bite of the turkey sandwich she'd ordered, sipping at the cup of tea, watching for the brown truck. She was beginning to feel like herself, as if she'd finally managed to take herself in hand, get a grip on herself — yes, that was it. She was getting her grip.

"Those men in the truck," she said. "They killed Raymond Trublood. They got away with murder. They don't want me to reopen Travis's case." She turned back to the window and went on: "There's more, John. I think Travis and Raymond took the petroglyph seven years ago."

That got his attention, she knew, even

though John O'Malley didn't say anything. He set his sandwich down and began sipping at his coffee, not taking his eyes from her. She told him how Travis had tried to talk his lawyer into filing an appeal on a contingency basis. How Travis had said that he'd pay him as soon as he was free.

"Where was Travis going to get any money?" Vicky continued. "His grandfather had already spent everything that he and the rest of the family could get their hands on for the trial. There wasn't anything left for an appeal."

"You think Travis was expecting payment from the sale of the petroglyph?"

Vicky nodded. "He didn't have the money yet, or he would have offered it up front to Gruenwald. He was *expecting* the money, but he had to be free to get it. I think he knows what became of the petroglyph, and the minute he was free, he intended to collect his share from whoever had sold it. It still doesn't make Travis a killer."

John sipped at his coffee a moment. Finally he set the mug down and leaned toward her. "It makes sense," he said. "Artifact thieves don't work alone. They work in tightly knit gangs. The man who contacted me . . ."

"The Indian."

"His name is Benito Behan. Navajo. Gianelli says he's been the intermediary between a gang of artifact thieves who work around the West and the locals — the Indians who know where the artifacts in their area can be found. Travis and Raymond could have been the locals. They knew Red Cliff Canyon. They knew which petroglyphs were the oldest and most valuable. They could have cut out the petroglyph and delivered it to Behan. The Indian had already contacted the tribes. They were ready to pay the ransom, then something went wrong . . ."

Vicky cut in. "He's probably come back. He found other locals willing to do the dirty work. They stole the Drowning Man, and they expect to collect from the tribes. What's his name, Benito Behan? I think that Benito Behan doesn't want me to reopen Travis's case. He's afraid of what a new investigation might turn up. It could link him to both stolen glyphs. It could even link him to Raymond's murder."

She stopped. At the periphery of her vision, she saw a brown truck move slowly past the window.

"What is it?" Father John said.

Vicky tried for a shrug. "I have to keep

reminding myself there are dozens of brown trucks around here." A couple had taken the next table, and she leaned forward, keeping her voice low. "I thought that maybe Marjorie Taylor was involved in the thefts," she said. "The woman could use the money. She's struggling to hold on to the family ranch, and she visited Travis in jail several times before the trial."

"What made you change your mind about her?"

"There were two men in the truck, John. I'm certain of it. I had just left Marjorie at the ranch today when the brown truck appeared on my tail. It was as if it had been waiting for me to turn onto the highway."

"Anybody else on the ranch who might have been waiting for you to leave?"

Vicky shook her head. "I didn't see the foreman anyplace. His name is Andy Lyle. Marjorie said he was in Riverton on ranch business."

"She could say anything. It doesn't rule him out," Father John said after a moment. "It just means there was another cowboy with him."

"Travis knows who they are." Vicky tightened both hands around the warm cup of tea. She was certain of it. Travis Birdsong hadn't leveled with her; he'd told a story that he'd hoped she would believe. And she had almost believed. "He knows who's behind the thefts. I'm going to see him again tomorrow. If he wants me to help him, he has to tell me the truth."

"That's not a good idea."

Vicky had to glance away from the worry in his eyes.

"The cowboys know the Firebird. They could follow you again."

"I'll be watching my back." Watching the brown truck closing in behind her. The image made her shudder, and she took another drink of tea.

"Let me have your cell."

Vicky stared at the redheaded man across from her a moment, then found the cell in her bag and handed it across the table. She watched him press the keys and ask for the number of Phil Mahoney's Auto Sales on the east end of Main. He tapped his fingers on the table and gave her a smile.

"This is Father O'Malley," he said. "Let me speak to Phil." A second passed, and he was exchanging the polite pleasantries. Yeah, the Red Sox were looking better than usual. Then he explained that a friend of his needed a car for a while. He waited a moment — tapping, smiling at her. "Thanks, Phil," he said. He pressed a key and handed her back the phone.

"What do you think about a blue Impala? It'll be waiting in front of the dealership with the key in the ignition. It's a loaner, and Phil says it's yours as long as you need it. I suggest you park it away from the apartment."

Vicky leaned against the back of the booth, tilted her head, and stared at the square patches of ceiling tile. She didn't want to start weeping. What was wrong with her? She had been alone for so long. Even with Adam, she had been alone, and the fact was, she had become accustomed to being alone. It was familiar and comfortable, a comfortable bubble of aloneness in which she walked around, and this sense that she was not alone, what good would it do to give in to that?

She said, "I think I'll like an Impala just fine."

"Let's go get it." Father John stood up and tossed a few dollar bills on top of the check that the waitress had delivered.

Vicky pushed the bills toward him, fumbled for the wallet in her bag. "I thought your donors always tell you to help the Indians." She set her money on the check and got to her feet.

"That's what I thought I was doing." He

gave her another smile as she started for the door, aware of the comforting sound of his footsteps behind her.

27

Evening was pressing down, and the sky had begun to turn to slate as Father John drove north on Rendezvous Road. He had followed the blue Impala through Lander. Vicky had left the car a block from her apartment, and he'd taken her home. He shouldn't worry, she'd told him as she'd gotten out of the pickup. She was used to taking care of herself, and the door had closed on that.

He'd watched her disappear into the building before he'd driven off, hunched over the wheel, trying to fight off the sense of helplessness. The cowboys in the brown truck had tried to kill her twice. What would prevent them from trying again?

He turned past the sign and drove through the corridor of cottonwoods. Beyond, the mission buildings seemed far away in the shadows. "This place will break your heart," Father Peter had told him when he'd first come to St. Francis. The old priest had been behind the desk in the study, the ceiling light shining through the fluff of white hair. "Break your heart, over and over again, the way you'll come to love the people. You won't be able to help yourself."

"Perhaps," he remembered replying, but he had never imagined the helpless love he would feel for a woman he'd yet to meet.

"It's not a bad thing, a broken heart," the old priest had said. "It makes us human."

The only sound was that of his own tires raking the gravel. Ian's blue sedan stood in front of the residence, like a beached boat at the edge of an empty sea. The carry-in supper for the volunteers who sang and drummed at Sunday Mass was on tonight's schedule, but there weren't any pickups about. He parked next to the sedan and got out, half expecting Father Lloyd to material-ize out of the dusk. But the old man wasn't there.

The minute that Father John let himself into the residence, Walks-On came skitter-ing down the hallway. He scratched the dog's head a moment, then followed him into the kitchen where Father Ian was work-ing on a plate of lasagna, a book propped open against the sugar bowl.

"Sorry, I started without you," he said,

glancing up. "Elena left another helping in the oven, if you want some."

"I've already eaten," Father John said. He walked over to the counter, the dog staying close, nudging him forward. He shook some dry food into the dog's dish and set it on the floor, then lifted a mug out of the drying rack in the sink and poured some coffee.

"Lloyd took a plate over to the guesthouse," the other priest said behind him. "Didn't want to stay around. Can't blame him, I guess. Everything okay?"

Father John sat down across from the other priest. Everything was not okay, he was thinking. "What happened to the carry-in supper?"

Father Ian shook his head. "Martin Black Bull called and said they wouldn't be having the supper here after all. He didn't actually say, you understand, but I got the idea they'd decided to hold the supper somewhere else. Oh, almost forgot . . ." Ian set his fork down, stood up, and went into the hallway. He came back carrying a small notepad, which he slid across the table. "Message for you," he said.

Father John glanced at the pad. Scrawled across the top sheet was an address on the east side of Riverton. "What's this?"

"A man called about an hour ago. Wanted to speak to you."

Father John sipped at the coffee. He didn't take his eyes off the unfamiliar address. Next to the address was the number 6.

"Said there was a message for you at that address. I thought it very strange, John. What does he expect? That you're going to drive across Riverton to get a message?"

It was exactly what he expects, Father John thought. He stood up, folded the message, and stuffed it into the pocket of his shirt. And then he *knew*. The address was the motel where the Indian was staying. The man expected him to go to the motel and get the message from the Indian.

"I'll be out for a little while," he said, heading back down the hallway.

"What? Whoa, hold on a minute." Ian's boots thudded after him. "What's this all about?"

"It's about the stolen petroglyph." Father John turned back to the other priest. "I'm going to a motel to pick up a message from the man who has the petroglyph."

"You think you should do that? You think you'll be safe?"

"There's a cop watching the motel, Ian. I'll be safe."

Before Father John banged out the door, he saw in the other priest's eyes that he hadn't convinced him any more than he'd convinced himself.

The Butte Motel sprawled like a derailed freight train at the back of a potholed parking lot. Father John turned into the lot and crawled in and out of the splotches of light from the fixtures mounted on metal poles, past the few vehicles scattered about — a pickup with a dent the size of a barrel in the door, a truck that sloped to the side, a battered-looking green sedan. Several cars parked at the edge of the road looked abandoned. He wondered which old truck or car the undercover cop was sitting in. None of the vehicles looked occupied.

Father John pulled into the vacant slot in front of the unit with a black 6 hanging sideways on the door and curtains drawn across the window. He crossed the cracked sidewalk that pitched upward and knocked on the door. From inside came the drone of TV noise. He knocked again and glanced around. Nothing moved in the shadows. A band of cream-colored light clung to the edge of the dark sky.

"It's Father O'Malley," he said, leaning closer. It occurred to him that Ian might have written down the wrong number. He was about to walk toward the end unit where an overhead sign alternately blinked *OFFICE* and *VACANCY* in orange neon lights when a loud guffaw erupted from the other side of the door. He waited a moment. Another guffaw, and he realized that it came from the TV.

An odd sense came over him then. It was as if the TV noise were crackling into the dusk and shadows that the motel had gathered into itself. He knocked again, then tried the knob. It turned in his hand, and he inched the door inward. "Hello?" he called. "Anybody here?"

"Now what'd ya say? You comin' with me or not?" the TV voice demanded.

"You crazy, man? We stick our heads out there, he's gonna blow 'em off."

Father John shoved the door open and stopped. Light from the television on top of a dresser flickered through the shadows, across the walls and the carpet, and over the body of the Indian toppled onto the bed like that of an animal that had stumbled into death. The blanket falling off the bed beside him was soaked in blood.

"So we sit tight and wait until he comes for us. That your plan?"

Father John patted the wall for the light fixture. His fingers finally found the switch, which he pushed upward. Light exploded into the room. He looked around, waiting for someone to rush past the opened door to the bathroom, except that light was flooding into the small bathroom, and he could see that no one was there.

He moved closer to the bed. The Indian lay on his side, black hair splayed like a feathered headdress, one arm thrown behind him, the other hanging off the side, as if he'd been asleep when he'd died. He had on blue jeans and a white shirt, matted with blood across his chest and sleeve.

"I don't know about you, but I like livin', man. You ask me, we sit tight."

God. God. God. How many times had the man been stabbed? And with what? A knife? "Have mercy on his soul," Father John said out loud, the sound of his voice a counterpoint to the TV voices.

"Yeah, well, I'm not hangin' around here waitin' to die."

Father John backed out of the room and closed the door behind him. Then he broke into a run down the sidewalk toward the flashing neon sign. He yanked open the glass door and threw himself toward the counter on the other side of the room.

Behind the counter, a squat, bald man in a tee shirt with arms the size of clubs crossed over his chest stared up at the TV under the ceiling in the corner. The same crime show was blaring.

"Hey, you ready? I'm ready."

"Get the police." Father John shouted over the TV voices.

"What?" The bald head swung around, and red-rimmed eyes blinked over the countertop. "Who the hell are you?"

"A man's been killed in number 6." He was still shouting. "Get the police."

But the police were already here. Through the rectangular window alongside the counter, he saw a man in blue jeans and light-colored shirt running across the patch of dirt that divided the parking lot from the next lot. He hopped across a short fence and kept coming.

"What the hell you talkin' about?" The bald man pushed himself upright, one hand groping toward the telephone on the ledge beneath the counter.

The door crashed open behind them. "Police!"

Father John swung around and faced the man in the light shirt. He was in his thirties with hard, intense eyes that took in the entire room. And the officer knew who he was, because he said, "What's going on, Father?"

"The Indian in number 6 has been murdered," Father John said.

At that, everything went into fast-forward: the officer whirling about, darting through the door, rushing past the window, shouting into a radio. The motel clerk, banging on the counter, shouting, "Murdered! This is a reputable place. Jesus, the boss hears about a murder, I'm gonna get fired. Gonna be my ass. Why'd you have to get the police? We could've taken care of things."

"Hold on." Father John tried to get the man's attention, but the clerk was hopping about, throwing up both arms, eyes darting around the room. "Listen," he tried again, leaning over the counter. "The police are going to ask you some questions. Try to think. Did you see anyone go to the Indian's room?"

The man stopped hopping; his eyes seemed to come into focus. "What am I? His keeper? I don't know what he's up to. Last night, I heard his car leave. He kept it parked out back, crazy Indian. He come back real fast, probably went and got himself some food. Booze, probably. I figured he was holed up in the room on a drunk. Not my business. Paid up through Tuesday, that's all I care."

Sirens had started up, a cacophony of noise in the distance, gradually moving closer. Sometime during the day, Father John was thinking, someone had gotten into the room and killed the Indian. Yet the police officer had been parked in the next lot with a view of the motel. He must have seen someone entering the room.

Father John started for the door. Noise of the sirens cascaded into the parking lot, and red, blue, and yellow lights flashed across the window. He turned back. The clerk was bent over the counter, a fist thumping the surface. "You going to be all right?" Father John said.

"Imelda."

"What?"

"Cleans up the rooms. I was thinkin' about her cart."

"What about it?" Father John moved back into the room.

"Said she was cleanin' number ten down at the end this morning. She comes out, and somebody's rolled her cart halfway down the motel. Had to go get it and push it back. Some kids playin' a joke, she said."

"Where does she keep her keys?"

"Shit!" The clerk brought his fist down hard on the countertop. "I tol' her a hundred times, don't hang the keys on the cart. Got in the way of her cleanin', she said. Some fool can walk off with 'em, I tol' her, but she kept doin' it anyway. So some fool got her keys, got into the Indian's room. I'm gonna fire her ass."

Got into the room by impersonating the cleaning woman, Father John thought. That took some thought, some planning. And that meant the killer knew the police were watching the room. He let himself out through the door and started toward the police cars piling up in front of number 6. An ambulance had pulled in behind the cars, and dark figures were darting past the swirling lights, moving in and out of the room.

The bulky figure of Ted Gianelli broke away from a group huddled next to one of the cars and came down the sidewalk toward him. "How come you're the one that found him, John?" he called out. He was still several feet away. "You want to explain that?"

Father John stepped forward and told him about the phone call that had come in to the mission this afternoon when he was out.

"Why didn't you call me?"

"I came here to get the message, Ted."

"Yeah? We haven't found anything in the

room that looks like a message."

"The Indian was the message."

"You're talking in riddles, man. Make sense, will you?"

"The caller had instructed me not to bring in the police," Father John said.

Light flashed past the opened door of number 6. A man in a plaid shirt, probably with the coroner's office, slipped past, carrying a folded gray body bag. Father John felt as if something heavy were wedged against his heart. He'd been wrong. The caller had been watching from the old cabin when Behan tossed the envelope onto the highway. The caller had seen him talking to Gianelli at the side of the road. He'd understood the Indian would be under surveillance, so he'd found a way to get into the room and kill him to make certain he couldn't talk to the police.

"We're conducting an investigation here, John," Gianelli said. "We're doing our job. We can't foresee how some psychopath might react."

"Two men tried to shoot Vicky today," Father John said.

"I heard."

"They tried to run her off the road yesterday."

The fed didn't say anything to that, and

Father John waited a moment before he said, "We've lost the chance to get the petroglyph back. The caller will take off with it. The locals will melt back into their daily lives, just like seven years ago, and they'll wait for the next chance to make a big score, if they don't kill Vicky first."

Gianelli glanced back at the room, and in the play of light and shadow, Father John could see the man's jaw working, but it was a long moment before he said, "Maybe not. My guess is that, as long as he thinks the tribes are ready to pay up, the caller will try to set up the exchange. He's pretty confident that you'll follow instructions now." He nodded at the motel behind them. "You know what he can do. No way can you go in alone."

Father John watched the three men hoisting a gurney with the lumpy body bag on top. They headed across the sidewalk and between two police cars toward the coroner's van. The rear doors hung open against the dim light suffusing the interior. Finally, he said, "It's our only chance. You want the killers. The tribes want the petroglyph. Let me get the petroglyph before you come in."

Gianelli shook his head. "I don't want you or anybody else ending up dead. You're out of this. You take the call, and you call me.

Understood?"

Father John didn't say anything. He turned and headed out into the parking lot toward the pickup.

28

It was a tradition after Sunday Mass. Greet the pastor in front of the church, comment on the homily. Always polite comments, even from parishioners he'd seen dozing off in the middle. Usually the line stretched up the steps and back into the church vestibule, but not this morning. There had been only a dozen people scattered about the pews. Three or four white people from Riverton. A few Arapaho elders and grandmothers. No families, no children. The Mass was half finished when Norman Yellow Hawk had let himself in through the door and slipped into the last pew. Father John had understood. The councilman had come to make sure that Father Lloyd Elsner was still leaving.

Father John had said the last of the prayers, taking his time, searching for comfort in the familiar words that fell around him like fine rain: *What shall I give to the Lord for all the things that He has given to me? I will call upon the Lord. Praising, I will call upon the Lord, and I shall be saved from my enemies. The Lord be with you and with your spirit. Thanks be to God.*

"Got the news about the Indian on the telegraph," Norman said now, shaking his hand. There was a fierceness in the man's grip. The elders were forming a circle around them.

"Spirits are upset," one of the elders said. "We're not protecting them, way we oughtta. That's how come the evil . . ." the old man gestured with his head in the direction of the guest house. ". . . came right into the mission. Wouldn't've happened if the spirits had been watching."

Father John told the elders that Father Elsner would be leaving the next day. Across the sidewalk, the three grandmothers were huddled together, brown faces shadowed with concern. He knew they were listening to everything.

It was then that he noticed the stocky white man walking across Circle Drive, thick arms swinging at his side. He didn't look familiar. Not one of the people from Riverton he'd gotten accustomed to seeing at Sunday Mass.

"We'll never hear from him again," Norman said, and for a moment, Father John thought he was referring to Father Elsner. "Guy that's got the Drowning Man. He's gonna take off like last time. Didn't want to leave any loose ends, so he killed the Indian. Nobody around that might know what he did with the glyph."

"Gianelli doesn't think so," Father John said, but a part of him believed that Norman was right. The idea had circled through his head all night. The man with the glyph — the raspy voice on the phone — intended to take it to Denver or Santa Fe or Phoenix, or wherever he'd taken the last glyph, sell it on the black market, and take the profits himself. There would be no Indian to connect him to the locals. No Indian or locals to pay off.

"How come you found the Indian?" Norman asked. The others moved closer, brown, wrinkle-streaked faces turning a little so that Father John could speak into their ears. He glanced at the white man, standing in front of the church next to the cottonwood, and said that he'd gotten a message to go to the motel. The heads of the elders nodded in unison, as if that made sense.

"You heard anything today?"

"It's still early," Father John said, but the councilman was nodding. He'd already proved his point. The stocky white man kept his eyes on some point across the mission, as if he were watching something in his head.

"I'm gonna call Mooney, guy that runs the bank," Norman said. "Have him come to the tribal offices this afternoon. Hope I can get him at home." The elders were staring at the ground. The grandmothers pulled blank faces, mouths tightened into silent lines. "No sense in keeping that much money around any longer," the councilman went on. "We're not gonna be needing it for the glyph. Mooney can put it back into the bank."

"I'm sorry," Father John said. It hadn't played out right at all. No cops, the raspy voice had told him, yet he'd managed to lead Gianelli and the whole Riverton Police Department to the Indian. Now the man was dead, the Drowning Man probably lost.

The little group started moving back, a circle pulling away from him. They turned almost in unison — elders, grandmothers, the councilman — and started for the pickups in Circle Drive. Father John waited until the engines coughed into life, one after the other, and the little procession of pickups had turned past the cottonwoods on the way to Seventeen-Mile Road.

"Welcome to St. Francis," he said, starting across the grass. The white man was dressed like a local — blue shirt, blue jeans, and boots — but he wasn't local.

The man came toward him, a slow, lumbering walk, as if he weren't sure of his footing. "That's funny," he said. "You're welcoming me here, real funny. You know who I am?"

"You're David."

The man stopped a few feet from him. He was in his midforties, Father John guessed, close to his own age, with the shadow of a beard tracing a prominent jaw and longish dark hair brushing the edge of his shirt collar. They'd been boys at the same time, and the thought gave Father John a sinking feeling. The priests he'd known then — the pastors, the teachers — had been so . . . so good. He had wanted to be like them.

The sun slanting across the man's face accentuated the pockmarks, as if he'd suffered from smallpox as a kid. The hair at his temples was sprinkled with gray, and there were gray hairs that stood upright in his bushy eyebrows.

"Thank you for letting us know," Father John said. He was thinking that Father Lloyd Elsner might have been counseling some kid tomorrow.

"How could you not know? How could you let him come here? That's a school over there, right?" He lifted one arm toward the school out by Seventeen-Mile Road. "You got kids around here."

"That's why I'm grateful to you."

The man blinked and ran the palm of his hand over the stubble on his jaw. He glanced away for a moment, then brought his eyes back. "I looked up to him. I trusted him."

"You don't have to tell me."

"No," he said. "I do have to tell you. I have to make you understand what he did to me. I was just a kid. Fourteen. I'd just turned fourteen when my dad died and Mom sent me to the Jesuit school. 'They'll make a man out of you,' that's what she told me. I didn't wanna go to that school, you know what I mean? It wasn't where my friends went, so I started raising hell, and they sent me to the counselor. Father Lloyd Elsner. I really got on with him. He had this fancy car, and he said, 'You wanna drive my car?' I said, 'Yeah.' I never drove a car before, so we drove out into the country, just him and me. We got way out where nobody was around, and he pulled over and let me drive. That was the first time it happened, while I was driving. He put his hand down my pants."

David Caldwell glanced away again and bit at his lower lip.

Father John didn't say anything. He was still wearing his vestments — the priest's vestments. The sun seared his shoulders. Even the breeze was hot, and branches of the cottonwood seemed to move with effort. He felt fixed in place by the man's pain and the force of his own anger.

"I didn't know what the hell he was doing," David went on. His hands were shaking. "He said, 'It's okay. I'm not hurting you, am I?' he says. And after that, it kept happening. Sometimes in counseling, sometimes in his car. I never told anybody. I thought I must've done something really bad for this to be happening to me. By the time I was a junior, I was bigger than he was, and I told him, 'No more of that.' He didn't care, 'cause by then he'd found younger boys. So I put it away, stopped thinking about it. Then I flunked out of college, and my wife, she left me and took my kids. I married again, and she left me, too. And the jobs. God, I've had a thousand jobs. Three years ago, I finally knew what I had to do. I had to make sure that Father Lloyd Elsner didn't ruin any more lives."

Father John waited a moment until he was sure the man had said what he needed to say. Then he told David Caldwell that he was sorry. Sorry for what another priest had done to him. Words — they were as flimsy as air. He made himself go on, saying that it was evil, that it never should have happened, and as he talked, he thought that something began to change and move in the man's eyes. It was like watching ice begin to melt.

"Father Elsner is leaving here soon," he said.

"Where will it be this time?" The hard stare had returned. "Which neighborhood? Which school will be down the block?"

"That won't happen again."

Now disbelief flashed in the man's eyes. The pastor of a remote Indian mission? What power did such a priest have?

And yet, sometime in the middle of the night, his thoughts jumping between the image of the dead Indian to the pedophile in the guesthouse, Father John had known what he would do, and he'd realized that Bill Rutherford also knew. Lloyd Elsner would be sent to a place where he could not harm anyone else. Otherwise, he would call the Jesuit Conference, explain how the provincial had violated canon law by placing a pedophile at the mission without informing the pastor, and Bill Rutherford, his old seminary drinking buddy, would no longer have his job.

"I give you my word," Father John said. Out of the corner of his eye, he caught the faintest movement in the alley, like a shadow flitting over the ground. The old priest appeared at the corner of the church and stopped.

David Caldwell spun around, as if he'd sensed another presence, and for a long moment, the two men locked eyes. Then Father Lloyd turned and started back down the alley.

The other man watched until the old priest had disappeared from view. "He's always younger in my mind," he said.

"He'll be gone soon. You won't have to worry anymore. The offer that the provincial made is still open."

"What? Money? You Jesuits think you can buy back my life? I don't want money."

"Counseling."

The man didn't say anything for a moment. Then he shrugged and started across the grass toward a tan sedan, the only vehicle still parked in Circle Drive. He glanced back. "I'll think about it," he said, before lowering himself behind the wheel.

The sedan moved slowly, then sped up around the drive, tires spitting gravel. For an instant, Father John thought the sedan might miss the turn and slam into one of the cottonwoods, but it held the road and shot into the tunnel of trees.

Father John went back into the church. He knelt at the altar a few moments — *We are in need of your mercy, Lord* — then headed into the sacristy, took off the chasuble and alb, and hung them in the closet. He checked to see that the Mass books and the chalice were in the cabinets, then let himself out the back door and walked over to the guesthouse.

He could tell by the hollow sound of his fist against the door that the house was empty. He stepped off the stoop and headed down the alley in the direction of the river. He could see snatches of white hair moving among the trees.

"I don't know that man," Lloyd Elsner said when Father John caught up with him. "I have never seen him in my life."

"He recognized you."

"He's lying. You're all lying."

Father John waited a moment before he said, "I have to take care of my people. You're going to have to leave."

"He'll come after me. Distributing his filthy flyers, talking to the newspapers."

"I don't think so."

"I'll never have any peace."

"He's suffered a great deal."

"Lies!" The man swung around and walked over to a fallen log. He turned back, and Father John could see that he was trembling. He clasped his hands together, as if he might keep them from flying away. "It wasn't what you think. I loved him. I loved those boys. I never hurt them. You wouldn't understand, would you, about love? Love doesn't hurt people."

"I'll pray for you, Lloyd."

"I don't need your prayers. God knows what was in my heart. You can't understand."

"I want you to pack your things," Father John said. He was thinking that there were so few. A worn suitcase with a red belt around the middle.

"There's no place for me, is there? I shall always be hounded. Wherever I go, David will be there, or another one . . . I'll never have any peace."

"I'm sorry," Father John told the old priest. Then he turned and headed back through the trees, down the alley, and across the grounds to the residence. Father Ian burst through the door as he was coming up the steps. "You have a call," he said. "I was coming to get you."

"The provincial?"

The other priest shook his head.

Father John brushed past and hurried into his study. He picked up the receiver. "Father O'Malley," he said, but the line was silent, the receiver a dead object against his ear. He pressed the numbers 57. "Unavailable" appeared in the readout.

"Who was it?" Father John turned to his assistant, who had followed him into the study.

"Man, asked for you. I told him you were on the grounds. He said, 'Go get him. He'll want to talk to me.' He'll probably call back."

Father John stared at the phone. He felt a surge of relief. It was a good sign. The man was still in the area.

The phone started ringing.

Father John picked up the receiver. "Father O'Malley," he said again. His voice was tense.

"You got my message?"

"You killed your own man."

"Your fault, Father. Surely you can't believe I would leave him in the hands of the police? We had an agreement, you and me. It made me start thinking maybe I can't trust you. Maybe I oughtta just call this off and get my money somewhere else. There's a lot of good buyers waiting for a petroglyph like this one."

"The tribes are ready to make the exchange," Father John said. His grip tightened around the receiver. He hoped that Norman hadn't sent the cash back to the bank.

"That a fact? You got the money?"

"I'll have it in an hour. I can meet you wherever you say."

"You're the one that'll make the exchange, understand? Don't try to give me any bullshit about bringing along somebody else, some detective disguised like a cowboy. You try it, and the Indian won't be the only one with a knife in him."

"I'll be alone." Father John gave his assistant a glance. Ian was shaking his head, frowning.

"Tonight. Nine o'clock. Go to the strip mall on west Main, the one with the bowling alley. Park in front, walk across the street, and wait on the sidewalk. Bring the money."

"Then what?" Father John said, but he was speaking into a vacuum, and in another second, the monotonous buzzing began.

He pressed the disconnect button, then tapped out Norman's number. Three, four rings, then the answering machine, and the deliberate voice of the councilman: "Leave your number. I'll call you back."

Father John dropped the receiver.

"You can't go by yourself," Ian said. He was wagging a finger, like a teacher admonishing a not-too-bright student. "It's too dangerous. The man's a murderer. Let the fed find a police officer built like you. Some guy dressed like you. Blue jeans and plaid shirt, cowboy hat. Somebody that's trained. He'll know how to handle things."

Ian was right, of course, Father John was thinking. Everything his assistant said was right and logical. He should call Gianelli now, make the arrangements, some plan to fool the man, get an officer next to him before he knew what was happening.

. . . won't be the only one with a knife in him.

Father John shouldered past the other priest, grabbed his hat off the bench and yanked open the door. Norman had a good hour's start on him. He had to get to the tribal offices before Norman turned over the cash.

"It's our only chance," he said before slamming the door behind him.

29

A Navajo tribal member was found stabbed to death last night at the Butte Motel. The victim has been identified as thirty-seven-year-old Benito Behan of Denver. According to a Riverton Police Department spokeswoman, the body was discovered by Father John O'Malley, pastor of St. Francis Mission, who had been called to the motel.

Vicky slammed on the brake and swung into the parking lot that fronted a restaurant on the outskirts of Rawlins. A dark sedan blared its horn as it shot past. She held on to the steering wheel and stared at the radio. The disembodied voice switched to something about negotiations on a new teachers' contract, and Vicky pressed the off button. John O'Malley must have gotten a call after he'd gotten back to the mission. For some reason, the caller had directed him to the motel.

And he had gone. He wanted the Drowning Man back with her people. But instead of the petroglyph, he'd found the Indian stabbed to death.

She swallowed at the lump tightening in her throat. What kind of people had Travis been protecting with his silence? The kind who had murdered Raymond and had now murdered the Indian? The kind who wanted to murder her?

It was a long moment before she felt steady enough to drive. A gust of wind whipped at the car, spinning contrails of dust down the street as she pulled out behind a pickup. The Sunday traffic was slow moving, meandering. She retraced the route she'd taken two days ago: west along an empty stretch of asphalt, left at the massive motel plopped down in the middle of the plains, then another empty stretch, the prison buildings shimmering in the sun ahead.

Officer Mary Connor escorted her again through the ID check and out into the van — moving deeper and deeper past the heavy chain-link fences and concertina wire. They reached the visiting room, where Travis sat upright on a plastic chair, staring at the white concrete wall, ignoring the TV high in the corner.

He jumped up and walked over as Vicky

signed in on the clipboard that the officer at the desk had pushed toward her. She motioned him toward the row of interview rooms where Officer Connor stood waiting beside an opened door. The minute the door closed behind them, the officer moved past the window out of sight.

Travis said, "You got good news?"

Vicky waited until Travis had slid onto the chair before she sat down across from him. The red emergency button protruded from the wall next to her. "I want you to level with me," she said.

"You file a petition? You talk to the judge? How's it look?"

"Are you listening to me? I want the truth."

"You got the truth. I told you everything. I didn't kill Raymond."

"The Indian was murdered last night, Travis."

That stopped him. He blinked into the space and swallowed. His Adam's apple jumped in his throat. "Murdered," he said almost to himself, as if he were trying to wrap his mind around the idea. "I didn't see nothin' about that on TV."

"I just heard it on the radio. His name was Benito Behan. I think he was the contact for both of the stolen petroglyphs. I think you know him. You know who he works for, don't you?"

"Jesus, murdered."

"The truth, Travis. Start with the petroglyph that you and Raymond chiseled out of the rock and removed from Red Cliff Canyon seven years ago."

The Arapaho was shaking his head, sliding his chair back from the table. "They tried to pin that on me, the fed and the prosecutor, but they didn't have any proof. No way were they gonna make that stick, and they knew it."

Vicky pushed herself to her feet. This was a waste of time. She couldn't help a man who wouldn't help himself. "You've already spent almost seven years here," she said. "You'll be eligible for parole in another three. You can do the time."

"I'll be dead."

She sat back down. "What are you talking about?"

"They killed the Indian. They're gonna kill me. There's rumors goin' around — I heard 'em — somebody here's got a contract for a hit. Could be anybody. I'm eatin', takin' a shower, I'm all the time waitin' for somebody to stick me. There's no way I'm gonna make it three more years. I gotta get out now."

"Tell me about the petroglyph."

Travis hunched forward, his gaze boring into the table. Finally he lifted his eyes to hers. "This is between you and me, right? It's not goin' outta this room."

"I'm your lawyer."

He ran his tongue over his lips. "I'm not proud," he said. Then he started talking, shifting his gaze to some point beyond Vicky's shoulder. "We drove up into the canyon, me and Raymond. We took a bag of tools, you know, chisels, hammers, crowbars. Hiked up the mountain and went to work. Heard the noise of a truck comin' up the canyon while we were still workin'. 'Geez, he's gonna hear us,' I told Raymond, so we stopped chiselin', just waiting for some yahoo to come hiking up the slope, lookin' to see what was goin' on. But the truck kept goin'.

"It was beautiful, that glyph. Looked a lot like the Drowning Man, like there was water all around the spirit image. It was hell to pry loose, I can tell ya. Took all day to pry it out of the rock, and we were sweatin' like pigs. I could feel the way the spirit was holding on, making it real hard, like he was givin' us the chance to change our minds. But we got the glyph onto a tarp and pulled it downslope over the rocks and brush, and sometimes that tarp started goin' so fast, we had to hold on to it. Other times, geez, it was like haulin' part of the mountain. We pulled it up a ramp into the back of Raymond's truck, covered it with the tarp, and drove down the canyon. It didn't look so big, but it was like — I don't know — something really big and powerful riding behind us. I couldn't get Grandfather's voice outta my head. 'It's sacred. You remember that, Travis.'

"And Raymond kept sayin', 'We did it! We got a real pretty piece of art, like they wanted . . .' "

Vicky interrupted: "Who, Travis? Who were you working for?"

Travis looked out through the window over the empty tables and chairs in the visiting room. He didn't say anything.

"Marjorie Taylor and her foreman?" It was making sense, Vicky thought. The owner of a ranch struggling to keep the place out of foreclosure and a foreman willing to help her. "Is that why Marjorie Taylor came to the jail to visit you? What did she offer to keep you quiet? Is that why you never said anything?"

And then she understood. The minute Travis admitted taking the petroglyph, he would have confirmed his own motive for killing Raymond, just as the sheriff and the DA and the FBI agent had suspected. Oh, it was clear, Vicky thought. Gruenwald assuring his client that he'd be exonerated, and Travis understanding that all he had to do was keep his mouth shut. "If you'd told the truth, you would have been convicted of homicide," she said.

Travis looked back and gave her an almost imperceptible smile. "That was part of it. I'm not proud of what I done." He looked away again. "I started gettin' nightmares, you know. I was underwater, and it was cold and black except for this light beamin' down. I couldn't breathe, and my lungs were burstin'. I kept flailing my arms, tryin' to swim to the surface, and then I saw the spirit, and we were both flailing. We were both drowning."

"Is that why you went to your grandfather's?"

"I told Andy I had a family emergency; I'd be back in a couple days. I still had the nightmare, even at grandfather's. It was like the spirit was following me; I couldn't get away. I tried to tell grandfather what I'd done, but I couldn't. I just couldn't let him know. So I went back to the ranch and told myself it was gonna be okay. We were gonna get ten thou each, Raymond and me. That was a whole lot of money, you know what I mean? I never had the way to get any money together before, and that was my chance. Maybe buy myself a little land, run a few head of cattle, build me a log house."

Travis leaned back in his chair and stared at some point past Vicky's shoulder. "Raymond came into the bunkhouse the night after I got back from Grandfather's. Said, 'The glyph's in a real safe place where nobody's gonna find it.' I said, 'You crazy? Why'd you do that?' 'We're going for the big enchilada, Travis,' he tells me. 'We did all the work, took all the risks, and our cut is peanuts. We're gonna get our rightful share of the money, or they don't see that glyph again.' He said he was gonna tell 'em we wanted half. Fifty thousand each. Then he ended up dead."

"What about you, Travis? Why didn't you end up dead?"

" 'Cause they'd worked it so the sheriff thought I was the one that shot Raymond. Wasn't til I was already in jail they seen the petroglyph was gone."

Vicky waited a moment before she asked what Marjorie Taylor had offered when she'd visited the jail.

"Offered fifty thousand, just like Raymond had wanted. All I had to do was tell her where the glyph was hidden. I told her, she got it all wrong. Raymond double-crossed me same as her. I reminded her I was at my grandfather's, so how the hell did I know where Raymond took the glyph? She knew I wasn't gonna say anything about stealing the glyph and get myself convicted. So she stopped comin' around, asking questions, trying to make me a deal. Everything was gonna be fine . . ."

"Except that you were convicted."

"Yeah, I was convicted, and Gruenwald wasn't gonna bother with any appeal, and I've been tryin' to get outta here for seven years. Sometimes I wake up in the middle of the night, and the sounds around here in the night, they're like the sounds of hell. Boots clackin' and doors slammin'. Even the quiet is a loud noise. I stare into that yellowish dark and I know I gotta get outta here before they kill me. They killed Behan; they're gonna kill me for sure."

"Who else was in on the deal, Travis? Benito Behan and who else? Who's running things? I need a name, Travis."

The man got to his feet and leaned over the table toward her. "I've said all I'm gonna say. Tell Michael Deaver he gets the judge to overturn my conviction and give me a new trial and I'll give him a name. I'll give him a murderer."

Vicky retraced her route through the prison complex — the van, the hot asphalt, the concertina wire gleaming above her in the sun, the officer at her side. She drove out of the parking lot and worked her way back to the highway, heading north now for the reservation, one eye on the rearview mirror. But there were no vehicles, nothing but the gray river of asphalt flowing behind.

And yet she knew that they would try again. Whoever they were, they would figure out that she was driving a blue Impala. She felt breathless, as if she were running. Running against time. They'd kill her and Travis for the same reason: They could not take the chance that the seven-year-old murder investigation might be reopened, not when it would lead directly to the ring or gang, or whatever they called themselves, that had stolen two petroglyphs and murdered two men.

She pulled her cell out of her bag, pressed the keys for directory assistance, and asked for Michael Deaver's number. No one by that name, the operator said.

Vicky pressed the phone hard against her ear and kept the wheel steady with her other hand. What had she expected? That the prosecuting attorney would have a listed home number? She asked for the Fremont County Prosecutor's Office. There was a blank silence at the other end, followed by the voice-mail message: "Michael Deaver's hours are Monday through Friday, 9:00 a.m. to 5:00 p.m. If you have called outside of those hours, please leave a message. If this is an emergency, please hang up and dial 911."

"This is Vicky Holden," Vicky said after the beep had sounded. The phone was like a cold rock against her ear. "If you pick up your messages, call me right away. It's about the murder of Benito Behan."

30

Father John parked in the vacant slot across from the entrance to the bowling alley. Constellations of light broke through the darkness: neon red and white bowling pins twinkling in the plate glass windows, an iridescent river of white flowing through the double glass doors, yellow circles flaring from the light poles scattered about the lot. He pulled the boxlike briefcase across the passenger seat and walked over to the curb. At the first break in the traffic, he jaywalked across the street, his fingers welded to the handle of the briefcase. Odd how heavy it seemed.

He'd reached the tribal offices that afternoon just as Norman Yellow Hawk and the Shoshone councilman Herbert Stockham had pulled into the lot. A black sedan was waiting. Father John had parked next to the truck and hurried around to the driver's side as Norman lowered the window.

"The man called," Father John said. "He wants to make the exchange tonight." The door swung open, and a corpulent man with a ring of gray hair around a pinkish dome lifted himself from behind the steering wheel and started limping over, as if he were trying to work out the kinks in his thick legs.

"Tonight?" It was a duet, Norman and Herbert uttering the word at the same time.

"You sure you want to go through with this?" Norman said.

"Mr. Yellow Hawk." The corpulent man worked his way down the side of the truck. "If you'll come with me, we can take care of the matter. I'm sure you'll be relieved not to have so much cash in the office."

Norman kept his eyes locked on Father John's. Finally he looked in the direction of the banker. "We're in your debt for coming out on a Sunday afternoon, Mr. Mooney. It's just come to our attention that we may need to hold on to the cash for a little longer. This here's Father O'Malley."

The banker turned toward Father John and stuck out a fleshy hand with brown blotches on the top. "Al Mooney, bank president." The man's handshake was brief and perfunctory, his palm moist. "I know it's not my business why these two good men want to hold on to a wad of cash, but naturally, Father, I wonder if there's any trouble that we — that is, the bank — could help with."

"Appreciate your concern." Norman was staring at the man through the opened window. "Sorry to inconvenience you. We'll be coming in tomorrow to deposit the money. Bring it during regular business hours." He gave the man a salute with his index finger.

"Well," the banker said, a slow drawl, "I guess you people know what you're doing." He'd started backing away, crashing against the side-view mirror, tilting it forward. "Sorry," he said, pulling the mirror back into place and finally extricating his wide girth from the narrow slot between the two vehicles.

It wasn't until the banker had stuffed himself back into the sedan and driven away that the two tribal chairmen got out of the pickup. "Money's inside," Norman said, ushering Father John and Stockham along the sidewalk to the front door of the tribal offices. "Two hundred and fifty straps. Bundled up real tight with rubber bands. One thousand dollars in each strap."

A quarter of a million dollars, Father John thought, and he was standing in the dark on Main Street, traffic flowing past, head-lights bouncing over the pavement, holding on to a brown leather briefcase that might be crammed with papers and files and books, the usual paraphernalia of a Jesuit priest, the pastor of a small Indian mission. Isn't that what people would think as they drove past? The Indian priest, probably on his way to some meeting.

The four-door, brown Chevy truck veered out of the right lane. Father John felt his fingers tightening around the handle of the briefcase. Two cowboys in a brown Chevy truck had followed Vicky, run her off the road, tried to shoot her. But there was only one cowboy in the truck slowing alongside the curb.

The passenger door flew open, and the driver — dark shirt and pants, dark cowboy hat pulled low, dark gloved hand motioning him — leaned over the passenger seat.

"Get in." It was a woman's voice, and he realized that he wasn't surprised. It was what he should have expected. Raymond Trublood had been shot to death on a ranch owned by a woman. Yet a part of him had expected the raspy voice of the man on the telephone. What did surprise him was that the woman had come alone.

Except that she wasn't alone. Father John

sensed the presence of someone else as he got into the cab, wedged the briefcase behind his legs, and slammed the door. There was a scuffling noise as someone rose from behind the seat. The truck shot back into the traffic, engine growling, and Father John saw the wide black cloth thrust over the rim of his cowboy hat in front of his face. Then the rough cloth was pulled tight against his eyes. The world went black. He pressed the heels of his boots against the briefcase.

"What is this?" he said.

"We're goin' for a ride." A baritone voice behind him. Father John tried to detect some connection with the caller's voice. There was none.

His hat had come off, fallen somewhere. He could feel the blindfold pressing against his temples. He raised his right hand and poked at the blindfold, but it was like a rubber band around his head.

A cold metal object about the diameter of a quarter — the muzzle of a gun, he realized with a spasm of panic — pushed against the back of his neck. "I wouldn't do that if I were you," the man said.

"Where's the petroglyph?" Father John managed.

"You'll see it."

"I expect you to bring me back to my pickup with the petroglyph."

There was a thumping noise, as if the woman were pounding the edge of the steering wheel. Laughing quietly and pounding the wheel.

"I don't see you have anything to worry about," the baritone voice said. "Unless you tipped off the police or your FBI buddy. See anything?"

"The usual," the woman said, but the amusement had drained from her voice. "White SUV a couple of cars behind. Looks like it's turning off."

They were driving straight ahead. If he was right, Father John thought, they wouldn't turn off until they came to 287 and went north. But how long would that take? He was in a stagnant world; there was no way to gauge the passing time.

The man had sat back, because Father John was aware of a cleared space behind him where the air could circulate unimpeded. The only sounds were the rhythmic whirr of the tires, the hum of the motor and the air conditioning, the barely perceptible exhalations of breath — his own and that of his captors, and all of it in a syncopated rhythm. Every once in a while the woman readjusted her position; he could sense the faint vibration running through the console between them.

God, what had he gotten himself into? Hurtling through a black world with two thieves — most likely murderers — and nobody knew where he was. *Our only chance.* The words kept repeating themselves in his head, like a mantra, and oddly enough, there was comfort in them, even a strain of logic.

"Where are you taking me?" he said, mainly to break the quiet, assure himself with the sound of his own voice in the blackness.

"Why don't you just shut up." The woman's voice, sharp at the edges and impatient.

"Now that was a stupid question," the man said. "If we wanted you to know, we wouldn't've blindfolded you, would we?" He gave a snort of laughter.

Still on the same road, and how much time had passed? Ten, fifteen minutes? They should be nearing the highway, which must have been the case because the car was slowing down, the motor backing off. There was the jerkiness of the brake being tapped, followed by a sliding halt, a halfhearted attempt at stopping and turning right at the same time. They were on Highway 287 now,

Father John was certain, traveling faster, the wheels droning on the hard-baked asphalt. He could hear the swish of passing vehicles in the oncoming lane.

And in the blackness, like an image burned into his retina, was the bright picture of the Indian sprawled on the bed in the dingy hotel room, the reddish-brown blood-soaked shirt and sheet and — strange, this — the cowboy boots with the scuffed toes and worn-down heels placed neatly side by side at the foot of the bed.

"Damn," the woman said. "Another SUV back there."

"Lots of SUVs around." The man didn't sound concerned.

They were taking another right turn, going slower now. A dirt road, pebbles spitting through the undercarriage, tires slipping. The car bounced over some kind of rut, throwing him forward. He thrust out both hands and braced himself against the dashboard. The briefcase slid sideways toward the door, and he jammed his heels against the side, a reflex motion, he realized. *Our only chance.*

They swung right again and bumped down an incline, the engine straining in low gear. Finally the truck rocked to a stop. The ignition clicked off, doors opened in sequence: rear door, driver's door, his door.

"Get out," the man said.

Father John reached for the handle of the briefcase, but it was sliding out of his grasp. He kicked his heels hard against it, holding it in place. "I'll take it," he said into the blackness, gripping the handle.

"Have it your way." The man's voice came across a chasm, as if he were already walking away.

Father John pushed at the blindfold until he could see the jittering glimmer of a flashlight swiveling about, punching through the blackness. He got out of the truck, keeping the briefcase close to his side. As he started after the retreating sound of the man's footsteps, he felt the pressure of a hand on his arm. "One foot in front of the other," the woman said.

The ground was rough, covered with unexpected ridges that jammed against his boots and put him off balance. For an instant, he saw himself tottering down the corridor of the prep school where he'd taught, one foot after the other with such effort — such concentrated effort — to appear sober. Sober as a judge, his father used to say when he was the drunkest, and that's what Father John would tell himself, over and over, tottering along, sober as a judge.

There was the sound of a door skidding on the dirt, and Father John stumbled across a threshold into what smelled like a barn. The air was stale, infused with odors of manure, leather, and old wood. The ground was hard-packed with dirt. Over to the right somewhere, horses were snorting and moving about, knocking against posts of some kind.

"You want to see the petroglyph? Have a look." The man's voice came out of the blackness.

Father John switched the briefcase to his left hand and, with his right, began fumbling with the knot at the back of his head. He managed to pull it loose, then ripped the cloth away, and tossed it onto the dirt floor. The light was dim, nothing more than the narrow flood of a beam. Still, it took a second for his eyes to adjust. At the end of the beam was the dark figure of a man, cowboy hat pulled low so that he seemed faceless. In the shadows he could make out the outline of a door, the tack and horse-shoes against the back wall, the saddles flopped over wood benches, and six or seven stalls, heads of horses bobbing above the gates. He glanced around at the woman planted a few feet behind him, as silent as the shadows.

"Where's the petroglyph?" Father John said, and in that instant, the light beam arched to the left and swept across the top of a gray, flat-faced rock. The beam started moving closer until all the light was focused on the carved white image of the Drowning Man. The image seemed to lift off the rock and float into space.

Father John walked over to the petroglyph. He'd seen it from the road, up the mountain slope, the sentinel of the canyon. He had never seen it this close. And now he couldn't take his eyes away. The image seemed to be looking back at him, the eyes wide and intent. Sticklike arms protruded from the sides, thin lines of fingers moving — they seemed to be moving! — paddling through water. The legs were also moving, truncated lines kicking sideways with squared feet, treading the invisible water. He could sense the water in the arcs billowing about the figure as it tried to move from the under-world into the light world. And that was what was so wonderful, the sense of life in the carved image.

He could hear the shallow spurts of his own breathing. The craftsmanship, the artistry of a shaman two thousand years ago — it was an amazing piece of art. He might have been in the hall of some great museum, drawn by a painting or a sculpture against the wall, drawn *into* it.

The beam flipped away and the Drowning Man retreated into the shadows.

"What was that?" the woman said. "You hear anything?"

"Forget it. You're just nervous." The man moved in close. "The money," he said, pulling at the briefcase.

"Not until the petroglyph has been loaded into the back of the truck."

"You don't seem to get it, Father O'Malley." The flashlight jumped up and down, blinding him a second before it dropped away. In the man's other hand was the silvery glint of a pistol. "You're not in any position to negotiate. We want the briefcase."

Father John allowed the briefcase to slide away, his eyes fixed on the pistol. Then he glanced sideways. The woman took the briefcase, dropped it onto a bench, and was fumbling with the catch. He was struck by the roughness of her white hands moving in and out of the light, the hands of someone used to shoeing horses or pitching hay. Fine lines of wrinkles creased her neck.

"The combination," she said. "What's the damn combination?"

The man was still at his side, shoving the

pistol into his ribs.

What was it Norman had said? One-eight-zero? You'll remember one-eight-zero.

Father John gave the woman the numbers, his lips so tight he could barely form the words.

"Damnit, I need some light." The woman was jiggling the metal circles below the clasp, leaning into it, back curved under her plaid shirt. The light bored into the briefcase as the clasp snapped open. She lifted the lid and stared at the stacks of bills, yellowish green in the light. She picked up a stack and flipped through the edges. The bills crackled in the quiet.

"Looks like it's here." She replaced the stack, closed the lid, and lifted the briefcase. "Get him back into the truck," she said, looking at the man with the pistol.

Father John felt an immense quiet settling over him, every part of him focused on this new reality. There was never going to be any exchange. Had he really believed that the couple would take the money and that he would drive the Drowning Man back to the reservation? He could identify them; Gianelli would have had them under arrest within a few hours. But Marjorie Taylor and Andy Lyle intended to take him somewhere else and kill him.

He said, "If you intend to shoot me, you'll have to do it here. The same place where you killed Raymond Trublood seven years ago. What story will you use this time? There isn't any Indian around to take the blame."

"You don't know shit." This from the woman, moving toward the door, spitting the words back over her shoulder. "Hold it." She stopped walking and stood very still, head tilted into the thin shaft of light cutting across the barn. "Somebody's out there."

"Could be it's . . ."

"Shut up, Andy." She spun around and glared at the man a moment, then turned to Father John. "You brought the cops, didn't you?" she said, her voice barely a whisper. "That SUV I seen out on the highway, that was the cops. Damn glyphs have been nothing but a shitload of trouble. We were doing fine, Andy and me, without them. Jesus, Andy, cut that light."

Darkness swallowed the beam of light. Father John was aware of footsteps crossing the barn, the dull thud of an object being pulled from the wall. It was a moment before his eyes began to adjust. In the slivers of moonlight breaking at the edges of the log walls and outlining the big double doors, he could see the woman inching sideways. She had a shotgun braced against her right shoulder. Andy Lyle was moving around to the other side. An elongated black shadow of a man with a gun slid over the walls.

"Don't do this," Father John heard himself say. "Put the guns down." It was like speaking into a black tunnel.

"Nobody's taking me from this ranch." The woman hissed the words.

"You sure about this, Marjorie?" There was a shakiness in the man's voice. "Maybe we could get out the back."

Father John wasn't sure what happened first — the back door flying open or the big sliding doors crashing back. Floodlights had bathed the barn, blinding him for a couple of seconds — that he remembered, groping through the light, and his own voice shouting: "Don't shoot! Don't shoot!" And the sound of his voice lost in the blast of gunshots. He dove to the ground and clawed his way through the dirt behind the petroglyph.

"Put your guns down and come out with your hands over your head!" The voice from outside was magnified. It reverberated around the barn.

"Go to hell!" Marjorie Taylor shouted, the words nearly lost in the volley of gunshots and the sounds of horses screaming and hooves stomping.

Bursts of orange light flamed in the floodlight, a bullet pinged against the petroglyph, chips ricocheted about and peppered Father John's face. He crouched against the rock, covering his head. *God, don't let anyone die.*

Then came the silence, like the silence at the end of the world. He'd just managed to untangle himself and peer around the edge of the glyph when noise erupted again. The horses whinnying and boots thumping the ground, an engine growling, voices shouting. He was aware of men moving behind him — when had they come through the back door? — and of dark uniformed figures looming in the wide doorway ahead, black cutouts in the white light, rifles swinging side to side like cannons swiveling about, zeroing in on the next target. On the ground inside the door was the crumpled figure of Marjorie Taylor. A few feet away, Andy Lyle lay stretched on his back, arms flung out, as if he had been lifted off his feet and knocked backward by some superhuman force. The blood blossoming on the front of his shirt had a deeper red cast in the white light. The metal pistol on the ground beside him gleamed against the dirt.

Father John felt the hot muzzle of a gun

against his neck. "Get to your feet," a man's voice said.

"For godsakes, that's Father John." Another voice attached to the boots stomping behind the glyph. "You all right, Father?"

The muzzle pulled back, and Father John got to his feet. "I'm okay," he said. He didn't recognize either man — sheriff's deputies in brown uniforms, like the other brown uniforms tramping about the barn, bending over the bodies of Marjorie Taylor and Andy Lyle.

He remembered starting toward the bodies just as Gianelli came through the door. The fed made a straight line for him, parting the floodlight. "Jesus Almighty Christ," he said. "What the hell do you think you're doing? You could be dead."

31

Vicky watched Michael Deaver lift himself out of the black SUV, grab a briefcase from the backseat, and come up the sidewalk flooded with morning sunshine. She glanced at her watch: 8:25. She'd been waiting in the entry to his office for twenty minutes. When she threw open the glass door, the prosecutor's head jerked backward, traces of surprise and amusement in his expression.

"Can't wait to hear what brought you out so early, counselor," he said, shouldering past her.

"I left you several messages yesterday afternoon," she said.

Deaver bent toward the inside door next to the white plaque with his name and *County and Prosecuting Attorney* in black type. The thick ring of keys jingled in his hand as he maneuvered one of the keys into the lock. "I make it a point not to check my messages on weekends," he said, pushing the door open.

"It's an emergency, Michael." Vicky followed him across the reception area with chairs pushed into the wells of the scrubbed desks, down the corridor to his office on the right.

"I'm sure." He slapped the briefcase onto the desk. "Need some coffee?"

"I need to talk to you."

"Well, I need coffee." Deaver retraced his steps across the small office and disappeared again into the corridor.

Vicky dropped onto a chair in front of the desk and tugged a yellow pad out of her briefcase. A phone had started ringing in the outer office, a door slammed somewhere. There was the sound of a running faucet and the clink of metal. She found a pen and wrote the date across the top of the pad, then the name: Michael Deaver.

The prosecutor was back, angling his large frame past the corner of the desk, patting at the front of his blue shirt, running one hand through his hair. "Just the smell of coffee revives me," he said, perching on his chair. "So what's the emergency?"

"My client, Travis Birdsong . . ."

"Oh, yeah." Deaver shrugged. "Mr. I-Never-Did-Anything-I-Was-Framed. Why

466

does it not surprise me that you're still on his case? Don't you ever give up?"

"Not when my client is innocent. He wants to make a deal."

"No kidding! A deal. What kind of deal does he think I would possibly want to make with him?"

"Travis can give up a murderer, Michael. He can give you information on a criminal ring that's been looting artifacts in the county for years. Does that interest you?"

"That a fact?" Deaver rocked back and forth for a moment, as if he were on a trotting horse, then jumped to his feet. "Ah, coffee smells good and ready. Sure you don't want some?" He darted around the desk, past her chair, and out the door, not waiting for an answer.

Vicky jabbed the ballpoint at the pad, making a series of half circles. The phone had started ringing again in the reception area. She drew a miniature figure in the center and gave it truncated legs and arms, long spindly fingers. She could hear Deaver's footsteps padding back down the corridor.

"Somebody get that damn phone," he yelled. "Anybody out there yet? Christ," he said, coming through the door. He set a mug on the desk in front of her and dropped back onto his chair, cradling his own mug in both hands. "Too much to ask people to get to work on time?" He slurped at the coffee. "So who's the murderer Birdsong's gonna give me?" he said, nodding toward the other mug. "Better have some coffee. Only way to start the day."

Vicky picked up the mug and took a sip. "He can give you Benito Behan's killer," she said. The mug was warm in her hands, and she realized that she'd felt chilled all morning. She'd been up for hours; it was still dark beyond the bedroom window when she'd finally given up tossing and turning and had headed into the shower. She'd munched on a piece of toast before she'd left the apartment. She could feel the coffee sloshing in her empty stomach.

She realized that Michael Deaver was staring at her, working at his coffee, watching her across the rim. "You're kidding, right?" He set his mug on the desk. "I take it you haven't heard the news. We've already identified the people responsible for the homicide. Marjorie Taylor and Andy Lyle. You know them?"

Vicky didn't say anything. The sound of a ringing phone seemed to come from a great distance.

"They're dead, Vicky. Case closed. I'm not

making any deals for dead murderers."

Vicky got to her feet and braced her hands against the edge of the desk. "What happened, Michael?"

"I got the call late last night . . ."

"A call you returned."

"Yeah, yeah." He waved away the reprimand. "Caller ID says the sheriff, I take the call. Everything came down last night. You're behind the news, counselor. Father O'Malley was on his way to get the stolen petroglyph. Had a quarter million dollars in a briefcase, which he was gonna turn over to Taylor and Lyle." He shook his head. "The man took a big risk. Could've ended up dead. They picked him up, blindfolded him, and took him out to the Taylor Ranch. Riverton PD and the sheriff's department had been watching for the good pastor's red pickup. They saw him leave it in a parking lot and get into a brown truck."

"What kind of truck?"

"What does it matter?" The prosecutor gave a halfhearted shrug. "I don't know. Chevy truck, I think the sheriff said."

Vicky stepped backward and gripped the top of her chair. "What happened, Michael?"

The prosecutor shrugged. "Sheriff's officers surrounded the barn. The woman started firing a shotgun before the deputies got control of the situation, and Lyle was backing her up with a pistol. You got two nutcases shooting at anything that moves, and the only things moving were deputies. They didn't have any choice."

"What about Father John?"

"He's okay."

Vicky sank back into the seat of her chair. She felt weak and shaky, tossed about in the waves of relief coming over her. "They tried to kill me," she said.

"What?"

"They ran me off the highway when I was coming back from Rawlins. They shot at me out on the highway by the Taylor Ranch."

"Yeah, I heard about those incidents. State patrol and sheriff are investigating. No-body's been charged."

"It was Marjorie Taylor and Andy Lyle." She'd thought it was two cowboys, but behind the masks — She had to fight off the urge to laugh. But then she would start weeping. She'd *told* Marjorie and her fore-man that she intended to visit Travis on Friday; they had followed her. Then, yester-day, when she'd left the ranch, they must have taken a back road and come out on the highway behind her. Determined to kill her then, finish what they'd bungled earlier.

And now they were both dead. Vicky pressed her hand against her mouth and swallowed hard. The relief she felt was so strong she could almost taste it. She was aware of the man leaning across the desk, watching her, concern and impatience mingling in his expression.

"You don't have anything to worry about," Deaver said. "They won't be coming after you again."

Vicky nodded, then ran her fingers over the moisture that had started leaking from the corners of her eyes. Finally, she said, "They were part of a gang of artifact thieves, Michael. They were working with an outsider. The Indian was the intermediary."

The prosecutor was shaking his head. "Look, we're going to find the evidence that connects Taylor and Lyle to Behan's homicide. Sheriff's deputies are still searching the ranch house, office, barn, the whole damn place. Mark my words, won't be long until they come up with the knife. They were involved in the theft of the petroglyph, and the Indian ended up dead. Now they're dead, Vicky. End of story."

"I'm telling you, Michael, it's a bigger story. They were part of the gang seven years ago. They were responsible for stealing the petroglyph then. They killed Raymond Trublood and made it look like Travis was guilty. It worked, Michael. They got away with murder."

"Oh, God." The prosecutor lifted his eyes to the ceiling. "Here we go again. Let me state for the record, there is no evidence. The guilty party was convicted. His name is Travis Birdsong."

"Then why is someone trying to kill him?"

"What?"

"You heard me. Word is out at the prison that someone has a contract to kill my client. It's curious, isn't it? Anyone who might get in the way of whoever is behind the thefts ends up dead. Raymond Trublood. Benito Behan. I started looking into Travis's case, and suddenly I became a target. Travis knows too much, Michael. He can blow this whole ring out of the water. He can identify whoever is running it. He can give you names, dates, times, meeting places for the petroglyph that was stolen seven years ago. He knows who's in charge. We want a deal. Travis will tell what he knows, and you ask the court to overturn the conviction. He's innocent, Michael."

"Sorry, not interested in any conspiracy story about rings of thieves that steal artifacts from public lands." The man shook his head and flicked his fingers at the mug. "Not my jurisdiction. Take your story to Gianelli. Maybe he can convince me that what your client knows is so damn important I oughtta get my office involved. Stealing artifacts isn't exactly a big crime, you know what I mean? Worth five years max in some federal prison, and you count on your fingers the number of thieves doing that kind of time."

"Travis could be killed to keep him from talking."

"He can make a report to the warden. They'll put him in isolation."

"Whoever is running things gave the order to kill Behan. He's given the order to kill Travis. He's tried to kill me."

A buzzer sounded. Deaver stared at the phone a moment, then picked up the receiver. "Yeah?" he said. A moment passed. "Tell him to hang on. I'm just winding up here.

"Sheriff's on the line; I gotta take the call," he said. "Look, manslaughter case seven years ago was solved. Homicide last week, solved. Stolen petroglyph, recovered. My guess is, Gianelli's gonna tell you the same thing. This case is over."

Vicky stuffed the yellow pad into her briefcase and started for the door. She turned back. The prosecutor was tapping the phone keys, pressing the receiver to his ear. She had the sense that he was making an effort to keep his gaze on the desk, ignoring the fact that she was still there. The man was like a block of stone, and she was chipping at stone with words. Flimsy tools lost in the air.

She pulled the cell out of her briefcase as she hurried down the corridor. Outside in the bright sunlight, she pressed the key for the office. Annie's voice interrupted the rings: "Lone Eagle and Holden Law Offices."

"It's me, Annie." Vicky started down the sidewalk toward the Impala at the corner of the lot.

"Adam's been wanting to talk to you." There was a light nervousness in the secretary's tone. "Wait a sec. I'll put him on."

Vicky folded herself behind the steering wheel, turned the ignition, and rolled down the windows. Cottonwood branches lifted like an umbrella over the lot; the breeze blowing through the Jeep felt cool.

"Vicky, where are you?" It was Adam's voice.

"I'll be in later," she said, dodging the question.

"Bud Ladd over at the BLM called first

thing this morning. What's going on, Vicky? He's spouting fire. Said you're trying to blackmail him."

"That's ridiculous."

"He didn't like the newspaper article, Vicky. Neither did Norman. I thought we had agreed."

"We agreed that I would manage the BLM case, and that's what I'm doing, Adam."

"When are you coming to the office? We have a lot to talk about."

"I'll be in later," she said, her finger searching for the end key.

We have a lot to talk about. Vicky fit the cell back into her briefcase and closed her eyes a moment. She was going to have to convince Gianelli that Travis had information on a ring of artifact thieves. Then Gianelli might be able to convince Michael Deaver to help her get Travis's conviction overturned.

She punched in the number for the local FBI office. "Be there, Gianelli," she said over the whirr of a ringing phone.

"They picked you up at 7:45 on Main, right?" Gianelli said. The fed looked like he'd been stuffed into the side chair, Father John thought, two-hundred-and-some pounds of linebacker muscle that hadn't yet started running to fat. A small notepad in his left hand, pages scribbled in black ink flipped back, ballpoint in his other hand poised over a new page. "That right?" the agent said again.

Father John got up and walked over to the window in his office. A few white clouds drifted lazily across the cobalt sky. "We've been over this a dozen times," he said. Lines of sunshine and shadow crisscrossed the mission grounds. He could feel the warmth working through the walls of the old building. He watched Walks-On dart around the corner of the residence and trot across Circle Drive, intent upon something in his dog world.

"People think of things later," Gianelli said behind him. Last night, the agent had ticked off the list of charges that he could file against him: obstructing justice, impeding a federal investigation, withholding evidence. "Only reason I'm not charging you," he'd said, "is because Father McCauley called and told me you were on your way to make the exchange. I'm going to assume he called on your instructions. Don't say anything." He'd thrown up one hand when Father John had started to correct the man's impression. "You okay?" he'd said, and his tone had seemed to soften.

But now the irritation was back. "When it's all over, people remember the details. It's the details that are important."

A shadow lengthened from the corner of the administration building, and Lloyd Elsner walked across the front, picking his way around the stoop. Then the old priest was gone, absorbed into the shadows of the trees on the far side of the building. He was like a broken piece of pottery, Father John thought. Pitiful but dangerous, with still-sharp edges.

He kept his gaze on the mission a moment, aware that the agent was waiting, impatience crackling the air like electricity. From the rear office came the clack of Ian's computer keys. St. Francis would return to normal soon. His parishioners would return. There would be meetings at Eagle Hall, kids darting about the grounds, the Eagles practicing out on the field. Tomorrow, he would put Lloyd Elsner on an airplane, and he would go . . . where? To a retirement home in a rural area in Wisconsin, Bill Rutherford had said. A secure place where he could be watched, and Father John intended to make certain that the provincial kept his word.

He turned back to his desk and sat down.

"The man called the mission yesterday afternoon and gave me instructions," he began. Then he went through the whole story again, probably for the third or fourth time. He could hear the hesitation in his voice. The images were carved in his mind: the flare of gunshots, the bodies stretched in the dirt, the uniforms rushing into the barn, shouting, cursing. The sound of horses screaming. He tried to relate all of the details — *details are important.* Gianelli filled the top page of the notepad in his hand, then flipped the page and started on the next.

"I think we can wrap this up," he said when Father John had finished. "Taylor and her foreman had quite a scam. Steal the petroglyph, hold the tribes up for a quarter million. Probably started thinking they wouldn't get anything if the glyph went to a dealer, so they decided to kill the Indian and cut their ties to the outside world. Nearly worked."

"Why did they try to kill Vicky?"

The agent locked eyes with him a moment. "We don't know it was them."

"Brown Chevy truck."

"Probably a thousand in the county."

"Then who, Ted?"

"There are a lot of folks who aren't happy about her taking Birdsong's case. Ask Norman. Ask your parishioners."

Father John stopped himself from saying that he didn't have any parishioners.

"Taylor and Lyle were opportunists," the agent went on. "They saw what happened seven years ago. Two Indians got away with stealing a petroglyph. They sold it and came to blows over the profits. Fast-forward to this summer. Taylor and Lyle decided to steal another glyph. They hedged their bets, got into contact with Behan on the chance that the tribes might not pay. But once they realized the tribes were willing to pony up a quarter of a million, they decided to collect the ransom themselves."

It made sense, Father John was thinking. It even seemed logical, and yet . . . the reasoning was slightly off, not quite right somehow. "How did Taylor and Lyle know how to contact Behan?" he said.

And then he understood. "They had to have been part of the theft seven years ago." Father John held up one hand before the agent could object. "It wasn't the Indian that they contacted. They contacted the dealer. He's the one who has been operating gangs of artifact thieves. He's the one who sent Behan here with a message for the tribes, just as he did before. Listen, Ted," he leaned over the desk, locking eyes with the man on the other side. "Taylor and Lyle could have shot Raymond Trublood and set up Travis to take the blame. Travis could be innocent."

The phone started ringing, and Father John reached for the receiver before he realized that it wasn't his phone. The agent was tugging at the cell clipped onto his belt. "Gianelli," he said, clamping the plastic object against one ear, not taking his eyes from Father John's.

A couple of seconds passed before he said, "I'll wait for you at the mission."

He pressed a key and stuffed the cell back into its case. "That was Vicky," he said. "She's on the way over."

32

Vicky drove through what passed for a morning rush hour in Lander, then turned onto Highway 789 and stayed in the wake of a truck with tires almost as high as the Impala's hood. Outside her window, the narrow ribbon of the Popo Agie River shimmered in the sunshine. Past Hudson, the truck continued down the highway as she turned onto Rendezvous Road and plunged into the reservation, the breeze lifting little clouds of dust over the asphalt.

She'd felt a surge of hope when Gianelli said he'd wait at the mission. John O'Malley would be there and together — they were always stronger together — they had a chance of convincing the fed that Travis Birdsong knew enough to stop a gang of artifact thieves. If Gianelli could convince Deaver that Travis had important information, then — the best she could hope for — Deaver wouldn't object when she asked the court to overturn Travis's conviction, grant a new trial, and release Travis on bond. She had to get Travis out of Rawlins before someone killed him.

Vicky gripped the wheel hard; she could feel her knuckles popping against her skin. First, she had to convince Gianelli.

When had the brown truck pulled onto the road? It wasn't there a few moments ago. She'd found herself still checking the rearview mirror — it had become a habit during the last three days. One eye on the road ahead, one eye watching for the truck. And now it was there.

"They're dead." She shouted and pounded the steering wheel, then made herself draw in a deep breath. The two people who had tried to kill her were dead.

And yet . . . there was something about the truck that caused her heart to start thumping: the way it matched her own speed and maintained the same fifty yard distance, the two dark cowboy hats framed in the windshield. *Breathe,* she told herself again. She wasn't out on a highway alone like before. She was on the reservation. There were turnoffs onto dirt roads that led to houses. The small town of Arapahoe was ahead, white houses with dark roofs dotting the horizon. She could drive into town, honk her horn, yell out the window. Doors would fly open, people would run outside. What could the cowboy hats do with her own people shielding her?

It was as if the Impala were on automatic, taking itself down the road while her eyes stayed on the truck. She reached blindly for her briefcase on the passenger seat and extracted the cell. Her fingers fumbled for the feel of the 911 key. Still the same distance behind, the same, unvarying speed. She felt slightly sick.

A woman's voice came out of the void. "Emergency."

"This is Vicky Holden. I'm being followed again by two men in a brown truck. I think it's the same men who are trying to kill me."

"Where are you, Vicky?" The operator *knew*. The state patrol investigator had said he'd alert the emergency operators. At the first sign of the truck, all Vicky had to do was call.

"Rendezvous Road, a mile or so south of Arapahoe."

"Wind River police are on the way."

She pressed the end key, set the cell on the console, and made herself take in another deep breath. *In and out, in and out.*

She kept her own speed steady. The turnoff to Arapahoe spilled into the road ahead. She could speed up, race into town, honking and shouting for help, and . . .

People would think she was mad. The brown truck would drive on, of course. It would disappear, and she would be in town with people gathering about, jabbering and shaking their heads, staring out across the plains toward Rendezvous Road where, if she was lucky, there might be a little cloud of rising dust. The moccasin telegraph would bog down for days with the story.

The truck was still there, still the same, steady pace. There was no sign of a police car. She'd never make it to the mission. She shifted her foot to the brake pedal and slowed for the left turn. The truck also began to slow down. Her heart was banging in her ears. The cowboys would shoot at her again; they'd shoot at anyone nearby. She would bring snipers to her own people.

Then the truck banked to the right. She stared into the mirror, scarcely able to believe what she saw — the left side of the truck perpendicular to the road. Then the rear end swayed and bounced across the barrow ditch, and the truck headed east on a dirt road, the top of the cab visible above the brush, swirls of dust rising behind.

Vicky felt her hands relax on the steering wheel; her heart was beginning to slow into its regular rhythm. There were so many brown trucks. She couldn't fall apart every time she spotted one. Besides, Marjorie Taylor and Andy Lyle had died trying to collect the ransom for the stolen petroglyph. As soon as Travis had a deal, Gianelli would arrest the dealer that they had been working with.

But another thought hung like a shadow at the edges of her mind. What if Marjorie Taylor and Andy Lyle hadn't tried to kill her? What if the cowboys had been Raymond Trublood's brother and somebody willing to help him? She was still trying to get Travis released from prison. She had no intention of giving up. What if Hugh Trublood felt the same?

Vicky tried to blink back the thought. It was crazy. Andy Lyle with the dark mask and dark hat, that was the cowboy who had shoved a shotgun out the window at her and pulled the trigger. He was dead. Marjorie Taylor peering through her dark mask over the steering wheel — she was also dead.

She stopped at the sign on Seventeen-Mile Road, picked up the cell, and called 911 again. She gave her name and told the operator that the brown truck had turned off. It hadn't been following her after all. She tried to ignore the warm flush of embarrassment that crept into her cheeks.

"Officers are on the way, Vicky." The operator's tone was soothing, as if it were perfectly logical for Vicky Holden to report any brown truck in the vicinity. "They'll probably want to contact you anyway."

Vicky thanked the woman, hit the end key, and sat at the stop sign for a moment, glancing both ways on Seventeen-Mile Road, still gripping the cold plastic cell, almost expecting the truck to appear. An SUV lumbered past, then an old white sedan spitting puffs of black exhaust. The truck was gone. She made a right, then another right past the sign with *St. Francis Mission* in black letters — a comforting sign, she thought.

She drove between the stands of cottonwoods, past the school on the right, sunshine sprinkling the asphalt. Just as she was about to swing into Circle Drive, the brown truck loomed in the passenger window: cutting past the edge of the baseball field, barreling through the brush and wild grasses, it bore down on her. She felt as if her bones had fused together. She couldn't catch her breath. The cowboys had turned onto the dirt road to throw her off. They'd

486

guessed where she was going. They'd followed the road a short distance, then headed cross-country for the mission.

She had brought them to St. Francis! And they were going to kill her.

The Impala seemed to bank into the turn on its own. She pushed down the gas pedal and shot around Circle Drive, rocking sideways, tires skidding. The engine roared in her ears. The truck was bucking in the rearview mirror, turning onto Circle Drive, not more than five . . . four car lengths behind. The mission was empty and quiet, suspended in time. There was no one around, no sign of life apart from John O'Malley's pickup in front of the residence and Gianelli's white SUV parked outside the administration building.

She drove for the SUV, pulled in on the far side — a flimsy shield of metal and fiberglass between her and the truck — and jumped out, leaving the engine running, the door hanging open. She threw herself around the front of the SUV and started across the infinity of space between the vehicle and the front steps of the building. At the edge of her vision was the brown truck, pulling a U-turn, engine roaring, gravel shooting around the tires. And the shotgun . . .

She saw the shotgun clearly, the long black metal jutting out the passenger window, blocking everything else — the steps, the administration building — as if it were the only thing in the world, and she realized with a sharp surge of panic that she was in the open. There was no place to duck, no place to hide. She tried to reach the steps, paddling as fast as she could, but the steps kept retreating. Her arms and legs were numb, heavy weights. She felt as if she were drowning.

A shadow lengthened around the corner of the building, coming out of nowhere. Then, at the edge of her vision, she saw the old man with white hair loping toward her, the black slits of his eyes fixed on the truck.

"Go back," she screamed, trying to wave numb arms. "Go back!"

The force of the man's weight crashed against her, and she felt herself falling sideways in slow motion, scrabbling for balance, clawing the air. She was abruptly conscious of the old man knocking into her again, pushing downward in an explosion of gunshots. A hot, sharp pain ripped through her as the sidewalk bucked upward and slammed into her shoulder. Another gunshot. The percussion roiled over her; the ground rocked beneath her. She felt the heavy weight of the old man pressing her downward, and the darkness of his body merged with the darkness that closed around her.

"Shots!" Gianelli said.

Father John was already on his feet, lunging for the window. He took it in at once — the brown truck whipping around the drive, the black barrel of a gun receding past the window, the two bodies crumpled together on the sidewalk a few feet from the front steps. And the blue Impala parked next to the SUV.

"Vicky!" He was running now, across the office, down the corridor.

"Hold it!" Gianelli was already at the front door, gripping a revolver that he'd pulled out of a holster somewhere. There was the noise of a vehicle boring into gravel. The fed started inching the door open, and this was strange — the man was quiet, rooted in place, focused — while Father John felt himself flying apart.

"Wait," Gianelli said. Even his voice was calm and controlled.

"They're leaving." Father John pushed past him, rammed the door open, and threw himself down the steps. "Brown truck with two cowboys," he yelled to the man behind him.

"John, get down!" Gianelli yelled.

Father John dropped next to the crumpled bodies: Lloyd Elsner half covering Vicky, an arm flopped across her back, the man's legs twisted grotesquely to the side, like the truncated, angled legs of a petroglyph, and the blood matting the dark shirt and pooling onto the sidewalk.

A motor raced, wheels screeched. Father John looked up as gunshots burst through the air. The truck had hurled itself into a U-turn and was barreling toward the administration building, cowboy hat leaning out the passenger window, the long barrel of a shotgun leveled on the white police car swerving in behind. Another police car shot out from the tunnel of cottonwoods and drove onto the grass in the center of Circle Drive, then turned left and rammed the side of the truck.

There was the crack of another gunshot. Father John saw Gianelli crouched at the side of the steps, revolver trained on the truck. The police car rammed the truck again — a deafening crunch of metal against metal. Then another shot, and the truck's right front tire burst into a fireworks display of black shreds. The vehicle skidded across the brush and bumped to a stop against a cottonwood, with the two police cars pulling alongside. A blur of light blue uniforms swarmed the truck. Gianelli bolted down the sidewalk and through the brush.

Father John took hold of Vicky's wrist, probing for a pulse. She lay pinned under the old priest, but her right hand was flung free — lifeless — and that was the hand he was holding now. His heart thudded against his ribs. His pulse galloped, almost obscuring the faint beating in the blue veins of her wrist.

"Vicky," he said, dimly aware of the blue uniforms milling about across the drive, the angry voices shouting and barking orders, and Gianelli hunched down beside him now, fingers searching for Father Lloyd's carotid artery. There was a rapid scrape of footsteps, and Father Ian drew up next to the agent.

"My God, what's happened here?" The other priest placed a hand on the old man's head.

Father John felt Vicky's hand moving beneath his own. She was beginning to stir, and he had to brace himself against the rush of gratitude and relief flooding over him.

He brought his lips close to her ear. "Can you hear me?" he said, making his voice as steady as he could manage.

Her hand was squeezing his then. "He's heavy," she said. "I can't move." Her voice was a whisper so faint that he had to keep his head near hers.

"Vicky, listen to me," Father John said. "Were you shot?"

"There's no pulse." Gianelli pulled back and got to his feet. The flaps of his leather vest hung open, and Father John could see the black straps plastered against his white shirt and the black handle of the revolver in the holster under his armpit as he walked over to the SUV. He yanked open the door and lifted out a radio. "Get some backup to St. Francis Mission. There's been a shooting. Two people down. Wind River officers have stopped the shooters."

"Dear God, the poor old man," Ian said, his hand cupping the top of the man's head.

"He pushed me away." Vicky was moving now, trying to slide out from under the dead weight of Lloyd Elsner. "He pushed me down."

"Are you okay?" Father John said, but he knew the answer in the way that she was extricating herself from beneath the old man's body. He lifted Lloyd's shoulder as Ian raised the man's arm. Vicky slid sideways and rolled free. It was then that Father

John saw the blood smeared across the side of her face, the dark redness soaking into her tee shirt.

"Don't move anymore," Father John said. "You could have been shot."

She shook her head and started pulling herself upward.

"Are you sure?" He placed his arm around her shoulders to help her sit up, unable to take his gaze from the bright smear of blood down the side of her shirt. He realized that she was crying, the palm of her hand flattened over her mouth.

"He came out of nowhere." The words were blurred with grief. "I shouted for him to go back, but he kept coming. He was looking at the truck, and he hit me so hard, I went down. They started shooting at us."

Father John looked over at the twisted body of Lloyd Elsner, the gray, shrunken face, the slack jaw. The old man might have fallen asleep with his eyes open, staring into the sky, except for the pool of blood widening around him. "I have to take care of my people," he'd told the priest. "You're going to have to leave."

Father Ian made the sign of the cross on the old man's forehead. "Dear Lord in heaven," he said, "have mercy on his soul."

Father John repeated the prayer, then

pulled Vicky closer, nearly sick with relief that she was alive.

There was a new outburst of shouting. Gianelli started across the drive, taking long, purposeful steps, swinging both arms, loosening the muscles, Father John thought. A tall, thin man was grappling with two officers, who swung him around and pushed him facedown onto the hood of the pickup. Another officer snapped handcuffs around one of the man's wrist's, then the other. The cowboy hat slipped off revealing a blond head and a reddened, wrinkled scar across one side of his face. Other officers were leading the slim man with rounded shoulders over to a police car. The man's cowboy hat was pushed back. A mass of black hair fell over his forehead.

Vicky gasped.

"Who are they?" Father John said.

"Ollie Goodman and the man he'd said was an assistant. Justin Barone."

33

The door buzzer sounded just as the phone started to ring. Vicky tightened the belt on her white terry-cloth robe and hurried down the hall. She lunged for the phone with one hand and held on to the towel wrapped in a turban around her head with the other.

"Hello?" She had to shout over the buzzing noise.

"You got what you wanted, Vicky." It was Deaver's voice.

"Hold on a minute." She carried the receiver over to the intercom. "Who's there?"

"Adam."

Vicky pressed the intercom button and turned her attention back to the phone. "What did I get, Michael?"

"Your client is being transported as we speak to the detention center in Lander. He'll be kept separate from Goodman and Barone. We find out that he's lying about a contract on his life, and he's gonna find himself back at Rawlins in solitary."

"Travis won't be going back," Vicky said, striving for more confidence than she felt. She could hear the elevator whirring in the corridor. "I'm counting on your help in court, Michael."

"Yeah, well, that depends on your boy spilling his guts. Just so you know, Ollie Goodman and Justin Barone have been charged with first-degree murder, attempted murder, assault, battery. You ask me, you're the luckiest lady around. Could've been you dead this morning. Gianelli said you were the target."

Vicky swallowed hard and blinked back the moisture welling in her eyes. She didn't feel lucky. She'd stood in the shower for a long time, staring at the water washing down the drain, pink with Lloyd Elsner's blood.

". . . said Barone has been operating gangs of thieves for years," Deaver went on, and it took Vicky a moment to realize that he was still talking about the fed. "Goodman has been his right-hand man in this area. Benito Behan was their intermediary. The feds have had Barone in their sights in the past, but he always managed to slip away. It's possible that Goodman might decide to talk. He was hollering for an attorney the minute he was cuffed. Officers that took them to Lander say he was crying like a baby, saying he was just taking orders. Thought Barone wanted to scare people, not kill anybody. Bottom line, Vicky, I'll support your petition and ask the judge to grant bond pending completion of another investigation. If it turns out there's evidence that Travis didn't kill Raymond Trublood, I'll stipulate to vacating the conviction totally. Your client still won't be out of the woods, though. Gianelli will probably expect a guilty plea on the theft of the petroglyph. If Travis is lucky, the fed will go for time already served, and your client will be free."

"Thanks, Michael." There was a single sharp rap on the door, and Vicky started fumbling with the safety chain.

"Gianelli is gonna interview your client at five o'clock. I'm giving you a heads up. Like I said, if he's full of bullshit . . ."

"I understand." Vicky pushed the end key and opened the door. She stared for a moment at the handsome Lakota filling the doorway: The broad, straight shoulders, raised chin, and narrowed eyes focused on her, like a warrior face-to-face with the enemy. She backed away, dropped the receiver into its cradle, and rebalanced the damp weight of the towel on her head.

"You okay?" Adam said after a moment. He moved inside and shoved the door shut with his boot.

Vicky nodded. She let herself down onto a stool at the bar dividing the kitchen from the dining area. She could still hear the cacophony of sirens and see the police cars pulling into the mission, the phalanx of officers swarming about. Somehow she'd made her way into John O'Malley's office, reporters following. Questions had burst like gunshots. *Why did they want to kill you? How did the priest get shot? A pedophile, right?*

And she, with Lloyd Elsner's blood crusting on her blouse and skin, trying to unscramble the questions jamming in her head, until John had stepped between her and the reporters. "Take your questions to the fed," he had told them.

She'd stayed at the mission awhile, giving the fed an initial statement, sipping at the coffee that John O'Malley had handed her. Outside, she knew, men from the coroner's office had rolled the old man's body into a gray bag, placed it in the back of a van, and driven away. Finally she had said that she wanted to go home. "I'll have an officer take you," Gianelli had told her. John O'Malley had said he'd take her, but she remembered getting to her feet and telling them that she would drive herself. She had wanted to be alone, and now she had to face Adam.

"We have to talk, Vicky." He sat down next to her.

"Travis has been moved to Lander." She'd blurted out the comment, making an effort to focus on the present.

"I don't give a rat's ass," Adam said. The vertical lines between his eyebrows deepened. He pulled his mouth into a tight line.

Vicky took her eyes away. Travis Birdsong was her client. Everything that had happened, her doing: the brown truck following her, the gunshots meant for her and striking the old priest.

"I care about you," Adam said. "I want you alive, which doesn't seem to be high on your priority list. You would have been killed this morning if that priest hadn't happened to get in the way."

"He saved my life, Adam." Vicky held on to the edge of the counter to keep from sliding onto the floor. She could see the old man loping toward her — the image was seared into the back of her eyelids. She could hear herself yelling, "Go back! Go back!" But he'd kept coming, looking at the truck — daring the men inside — as if he'd wanted the bullets that were meant for her.

"It's been a rough day," she managed. "Can't we talk later?"

"It's now, Vicky." Adam got to his feet and walked to the other end of the bar. It was a minute before he locked eyes with her again. "There won't be any logging trucks going up and down Red Cliff Canyon. Bud Ladd called this morning. Said the timber companies had decided on the alternate route. Didn't sound happy about it. Said the BLM believed they had made the correct decision on Red Cliff Canyon. The alternate route has its own problems. A short section crosses a wetlands; a lot of people won't be happy. But I got the impression that the timber companies didn't want the publicity. They didn't like the idea of the public thinking they were destroying a sacred place. That was your doing, Vicky. It's what you do best, getting the best deals for your people from the white folks that run things around here. What I don't understand is why you don't want to do it."

"That's not true, Adam."

"Oh, it's true, all right. You intend to file a motion to vacate the conviction of a killer that nobody wants out of prison. I had a long talk with Norman Yellow Hawk this morning. The tribes are grateful to have the

Drowning Man returned. They're very happy about the BLM decision, but that doesn't mean they want Travis Birdsong back. I can read between the lines, Vicky. The tribes don't want to work with a law firm that tries to get new trials for killers like Birdsong."

"What are you suggesting, Adam?" Vicky knew the answer, but she wanted him to say it. It would be his call. There would be no going back, and she could see the truth of it fluttering behind the stone mask he'd pulled on.

"Say it," she said.

It was a moment before the fluttering stopped, and Adam's expression became quiet and resolved. "We can't go on like this. I assumed you were working things out with the BLM, when you were in an ambulance on your way to the hospital. This morning, Annie rushed into my office screaming. She was hysterical. She'd heard you'd been shot. You were dead. I was on my way out the door when the phone rang. You weren't dead after all. Some poor old guy that got in the way — he was dead. I needed time before I came over here. I had to do some thinking."

For a moment, Adam let his gaze linger on the yellow legal notepad she'd pulled out of her briefcase and left on the bar: the scribbled notes about the BLM and Red Cliff Canyon, the stolen petroglyphs, Travis's case — all of it mixed together.

She would not be the one to say it, she was thinking as Adam started pounding the edge of the bar with a clenched fist. Finally, the rapping noise folded into a solid, final thud that sent a shiver running beneath the tile. The white knuckles disappeared into his brown hand the way snowcapped peaks dissolve into the clouds.

"I'm in love with you, Vicky," he said.

She flinched backward. This was not what she'd been expecting.

"That's my problem, I realize. I'm under no illusions that you love me. I've been hoping that would change. Maybe it's time . . ."

The mask began to change; it was like watching spider cracks run through stone. Vicky held his gaze and nodded. "You're right. It's time." She saw herself back in a one-woman office handling DUIs and leases, writing an occasional will, representing Arapahos accused of murder or rape or who knew what other heinous crime, and some — oh, this was the thing — some would be guilty. And what good was that? Her own people would turn to Adam Lone Eagle for the cases that mattered, the cases that involved oil and gas and timber and water.

She hurried on: "We'll split up the firm. I'll start looking for new office space."

"What? That's not what I want. I want to keep the firm. You can practice the kind of law that you want. It's what you have to do; I know that now. I'll practice the kind of law I want. We'll collaborate on important cases. We're a good team, Vicky."

Vicky got to her feet and walked over to the window on the other side of the dining table, wanting to put some distance between them. It would be so easy, she knew, to give in to the tears and sense of relief growing inside her. "What about Julie?" she said.

Adam looked away. It was a moment before he said, "She has a line on a job. I've worked out arrangements for her to settle matters with the IRS. She's all right." Then he locked eyes with Vicky again and added, "She'll probably need me again in the future. I'm all she's got."

So that was how it had to be, Vicky thought, a compromise on both of their parts, each trailing remnants from the past. She said, "I intend to do everything possible to see that Travis is exonerated."

Adam nodded.

"The tribes might drop the firm."

"I've spent a lot of time today thinking about that." He circled into the dining room toward her, his hands jammed into the pockets of his khakis. "The tribes might drop us, but they'll come back because we're the best and they know it. You saved Red Cliff Canyon; you saved the petroglyph. They'll come back, once the controversy over Travis Birdsong dies down."

"There won't be enough evidence to convict him again. I doubt that Deaver will refile the charges. The truth is, no one may ever be convicted of Raymond's murder. It could have been any one of them: Lyle, Marjorie Taylor, Goodman. Even the mastermind, Barone. Any one of them could have been in that barn. The problem is that Raymond's brother and Norman and the rest of the Joint Council will always assume that Travis is guilty."

"It'll be old news tomorrow."

"I'm not going to make any promises."

Adam lifted a hand into the space between them. "I don't want to hear any. The next time one of the grandfathers or grandmothers comes begging for your help, I know what you'll do." He left the rest of it unspoken, ghosts of words hanging between them. "The point is, we're partners, right? If you're in danger, I want to know. I want to be there to protect you."

"Oh, Adam," Vicky said. "I don't expect anyone to protect me."

"You hear what I'm saying? I don't want you to feel alone. I want to stand with you, whatever you're doing."

"The smaller cases can still go to Roger," Vicky said, wanting to give a little.

Adam nodded, as if that were another promise he'd just as soon she hadn't articulated.

"Gianelli's interviewing Travis at five," Vicky said, throwing a glance at the clock over the stove. It was close to four.

Adam nodded, then started backing toward the door, holding up both palms in the Plains Indian sign of peace. "It's settled then, right? I'll see you at the office tomorrow. We'll go on, Vicky, you and me."

She gave him a smile and watched him pull open the door and head into the corridor. "Law partners," she said as the door closed on Adam's large, retreating figure.

Travis Birdsong was already seated at the table in the interview room when a deputy waved Vicky inside. She took the chair next to him, still feeling rushed from hurrying about, glancing through her notes while she pulled on a dark skirt and a blue silk blouse and stepped into a pair of black pumps. Her hair was still damp. She tried to slow herself down, regain her balance.

"How are you?" she managed.

"Better now that I'm outta Rawlins."

"You should know that Ollie Goodman and Justin Barone tried to kill me this morning. They shot a priest at St. Francis Mission. The man is dead."

"I heard on the radio," he said. "You think I'm surprised? The way I got it figured, it was Goodman that shot Raymond."

"You said that Goodman had left the ranch. You didn't see him when you rode down from the pasture."

Travis tossed back a strand of black hair. "I guess I came to some wrong conclusions. Maybe he never left the ranch, that's how I see it now. He could've driven around to the back of the barn where there's a real good view of the red bluffs. I seen him out there workin' once. Had half a picture of the bluffs painted on his canvas. Truck was over in the trees in the shade. He could've gotten into the barn through that back door we never used. I figure he was waitin' for Raymond inside. Raymond never seen what hit him. Goodman went out the back, got in his truck, and took one of the back roads off the ranch."

It was only a story, Vicky was thinking, told by a convicted man desperate for a new trial. "Gianelli's going to want evidence, Travis," she said.

"I got proof of what was going on," he said. "I haven't told you all of it."

34

There was the thud of a door shutting, the scuff of boots on tile. Vicky saw the brown uniform moving on the other side of the window that separated the interview room from the corridor. Then, a knock and the door swung open.

"Fed's here," the officer said. "You ready?"

Vicky nodded. She could sense Travis tensing beside her as the sound of the officer's footsteps retreated in the corridor.

"You sure the fed's gonna help me?" he said.

Vicky turned toward the Arapaho. "There aren't any guarantees, Travis."

He slumped toward the table and dropped his head into both hands, a perfect picture of despair. "All I got," he said, "is what I seen and heard."

"It's your best chance." Vicky waited a moment; then she told him that he would have to give up the petroglyph.

"What?" The man's head snapped back; his hands drifted over the table. "What're you talkin' about?"

"The truth, Travis," Vicky said. She was taking a gamble, she knew. She had no proof, yet it made sense. She pushed on: "The only way you could have gotten the money to pay Gruenwald *after* you were released from prison was by selling the petroglyph that you and Raymond had taken. That means you know where it is. Raymond must have told you where he put it."

It was a long time before Travis said anything, and for a moment, Vicky thought that he might jump to his feet, bang on the door for the guard, and walk away. But where could he go? Back to Rawlins where someone was waiting for him?

"That glyph's all I got," he said finally. "It's my ticket outta the rez. I paid for that glyph. I paid . . ."

"It belongs to the people."

". . . seven years of my life."

"Gianelli is going to want to know where it's hidden."

"C'mon, Vicky. It's not like it's the Drowning Man. I wasn't gonna take a sacred glyph."

"All the petroglyphs are sacred. You know that."

Vicky was aware of the rhythm of footsteps, the rustle of movement in the corridor. The door opened again and Ted Gianelli stepped inside. He let the door close behind him, then pulled out the chair across the table and sat down, not taking his eyes from Travis. "Your attorney tells me you're ready to talk about the stolen petroglyphs and other artifacts," he said.

Vicky exchanged a quick glance with Travis. The Arapaho exhaled a long breath, as if he were letting go of some deep, hidden part of himself. "What do you want to know?" he said.

"How'd you get involved, Travis? Suppose you start your story there."

Travis leaned back and clasped his hands on the table. He ran his tongue back and forth over his lips for a moment before he began: *"I'd been workin' at the Taylor Ranch maybe two, three weeks, when Raymond rides up alongside me and says, 'You interested in makin' some extra cash?' We was out in the pasture pitchin' hay to the cattle. Nobody around, just him and me. It was freezin' cold, I remember that, and I was tryin' to keep movin' just to keep from freezin' to* death. 'Sure, I'm interested,' I told him. So he says that Mrs. Taylor and Lyle know a guy that wants to buy a petroglyph. Gonna pay a lot of money. All we gotta do is get the petroglyph.

"Well, that wasn't gonna be easy, I was thinkin'. Lyle says, don't worry. He's got the hammers, chisels, and crowbars. It was gonna take some time, but nobody goes up Red Cliff Canyon in the winter. I said I had to think on it. The canyon's sacred, you know. Spirits live up there. I wasn't real anxious to disturb the spirits.

" 'Think about ten thousand dollars,' Raymond said.

"That was more money than I'd ever seen, so I said, Okay, I'm in. That afternoon — it was startin' to get dark — we drove up into the canyon to meet Mrs. Taylor and Lyle and decide on the glyph to take. We got to the curve where you could see the Drowning Man. Well, there were four pickups parked right in the middle of the road. Beyond was nothin' but snow as smooth as glass. You couldn't see the petroglyph for the people standin' in front.

"Raymond and me hiked up the slope through the snow, and Mrs. Taylor says, 'This is the glyph we want. You think you can handle it?'

"I was feeling real strange now, wishing I hadn't gotten into this. Besides Mrs. Taylor and Lyle, there were a couple other white guys. Tall, blond guy with a scarred face came around the ranch to paint his canvases. Name was Ollie Goodman. Standin' there, leanin' on his crutch. The other white man was shorter, had black hair with snow sprinkled in it, like he'd walked under a branch. He was dressed real nice in a gray overcoat with a red scarf tucked in the front and fancy boots that he kept stompin' around in, like he wasn't happy with 'em gettin' messed up in the snow. I remember he kept smokin', lighting a new cigarette off the last, tossin' the butts into the snow.

"That was when I started thinking this was the guy that wanted the glyph, and he wanted the oldest, most beautiful glyph in the canyon. I knew the spirits brought me there for one reason: I had to protect the Drowning Man. So I said, 'We can't get that glyph.'

"The man in the gray coat says to Mrs. Taylor — I mean, it was like Raymond and me wasn't even there —'You told me they were up to the job.'

512

"Don't worry, Justin," Mrs. Taylor said. She was bowin' and scrapin'. She looks me in the eye and starts goin' on how he's an expert on Indian artifacts and knows what artifacts are gonna sell, and me and Raymond would do like she tells us.

"I knew then that they was the ones diggin' up grave sites and stealin' Indian artifacts for years. There were all those rumors about outsiders taking our artifacts, since nobody ever seen any for sale in the local shops. All the time, it was locals stealin' 'em for this outsider named Justin.

" 'It's really quite wonderful,' the Justin guy says. I mean, he talked like some fuckin' professor. He had on black leather gloves, and he kept rubbing 'em together, like he couldn't wait to get his hands on the Drowning Man. 'Look at the way the artist has carved the image with such definition and precision. A true artist, a Michelangelo of the plains. The patina couldn't be more beautiful. This petroglyph is very old, fifteen hundred, two thousand years. There'll be no problem moving it. If the tribes don't pay for it, half a dozen clients will bid against each other for it.'

" 'We'll cut it out okay,' Raymond said. All he was thinking about was getting his hands on ten thousand dollars.

"I was real nervous. If I said I didn't want no part of it, what were they gonna do to me? Let me walk down that mountain? I didn't like the way Andy Lyle was watchin', just waitin' for me to say something stupid.

"So I said, 'You want a beautiful glyph that's real old with perfect patina? I know a better one.'

"Mrs. Taylor looked real hesitant. She started to say something, when Justin clapped his gloves and interrupted. 'Better petroglyph than this? I'd like you to show me,' he said.

"I started climbing upslope through the snow. They were huffin' and puffin' behind me, all except for Goodman. No way was he gonna make it up the slope. 'How much farther,' Mrs. Taylor shouted, but I just kept goin', trying to remember where my grandfather took me to when I was a kid. The petroglyph was real beautiful, I remembered, but it wasn't the Drowning Man, and it was high enough up the mountain that it'd be awhile before anybody would see it was gone. I was hopin' the spirits wouldn't know either. I was thinkin' that maybe we could just take it, and everything would be all right.

"Mrs. Taylor kept shoutin', 'Where is it?' and

514

I could hear Justin grunting like he couldn't catch his breath, probably mad as hell that the snow was ruining his fancy boots and the bottom of his fancy slacks. Then Lyle gets next to me. 'You wouldn't be leading us on a wild goose chase, would you?' he says. 'Justin Barone is a very important man.'

"I closed my eyes, and I said to the spirits, 'You gotta help me find the glyph, 'cause I can't find it, and they're gonna take the Drowning Man.' When I opened my eyes, I seen the glyph upslope a little farther ahead, right in front of me.

"Justin Barone said it was beautiful all right, every bit as old as the other glyph, and what he liked about it, I could tell, was that the carved image was bigger, and it was a similar motif, he said. That's what he called the image. Motif. He started clapping his hands, sayin', 'Perfect, perfect.'

"'Any problem getting it down the mountain?' he wanted to know. I said no problem. We'd put it on a tarp and pull it down like a toboggan.

"Then Mr. Justin Barone said, 'This is the glyph I want.'"

Gianelli was filling in the lines of the notepad, working fast, his pen making little scratchy sounds. "Did you see this man again?" he asked without looking up.

Travis shook his head. "Took Raymond and me about a week to cut out the glyph, and every night, Mrs. Taylor wanted to know how we were doin'. She'd say, 'I gotta call the gallery and let Mr. Barone know.' Always wanted to make sure we didn't hurt the carving. 'The boss wouldn't like that,' she'd say. She called him the boss."

Travis leaned over the table. "I didn't kill Raymond," he said. "I think he told Mrs. Taylor and Lyle that if he didn't get more money, he was goin' to the fed and blow the whole deal. He was gonna name everybody involved, including Mr. Justin Barone."

"Well, what do you think?" Vicky tried to match her stride to Ted Gianelli's as they crossed the parking lot. The sun hovered in a white haze over the mountains, and the day's heat was still lifting off the asphalt.

The agent stopped and turned toward her. "Justin Barone owns the Barone Fine Arts of the West Gallery in Santa Fe. We've suspected him of trafficking in illegal Indian artifacts for some time, but we've never been able to connect him to any specific thefts. There are always layers of people

516

between him and the people he hires to steal the artifacts. All I've got now is the word of a man convicted of manslaughter. If his story is true, it's the first time I've heard of Barone venturing into the field himself. He relied on Belhan for that. Hard to believe he let his guard down."

"I met him at Goodman's cabin in Red Cliff Canyon."

Gianelli stared at her for a second or two. "You're certain?"

"Goodman was the main local connection," Vicky said. "He sells his paintings in Barone's gallery."

And then she had it. "Travis and I could both identify Barone. Travis could connect him to the theft of the petroglyph seven years ago. I could connect him to Goodman and the local gang. It made us dangerous, Ted. Raymond was dangerous, and Barone ordered him killed. He ordered Behan killed before the police could question him. He wanted Travis dead. He wanted me dead. Everyone who was dangerous had to be killed."

"We have him, Vicky," Gianelli said. "We finally have that bastard."

35

Father John pulled up in the Toyota pickup behind the line of vehicles parked on what passed for a road across the high mountain valley. He got out and started across the meadow toward the little crowd assembled near the only tree visible: a gnarled, stunted pine that looked more dead than alive. Vicky stood next to Gianelli. The Indian next to Amos Walking Bear had to be Travis, thinner, older looking, shoulders sloped in resignation. There were several uniformed deputies and two men working shovels in the ground and tossing dirt onto the pile growing under the tree. The sun stood overhead in a blue sky scrubbed clean of clouds, as placid and clear as the pond that glistened across the valley. An almost imperceptible breeze rustled the stalks of grass. Rising over the valley were the jagged peaks of the Wind River Range. Except for the clunking and scraping sounds of the shovels, the valley was suffused in quiet, like the quiet of outer space.

Vicky broke from the crowd and came toward him, one hand holding her hair back in the breeze. "Glad you could make it," she said, falling in beside him.

"Thanks for letting me know."

"I figured you'd want to see another petroglyph recovered."

That was true, Father John thought. He wanted to see both petroglyphs back where they belonged. Not in Red Cliff Canyon — that was impossible. They could never be returned to the place where they had stood for two thousand years. But they would both stand in front of the tribal offices in Fort Washakie, fixed in cement, safe. At least, that was the news on the moccasin telegraph, and Vicky had confirmed it when she'd called yesterday.

"Goodman's started talking," Vicky said now. She stopped walking, and he turned toward her. "He's scared, John. He knows he's in way over his head. He's been passing small artifacts to black-market dealers in Santa Fe and Scottsdale for years. Stealing the petroglyphs was the next step. Then, it was murder. The sheriff's deputies found an eight-inch knife in Goodman's studio. They think the lab will confirm that it was used to kill Behan. He's already been charged with homicide for Father Elsner's death."

She shook her head, and he realized that there were images imprinted in her mind, just as there were in his, that she would like to shake away. "According to Deaver, Goodman's telling everything he knows about Barone's operations in five or six states. He's hoping that by cooperating, the court might spare him from the death penalty."

"It's over," Father John said, and in that instant, someone standing at the tree let out a cry of joy. The little crowd pressed together, heads bent. Amos Walking Bear folded himself onto both knees and peered into the wide depression in the ground.

"They found the petroglyph." Vicky broke into a run.

Father John ran after her, careful not to pass her: she should see it first.

Vicky reached the group and dropped beside the elder. No one else moved. They might have been in a trance, Father John thought, everyone staring down. Amos pulled a handkerchief from the back pocket of his trousers, leaned over, and began brushing at the thin layer of dirt, a slow, reverent motion. Travis lifted his chin and looked away, across the meadow at the traces of snow lining the high peaks.

"Seven years," Gianelli said when Father John stepped next to him. "And it's still beautiful."

Father John stared at the carved image emerging beneath the swipes of the white handkerchief. It might have been a duplicate of the Drowning Man, the boxy, human figure with a flattened head, truncated arms and legs, deeply incised in the pinkish-gray rock. The rounded eyes stared up at the sky with a look of surprise. With each pass of the white handkerchief, the image became clearer and sharper. The bronze-toned patina glistened in the sun.

It was then that Father John noticed the moisture leaking from the corners of the elder's eyes.

The two officers laid down their shovels, picked up crowbars, and began gently edging the petroglyph onto its side. One of the deputies withdrew two thick leather straps from a green duffel bag slung against the tree trunk. Father John knelt down and set both hands on top of the cool rock to steady it as the other men, working with crowbars, slipped a strap around first one end, then the other.

When the straps were tight, they began hauling the glyph out of the ground. Father

John held on to the edge of the stone, try-ing to keep it steady as it rose into the daylight. And then the petroglyph was free.

The officers pulled it onto a tarp that was spread on the ground. Then they pulled the tarp across the grass and up a metal ramp into the back of a white pickup with *BIA Police* stamped in blue and yellow on the side. They slammed the tailgate, got into the cab, and headed down the road, trailing a brown cloud of dust.

Other officers were leading Travis Bird-song toward a Fremont County Sheriff's vehicle, a gray SUV. Amos Walking Bear started after them, then turned to Father John and Vicky.

"Ho'hou'!" he said, lifting a weathered brown hand in a half salute. "My grandson's gonna be free. He shouldn't've gotten mixed up in this." He nodded toward the tree that had sheltered the hiding place. "He was wrong, but he never killed anybody. Fed says he's gonna have to go to federal court. Probably get probation and time served for taking the glyph. Might have to pay a fine. But he's gonna come back, live a good life. That's what he wants. Live back with the people, like the petroglyphs."

Father John and Vicky walked the old man

over to the gray SUV where a deputy held open the rear door. Another deputy was inside, bent over the wheel, jiggling the ignition. The engine coughed into life, sending a thin black stream of exhaust out of the tailpipe. The old man slid into the back seat next to Travis. After shutting the door, the officer got into the front and pulled the door shut as the vehicle swung back onto the road following the pickup that had shrunk into a white square far down the mountain. Gianelli's SUV pulled out behind.

Vicky tilted her head back and stared at the sky a long moment, working her fingers into the muscles of her shoulders. "I started thinking . . ." She paused, looking up at Father John out of the corners of her eyes. They were the only ones left in the high meadow, the breeze riffling her hair. "In the middle of the night, I started thinking about you and the mission and wondering whether your boss, the provincial, will retaliate."

Father John hesitated. It was true that he'd refused to allow Lloyd Elsner to remain at St. Francis, and now the man was dead. When he'd called the provincial, Rutherford's voice had been as hard as stone: "I'll get back to you."

Father John had hung up with a sense that, in the corner office of a gray-stone building on a traffic-snarled street in Milwaukee, Bill Rutherford and the other Jesuits who administered the province would reach the same conclusion: If Father John O'Malley had been taking care of his job as the pastor of St. Francis Mission instead of involving himself with stolen petroglyphs and homicides, an old priest might still be alive, living out his days in seclusion somewhere. And that Rutherford would . . .

"Transfer you somewhere else." Vicky's voice cut through his thoughts.

He looked away. He'd tried to ignore the possibility, but it was like a chisel scraping at the edge of his consciousness. He couldn't get away from the rhythmic, grating noise of the words: *somewhere else, somewhere else.*

"Tell me, John. Did he put you on notice?"

Father John shook his head. It wasn't like that. Nothing definite, just a lingering sense that time was running out. He said, "I'm always on notice, Vicky," trying to make light of it, smiling at her.

"The provincial's wrong if he thinks you could have prevented Father Elsner's death," Vicky said. "There wasn't anything you could have done to save him, and that's the truth."

The truth. Ah, that was hard to grasp, hard to wrap up in a tidy package. There were always pieces that kept flying away like the motes of dust in a sunbeam.

"I can't shake the image of the old man coming toward me," Vicky said. "Last night, I kept seeing his eyes, like dark slits, pencil marks, and the expression on his face! It was more than just determination. It was fierce resignation. God." She shook her head, as if the image might fly away. "I'd thought that he pushed me down to save my life. I've been feeling so guilty. I was the one who was supposed to die, not that old man. But he wasn't even looking at me. He was looking at the truck and walking straight toward it, half running toward it, doing a little hip-hop. He was going toward the gun, John, and I was in his way, so he pushed me down. He wanted to die."

Father John kept his eyes on hers a moment. He'd been unable to shake his own images of the white-haired, stooped old man, and the sound of despair ringing through his voice: "There's no place for me, is there? I shall always be hounded."

Father John placed his hands on Vicky's shoulders. He could feel her trembling. "What matters is, he pushed you down, Vicky, and you're alive. You'll go on. Lloyd

Elsner is in the hands of God."

"But what about . . ."

Father John held up one hand. "And so are we," he said.

ABOUT THE AUTHOR

Margaret Coel is the *New York Times* bestselling, award-winning author of the acclaimed novels featuring Father John O'Malley and Vicky Holden, as well as several works of nonfiction. Originally a historian by trade, she is considered an expert on the Arapaho Indians. A native of Colorado, she resides in Boulder. Her Web site address is www.margaretcoel.com.

The employees of Thorndike Press hope you have enjoyed this Large Print book. All our Thorndike and Wheeler Large Print titles are designed for easy reading, and all our books are made to last. Other Thorndike Press Large Print books are available at your library, through selected bookstores, or directly from us.

For information about titles, please call:
(800) 223-1244

or visit our Web site at:
www.gale.com/thorndike
www.gale.com/wheeler

To share your comments, please write:
Publisher
Thorndike Press
295 Kennedy Memorial Drive
Waterville, ME 04901